StarBridge

★★★★★★★★★★★★★★ *Book Three*

SHADOW WORLD

A. C. CRISPIN and
JANNEAN ELLIOTT

ACE BOOKS, NEW YORK

This book is an Ace original edition,
and has never been previously published.

SHADOW WORLD

An Ace Book / published by arrangement with
the authors

PRINTING HISTORY
Ace edition / January 1991

Cover art by Dorian Vallejo.

For information address: The Berkley Publishing Group,
200 Madison Avenue, New York, NY 10016.

ISBN: 0-441-78332-5

Ace Books are published by The Berkley Publishing Group,
200 Madison Avenue, New York, New York 10016.

PRINTED IN THE UNITED STATES OF AMERICA

10 9 8 7 6 5 4 3 2 1

RAVE REVIEWS FOR THE *STARBRIDGE* SERIES!

"This is the type of rousing adventure story which Heinlein made so popular a generation ago . . . Excellent!"

—Andre Norton, author
of the *Witch World* series

"A great success . . . An adventure novel with some thought in it!"

—Vonda N. McIntyre, author of *Starfarers*
and *Enterprise: The First Adventure*

"A solid, highly readable piece of work!" —*Locus*

"An interesting supporting cast of aliens and a strong theme of understanding and acceptance among races." —*Booklist*

"A space adventure series patterned strongly after much of [Andre] Norton's early work . . . Fascinating!" —*Dragon*

"A good, lively, fast-moving story . . . I'm delighted to recommend it." —Judith Tarr, author of
The Hound and the Falcon trilogy

★ ★ ★

DON'T MISS THESE *STARBRIDGE* ADVENTURES:

Book One: *StarBridge*
Book Two: *Silent Dances*

The STARBRIDGE Series

STARBRIDGE by A.C. Crispin

STARBRIDGE 2: SILENT DANCES by A.C. Crispin
and Kathleen O'Malley

STARBRIDGE 3: SHADOW WORLD
by A.C. Crispin and Jannean Elliott

Also by A.C. Crispin

V
YESTERDAY'S SON
TIME FOR YESTERDAY
GRYPHON'S EYRIE *(with Andre Norton)*

Acknowledgments

I don't know if it's appropriate to acknowledge one's collaborator, but, in my case, it would definitely be inappropriate if I did not. Seven years ago, just as her own career was taking off, Ann Crispin took the time to befriend a fan who wrote her a letter. Her critiques of my first book attempt and her call two years later with an invitation to join the StarBridge team provided a rare apprenticeship in the writing craft. Thank you, Ann.

I appreciate also our agent, Merrilee Heifetz, and our editor, Ginjer Buchanan, for, along with Ann, taking a chance on new, unknown writers. I hope the *StarBridge* series will continue to be an open door for new talent.

Sincere thanks also to the following:

My entire family, particularly Dorothy Craig Elliott (for loving me at my most difficult, as only a mother can), Suzanne E. Rule (the sister who said, "Over the transom can also work," and then proved it by calmly submitting two books that hit the bookstores long before this one, the rascal), and Katrina E. DeBusk (for her own work of creation in producing the dearest nephew ever). I love you all.

Michon, for years of listening and encouragement on all my projects.

Kathy, for laboring over a long, in-depth review.

My bosses, for always inquiring how the book was going and never mentioning bloodshot eyes.

So many friends who, with patient anticipation that this book would actually materialize, supplied buckets of support, reader duties, and innumerable kindnesses—friends like Judy, Jerry, Joan and her wonderful group, Kary, Tom, Jim, and the lunch bunch (Elaine, Michelle, Helen, Kim, and Nancy).

And, finally, I wish to send a big thank-you to all the readers of this book who are joining in the environmental effort to save our precious earth. That human beings *will* explore the galaxy someday is a cherished dream for us science fiction types—but let's keep a home to come back to.

—Jannean Elliott

This book is dedicated to my fifth-grade teacher, Mrs. L. Blum, with gratitude for the very first vote of confidence,

and

to the wonderful students of Brainerd, Howard, and Tyner Schools, Chattanooga, Tennessee, 1970–1980, from a teacher who remembers the lessons of life we shared.

—Jannean Elliott

Prologue

The four moons of Elseemar rose one by one over the mountain peaks, sending multiple shadows gliding along the ground. Shadows flowed beneath the tall trees, chasing along the furrows of the field where Lieor worked, loosening thc soil around each of the sestel seedlings with a hoe.

The Elpind labored steadily, carefully, but Lieor's mind was far removed from the job at hand. Tomorrow would be the most important day of the Elpind's life. Soon after dawn, Lieor and many other Elspind would receive the first dosage of the new drug the team of alien scientists had developed in the mountain lab. They were calling their recently synthesized discovery Elhanin, which meant, in Elspindlor, "life-more-long."

Tomorrow a new life for Lieor would begin—a life that might prove twice as long as an Elpind could otherwise expect. The scientists believed that Elhanin would roughly double the years Lieor would remain a neuter, a "hin," and also increase the time that the Elpind would have after hin's Change, when Lieor would become either "heen" (male), or "han" (female).

Unlike Lieor's parents, hin might actually live to wean all of heen's or han's children, see them growing up, before dying.

Lieor reached the end of a row, then halted work for a moment to look up at the lab nestled into the mountainside.

The Elpind's huge, round eyes shone with more than reflected moonlight, bright as they were with expectation and eagerness. *Tomorrow*, hin thought, feeling the chill night wind stir the downy hair on hin's spindly but wiry-strong arms and legs. *Tomorrow life truly begins anew for all of us . . .*

The Elpind shivered, but hin's shudder was born of eager anticipation, not cold. The lab, every light shining, glimmered like a beacon of hope against the dark mountainside. The scientists from the Cooperative League of Systems, along with Elpind herbalists, were evidently working the night through. Lieor knew from talks with hin's Heeyoon friend, Moonrunner, that the scientists were determined to stay on schedule with their testing program.

The Elpind moved to the new row of sestel seedlings with a skip and a bounce that was even more energetic than usual. It was odd to think of Moonrunner and the other CLS scientists awake the entire night, for the off-worlders usually slept when it was dark. Lieor still found the idea of sleeping every night of one's life one of the most alien things about them.

Elspind almost never slept. Instead, they remained busy: tending their crops, constructing dwellings and outbuildings from native stone and wood, spinning plant fibers to weave into clothing for the han and heen, as well as blankets and rugs for their homes. Even Elpind times of relaxation were filled with "Tellings"—history, legend, and cultural beliefs combined in a rich oral tradition.

As Lieor worked, hin thought longingly of hin's sibling Eerin. Lieor missed Eerin with an intensity that surprised even the Elpind. They were the last two surviving neuters in their family. Their other siblings had all entered Enelwo, the Change from which neuters emerged as males or females . . . or died in the process. Nine sunrises ago, Eerin had boarded one of the off-worlders' shuttles and had left Elseemar behind.

Not so long ago, we still believed that Elseemar's sky was the end of creation, Lieor thought. *We thought we were the only people there were . . .*

Now everyone knew of the vast, dark void behind the sky, the void the off-worlders called "space." The aliens who had traveled to Elseemar from other worlds were of different species, but all belonged to the CLS, the Cooperative League of Systems. Lieor pictured the strangenesses of the off-worlders in hin's mind: the long, limbless creatures called "Mizari"; the small flying beings from a world called "Apis" (though the beings themselves had another name for it); large, strong, maned Simiu who walked on all fours; and the tall, fanged, furry beings that walked two-legged, like the Elspind, and were called "Heeyoon."

And even these were not all the varieties that belonged to the CLS. Eerin had said that at StarBridge Academy, hin would be meeting many others, among them humans . . . certainly one of the oddest species, from everything Lieor had heard.

Surely, Lieor mused, *Eerin will return to Elseemar with many fine Tellings to share with us!*

Suddenly the Elpind's round, softly furred head turned as hin listened intently. Hin discerned a faint sound in the woods surrounding the sestel field—the sound of footsteps, but not ordinary, friendly footsteps. These soft patterings held something furtive and stealthy about them.

Alarmed, Lieor peered into the trees, and finally made out several Elspind stealing through the forest. A stray shaft of moonlight caught the design on one of the tunics they wore. Lieor could not see the device clearly, but hin did not have to—its general shape betrayed it. Only the Wospind, the People of Death, wore the image of a diving Shadowbird embroidered on their clothing!

And they had come from the direction of the CLS laboratory. Realizing that, Lieor's heart contracted with fear. Throwing down the hoe, hin broke into a run. The Elpind raced through the woods, driving hinself up the mountain's slope, bounding agilely over fallen trees and low-lying shrubs. All the while, Lieor was filled with a terrible urgency . . . and a sense of foreboding.

The Wospind were a small—but increasingly vocal—group of Elspind who had protested the presence of the CLS scientists from the beginning. "Our lifecycle may be short," they vehemently maintained, "but it is the one nature intended for us. To defy nature is wrong. No one—especially no off-worlder—should tamper with what we are and what we will be!"

"I'm not sure it's wise for your leaders to ignore the Wospind as they are doing," Moonrunner, the Heeyoon scientist who was Lieor's special friend, had commented recently. "Ignoring a problem doesn't make it go away."

"The Great Council's position is that if the Wospind do not wish to take Elhanin, then that is their choice," Lieor had replied heatedly. "But they must not take our right to do so away from us! Let them reject Elhanin—we will outlive them all!"

"They are growing angrier every day." Moonrunner's long gray muzzle wrinkled at the memory. "Some have shouted threats at us as we leave the confines of the lab. I can smell their hate and fear; it is increasing as we approach the large-scale testing."

"The Wospind have never hurt anyone," Lieor reminded hin's friend. "Except for the clan feuds—and the last of those ended many generations ago—we Elspind have always been a peaceful people."

Now those dismissive words returned to haunt Lieor as hin dashed up the mountain slope, a nameless fear filling hin's mind and heart. Wospind could have had no good reason for visiting the CLS laboratory under the cover of darkness.

Lieor had almost reached the lab's lighted grounds when a terrible thunder shook the mountainside and the lab erupted in a searing inferno of light and heat. Chunks of native stone and the aliens' building material rained down as Lieor fell and rolled, sheltering hin's head with hin's arms.

When Lieor dared look again, long, leaping flames had engulfed the main laboratory complex and were spreading toward the rest of the buildings. The roar of the fire almost masked the sounds of screams. Squinting against the glare, Lieor made out several dark forms silhouetted against the brightness as they staggered away from the burning portion.

Shocked, numbed with horror, Lieor climbed to hin's feet, hesitated, then, seeing a motionless dark form, hin darted forward. Terrible heat singed hin's downy fur as Lieor grabbed the alien's legs and began dragging the other toward safety. Reaching the sheltering darkness of the trees, Lieor looked down, and realized that the rescued alien was a Simiu.

Turning toward Lalcipind, Lieor began shouting for help, but suddenly a howl of purest agony drowned out hin's voice.

The Elpind whirled to see a fiery figure running toward the woods, leaping and capering in a frenzy of pain. Its death cry filled the air, resounding off the mountain slopes. Even as Lieor started toward it, trying to think of a way to tackle the victim, smother the flames, the runner collapsed, still writhing. By the time the Elpind reached it, it was mercifully dead.

Lieor shuddered as the rankness of burned flesh filled hin's nostrils. The body was hideously charred, but still . . . hin knew.

It was—had been—Moonrunner.

The Elpind started nervously as a shadow before hin suddenly became substance, stepping out from between the tree trunks. The newcomer was a dun-colored neuter like Lieor.

"Tell everyone," said the stranger, "tell them that this"—hin waved a slender arm at the lab—"this is what will happen to all those from other worlds who come to Elseemar. Warn any aliens who still live to leave our world and never return. Tell the WirElspind—Elseemar's precious Great Council—that the research aimed at altering our lifecycle must *stop*. Tell them that Orim, leader of all Wospind, has so decreed it!"

Orim melted back into the shadows and disappeared.

Later, after the survivors were being helped, and the flames were finally under control, Lieor knelt beside Moonrunner's body. "Moonrunner," hin whispered the ritual words, "El is life and Wo is death and each completes the other. In the quick flight of a Shadowbird El becomes Wo. Let it be, and let it be ever so." The words comforted hin; death, after all, was an old friend on Elseemar.

Then Lieor rose and left the fitfully burning lab, climbing quickly up the mountain path behind the aliens' still-untouched living quarters and secondary lab buildings. Three of the moons were already gone; only Orood hung stubbornly in the sky. Dawn was breaking.

Reaching the clearing, hin began the Mortenwol, dancing for hin's shattered dreams of a new life, dancing for those who had embraced Wo and begun the final journey this past night . . . dancing especially for Moonrunner. *Hin will always remember*, Lieor promised silently as hin leaped and turned, feeling the terrible heaviness in hin's chest lighten a little.

And then, when the sun had risen fully into the sky and the Mortenwol, the death dance, was finished, Lieor went to tell the Council what Orim had said.

CHAPTER 1

◆

Wins and Losses

Cara Hendricks straightened up suddenly, convinced she'd just heard a soft, slithering sound from the other side of the door. Quickly she activated her camera with an abrupt, nervous gesture, and the small, tubelike device rose into the air and took position over her left shoulder. As she glanced anxiously around, the tiny, gold sensor patch attached to the dark skin just above her left cheekbone signaled the little instrument to follow her gaze. The autocam whirred softly, recording everything she saw.

Long seconds passed. Nothing happened.

"Camera off," Cara muttered, though she left it hovering in the air. With a sigh she settled back in her seat, running a hand over her hair, checking that no strands had escaped from her sleek chignon. Usually Cara let her black hair fluff around her face naturally, but today she wanted to look every inch the professional journalist. After smoothing the skirt of her best blue suit, she folded her hands in her lap with an outwardly relaxed air.

Her pleasantly bland surroundings resembled a hundred other waiting rooms the seventeen-year-old black girl had seen back on Earth. Cara still found it difficult to believe that she was far below the surface of an airless asteroid in outer space, light-years away from Earth.

Any minute now, she would meet her first extraterrestrial.

Her autocam hovered faithfully beside her. The latest in microvideo technology, it was on loan from the Associated Earth Press. Frank Madden's words as he'd placed the expensive piece of equipment in her hands echoed in her memory, making Cara smile.

"You won't have to think about your equipment at all," he'd promised. "This little gem is state of the art. It'll track, zoom, focus, adjust, and frame automatically. All you have to worry about is what you're going to ask during your interviews."

As if that's not enough to worry about, Cara thought, *since the second person I'll be talking to here at StarBridge Academy is an eminent diplomat who just happens to be a . . . big snake!* She'd seen Mizari on holo-vid many times, but that wasn't the same as coming face-to-face with one of the aliens.

Cara tensed, thinking again she'd heard a sound, but it was another false alarm. She glanced at her watch, seeing that ten minutes had passed since Dr. Robert Gable had left her here to wait for the elderly Mizari who was the Liaison between StarBridge Academy and the CLS.

To think that I've actually met someone who was aboard the ***Désirée,*** she thought. Somehow she'd figured the famous Rob Gable would be taller, but the slender, dark-haired psychologist had barely topped her own modest height. He was close to forty, Cara knew, but his unlined face and easygoing grin made him seem nearly as young as the students he counseled here at StarBridge.

He promised that we'd talk more later on, she mused. *Maybe . . . just maybe . . . I can get him to reminisce about his experiences fifteen years ago when he and Mahree Burroughs made their First Contact with the Cooperative League of Systems. Everyone knows how closemouthed he is about his personal life, so getting him to talk about that would be a real feather in my cap . . .*

For all her anxious listening, Cara never picked up any kind of warning—any whisper of scales, any slithery sound. Suddenly the door slid open, and the Liaison Officer between the

CLS and the Academy at StarBridge flowed into the room.

"Ms. Hendricks," said the Mizari in English, with a graceful inclination of his wedge-shaped head, "I am Ssoriszs. Forgive me for making you wait. I bid you welcome to StarBridge." His voice was thin, but pleasant, and the extra hiss on the "s" sounds was only a minor distraction.

Cara stood up hastily to face the alien. "Thank you, Esteemed One," she said. "I'm very glad to meet you, sir." There! The greeting she'd memorized had come out perfectly, but then her rehearsed sentiments abruptly deserted her. Instead, to her horror, she heard herself blurt, "I—I didn't know you'd be so beautiful!"

Ssoriszs dipped his head a second time. "You are most kind."

The Mizari was easily three times as long as Cara was tall, and as thick around as her waist. He faced her with the first third of his supple body reared up like a cobra; the rest was neatly coiled. His sleek scales glittered palest mint-green, with amber and emerald diamond shapes patterning his back. His pupilless eyes were golden, and his entire head was haloed with long, slender appendages that waved constantly. The effect created by the iridescent tendrils was that of a shimmering, rainbow-colored cloud that floated and danced with each small movement of the Mizari's head.

The alien regarded Cara steadily with his lidless eyes. "Allow me first to compliment you on your recent achievement. I watched your winning documentary on the socioeconomic effects of the First Contact on the major Terran governments. The Associated Earth Press made a fine choice when it awarded you the title of 'Young Journalist of the Year.' We here at StarBridge are most fortunate that your prize was the chance to come and visit with us."

Cara flushed with pleasure. "Thank you, sir. It's a pleasure and an honor. Did they tell you I'm to do a documentary while I'm here, a student's perspective on StarBridge? I'd like to begin filming you now, if I may." *Good recovery,* she congratulated herself. *Maybe he'll never guess you were so flustered meeting him that you forget to activate the camera!*

"Certainly," he agreed.

She waved to the autocam and continued smoothly, "Since my knowledge of people from other worlds has so far been gained through books and the networks, I'm looking forward to meeting the students here at StarBridge." The words of her planned speech were surfacing in her mind.

"They are looking forward to meeting you, also," he assured her. "And as for meeting people from other worlds, you will have a rare opportunity while you are here: a chance to meet an Elpind."

Cara's heart leaped excitedly. "You're getting one of the ten!"

"Well informed, as a journalist should be," said the Mizari approvingly. "I had wondered whether the long trip in hibernation might have caused you to miss the latest news."

"I only spent two months in hibernation," Cara explained. "The last month I caught up on all that had been happening while I was asleep. One of the biggest stories, of course, was that ten Elspind had been chosen to be the first of their kind to leave Elseemar and visit selected CLS-member planets. StarBridge isn't exactly a planet; it didn't occur to me that one of them might come here."

Cara didn't try to conceal her excitement at the Mizari's news. Until now, contact with the people of Elseemar had been carefully screened and limited by the CLS. As a result, anything Cara could discover about this relatively unknown world would be news to the average human viewer.

"We were unsure ourselves after that regrettable episode of violence on Elseemar," Ssoriszs said. "The ten emissaries had just departed a few days earlier, and we thought the CLS might rescind their offer to sponsor the trip and send them back home. But they elected to let the goodwill tour continue."

Cara nodded. "I'm glad they did, though what happened at that lab was a terrible tragedy. I understand that some radical group is demanding that the planetary government ban all off-worlders."

The Mizari nodded. "That is what I heard, also."

"I'd like to get a chance to interview this Elpind about the entire incident. Maybe he or she can explain what was behind it all."

"You will have that opportunity, though, of course, I cannot promise that Eerin will wish to answer those particular questions. None of the ten are scheduled to visit Earth," Ssoriszs added. "You may well be the first human journalist with an opportunity to interview an Elpind."

"That thought has been uppermost in my mind ever since you told me about this visit," Cara confessed with a grin.

The Mizari hissed softly, and Cara decided it was his equivalent of laughter. *I know because his fangs are folded back,* she thought, pleased that she could "read" an alien and pleased, too, to realize that her nervousness was gone. "When will Eerin," she tested the name's pronunciation, "arrive?"

"Twelve, perhaps fourteen days from now. You will have time to get acquainted with StarBridge first. I can give you a brief tour of the school now, if you wish."

"Yes, please!"

Ssoriszs uncoiled, and Cara followed her escort out the door. The smooth slither of the alien's limbless body over the floor fascinated her . . . and so did the fact that she had to stretch her legs to keep up.

As they followed the gentle curve of the corridor, Ssoriszs explained that this large asteroid, rich in the energy-producing substance humans called "radonium," had been donated by his people, then towed into position by CLS engineers. Most of the Academy was constructed beneath its rocky crust. Four domes protruded above the surface. One of those domes, the smallest, was the shuttle hangar where Cara had disembarked.

The second largest dome, an observation and lounge area, was the first stop on their tour. The view of the stars through the dome's transparent plas-steel was glorious. Sharp and unwinking because there was no atmosphere, they glowed with subtle variations in color, seeming amazingly close.

Cara sank down on one of the couches intended for human occupants and stared upward raptly. "They're so beautiful," she whispered finally. "Which one is Sol? Earth's sun, I mean?"

"I regret that your sun is too small to be visible from here," the Liaison told her, and the young journalist had to swallow down a sudden wave of homesickness. Determined not to give in to it, she concentrated fiercely on the view, turning her head so her camera would pick up every angle. Cara could also make out the shape and docking lights of nearby StarBridge Station silhouetted against the stellar profusion.

"Our Academy is named for this sector of space," the Mizari

said. "We have no sun nearby, so here it is always night . . . and always beautiful. Because there is no nearby sun, this sector of space has long been a place for the S.V. ships to change course—far enough from the gravitational pull of any star that the ships may safely leave and reenter metaspace. Vessels traveling to and from most of the Fourteen Known Worlds pass through StarBridge Sector. Thus this central, 'bridge' location made this site ideal for our school."

They left the observatory with Cara promising herself to visit its view at least once every day that she spent at StarBridge. The next stop was the huge auditorium dome called the Arena, and then they took a quick look at the botanical garden dome, housing plants and trees from many worlds in a riot of living, colorful shapes.

"Some of our classes meet on this level," commented Ssoriszs as they left the botanical garden. "Would you care to see one in progress?"

"Absolutely."

Cara had thought she was prepared, but she still felt a sense of shock as the Mizari activated a viewing window. Perched on top of a lectern and waving feelers energetically was a creature that resembled an enormous wasp. The alien's antennae stroked what Cara knew was a voder and slurred, hissing sounds emerged.

"That's an Apis!" whispered Cara excitedly. "What is it saying? What subject is this?" She looked at the students, recognizing Simiu, Heeyoon, Mizari, another Apis, a couple of Chhhh-kk-tu, and, of course, several humans. All were listening attentively. Some keyed notes on pocket computer links to accompany their recordings of the lecture.

"Dr. Zenez is our chief dietician here at StarBridge," Ssoriszs said. "She's giving a guest lecture today on the psychological connection between the olfactory and the digestive systems in various species. Our students must be able to understand and control their instinctive reactions to odors and appearances of native foods if they are to eat on planets other than their own."

Dietician! Cara remembered what a fit her mother threw if a fly landed on the food at a family picnic. What would Mama say if Dr. Zenez served her potato salad? She choked back a giggle, trying to sound as if she were clearing her throat. "Ummmm . . . what language is she speaking?"

"My own," Ssoriszs replied. "Mizari is the official CLS language, therefore we use it here. Each student must be fluent in Mizari. That is in addition to whatever language they have chosen for their specialty."

After a few moments of intent observation, Cara indicated her readiness to move on. Rounding the next corner, she could hear the same rapid, sibilant speech that had come from the dietician's voder. This time, however, the hissing sounds were sharply accentuated and the voice was several decibels louder . . . and not, Cara realized quickly, just because the conversation was taking place in the hallway.

The speaker was another serpentlike Mizari, a smaller one than Ssoriszs, but just as beautiful, with pale golden scales and brown patterns. The alien faced a human male who appeared to be two or three years older than Cara herself.

"The teacher is angry?" Cara asked the CLS Liaison quietly, basing her guess mostly on the young man's defiant stance, but also on the stiff kinks in the alien's sinuous body and the jerky motions of the haloing tentacles.

"Yes," answered Ssoriszs softly. "It seems the student has failed to complete an important assignment, not the first such failure, I gather. The teacher reminds the student that he was formerly one of her best and claims he must be deliberately sabotaging his potential."

Cara studied the miscreant. He was of medium height, had dark blond hair, and a solid athletic build. *Good-looking,* she thought, watching him stand with his head up, his well-cut chin jutted out, stoically absorbing the teacher's tirade.

The young man's eyes shifted to hold Cara's for a moment. She saw that they were a stormy greenish gray. The journalist looked away quickly, embarrassed to have been caught staring.

"Come," said the Mizari. "We have much more to see."

As they moved away, Cara wondered how she could find this student again. It would be interesting to interview someone who obviously was having problems. *No school is perfect or has perfect students . . .* she thought. *Not even the Academy at StarBridge, it seems . . .*

"Do you know that student's name, Esteemed One?"

"He is a fourth-year student. Mark Kenner," Ssoriszs replied as his tentacles waved her aboard a nearby elevator. The lift pressed them gently against its walls as it went sideways, then dropped. "On the next level," said the Mizari, "we will see the library, the gym, and . . . "

"Mark, wait up!"

The moment he heard himself hailed, Mark Kenner remembered what he'd forgotten. With a sigh he turned and let Sulinda Carmel, his girlfriend for nearly six months now, catch up to him. Her ebony curls tumbled prettily as she half jogged through the crowd of students outside the Arena. Her olive cheeks were flushed with anger.

"I looked for you at lunch, but you didn't show. Did you forget you were supposed to meet me at the Spiral Arm?" Her black eyes sparkled with a mixture of irritation and concern as she stopped before him.

"Susu, I'm really sorry," Mark said humbly. "I had something else on my mind. I didn't get an assignment in to Esteemed Rissaz, and she was furious . . . and that was right before lunch, so I went to the library to try and catch up . . ." Mark trailed off, seeing a tally in the girl's eyes of how many times he'd let her down these past two and a half months since his mother . . . "Honest, it just slipped my mind, Su. If you'll forgive me, we could go to dinner instead."

"Now that I've accosted you in the hallway, you mean? We wouldn't have had a lunch date if I hadn't arranged it, because you haven't called me in days. I don't deserve that, you know. If there's something you're trying to tell me, have the courtesy to tell me to my face."

Two of Sulinda's traits that attracted Mark were her mercurial temper and her directness . . . but not at the moment. After an already trying day, Mark's own temper threatened to stir, but he made another attempt to soothe her. "Come on," he coaxed. "You know I didn't stand you up deliberately. Rissaz bawled me out thoroughly, and my mind was on that instead of lunch, that's all."

This time Sulinda picked up on his reference to the Mizari instructor. "Mark! Don't tell me the assignment you didn't complete was that one on Mizari art forms, not after Rissaz gave you a two-week extension!" She was aghast.

Sulinda ranked in the top five percentile, and Mark knew she'd never been late on an assignment in her life. *Up to three months ago,* he thought bitterly, *neither had I.*

"Do you want to wash out of here? With only a year to go?" Her tone held more irritation than sympathy. "Don't you think that would be pretty stupid?"

That stung . . . and came far too close to a topic Mark wasn't ready to discuss. "What I want," he growled, "is for people to get off my case for just one day!"

At his unexpected vehemence her eyes widened, and she backed away a step as if he'd threatened to strike her.

"Shit," Mark groaned, reaching out for her. "I didn't mean it that way, Su. You know you're the only one I can . . . " He had to stop, embarrassed by the unexpected lump in his throat.

Sulinda took another step backward. Her eyes beneath her soft, tumbled bangs brimmed with angry tears. "Mark, I've tried to keep us together, but I'm tired of being the only one trying. It's been nearly three months since your mother died and you're still punishing yourself for something that was in no way your fault. That's bad enough; it's causing you to let go of your grades, your friends, everything you've worked for. But lately you've started punishing *me*! I don't intend to take it anymore!"

"Well, no one's forcing you to. If all you want to do is fight today, I'll take a rain check, thanks." Mark turned his back on her and walked the short distance to his locker. He thumbed it open, then stood staring blankly at the inside, trying to remember just what it was he had to do for tomorrow. He had a lot of assignments due . . . some of them, like Rissaz's report, *over*due. *I'll go to bed early,* he rationalized, tossing his data cassettes inside, *and study fresh in the morning . . .*

Sulinda hadn't moved; he could feel her eyes on his back. Mark shut the locker and reluctantly turned to face her.

Her dark eyes were brilliant with anger, but her voice was deadly quiet as she said, "I don't want to fight any more either, Mark. You're right. No one's forcing me, and I don't choose to be a masochist. I can't make you happy, and you're making *me* miserable." She took a couple of steps toward him and held out an open palm. On it lay his fourth year pin. She'd taken it off the breast of her blue StarBridge jumpsuit while his back had been turned.

He stared at her incredulously. "You really want to do this over one missed lunch?"

"It's not one lunch and you know it. We've done nothing but go through the motions for weeks now. I think you pushed me into this because you didn't have the guts to do it yourself. Am I right?"

No! You're wrong, Susu! Breaking up with you is the last thing I want. Why can't I tell you so? Mark wondered. Instead it was as if his mouth had a life of its own. "You're the one who's got it all figured out," he said evenly. "Not me."

She nodded sharply. "Fine, then. Good luck, Mark. You're going to need it."

Somehow the pin was in his hand. Mark stared at it as if he'd never seen it before. It showed him a tiny, holographic image of a rainbow bridge linking two planets against a black, star-studded sky. Emblazoned across the arch of the bridge were his initials: WMK. William Mark Kenner.

He looked back up to find Sulinda gazing pointedly at the breast of his gold-colored jumpsuit where her own pin, identical to his except for the initials, rested. Somehow he fumbled it off.

Sulinda took her pin back with a calm dignity. Before Mark could think of anything else to do or say, she was gone.

Mark stood frozen by his locker, the little pin digging into his palm, for what seemed like a long time. Beneath the momentary anger and the hurt, he felt the bone-deep tiredness of depression that plagued him so often now. It coiled around his limbs, weighing him down. Finally he sighed and headed for the small suite he shared with a second-year student, Hamir Rajannipah.

Hamir's short, slender frame was sprawled on the couch in their common living room. The eerie clattering of a Mizari windweed recording blasted from their sound system. Like Mark, Hamir was majoring in the Mizari culture.

"Hey, Mark," he greeted over the din, "you're late."

The older student made a perfunctory gesture, but didn't speak as he stalked past his roommate into his bedroom. The message light was flashing on his computer link, but Mark ignored it. *It's just Rob Gable,* he thought with a grim certainty, *wanting to know why I missed my counseling session today.*

Throwing himself on the bed, he flung an arm across his eyes to block out the illumination from the ceiling panels. He couldn't muster the energy to order the lights to dim.

"Mark?" There was a quick knock at the door, then Hamir came in without waiting for an invitation. He surveyed his suitemate with concern. "Uh-oh. You look like you just lost your best friend."

"Yeah, well . . . " Mark shrugged without emerging from the shelter of his arm. "Rough day."

"You ready for dinner?"

"No," he mumbled. "You go on."

"Thetor and I waited on you. I told him I'd call when you got in. We were all going to study for tomorrow's test on Mizari generational taboos, remember?"

"I'll catch up to you later," Mark promised, knowing he wouldn't. "It's been a long day. I just need a few minutes to myself."

The boy hesitated, then shrugged. "Okay. Suit yourself."

Hamir's words lingered behind after he'd gone. *You look like you just lost your best friend . . .*

Mark blinked against a sudden sting of tears. That's what Sulinda had been to him, all right. His best friend. She was fun and she was sexy, but more important, she was a very genuine person whom Mark had come to admire. And, yes, depend on. They'd shared everything; he'd never known that kind of companionship before. *Dammit, Susu . . . why didn't I stop you? I could have, I know it . . .*

On impulse, to shut out the cry for her in his mind, Mark rolled off the bed. "Mirror," he commanded, and the wall opposite him flickered, then went reflective. He stared curiously at the face reflected there, wondering if it seemed different to others. Almost everyone he met lately who knew him had commented that he didn't look well . . .

His reflected countenance seemed much the same . . . perhaps a bit thinner, the slight hollows beneath the high cheekbones more pronounced. He'd lost weight, though he'd tried not to miss out on too many of his self-defense workouts.

Somehow yelling and punching and kicking had helped him exorcise—if only for a moment—some of his demons.

There were dark shadows beneath his eyes, but those weren't uncommon, especially around exam time. So what was it that made people say he looked different? Perhaps it was the expression in his eyes. Even to himself he appeared weary and beaten . . . as though nothing much mattered anymore.

Mark suddenly realized the little rainbow pin was still clenched in his fist. He tossed it on the nightstand where it caught the light as it tumbled to a halt between two small holo cubes, one of Sulinda and one of his mother. *Ironic,* he thought bitterly. *I'm studying to be an interrelator, a living bridge between worlds—and I can't even bridge the space between myself and the people I love . . . loved . . .*

He shook his head. Becoming a StarBridge interrelator had always been such a reachable dream for him. He'd always enjoyed being with people, learning about people—any kind of "people." Differences in outward form or customs didn't frighten or repulse him; they only intrigued him. "Mark's never met a stranger," his mother had bragged to the StarBridge testing panel that had profiled her son at age twelve.

At fourteen, Mark had left Earth to attend the Academy. From the first he'd taken readily to the alien languages, exotic foods, and weird mixture of living styles and mores that were commonplace in a school where beings from so many different worlds lived and studied together. While some human students spent their first year uneasily struggling to accept giant slugs or creatures resembling baby blankets as sentient beings, Mark had no trouble. "A natural interrelator," his teachers had declared. "One of our best ever."

Until now.

Mark scooped up the pin and dropped it in a drawer, where he wouldn't have to see its mute reminder of failed ideals and dreams. Sulinda was right. His grades weren't the only thing that had gone awry this quarter. One by one he'd antagonized his friends, rejecting their sympathy, driving them away. He had shut out those who wanted to help him, like Rob Gable.

It was his own fault, he knew that. He knew his feelings about his mother's death were tangled somehow with a growing certainty that he didn't belong at this school. What he didn't know was why he couldn't seem to escape from the whirl-pool of guilt and grief that was sucking him under. Everything he'd ever cared about, everything he'd tried to be, was swirling away, vanishing into that maelstrom.

The other thing he didn't know was what to do about it.

CHAPTER 2

◆

Decisions and Schemes

Cara decided she was in a mild state of shock. *To go from meeting your very first extraterrestrial in the morning to facing dozens of them by dinner is too much for anybody. Overload,* she diagnosed clinically.

Esteemed Ssoriszs had given her a choice: dinner with the school's Chhhh-kk-tu Administrator tonight or tomorrow night. Cara had chosen the postponement, figuring she'd see more interesting sights in one of the student dining areas.

And was I right! Though I'm not sure "interesting" is the word for it . . .

Incredible that there could be so many different ways of eating! She'd watched food siphoned, absorbed, crunched, or packed into orifices where orifices had no business being. At least she guessed some of the stuff she saw disappearing could be called food. Her own appetite had rapidly vanished.

After a while she'd sent her student guide back to do homework, promising she would go to her room and fall into bed after dinner. Now she was just relaxing, with her camera off.

Well, not exactly relaxing. Even with the new things to see and learn during her first day at StarBridge, she hadn't been able to get the Elpind's upcoming visit out of her mind. A documentary on StarBridge wasn't half the news that the interview with Eerin would be . . . and she intended to be completely prepared for what might be the chance of a lifetime.

She was finishing her second page of draft questions, sipping at a fruit drink, when she looked up to see someone she recognized coming through the door. It was the young man from the hallway.

Cara watched as he collected a tray and headed for a servo, admiring his build. *Wide shoulders, nice butt, and handsome, too. Wonder if he has a girlfriend?* The thought made her grin inwardly. *Where's your professional detachment? Those are hardly journalistic thoughts, girl.*

She looked him over again, searching for a clue to his mood. If she wanted to interview him while the emotions of his trying day were still fresh with him, now seemed like the best time. Waving her camera unobtrusively into position, but not turning it on, she got up and crossed over to where he sat.

"Hello! Mind if I join you?"

Listlessly he nodded at one of the empty seats. Cara sat down and took a deep breath. "I'm Cara Hendricks, a journalist from Earth. What's your name?"

"Mark Kenner," he said reluctantly.

"I'd like to interview you, Mark. May I activate my camera?"

"Why me?" he countered. "I'm sure there are plenty of other people who would enjoy the opportunity." As he finished, Mark seemed to realize how rude that sounded, and amended, "Sorry, no offense, but I'm just not in the mood." His hazel eyes were shadowed and unhappy.

He looks like he hasn't got a friend in the universe, Cara thought. "I can see that," she said, "but that's exactly why I want to interview you. You see, I'm doing a documentary, and every student I interviewed today, Mizari, Simiu, Chhhh-kk-tu, human, whatever, they all told me how wonderful StarBridge is and how much they love it here. I'm sure that's true, but as a journalist, I know it can't be true all the time."

"So you're looking for the other side of the story?"

"Right!"

"Well, I'm not it. I agree with the rest of them. The Academy is great." He took a determined bite of his sandwich.

"It didn't look so great for you in the hall today," Cara said bluntly.

Mark stopped chewing and stared at her, then shrugged. "School is school, no matter where. You don't do your assignments, you get a lecture."

"But isn't it weird to get that lecture from a big snake?"

For the first time strong emotion flared in the young man's hazel eyes; he glared at her indignantly. "We don't have *snakes* here, Ms. Hendricks. We have *people*. If you're going to do a documentary on this place, you need to get ideas like that out of your head. In fact, it's that kind of human-chauvinist, bigoted thinking that this school is dedicated to—"

He broke off, staring hard at her. "Wait a minute. You didn't mean that . . . you were just getting a rise out of me."

"Very quick," Cara said approvingly. "For a fish that hit the line hard, you sure spit the hook right back out. I used to go fishing a lot back home," she added in response to his quizzical look. "In the Appalachian wilderness park, only an hour's hop from home. I'm from Old NorthAm. Southeastern Metroplex—Atlanta division. How about you?"

"Uh . . . Earth. Old NorthAm." He didn't say what part.

"Look, I apologize for baiting you," Cara said. "I do understand the school's mission. I've read Mahree Burroughs' *First Contacts* three times, and admired the whole idea of this school ever since the project was first proposed."

He smiled wryly, but at least there was genuine humor in it. "When Rob Gable and Esteemed Ssoriszs first proposed this school, you were still in diapers. *I* was barely four."

She grinned back. "Okay, point conceded. But I do agree wholeheartedly with the StarBridge mission. However, a good journalist tries to examine all angles to a story. No place in the universe is perfect, right?" Mark had stiffened up again, so she shrugged and waved reassuringly. "Okay, never mind. Let's just chat a minute. Off the record."

"Off the record?" Mark asked skeptically, but then he sighed and smiled again. "Okay, I surrender."

"Great! Thanks," said Cara. "For one thing, I'm trying to boil down all the information I learned today into quick exposition for my viewers. Everyone knows about the human students who are telepaths, and are studying to go out on the exploratory ships. But lots of people on Earth are still foggy about the distinction between translators and interrelators. So will you correct me if I'm wrong?" she requested.

He nodded.

"Okay. Translators major in languages, perhaps as many as four or even five different ones. They learn to translate accurately and rapidly, and after graduation, most of them wind up working for the CLS on Shassiszss for several years. Right?"

"You've got it. After translators work for a while as interpreters, they're apt to go on to other professions—medicine, interstellar law"—he nodded at Cara—"interstellar journalism—you name it."

She made a note using her computerpen. "Good. Now, the interrelators . . . they learn only one or maybe two other languages, aside from the basic Mizari everyone has to know just to attend here. But they learn more than just a world's language. They learn about the people, the history, the cultures of a planet. Right?"

"Basically. But it's more than that, even. Interrelators study the laws, social customs, mores, taboos—all facets of the culture and the forces that shaped it. An interrelator's goal is to be prepared to live on a alien world, as part of the diplomatic team. They learn to truly understand the point of view, the *mind-set* of another species."

Mark smiled faintly, obviously reminiscing. "My friend Tesa—she's out working as an interrelator now, on Trinity—used to say that interrelators were the best guarantee against the type of exploitation that resulted in the eradication of far too many races back on Earth hundreds of years ago."

"But most of the diplomatic teams currently operating aren't StarBridge graduates," Cara pointed out.

"That's true, and it's caused problems, believe me. Don't forget that StarBridge was only founded six years ago. But eventually, Rob and Esteemed Ssoriszs hope that all ambassadors will be Academy graduates."

"So what are you studying to be?" Cara thought she'd guessed, but wanted to hear it from him.

His eyes grew shadowed once more, and he glanced away. "An interrelator," he said, sounding as if the admission were dragged out of him forcibly.

"What year are you in?"

"I'm due to start my fifth year in two months."

She did a quick calculation. "So that makes you . . . what? Nineteen?"

"I'll be twenty in a month or so."

"You said you'll be beginning the fifth year. That's a long time to be away from home. Don't you miss Earth?"

He shrugged, then shook his head, not meeting her eyes. "Not much."

"Someone else told me today that each student is allowed to take a long break during either the third, fourth, or fifth year, if he or she wants. But she also told me that many students elect not to take that break, since it takes six months just for the travel time, and most of them don't want to lose nearly a year. What did you decide to do? Did you take the long break?"

Mark's expression froze. He began feeding his dishes into the table's recycling slot. "I've just realized how late it's getting," he said abruptly. "Look, it was nice meeting you."

"Wait!" Cara protested. "Did I say something wrong? Is it about the breaks? Did you lose your chance to take one because of your academic problems?" she guessed, remembering the scene in the hallway.

"You journalists never let go, do you?" He stood up. "Get him talking, you figured, and eventually work back around to his personal life. Well, I don't consider that subject to be any of your business—or any of your viewers' business, either!"

Cara flushed, glad that, with her coloring, Mark probably couldn't tell. She *had* been trying to draw him out, that was true. But she'd said "off the record," and she'd meant it. She hadn't activated her autocam while they'd been talking. *What's he so damned touchy about?* she wondered, feeling a stir of righteous anger.

"I'm sorry if that's what you think of me," she said, keeping her voice level. "What I thought is that StarBridge students would be eager to talk about their school and their lives here, proud of what they're doing. Not defensive. And certainly not downright rude." Glaring at him, she finished sarcastically, "Is that what they teach you here? To be nasty?"

As soon as the words left her mouth, Cara was instantly ashamed. A good journalist was supposed to be objective, but she'd let Mark's attitude get under her skin. As her taunts penetrated, he actually flinched.

"I'm sorry," she began hastily. "I didn't mean to—"

But Mark was already moving. He mumbled something at her, something that sounded like "not the school's fault," before he disappeared out the door.

A nightmare woke Mark again that night. He jerked up in the bed with a stifled shout, his heart pounding violently. It took a second or two to realize he was awake, and then, shuddering, he waved up the lights.

He rubbed his eyes blearily, then managed to focus. *Look at this mess, dammit!* He used to be reasonably neat. Now there were clothes, cassettes, dirty laundry, and half-eaten snacks everywhere.

With a long sigh, Mark crawled out of bed and began to pick up the stuff littering the floor. Better to straighten up the mess than to dwell on his problems.

But his mind wouldn't cooperate, and when he found the message-cassette on the floor under the desk, his memory played it back to him with cruel clarity:

"Mark, honey, I received your hologram yesterday," he could almost hear his mother say. "So much nicer than just an audio, even if it is more expensive."

But she had sent only an audio message herself. *That alone should have made me suspicious,* he thought. He was sure now that she had not wanted him to see the ravages of her illness in her face.

Shit, Mom, you didn't have to work so hard to hide the truth. I probably wouldn't have noticed, no matter what kind of message you sent . . . unless, maybe, you'd held up a sign.

In his hologram Mark had told his mother he'd decided not to take the long break StarBridge allowed at the end of his fourth year, as they'd originally planned. "The trip to Earth takes so long," he'd said. "And if I forgo the break, I can start right into my last year; it'll move the whole program and graduation up earlier. Mom, I'll definitely come home for a good long visit after that," he'd promised, knowing how much she'd missed her only child these past four years.

How comfortless, bitter even, that promise must have sounded to her! Mark clenched his fingers on the cassette until his knuckles whitened. It hadn't been until weeks later, when Rob Gable called him in to gently break the news, that he'd learned that his mother knew—had known all year—that she was dying.

It didn't matter that even had he taken his break, he wouldn't have made it home in time. What mattered was that he had taken away her hope of seeing him for the last time. What mattered was that in all her messages during that last year, he'd never once picked up on her desperation and the need behind her increasingly frequent references to his trip home. What mattered was that he'd even missed the ring of finality in some of the things she'd said in her last communication.

How can I be a hotshot interrelator, someone who specializes in understanding the other person's viewpoint, if I can't even figure out that my own mother is dying?

Mark flung the cassette against the far wall so hard its cover cracked. He froze, wondering if he'd damaged it . . . then decided he didn't really want to know, not right at the moment.

He had to get out of that room. Cautiously Mark opened his door and stepped into the living area he shared with Hamir. It was empty and silent, and the door to the other bedroom was closed. With a sigh of relief that his suitemate hadn't awakened, Mark slipped out into the main corridor.

He took a long walk through the dimly lit hallways of the Academy's artificial night. Night wanderings had become almost routine these past couple of months, and Mark's feet led him automatically to his usual final destination, the observation dome.

Thoughtfully, for a long time, he stared upward at the glowing stars, mulling over the choice that had haunted him for weeks now. It lay at the root of his inner turmoil and, Mark recognized, was probably the main reason he hadn't been able to share his feelings with Sulinda lately. His feelings lay too close to the path of his decision, a decision that had to be made by him alone—a decision that it was time to stop postponing.

Some will say I'm taking the coward's way out by quitting, Mark thought. He knew differently, knew what the cost would be to him for the rest of his life. But he had to consider the consequences, not only to him but to others; he had to do the right thing.

And so he made up his mind.

And to think there was a time when I was naive enough to think that administering a school would be a dull job, Rob Gable thought with a wry smile as he strode toward his office the following morning, with Cara Hendricks at his side. The school's Chief Psychologist almost voiced the thought aloud, but caught himself, remembering that the girl was a journalist. Rob had been burned by the press enough times in his youth to have learned caution, even when the reporters seemed as pleasant and ethical as this young woman.

Rob liked Cara and was impressed by her work. He knew that she was hoping that their interview this morning would include his reminiscing about the past, and his relationship with Mahree . . . and Claire, their daughter . . . but it wouldn't. Rob Gable didn't talk on the record about the things that were most important to him.

With one exception . . . this school.

StarBridge Academy was his baby, nearly as much as his twelve-year-old daughter. The doctor cheerfully seized every opportunity to be interviewed about the Academy, eager to keep its goals before the public eye. StarBridge *had* to succeed. Effective diplomacy and peaceful negotiations were no longer just ideals—they were essential. The explored universe was now a place where modern technology could wipe out an entire planet in less time than it took Rob's students to finish an evening's studies.

A Simiu student came barreling down the corridor at a headlong gallop. "Dakk'ahrrr," Rob growled, his throat protesting against the harshness of the Simiu syllables, "in the name of honor, *slow down*!"

The student skidded slightly as she hastily moderated her pace. "Apologies, Honored HealerGable," she yipped back over her shoulder.

Rob nodded and waved her on with a resigned expression. "Freshmen!" he muttered to Cara, shaking his head.

She smiled and nodded sympathetically, but her attention was clearly divided. This morning Cara wore a voder, a Mizari-designed one resembling a jeweled ear cuff more than an extremely sophisticated translation device, and the largest part of her attention was given to the conversations going on all around her.

She's a very attractive young woman, Rob mused, glancing at her animated, heart-shaped face. The gold sensor patch accentuated her high cheekbones, adding a slightly rakish air. Her wide, dark eyes sparkled with humor and intelligence, and her smile always seemed easy and genuine.

To think that she's the same age as Mahree when I first knew her, Rob thought with an inward shake of his head. *Was I ever that young?* He smiled at the young woman's eager expression as she passed two Vardi, careful not to stare openly. *Already she's fascinated by other species. Just like Mahree.* He realized that Cara reminded him, in some ways, of her. The young journalist had the same kind of quick, instinctive understanding, and the same relentless curiosity. *She's strong, too,* he thought. *Strong and practical, just like Mahree.*

Cara grinned, her eyes indicating a small knot of students they were just passing. Rob followed her gaze to the girl holding court.

"—and then Windracer broke his own record on the Space Sweeper. With one claw! Honestly, I thought the lasers would short out!"

The little group groaned in unison, "Dot, lasers don't . . ."

By then Rob and Cara were out of range. Glancing down the right branch of the corridor, Rob hastily warned Cara to turn off her camera. They were about to pass by a Shadgui.

Cara quickly complied. "Esteemed Ssoriszs warned me yesterday. He said they have a strong opposition to representations of their bodies, that it's a part of the Shadgui belief system." She regarded the people ahead of them with interest. "Is 'they' the correct term to use for a symbiont?"

"Correct enough," said Rob. "At least, when you're using English."

A human male about Cara's own height and coloring faced

the Shadgui, a huge, eyeless being who rather resembled a sloth. The presence of pink-tipped mammary glands amid the coarse dark brown hair covering her chest identified her as a female. On her shoulder, attached to her neck, rested a fat, reddish, warty-skinned creature with bright button eyes.

"Hress, you're coming to the game this afternoon, aren't you?" Rob heard the human student ask. "I've been assigned to describe all the plays in Shadgui, informal dialect. I want you to tell me if I say the words right."

"Honored will I be to have my tongue in your mouth, Ahmed," replied the alien female solemnly in halting English.

Beside him, Cara choked with stifled laughter, and Rob saw, even with the dark skin, Ahmed's vivid, involuntary blush. Chuckling, Rob stopped.

"Hress, you just made his day," he informed the Shadgui in Mizari. Rob glanced at Ahmed. "Are you going to supply the language lesson on this particular colloquialism or would you rather I did?"

Hress smoothed her shaggy chest hair, concerned. "Is it that I say wrong?"

"That's okay, Dr. Rob, I'll explain," Ahmed said, recovering his aplomb. He caught Hress by one of her massive arms and led her away with him. Rob heard him beginning his explanation, this time in Mizari. "It's just a misunderstanding, Hress. The reason it's funny is that, on Earth, when two humans kiss . . . "

"This voder is great!" Cara exclaimed. "I can understand everything, no matter what language. With this technology available, do new students ever balk at having to actually learn Mizari and all the other languages they study?"

"When they do, I tell them about the time Mahree and I had our First Contact with the CLS, and how we learned that communication between worlds is too delicate an art to be entrusted to mechanized translation programs." Rob spoke with conviction. "Even the best translation program can have glitches, which can have serious consequences during delicate negotiations."

As he finished, a soft bell chimed; the corridor lighting flashed off, then back on, and the already-thinning crowd practically disappeared.

"Uh-oh, I'm supposed to be open for business by now," Rob said. He smiled at Cara. "I don't have anyone scheduled but you, though, and since we're already together, I guess I'm not late. Got your interview questions ready?"

"Of course." They rounded the last curve and she stopped suddenly. "Uh . . . Dr. Gable, you may not have anyone scheduled, but I think someone's here to talk to you anyway."

Rob's eyes narrowed in concern as he recognized the young man pacing before the door to his office. He'd been counseling Mark intensively since his mother's death, but lately the student had become more and more withdrawn, avoiding discussions of the things that were really troubling him. Yesterday's missed session hadn't been the first. Now here he was voluntarily.

As they say in one of my favorite movies, I've got a bad feeling about this, Rob thought grimly, taking in Mark's pale face and determined expression. Absently, he wondered what to do with Cara as they came face-to-face with the student. He didn't want to put Mark off; all his professional instincts warned him that the young man needed immediate attention.

"Hi, Mark," he said.

"Hi," Cara echoed hesitantly. She and Mark eyed each other warily.

Rob masked his surprise. "Cara, this is Mark Kenner, one of our fourth-year students, and Mark, this is—"

"We've met," Mark broke in, "and I owe her something. An apology.

"I'm truly sorry about last night," he said to Cara. "I took my bad mood out on you, and I was rude. Please don't judge the students at this school by me. I'm just . . . uh . . . " He trailed off awkwardly.

"Going through a hard time?" suggested Cara. Her smile forgave him.

Mark looked at the doctor accusingly.

"I haven't said a thing to her," Rob protested. "You know better than that. Hell, I don't even know what you two are talking about."

Neither smiled. Rob glanced at Cara and realized that her journalist-trained eyes probably saw in Mark's face the same tired-to-the-bone strain that he did.

"Cara," Rob began, "would it be possible for you to . . ."

She was already ahead of him. "You know, Dr. Rob, I really need to pull my notes together before our interview this morning. Is there somewhere I could work?"

Rob nodded, appreciating her quick perception. "There's a conference room here," he answered, opening the adjacent door.

"But first"—Cara paused in the doorway—"I owe you an apology, too, Mark. I was the rude one, and very unprofessional. I wouldn't want you to judge all journalists by me."

Mark smiled, the expression momentarily wiping the stress and fatigue from his face. "Let me set you up with some friends who'd love to be interviewed," he offered by way of acceptance. "After lunch?"

"After lunch," Rob interrupted firmly. *Can't let him get too comfortable; he'll lose the impetus to tell me whatever it is that's brought him here*. "Come on in, Mark."

Steering the younger man into his office, Rob shut the door and activated the "No Interruptions, Please," sign. Quickly he signaled his assistant to hold all calls. Before he could sit down at his desk, a small, sleek form bounded into the chair and sat smugly, tail curled primly around her feet.

"Morning, Bast. Why didn't you put the coffee on?" Rob asked as he scooped the little black cat up one-handed. Her purring increased geometrically. Plopping her in the middle of his desk, the doctor waved the lights up slightly, then ordered a pot of coffee.

As he sank into his seat and leaned back, he regarded Mark, who was still standing awkwardly near the door.

"Have a seat," he invited, waving at the nearest chair.

The student didn't move. "No, thanks. This won't take long, Rob. I just came to tell you that I've decided to withdraw from StarBridge. I'm meeting with Kkintha ch'aait," he named the school's Administrator, "this afternoon to tell her that I'm going back to Earth."

As a psychologist and M.D. Rob had had years of practice in keeping his inner feelings off his face, and he was grateful for that now.

"But you're telling me first?" he asked evenly, concealing

his shock and distress. "You must know I'd be . . . I am . . . totally opposed to such a thing. Running away isn't a solution to problems, you know that. If you leave, you'll be throwing away years of hard work, good work . . . you'll be abandoning the dream you've had ever since you were a child. Mark, that would be a terrible mistake."

"You've been my friend, as well as my counselor," said Mark quietly. "You've tried to help. I felt I owed it to you to be the one to tell you myself. But this isn't a subject for argument, Rob. My mind is made up."

"I wouldn't be your friend if I didn't try and talk you out of this. I'm going to try my damnedest to change your mind."

Mark smiled briefly. "Can't we consider the attempt made, and leave it at that? I already know everything you'll say . . . hell, everything you *have* said in our sessions, Rob. And I've listened. But I have to listen to myself first. This decision is the right one for me."

The coffee arrived. Stalling for time, Rob slowly poured two cups, even though Mark shook his head as he pushed the mug toward him, again indicating a seat for him to take. The doctor's mind was racing. *Let me find the right words to say. This one is truly gifted, if only he knew it . . . losing him would be a tragedy . . .*

Mark's mask of control was firmly in place, but Rob was too experienced to miss the anguish hiding behind the hazel eyes. *If he didn't want to stay in his heart of hearts, it wouldn't hurt him to leave. I've got to try . . .*

"C'mon," he urged. "Just sit down and have a cup of coffee. I don't have anything scheduled . . . "

"No, thanks," Mark said, politely but firmly. "I really need to be going."

But still he hesitated. Encouraged, Rob took a deep breath. "I know how much you love people," he began, feeling his way, "and I mean people, whether they have wings or claws or two legs or ten. You're good with people. Not everyone is. I hate like hell to see the CLS lose out on a talent like yours. We *need* you, Mark."

The younger man stayed stubbornly silent, but his face flushed, and the steady gaze of his eyes faltered for just a second.

Hmmm . . . Rob ran his last words back through memory. *Talent. That's the word that made him squirm.* He tested his observation.

"I know your classes haven't been going well, but that's only natural after . . . "

Mark shook his head. "I'm going to catch up on my assignments before I go. My grade average hasn't slipped that far. If you'll recommend me to a good university on Earth, I can channel the credits I've earned here into a decent major there. I'll probably only need a year or so more, even with changing over, since our programs here are accelerated."

Okay. He's not running from the work and the drop in grades. But still . . . something about the word "talent" got to him . . . and people; I was talking about people . . .

Rob thought back over his counseling sessions with Mark, not only those since his mother's death but those from over a year ago, and suddenly he knew the answer.

"You've decided it's three strikes and you're out, haven't you?" He hoped Mark knew the old baseball idiom. "You've added up your freshman mistake with the Mizari *shrizzs,* your guilt about Jon Whittaker's suicide last year, and, now, new guilt feelings about your mother's death. You've decided you don't have what it takes, the perception and the insight necessary to be an interrelator." He paused for effect. "You're worried that if you took a diplomatic post, somebody else might get hurt because you made a mistake."

The look of astonishment that filled Mark's hazel eyes before he blinked and glanced down was eloquent. *Eureka!* Rob thought.

"You don't have to look so surprised," the doctor said dryly. "Psychology is my job, you know. We've talked about each one of those incidents before, but let's look at what they mean together."

Mark opened his mouth to protest.

"That's what you've been doing, isn't it? Adding it up?" At the reluctant nod, he said, "Well, then, give me a shot at it. But first, open that door and ask Cara to come in."

"Mark and I are going to be a while," Rob said without preamble when Cara appeared. "Can we reschedule for another time?"

She darted one quick look, half curiosity, half sympathy, Mark's way, but observing his averted face, her expression smoothed into noncommittal professionalism.

"That's fine, Dr. Rob. There's a low-grav gliding contest in the Arena that I would have hated to miss anyway. It'll be great footage."

With that settled and the door once again closed, Rob took a long swig of coffee. Bast leaped lightly into his lap and began to purr. Petting her absently, the doctor sat back in his chair, outwardly relaxed, silently waiting.

Mark sighed and sat down.

Nearly two hours later, with Mark just gone, Rob checked the conference room to see if Cara had returned yet. There was a folded note with his name on it on the table.

"I'll call you late this afternoon to see when we can interview," it said. "Good luck with Mark. I'm sure that whatever's bothering him, you can help."

Rob smiled wistfully at her affirmation of faith in his abilities. He had failed to change Mark's mind with talking, and now he was contemplating more drastic action. But if he were wrong . . .

"Mistakes are too costly when you deal with people," Mark had admitted at one point in their session. "You're right when you say that I'm scared. What if my next mistake cost hundreds or thousands—or *millions*—of lives?"

Mark had learned as a freshman how easily mistakes could occur. He'd known of the taboo connected with the Mizari *shrizzs,* the combination drinking vessel/family heirloom that was assigned to each child as part of his or her coming-of-age ceremony, and had understood that, no matter what, the fragile object must *never* be touched by anyone outside the family.

"But when I saw Shissar drop it, that day at dinner," he'd reminded Rob today, "instinct took over. My cultural background said not to let such a beautiful thing break, and it completely overrode the knowledge I had. Even though Shissar's family forgave me, what if I'd broken a taboo that strong with a culture less"—he'd searched for words—"flexible, less tolerant than the Mizari? That one incident could have caused irrevocable harm!"

He'd shaken his head at the memory. "Good intentions just aren't enough."

Mark felt that his instincts had failed him again with Jon Whittaker . . . or rather that they had failed Jon.

Thirteen months ago, in the middle of the school's artificial night, with incredible coolness and misguided courage, sixteen-year-old Jon Whittaker had slit the veins in both wrists and both ankles. The next morning Mark had opened the bathroom door and found his roommate's nude body sprawled halfway out of the bathtub, as though Jon might have changed his mind and been trying to summon help—too late.

"I should have seen it coming," Mark had repeated over and over during their subsequent sessions. "I should have guessed Jon would try something. He was so down. Why didn't I see? I might have stopped it!"

"It was my job to see it coming, and I didn't." Rob didn't try to conceal the bitter regret in his own voice. "We've talked about this before, Mark. It will haunt both of us until we die, I expect, but if anyone is to blame, I am. I'm the counselor. I'm the doctor. You were just Jon's friend, and believe me, you were the best friend anyone could have been to him." He straightened his shoulders with an effort. "I learned long ago that you have to forgive yourself and go on, or you're no use to anyone. You've got to learn to let it go, Mark."

The younger man nodded. "I know. I think I was learning to, when my mom . . . died. That brought it all back again, more painfully than ever."

"Mark, I think you should try looking at your remaining unaware of your mother's illness as *her* triumph, rather than *your* failure."

Mark looked thoughtful, as though that had never occurred to him before. Rob pressed his momentary advantage. "She went to great lengths to keep from burdening you with that knowledge," he pointed out. "It would have broken her heart if she thought her decision to keep her ill health a secret led to the end of your dream. And don't forget, Mark, your becoming an interrelator was *her* dream, too."

Now, standing in the empty conference room, Rob gave a long sigh. "He agreed with every single damn word I said," he muttered, "but not one of them changed his mind."

He's just too conscientious, the doctor thought. *But he doesn't realize that that very quality will make him a top-notch interrelator. I know he's got the courage to live with the risk and carry that burden. But I've got to make Mark realize that, too.*

Bast padded through the doorway and meowed loudly. Rob turned to face her.

"Which is why," he announced solemnly to the cat's unblinking green eyes, "I'm going to talk Kkintha ch'aait into going along with my . . . plan. After all, it's not as though I *arranged* to have the Elpind drop in for a visit." He smiled faintly. "Can I help it if the timing just happens to be right?"

CHAPTER 3

◆

Tapped!

The crowd hopped, flew, scuttled, loped, and jostled its way down the corridor toward the Arena.

All these different kinds of beings, all in motion together, all excited. Great stuff for my documentary, Cara thought, excited herself. She turned her head from side to side, trying to see everything, wanting her camera to capture all of this, the most colorful, exotic crowd she'd ever been in.

This is going to be a wonderful lead-in for my coverage of the Elpind's visit. Hundreds of beings practically stampeding to the assembly so we can all get our first look at yet another species from the galaxy's incredible variety.

Carried by the crowd's momentum, Cara plunged into the noisy melee of the Arena. Large enough to hold the entire student body and faculty at one time, with movable floors, adjustable gravity, and a sound and light system that put Earth's finest arts or sports complex to shame, the Arena was a gymnasium, the low-grav hang-gliding site, a theater, and even an ice-skating rink. Right now, it was a bowl-shaped assembly hall with seats of various configurations for alien forms rising away in stacked layers from the low center stage.

The noise level was almost uncomfortable as the students poured in. Cara smiled at the strange mixture of sounds that so many alien tongues created. Grunts, whistles, gutturals, clicks, and growls mingled with more musical tones, producing a fascinating cacophony. Underlying it all was the ever-present sibilant hiss of the Mizari language. Cara caught a sudden whiff of overripe melon as two Vardi conversed in their olfactory-based language.

The young journalist considered where to sit. She'd made several friends in the weeks since her arrival, and one of them, a Simiu, was waving at her now. She began to make her way toward Frrkk'eet, then hesitated as she noticed another familiar face two rows over.

She hadn't seen Mark Kenner except to wave at in passing since the day he'd introduced her to his friends as he'd promised. But then he'd rushed away, leaving her with them, explaining that he had to cram for a makeup test. Waving back at the Simiu, Cara indicated her new direction.

"It's a good thing I'm not doing my documentary on *you*," she said with a grin, dropping into the seat next to him. "You went into hiding on me."

Mark laughed. "I told you from the very beginning I'd be a poor subject. No, really, I have been in hiding. Getting my coursework caught up," he explained. "How is the documentary coming?"

"Really well. Everywhere I look there's something new and interesting to film."

He raised his eyebrows. "*Film?*"

Cara grinned. "A figure of speech. Of course nobody has used actual *film* for centuries . . . but the term lingers on. Anyway, I think the only time I turn the camera off is when I'm in bed. And, of course, the chance to interview the Elpind . . . I can't wait!"

She watched Mark as she spoke, noticing something different about him. He looked more relaxed, more at peace with himself.

"So, besides the coursework, how are you?" she asked, wondering if she dared say what she really meant. *Why not?* she decided. The journalist in her still wanted to discover the story she sensed in Mark Kenner. "I mean," she added, "you look . . . uh, happier, I guess, than when I saw you the other day."

"You mean, happier than when you saw me waiting for the shrink?" He grinned to take any implied sting out of his words.

His smile was marvelous, warm and high-powered, Cara noted. The impact of it distracted her for a moment. When she recovered, he was saying, " . . . and so, I made a decision. You know, you always feel better when you've made up your mind what to do about a problem."

"What problem? What did you decide?"

"Whoa! My turn to ask a question. Don't you need to be down front to film this?"

"Dr. Rob let me set up a second camera on stage. They always record special events like this anyway, so I'll just piece together the best footage from the different cameras. That leaves me free to go for crowd shots with my autocam."

Cara paused, wondering whether she should let Mark get away with changing the subject. But just as she was about to try again, a hush, ripe with anticipation, abruptly fell over the Arena. She looked down at the stage and saw the school's Administrator, the Chhhh-kk-tu named Kkintha ch'aait, step to the small podium to begin the assembly.

Cara had begun to pick up a smattering of Mizari, but this was too important to miss a word. Hastily she switched on her voder.

" . . . and I think you are all aware," the Administrator was saying, "of the disclosures made ten months ago by the CLS concerning Elseemar. The people of Elseemar, the Elspind, following several years of limited interaction with CLS sociological teams, recently expressed an interest in visiting and learning about other worlds. The CLS agreed to sponsor the visits, and as a result, the WirElspind, Elseemar's governing body, chose ten of their members for this very special mission.

"These representatives are the first to ever leave their planet. Their reports will have a major impact on the people of Elseemar, as well as future relations between Elseemar and the Cooperative League of Systems."

I know all this, Cara thought impatiently, forcing herself not to wriggle in her seat.

"StarBridge has been given the honor of receiving a visit from one of these Elpind emissaries. Students and faculty of the Academy at StarBridge"—Kkintha ch'aait paused for emphasis—"I would like you to welcome Eerin."

Cara jumped to her feet, clapping as hard as she could. So did Mark. Since every student in the Arena was just as eager to express delight and since every species had its own way of doing so, the uproar was astonishing.

The being who stepped out into view didn't exactly "step." Instead it bounded out, skipped across the stage, then skidded to a halt beside the Administrator. Even from halfway back in the huge Arena, Cara could feel the boundless energy radiating from the small creature.

The alien was humanoid, with a head, two arms, two legs, and upright carriage. Cara couldn't distinguish facial features from where she sat, but she noted that the head appeared uncomfortably large and startlingly round in contrast to the thin, angular frame. The effect was softened somewhat by the cream-colored down covering both head and body.

Cara compared the Elpind with the Chhhh-kk-tu. Adult Chhhh-kk-tu, on the average, stood about as high as her collar. The Elpind was about the same height but there the similarity stopped. Kkintha ch'aait was rounded and densely furred and, while small, looked solid and stable. The Elpind, thin and much more lightly furred, appeared fragile in contrast.

Cara wondered at its age. Its sex she knew . . . or rather, she knew about its lack of sexual identity. Recent newscasts about the scheduled visits had revealed to the general populace of the CLS for the first time that Elspind were either male, female, or neuter, and that all of the ten emissaries were neuters. They would be referred to with the Elspindlor pronoun for neuters, "hin," the Mizari journalist had reported.

The noise was finally dying down. The Administrator spoke again. *Still in Mizari,* noted Cara. *Hin isn't wearing a voder, therefore Eerin must know Mizari.*

"Our students represent the Fourteen Known Worlds of our galaxy, Eerin. More than that, they are the finest young people their planets have to offer. They come here to form a very special community and to learn how to advance the peace and prosperity of all systems. The welcome you heard means they are eager to make you one of them."

It happened all over again: the yelling, the clapping, the barking and whistling and hissing and yipping and stamping.

Kkintha ch'aait waited patiently, seeming to enjoy herself. The Elpind made constant, tiny motions. Cara wondered if it . . . *hin,* she reminded herself, was nervous.

Finally the students settled back down.

"Eerin expressed the desire, in a government communiqué prior to arrival, to experience something uniquely StarBridge," Kkintha ch'aait said. "We have decided a pair project will allow Eerin to experience a unique feature of StarBridge, and will offer the best opportunity for hin to interact with another CLS-member species. In addition, it works well with hin's plans to visit another system before returning to Elseemar. The death of two birds with one rock, as you human students might say."

A rumble of appreciative laughter rose from the members of the audience to whom she referred.

Cara had learned during the past weeks about pair projects. Two students of different species were paired and sent away from StarBridge to accomplish a special project set by the Academy. All interrelators were required to complete a pair project, and many of the telepaths and translators elected to, also. It was considered the best way to learn teamwork across cultural lines.

Pair partners were seldom chosen for each other from the cultures each student was majoring in; the idea was to have them learn from each other without prior preparation.

Sort of a field test, she found herself thinking, then she focused again on what the Administrator was saying: " . . . a special Tapping right now. The faculty felt Eerin would enjoy watching the Tapping ceremony itself. I will tell you that the choice announced through our light system will be a surprise to both Eerin and the chosen student, but we have put a great deal of thought into selecting the person we felt would be the best pair partner for Eerin."

Cara could feel the excitement level rise another notch. "Did I understand correctly?" she whispered to Mark. "Someone's already been chosen, but that person doesn't know it yet . . . and is going to find out right now?"

"Right. You'll like the Tapping ceremony," Mark replied.

"What if it's you?" she kidded. "I'll get the best camera angle possible, totally by chance."

Mark smiled tolerantly. "Nope, once again, you'll have to go elsewhere for your story. I did my pair project over a year ago."

"Who did you get?"

"A Heeyoon, Starchaser. We got to be great friends. She—" He interrupted himself. "They're ready to start! Is your camera on?"

"Naturally." Cara gazed about her expectantly. The term "Tapping," she knew, came from the ancient custom of choosing members for exclusive clubs or special honors by sending someone to actually "tap" a chosen person on the shoulder. While the old terminology lingered, Cara felt sure she would witness a very different method of selection.

Mark nudged her. "Put your palm over this," he said, demonstrating by pressing his hand against a small sensor plate embedded in the arm of his chair.

Gradually the lights dimmed until the Arena was totally dark. Suddenly she saw a yellow glow several rows away. Cara jumped as a green light illuminated the arms and back of her seat. A soft orange glow outlined the chair in front of her and to the right. Throughout the Arena different colored lights winked on, one by one, at random, until the audience shimmered like a huge rainbow.

Mark leaned over to whisper again. "The computer activates a white light when it recognizes the presence of a Tapped student." His chair was still dark, but it wasn't the only one. There were still many dark spots scattered between the bright islands of lighted seats.

The lights that were winking on did so more slowly now, adding to the suspense. A dark spot two rows away glimmered into blue.

Even as Cara craned her neck to see who would be next, something flashed at the corner of her eye. She turned her head quickly.

Bright white light bathed a wide-eyed, openmouthed Mark.

"Congratulations!" cried Cara. "Mark, it *is* you!" She had to practically shout to be heard over the exuberant noise that had started up again in the Arena.

He was shaking his head no, and his shocked distress was evident. Cara grinned at him. "Hey, don't take it so hard. So, you'll have done two pair projects," she said. "It'll look great on your résumé." He was obviously supposed to walk down to the stage, but he didn't move. "Go on, Mark. Get down there."

"You don't understand!" he hissed frantically. "I *can't* be Tapped. This is a mistake!"

Computers can't make a mistake; they only make hundreds at a time. The worn, old joke flashed across Cara's mind, but she dismissed it. This wasn't the time for humor; Mark's face told her that.

"Why, Mark? Why can't you be Tapped?"

Mark still looked stunned. "Because I'm leaving StarBridge. Dropping out. They know that; they're supposed to be starting my transfer."

Cara's mouth dropped open in her turn. "Oh, no!"

Kkintha ch'aait was speaking. She'd grown impatient waiting for Mark to come forward on his own; she was calling his name. The excited sounds in the Arena were dying down into puzzlement. The brilliant white light of Mark's chair, glaring among all the softly colored ones, was like a giant finger pointing at him.

"Damn!" said Mark softly. "I can't let the Elpind be embarrassed in front of this crowd. They'll just have to straighten this mess out later." The instant he stood up, the Arena burst into fresh sounds of congratulations.

Cara watched him force a creditable smile, climb over feet and paws to get out of the row, then start down the aisle toward the stage.

Dropping out! she thought incredulously. *So that's the decision he wouldn't discuss. But why? He's bringing his grades back up, he said, so that's not it. What then?*

As a journalist, Cara was fascinated, but as a friend, she resolved to wipe Mark's verbal reactions to his Tapping out of her documentary. *He'd better never make another crack about journalists prying into his personal business,* she thought ruefully, watching him as he mounted the ramp up onto the stage. Slowly the lights in the Arena winked out, one by one, until only the stage was lighted once more.

• • •

From the stage, the darkened audience appeared to Mark like a vast, tranquil ocean of muted sound and movement. The faint shufflings and hushed conversations died away as he approached the podium.

His first impression was of his own awkward height. As a human male of average height, he towered over both the Chhhh-kk-tu and the Elpind.

"Congratulations, Mark," said Kkintha ch'aait.

He glanced at her sharply. The Administrator had okayed his transfer two weeks ago, so she, too, knew this was a mistake. *I guess we both have our roles to play,* Mark thought. *For now, at least.* He nodded to her and turned his attention to his supposed-to-be pair partner.

Not as fragile as hin looks, he thought, his eyes tracing the ropy tendons and long muscles clearly outlined beneath the fine, cream-colored down. The Elpind's size and slenderness concealed a tough, wiry strength.

Mark consciously used the pronoun he'd heard in newscasts about Elseemar. StarBridge classes had been buzzing for weeks with the news that the visitor would be a neuter. So far, Dr. Blanket, the intelligent Avernian fungus creature, and the one Rigellian student were the only neuters in residence at the Academy—and the Avernian might more properly be called asexual than neuter. Species with three distinct sexes were rare.

Eerin's stick-thin legs ended in narrow, well-arched feet. Here hin's down gave way to light orange bare skin that appeared leathery. They weren't really big feet, Mark decided; they just appeared too long by human standards—especially in contrast to the thin legs. The alien had toes, prominent kneecaps, and long, sinewy hands that resembled the feet.

"I am honored to meet Eerin of the Elspind," said Mark in his flawless Mizari, making the Mizari greeting bow, tented hands above his head and a deep inclination of his body. Only then did he allow himself to look directly into the alien's face.

Eerin had no ears, only recessed ear slits, and the same creamy layer of down that covered hin's body grew up the graceful neck and over the head. There was a roundness to the head, a round shape to the face, that the human eye found disconcerting.

The fine down thinned away to nothing on the Elpind's face, and the skin revealed was softer-looking and less orange than that of the feet and hands. A broad, snubbed nose made a blob in the middle of the face, but the mouth had an almost-human shape with its full, apricot-colored lips.

"Mark Kenner," said the Elpind clearly.

Mark nodded again, fascinated by the alien's eyes. They were enormous and as round as the Elpind's face, but that wasn't what made them spectacular. It wasn't even their color, which was the shade of old, beaten gold, with huge, dark pupils. What made them striking was their depth and clearness, the light in them, and the intensity of expression. Life and warmth and an unmistakable happiness poured out of those eyes.

Mark couldn't hold back his own response. His smile broadened to a silly grin. "Welcome to StarBridge!" he cried.

The rest of the program was a blur. Kkintha ch'aait presented Eerin with a StarBridge pin, and then the Elpind spoke to the audience in careful but excellent Mizari. Mark thought of the confidence with which Eerin had said his name and decided the alien had known and practiced the strange sounds well before the ceremony.

Not a mistake then. *I've been set up. And I bet I can guess by whom, and why.*

At the end of the program, when he glanced offstage, Mark knew he was right. He politely excused himself to the Elpind and went over to speak to the slender, dark-haired man who awaited him.

"You're hoping this will change my mind," he said bluntly.

"Of course," Rob Gable admitted. He smiled warmly. "What kind of friend would I be if I didn't try?"

Mark sighed. "I thought maybe the kind who'd believe I know my own mind."

"Mark, when you get back from this pair project, the transfer applications will have gone out, and you'll probably have half a dozen scholarships lined up to choose from. Then, if you still want to, you can take one of them and withdraw from StarBridge. But it's a big galaxy out there, and you've only set foot on one alien world so far." He was referring to

Mark's third-year pair project when he'd gone to Arrooouhl, the Heeyoon's mother world.

"Now tell me," Rob said, "you wouldn't like to visit just one more planet before you go back to Earth, maybe for good."

Mark hesitated. He wasn't meant to be an interrelator; he'd accepted that, but his curiosity about other worlds and their people endured.

"Yes, you're right. I'd like that," he agreed. "But isn't the situation with the Elspind very important to the CLS? This visit is going to have a lot of impact on Elseemar, don't forget. And with the unrest on that planet right now . . . " He shook his head. "StarBridge needs to assign its best person to be Eerin's companion."

"It's not as though you'll be going to Elseemar during your pair project," Rob pointed out. "Mark, we had to have someone experienced, someone with flawless Mizari, whom we knew could handle a pair project. I know you don't feel you're the best person for this assignment, but Kkintha ch'aait and I and the rest of the faculty do. Trust us." His dark eyes held Mark's steadily. "Put your decision on hold for a while, and concentrate on doing a good job with Eerin. Okay?"

"I am . . . honored," Mark said, "that you think this highly of me." He had one more protest. "But won't this be a lot of money for the 'Bridge to waste on someone who's leaving?"

"If you come back with a different outlook and decide you'll be an interrelator after all, it won't be a waste."

"And if not?"

"I've gambled before and lost. We'll handle it."

Mark nodded. Excitement churned in his stomach. "Okay, I'll do it."

The doctor grinned, then indicated Eerin, who was still talking to the Administrator. "The bets are placed," he said. "Let's get this project under way before your partner starts to feel neglected. You know the drill?"

Mark nodded. "First order of business is to pack a few things and move into the room we'll share together during orientation. Where's Eerin's stuff?"

"Still in the shuttle. Hin barely got here in time for the program."

They walked over to join Kkintha ch'aait and the Elpind. The

Administrator was also discussing the "drill," but her attention was distracted when Cara and her camera suddenly appeared and waved at Mark from the other side of the stage.

Mark chuckled at the eager look on the journalist's face. "Eerin," he said, speaking Mizari, "I want you to meet a friend of mine."

CHAPTER 4
♦
Eerin

By the time the StarBridge corridors dimmed to signify the rest cycle—night, as human students referred to it—Mark was exhausted. He'd talked until he was hoarse, but each answer seemed only to generate another dozen questions from Eerin.

The human student had been astounded to learn that it had taken Eerin only four weeks to learn Mizari. The Elpind spoke it almost as well as he did. "I suppose they must have given you hypno-learning sessions," he said during their orientation tour. Each new sight seemed to make the Elpind's golden eyes grow wider as hin tried to take in everything at once.

Eerin glanced at him. "No. Hin learned quickly because ours is an oral culture. Elspind know how to listen carefully, learn quickly, and how to hold knowledge firmly in mind. It is important, for each learner will, at some time, be a teacher of the young and there is much to pass down."

Mark gazed at the Elpind skeptically. It was true that Eerin hadn't used any kind of recording device all afternoon, but he'd attributed that to first-day excitement. "You mean you'll remember everything you see and hear well enough to report on it when you get back to Elseemar? From one exposure?"

Eerin nodded, a gesture hin had already picked up from Mark in their short acquaintance, claiming it was "economical."

"Okay," Mark said. "I'd like to see you in action. Tell you what, look through this doorway for thirty seconds and then I'll ask you to describe everything you see."

The portal in question opened on the Spiral Arm, the students' favorite hangout. The Elpind stood in the doorway, utterly still for the first time, as hin's huge, golden eyes intently scanned the place.

"Time's up," Mark announced, and Eerin stepped obediently back into the hallway.

"Okay," the young man challenged. "Describe what you saw." He was expecting four or five accurate details, mixed in with a greater amount of vague and uncertain half memories.

What he got was a flood of sharp, clear images. Eerin described the pattern in the tile, the layout of the tables, each hanging plant, each holo-vid decorating the eatery. Hin verbally sketched the foods on the tables by the door so accurately that Mark recognized each item. The Elpind was just starting in on the various beings themselves when Mark held up a hand.

"I believe you," he said simply. The remainder of the day Mark was very much aware that everything they did, every word he said, was literally being recorded in that amazing brain of Eerin's. It made him speak carefully, and think before he spoke.

That was one of the main reasons he was worn out by bedtime.

"Eerin," he said when they were finally settled in their new suite for the night, Mark on the couch and the Elpind perched restlessly in a chair, "this ability you have to learn and remember is marvelous. I'm envious. But with the recording technology the CLS can offer, your people wouldn't have to spend time memorizing things to preserve their knowledge. Instead you could use your mental talent for other things."

The Elpind blinked, considering. "It is difficult to think about changing something that has been part of our lives for so long," hin said. "Our people face many difficult choices now. Since that day eight of your years ago when a Heeyoon shuttle was forced to make an emergency landing on Elseemar, we Elspind have been examining our traditions and beliefs. The first decision the WirElspind made was the day the Heeyoon landed. The aliens offered to leave, at the risk of their lives, rather than encounter our culture, but our leaders said no. Instead, Elseemar welcomed them."

"The Heeyoon offer was made in accordance with standard procedure for CLS-member worlds," Mark said. "Why did your people decide to welcome them?"

"Many reasons," Eerin said. "Foremost among them, I believe, was curiosity. Elspind are a curious people. We like to learn."

No kidding, Mark thought, remembering their day together.

"Now the CLS cultural team has been on Elseemar for seven of your years," Eerin was continuing. "While they live, in many ways, as simply as any Elpind, they have shown us many wonders. Images of worlds beyond our own, glimpses of machines and devices that can replace our own labor in the fields, of new philosophies and ideas. Most Elspind are eager to learn new ways, but some feel threatened. They fear new ideas will push away the old."

"What do you think?"

"Hin sits on the ruling council, the WirElspind. It is hin's duty to investigate the new possibilities and help hin's people make wise choices," Eerin said evasively.

Mark's first impulse was to press for more details, but his training cautioned him to go slow. Besides, a great wave of sleepiness suddenly washed through him. *Later,* he thought. *There will be time to learn all about each other. That's what a pair project is all about.*

"That's a heavy responsibility," he said aloud. "I know this trip is part of your investigation, and I'm honored to be involved. I hope I can help you learn what you need to discover." He leaned back on the couch, unobtrusively easing his shoes off with a sigh.

"When can hin see the rest of the school?" Eerin asked. The Elpind had asked so many questions that they'd only covered two of the domes and part of the underground facilities.

"We'll have some free time tomorrow after our first training session," Mark replied. "There are a lot of people eager to meet and talk with you, and many activities you might like to try." The last words of his speech were half swallowed by a massive yawn that erupted before he could stifle it.

It didn't seem possible that the Elpind's eyes could grow any rounder—but it certainly appeared as though they did.

"What was that?" Eerin asked, ignoring Mark's response and pointing at his mouth.

"Uh . . . we call it a 'yawn.' " Mark gave the last word in English. "Humans yawn when they need to sleep. And I'm really beat—uh—tired. Sleep's going to feel great tonight."

"Sleep," Eerin repeated thoughtfully. "Yes, hin heard of that, but hin has not had the opportunity to study it closely." The Elpind examined Mark's reclining form with avid curiosity. "How long will Mark do this sleeping activity?"

"What?" Mark sat back up. "Are you trying to tell me you don't sleep? That Elspind don't sleep?"

"Correct." The alien considered a moment and then offered, "No, not fully correct. There are rare times in the lifecycle when Elspind require inanimate rest to store energy. At those few times, we sleep, but only then."

"As much energy as you put out during the day"—Mark was remembering the pace Eerin had set during their tour—"I'd think you'd need to store energy every night. Don't you get tired?"

"If hin is tired, hin thinks quietly or hin eats. Food creates energy, of course, and so do hin's thoughts."

"I am eager to learn more," Mark said. It was, he'd discovered, the polite Elpind response when a speaker introduced new information. "But I would like to learn it in the morning. Humans don't learn well when they are tired. We must sleep every night." Remembering Eerin's earlier words, he asked awkwardly, "Uh, did you really mean you would like to observe someone sleeping?"

Eerin nodded eagerly.

"Well then, I'll sleep out here. Feel free to observe." His grin got lost in another huge yawn, and in spite of feeling like a prize specimen about to stretch out on a lab slide, Mark slid back down on the couch. "What will you do all night?"

"Think and remember, of course."

"Of course," echoed Mark wearily. "Have fun. And listen, wake me if you need me."

"Hin will not need Mark," said the Elpind serenely.

Shutting his eyes, Mark rolled onto his stomach, instinctively seeking his favorite sleeping position. He'd been so busy ever since the Tapping that he'd had no time to dwell on his problems, but now his depression returned like an unwelcome visitor. Tired as he was, the image of Sulinda formed behind his closed eyelids.

He'd spotted her in the crowd that surrounded him after the Tapping, buzzing with congratulations and curiosity. Leaving Eerin to Cara and Rob for a moment, Mark beckoned to Sulinda and the two of them went down the steps to the backstage area and found a private nook. "Congratulations," she murmured, and leaned forward to give him a quick kiss. But Mark didn't let her get away with that—instead he put his arms around her and returned her kiss like a starving man finally set before food. He felt guilty as hell for doing it, but he'd missed her so much during these last two weeks!

The young man shifted uneasily, remembering how Sulinda's eyes shone when he finally raised his head, how she nestled close to him. "It's been a long time," she whispered, and her dark eyes said, "I want you back."

It was then that Mark had told her he was dropping out of school. He watched her face change, felt her step back, out of his arms, knowing that Su now understood, as he did, that his leaving the Academy meant it was *really* over between them. "I'm sorry, I shouldn't have done it," he said, referring to the kiss, "but, SuSu . . . I couldn't help it. I still care."

"I care about you, too," she admitted, "but under these circumstances, I don't think we'd better see each other again."

"Maybe we could talk . . . " he began, but her hair rippled like an ebony wave as she shook her head no. "There's nothing for us to talk about. It's over, and you don't want to listen to me tell you what a mistake you're making—leaving StarBridge, I mean. Good-bye, Mark."

He sighed softly against the couch cushion. *She's right, it's over . . . but that doesn't mean it doesn't hurt.* He knew he'd respect her wish not to see him again. Today's slip had been too painful to risk a repetition. He could hear Eerin moving about the room. *Since I can't sleep, I ought to get up and talk to hin again,* he thought fuzzily. *I'll just rest my eyes for another minute . . . just a few seconds, that's all . . .*

• • •

Ri-El Eerin, The Part of Enduring Life known as Eerin, moved about the small room, flexing hin's long, narrow feet. Hin missed the cool softness of grass, the damp firmness of soil, the rough textures of the wide tree roots that laced the paths of hin's mountain home. Here the surfaces beneath hin's feet were all smooth and hard and cold or else blandly soft—"carpet" was the English word, hin recalled—so that one could not know the true texture of the floor it hid.

Lieor, hin's sibling, had been envious when Eerin had left, but now Eerin knew that Lieor would have been miserable out here, away from the fields, forests, and streams hin loved so well. Lieor would have felt as rootless and dead as one of hin's sestel plants ruthlessly torn from the ground.

Eerin had learned on the long journey to StarBridge that to think too often of home was to make hinself sad; deliberately, hin switched back to the present. *Is it safe to turn and look at Mark yet?* Eerin wondered.

Hin knew that it often took humans several minutes to enter this strange state called "sleep." In spite of Mark's invitation to watch, Eerin feared it might be impolite to do so during the transition phase. Transitions on Elseemar were special times in the lifecycle and reserved for the family. It would do no harm to grant the human the same courtesy.

Finally, though, hin felt it would be permissible to begin observation. Quickly reviewing the scientific facts about sleep that hin had learned, the Elpind padded over to the couch—quietly, for the information had listed some common deterrents to human sleep, and noise was one of them.

Eerin leaned over the prone figure, comparing Mark's respiration pattern, the movement of his eyes beneath the eyelids, and the other outward aspects of sleep with the knowledge stored in hin's memory.

After a few minutes, the Elpind nodded with satisfaction. The description had been accurate. Hin's observations confirmed that human sleep was not unlike the inanimate state that came over Elspind before the Change.

But humans did this activity every day! How could they bear to lose so much time from their lives? The waste was appalling.

Eerin sighed quietly, retreating back to the center of the room. To see new things, learn new concepts, enrich one's time . . . but so much had proved deeply unsettling. To be always enclosed, away from the sky, for example. To meet so many different kinds of people in one place—when all on Elseemar were obviously from the same beginning seed. And to be paired with a human who must sleep away part of each precious day.

It is not hin's task to judge what is a waste of time and what is not, Eerin thought sternly. *Each moment is a chance to observe and nothing learned will be wasted. The WirElspind cannot know which knowledge will prove valuable and which will not until all knowledge has been Told and sifted.*

Eerin pictured the faces of hin's peers on the Council. Not since ancient times had a Council faced decisions such as awaited this one . . . nor such opposition to the voice of the people as the Wospind offered. Hin must do hin's best to bring back wisdom that would help.

Eerin sank to the floor, legs folded beneath hin, and began to change hin's breathing pattern. Deeper and slower the Elpind breathed, flushing the wastes of fatigue from the cells of hin's body. Then, erecting a temporary mental barrier against sensory input, the Elpind began reviewing the day's impressions, facts, conversations, and visual memories.

In spite of the fact that hin did not wish to censor any knowledge before it was laid before the WirElspind, there were obvious duplications and irrelevancies that could be discarded. The rest would be processed and stored. Later, hin would thoughtfully sift and prepare the stored information for a *reci*, a "Telling." *Though it will take many* **reci** *to convey all that hin has learned on this trip,* Eerin decided. *And there remains so much yet to learn!*

Eerin's mental review and compilation of information took nearly three of the human measurement called hours. Finally the Elpind opened hin's eyes, only to see that Mark still slept!

Eerin sighed, then jumped up with fresh impatience. Hin's knowledge of humans said that sleep consumed an average of six to eight hours daily . . . but it had also said humans had different sleep patterns. Some required very little, others more.

The Elpind studied hin's pair partner. Mark Kenner's size and weight, which hin had demanded to know this afternoon, put him in the average range for adult human males. Did that mean his sleep period would also be average? There was nothing to do but wait and see.

Restlessly, the Elpind wandered into the adjoining bedroom and was overjoyed to see, in the corner, a computer link. Eerin had learned to use one on the ship. Now learning could be accomplished, even while the human slept.

Activating the machine, Eerin, with mind freshly cleared, prepared to gain new knowledge.

Mark emerged from sleep with a start, realizing that he'd just heard a high-pitched protesting *beeeep!* from the computer link. The Elpind was nowhere in sight.

When he reached the bedroom door, staggering a little, the Elpind looked up, plainly ecstatic. "Mark is awake! That is wonderful! Four human hours. Long, but shorter than average."

Mark shook his head groggily. "Eerin, what are you doing?" The desk console was flashing urgently. The human stumbled over and hit the "escape" control.

"Hin was modifying this setup so the computer would speak faster, but it stopped and made a noise."

"Oh." Mark blinked stupidly, still trying to come all the way awake. He rubbed his eyes hard, then checked the link's STATUS. "Uh, this is as fast as it will deliver in oral mode, Eerin. I didn't know you could already use a computer. I was going to teach you tomorrow."

"Tomorrow!" Eerin's shocked tone indicated that Mark might as well have said "next century." "There is much to learn before going home. Hin will not be postponing things for tomorrows. Hin learned to use these tools on the ship."

"Oh." *All that and learning Mizari, too? Damn, but these beings learn fast!* "What do you think of the computer?"

"Hin has discovered hin likes the computer's speech." The golden eyes shone. "Machines tell knowledge very efficiently, if not elegantly."

"What do you mean, not elegantly?"

"Without rhythm, measure, and style, gaining knowledge is not as pleasurable for hin."

Mark stifled a yawn, intrigued despite his weariness. "Can you explain more? About the rhythm and style, I mean?"

"Listen." The Elpind activated a file sitting in buffer.

"Elspind. Lifecycle," said the computer in a soft, stilted voice. "Each Elpind is born neuter and remains so for the rough equivalent of ten standard years. Hin (the term denoting the neuter state) then enters the Change and emerges as either han (female) or heen (male). The adult mates for life soon after the Change and begins to reproduce the species. Death occurs four to six years after the Change."

"Pause," said Eerin. "Does Mark hear? Without rhythm, there is no flavor. A Telling would—"

"Wait a minute," Mark broke in. "I'm confused. Eerin, which are you going to become, han or heen?"

"Hin does not know."

"You don't know whether you're going to change into a male or a female? Surely you have some idea, sometime before this Change thing, how you'll come out."

"No."

"Well, which do you want to be?" Mark restrained the urge to kiddingly add "when you grow up." If Eerin was any example, the hin were, indeed, "grown up." He'd already gathered from Eerin's conversation today that the neuters built, administered, and maintained Elpind society; the han and heen built families.

"Hin will be happy to be either. Both han and heen are valuable and needed to give life to the people. But"—the Elpind showed signs of impatience—"hin wished to show Mark the difference between the computer's speech and a Telling. Mark will hear the rhythm, the measure, the style."

"Okay. I'll just sit down, if you don't mind." He sank into the armchair in the corner of the bedroom as Eerin dropped down to the carpet and sat cross-legged, thin knees sticking out like exclamation points. Hin began to rock gently back and forth on hin's bony rump.

"Hear these words and carry them through your days. The strongest words grow from deepest roots. Understand these words."

Even translated into Mizari, Eerin's speech carried a sing-song rhythm. Mark found it easy to let his mind follow the flow.

"El is life and Wo is death, and each completes the other," chanted Eerin. "We are Elspind, the people of life, for the life of the people endures even as death swallows us one by one. Our lives are cast like the shadows of the four moons from the ever-shining light of the people. We are born for the rizel. In the rizel, life is taken each from the other and given each to the other, and El walks so far ahead of Wo, there is no catching."

"Hold on a second. I'm confused again." Mark waved a hand. "What is the rizel?"

"Hin just told Mark. It is the coming together of han and heen so the people will endure, generation after generation," Eerin answered matter-of-factly.

"You mean, uh . . . sex?"

"Not gender, but the coming together of the two fertile Elpind for creation of new life," Eerin said.

"That's what I . . . " Mark searched hastily for a word that would not be either misinterpreted or vulgar. "You mean, the act of mating," he amplified. At Eerin's confirming nod, he continued, "Elspind teach that they are born to mate?"

"Is it not so with all peoples? Is it not how the life of the people endures?" The Elpind looked thoughtful at having to explain the ancient philosophy and added, "Perhaps Elspind value their collective life more because our individual lives are fleeting, like the shadows of our four moons."

Fleeting, thought Mark. *Like shadows*. He was remembering Eerin's Telling and how beautiful it had sounded—how oddly positive. Then he repressed a shudder, recalling the nightmares that had begun with Jon's suicide . . . and again with his mother's death. There had been shadows in those dreams.

"It is said that, in ancient times, our lives before Enelwo were longer, but then something—perhaps the sun, perhaps our environment—something changed and Enelwo came more quickly."

Mark frowned at the barrage of information. "What's Enelwo?"

"It is what the computer called the Change."

"Enelwo." He tested the sound slowly. "I hear the words for both life and death in there."

"El and Wo step close together at that time, and no one can know beforehand which hin will embrace."

"Or whether you'll live the rest of your days as male or female," Mark added thoughtfully. He tried vainly to imagine what it felt like to have two huge unknowns bearing down on you from the moment of birth. Humans had trouble handling just one.

Eerin bounced up off the floor. "How do humans ever learn?" hin said. "They cannot listen in long pieces; they must talk, also. Talk and get a small answer, talk some more and get another small answer."

"I'm sorry for interrupting," Mark apologized. "I want to hear all the long pieces you have to say, but I also need to be sure I understand them."

"Mark does not need to say heen is sorry," Eerin was quick to point out. "It is only that hin truly wishes to know how humans learn . . . it is obvious that humans do, but not plain to hin *how* such learning is accomplished. Obviously very differently."

"Uh, yeah . . . " Mark said, and a wide yawn caught him unawares. "That's a big subject, Eerin, and it would take me a long time to tell what I know about it."

"Then hin will ask the computer. Does Mark wish to help the machine answer?"

Since he'd turned out to be a less-than-satisfactory pupil, the Elpind was eager to get back to the computer. Mark decided it wouldn't bother Eerin if he was honest. "I'd really rather go back to sleep if you don't need me," he admitted.

Eerin's tone managed to convey both resignation and pride. "Mark may resume sleep. Hin does not need help."

Gratefully, Mark padded back into the living room and flopped back down on the couch. Dimly, through the open door, he could hear Eerin at the computer link. Hin was busily retrieving the computer's files on human learning methods—and also, Mark noted, with a wry grin, human sexuality.

So hin can hear them all in one "long piece," Mark thought, wondering whether it would be worth getting back up just to watch the Elpind's face. Eerin was in for some surprises, to say the least. Compared with the Elpind lifecycle, Eerin might well find human sexuality pedestrian by comparison.

Born to reproduce, he thought with an inward shake of his head. *Well, in a way that describes every species, I guess. But for most species mating isn't fraught with such . . . urgency.* He resolved to do some reading tomorrow on Elpind sexuality. He had no idea how Elpind females gave birth. Eerin's body was certainly featureless.

That Change they go through must be a profound one, he thought. *Their metabolisms must take a ninety-degree turn . . .* He wondered how close Eerin was to hin's own Enelwo.

"Eerin," he called softly, "I was just wondering. How old are you?"

"Pause," the Elpind's voice said, then the alien appeared in the doorway. "Hin has lived for 6.5 of your years."

About three and a half more years, then, Mark thought as the Elpind disappeared, remembering that the neuter stage lasted approximately ten standard years before the Change. *And then, maybe six, maybe only four years more before . . .*

It was difficult to finish the thought. By the time Mark turned thirty, gentle, inquisitive Eerin would be dead.

He heard his companion's voice again. "Computer, resume."

No wonder you don't sleep, Mark thought, feeling a wave of pity for the Elpind. *You can't afford to waste any time.* And now, thanks to this pair project, Eerin was being forced to live some of hin's brief life at a snail's pace—a human pace.

Mark shivered and closed his eyes. *It's natural for them,* he told himself sternly. *For Elspind, their life is just like your life is for you. All there is . . . is all there is. It's the same for everybody.*

The human fell back into a restless doze, but the nightmare came again for the first time in two weeks, the first time since he'd made his decision to leave StarBridge. The dream had variations, but in it, a shadow hovered over his mother, slowly descending, until it engulfed her, and he watched her die. If that didn't wake him, he always came to a door and opened it. Slowly. Too slowly. He could never get it open in time to stop the blood from seeping out from under the door onto his bare feet. *Jon is dead. My fault!*

When he opened that door, saw his friend's body, the horror always woke Mark, and this time was no exception. He opened his eyes and sat up with a jerk, gasping.

Rubbing his hands across his face, he felt his heartbeat hammering within him and took slow breaths, trying to calm himself. Damn! There'd been a variation in the dream this time, too. Just now, when he'd opened that door, he'd seen Eerin on the other side of it, withered, ancient . . . and dead.

He glanced at his watch. 0600 hours. The room was completely silent.

"Eerin?" Mark got up and glanced into both bedrooms. The Elpind wasn't in either.

His heart pounding again, his stomach in a knot, Mark padded barefoot across the floor to the bathroom. Memories of Jon made him swallow hard. His dream . . . and finding Eerin . . .

"Eerin?" He tapped. "Hey, Eerin! You in there?"

No answer.

Hesitating for only a second, Mark opened the door.

Eerin wasn't in the bathroom.

Mark's mind seethed with worry as he jammed on his shoes and bent to seal them. The Elpind was his responsibility, in a way that a pair partner chosen from the population of regular StarBridge students would not have been. Eerin was extremely intelligent, more so than he was, Mark had decided, but hin was still new to technology. StarBridge could hold dangers for someone totally unfamiliar with elevator shafts, food servos, and recycling chutes. Swallowing, Mark realized that the things he'd always taken for granted could be potentially lethal.

He bolted out the door at a near run. The library's computer annex, several dining areas, and a quick jog through the botanical dome yielded no Eerin. On impulse, Mark turned his steps toward the observation dome. The Elpind had been enraptured with the breathtaking view of the stars.

His hunch was correct. His pair partner was kneeling in the center of the lounge, tying closed a long, thin case that he hadn't seen before.

"Eerin," he had to catch his breath, "what—what are you doing up here? I've looked all over for you!"

"Hin came here to perform the Mortenwol. It is how hin begins each day."

"Mortenwol?" repeated Mark blankly. "Well . . . uh, couldn't you have done it in our room? I don't think you should go out by yourself, not until you get a little more familiar with StarBridge."

"The Mortenwol is not quiet. Mark said he required more sleep. Hin wishes Mark to remain healthy."

"Oh. Well, uh, thanks. Listen, is this Mortenwol something I would be allowed to watch?" he asked.

"Certainly. Close friends and family share it on Elseemar every morning."

"Well, if you do it every day, it's obviously an important part of your culture. I'm supposed to be learning about your culture just as much as you are mine, remember?"

"Mark can watch tomorrow," promised Eerin solemnly.

"Okay, good. What is it, by the way?"

"Mark will see." The Elpind's golden eyes sparkled with mischief . . . and anticipation. "Tomorrow. But what will we do today?" Eerin appeared ready to race off in any direction the human might point.

So much energy! Mark sighed, but he couldn't help smiling in return. "Let's start with food," he suggested. He'd learned yesterday that eating was second only to learning as Eerin's favorite activity.

He was rewarded with a joyous bounce and skip of the sort that humans usually reserved for momentous occasions.

So they went to breakfast.

Before they were halfway through, Cara Hendricks joined them. She smiled excitedly as she brought her tray over.

"I've been given permission to spend the whole day with you two, if that's okay," she said. "Not for a formal interview yet, but just to get acquainted." Cautiously she tasted a yellow, gelatinous puddle on one of her plates, then grimaced.

"We call it slimefruit," offered Mark, grinning. "It's from one of the Apis homeworlds. Kind of an acquired taste."

"I've been bravely trying something new every meal, but maybe I'll just stick with the croissants this breakfast." She pushed the yellow goo away.

"Mark, will you explain to Eerin in Mizari about cameras

and what I'll be doing today? And talk slowly so I can try to follow along. I've been practicing for two weeks now, and I'm able to pick up a few words here and there."

"That's great," Mark said. "Congratulations."

"Well, there's nothing to celebrate yet." Cara chuckled. "I make clearer sounds brushing my teeth right now than I do speaking Mizari. But I'm going to keep on with it, even after I get back home. Knowing the dominant language spoken by the CLS councils and administrative offices can only help me as a journalist."

Mark explained Cara's request to the Elpind, to which Eerin responded in the affirmative. Then he turned back to Cara. "Okay, test time. What did hin say?"

"I think Eerin said he—uh—hin doesn't mind being filmed. And something about 'look inside'? I think?"

Mark grinned. "You're right. Eerin wants to look inside your camera to see how it works. And you'd better plan on showing hin the footage, too. Curiosity, I've discovered, is this Elpind's middle name."

Cara laughed. "I will show you," she said in halting Mizari to Eerin. Then ordering the camera into position and on, she began to watch the Elpind eat. Eerin was totally unself-conscious as hin busily stuffed purple and white stringy things into hin's mouth.

"Mark, can you explain what Eerin is eating? In English, for my viewers back home," she added.

"Sure. We did this yesterday, twice, so I already know. Elspind are vegetarians. They have no teeth, just hard, bony ridges extending the gums." He glanced at Eerin and said in Mizari, "Would you mind showing her your mouth?"

The Elpind obligingly pulled hin's lips back to display hin's lack of teeth for Cara's camera.

"Eerin is eating roots and stems from a plant called 'sestel,' " Mark continued. "Hin brought it from Elseemar, because their dietary needs are still being analyzed."

"Hin's not chewing," Cara said.

"Yeah, well, Eerin explained that. Hin's got a tongue, see." Again he prompted hin, and the Elpind opened wide. Hin's tongue was broad, orange, and looked tough enough to trowel mortar with.

"Under the tongue," Mark went on, "are . . . glands, I guess you'd call them. When Eerin holds the food under hin's tongue for a few seconds, secretions from these glands break it down and make it soft enough to swallow. Several stomachs finish the job, each in their turn, once the food gets there."

Mark grinned at Cara's aplomb as she took another bite of croissant during this explanation. She was toughening up fast. It took some human students months to be able to eat with aliens without gagging.

"Do they have taste buds?" she asked. "Do they enjoy eating like we do?"

Mark nodded emphatically. "Oh, they enjoy it, let me promise you. Hin drove me crazy yesterday asking when it would be time to eat next." But he turned to Eerin and dutifully asked the question.

Eerin's vigorous nod in Cara's direction was the answer.

The last of the Elpind's purple and white plant products disappeared, and the humans recycled their dishes.

"What's the schedule for today?" Cara rose to her feet, the little autocam readjusting its position in the air next to her.

"Eerin and I will spend this week boning up on survival skills, advanced first aid, and any special info we'll need to perform our pair project assignment—which we'll find out about from Rob this afternoon. All the while we'll be using our free time getting to know each other and each other's ways better, trading language skills, that kind of thing. Next week we'll learn what our specific assignment is going to be, so we can begin planning for it."

Cara gave Mark a long look. "You sound pretty enthusiastic about this pair project. Does this mean you've changed your mind about leaving StarBridge, Mark?"

He shook his head, feeling his own features tighten. "No, I'm just doing this because I was the most experienced student who was currently available. My way of saying thanks to Rob Gable and this school, I guess. I owe both of them a lot."

"Maybe you'll change your mind," she said, giving him a sideways glance as they moved along the crowded corridor.

"That's obviously what Rob's hoping, but I won't," Mark said shortly, hoping she'd take the hint.

Eerin, in hin's typical fashion, had forged ahead of them.

Finally, the Elpind halted and waited for hin's slow companions. "Hin has observed that humans are capable of moving faster than Mark and Cara," hin said with a hint of reproof.

"What did hin say?" Cara demanded.

"We're a pair of tortoises, it seems," Mark told her, chuckling dryly. "And Eerin is the hare."

Cara watched the Elpind bound ahead of them with all of hin's exuberant energy. "Don't they *ever* slow down?" she wondered aloud.

"No," Mark said slowly, suddenly sobered, "they can't afford to slow down. Eerin can't afford to waste time."

CHAPTER 5
♦
The Mortenwol

Morning came early, but a gritty-eyed Mark rolled out of bed without a grumble. Eerin had ignored every attempt yesterday to find out just what this Mortenwol thing was, and by that time his curiosity was acute.

After a quick shower, he felt better. "I'm ready," he told Eerin expectantly. "You can start the Mortenwol anytime."

"At home it is done in the part of our dwelling that is open to the sky."

"A courtyard?" Mark guessed. "Okay. You want to go back to the observation dome?"

Eerin nodded. Hin disappeared into the other bedroom and came back with the two cases Mark had seen the day before. Hin handed the long, thin one to Mark to carry. It was very light.

When they reached the observatory, Mark settled on one of the low couches to watch whatever was about to happen. Eerin took position in the middle of the room, beneath the peak of the great dome. Hin's creamy coloring glimmered palely in the starlight. The Elpind had not spoken since arriving, and there was a strange, distant look in the golden eyes.

Placing the long case on the floor, Eerin opened it, removing six feathers. Each was black-tipped and yellow-spined, but two were deep red, one a dark green, two a soft blue, and one a pure, startling white. The plumage was full and springy, not tired-looking the way Mark had seen old feathers become.

With quick motions of hin's long, slender fingers, Eerin wove the six feathers together until they became a chaplet. Hin slipped the headband over hin's head, where it made an attractive contrast to the Elpind's creamy down.

Next the Elpind slid a small oblong board out of the second case. About half a meter long, it appeared to be made of wood and was finely worked. Carefully Eerin twisted a short lever attached to the underside. *Some type of winding mechanism*, Mark decided. Then, standing, hin bent and spread long fingers to press the four corners of the board simultaneously. A low, powerful hum emerged.

A music box of some kind? Mark wondered. At Eerin's next touch, this time a gentle tap over a spidery-looking symbol in the center, the box began to play. The purity of its sound impressed Mark; each note was like a little bell.

The Elpind stood motionless for the first few notes, gazing distantly up at the stars overhead. Then, with an incredible leap straight into the air, Eerin was dancing.

Many heartbeats later, Mark realized that his mouth was still hanging open. The agility, the pinpoint control, the amazing strength and power that the movements implied: he'd never seen anything like it, not in holo-vids of professional ballet, not in tough gymnastics contests . . . not anywhere.

Mark himself was a good dancer. He was highly skilled, too, at the stylized, rhythmic movements that were the foundation of the self-defense training he'd taken for years; he knew how to think and move in patterns. But Eerin's dance was incredible. The intricacy, the quick repetitions, the grace with which every movement was made . . . it awed him.

The music from the little board swelled out in high, reedy notes, wild and sweet and joyous. It was full of energy, like the Elspind themselves.

Pattern after pattern of rising notes repeated and crescendoed. The weaving of the rhythms was complex, but simple to follow, and Mark felt a response rise from deep within him. The notes called to him, quickening the blood in his veins. He found he had to consciously keep himself on the couch, that the music was practically pulling him into joining the wild dance. He perched on the edge of his seat, feet twitching.

Mark kept his eyes fixed on Eerin. With each repetition of the musical theme Eerin seemed to leap a little higher, whirl a little faster. Yet there was no sense of frantic exertion. Each movement floated, as if a feather danced. The dance was gracefully effortless and obviously fraught with deep emotion.

A piercing new note sounded, and Mark sensed that it signaled the beginning of the end. Sounding again, it began a pattern of its own, moving in and out of the established melody, slowing the wild rhythm bit by bit. Then with a long trembling of the high, sharp note, it was over.

Eerin came back to the couch, eyes shining with energy and joy. Hin wasn't even breathing hard.

Mark hunted for words. "That was—that was worth getting up for!"

The Elpind nodded graciously, seeming to understand the depth of the compliment, coming, as it did, from a species that craved hours on end in a comalike state. Hin began unweaving the feathers, laying them carefully in the oblong case.

"Really, Eerin. I loved it, all of it!" Mark walked over to collect the music board and bring it back to Eerin. "Tell me what it means. It's more than just a dance, isn't it?"

"It is a ritual, the most important ritual of the Elspind. The movements are learned by all, but each individual makes stylistic variations meaningful to hin. The sequences of movements that form the internal patterns are handed down from family to family. Any Elpind watching a Mortenwol can tell from which family line the dancer has descended."

"Are you telling a story in the dance, the story of your family? What does 'Mortenwol' mean? And what do you call that thing?" He pointed to the music board that Eerin was now tucking back into its protective covering.

"This is a kareen," Eerin replied. "No, the dance is not a story. Mortenwol means . . . the best words are . . . death dance," hin said calmly.

Mark recoiled as if he'd been struck.

The Elpind did not seem to notice. "It is performed each

morning to greet a new day of life and to prepare the body and the mind should death come in the midst of that life. And there are other ritual times when the Mortenwol may also be danced. If death is imminent or inevitable, for example, an Elpind will dance the Mortenwol—or, if incapable of performing the dance, the Elpind has the right to ask any other Elpind to dance in hin's, heen's or han's stead."

"Death dance," whispered Mark, shocked. "*Every* day?"

"We Elspind live close to death," said Eerin serenely. "Don't humans wish to be ready when death comes?"

Mark was trying to get control of his emotions. This was an important part of Eerin's culture; it wasn't his place to criticize it. Interrelators were trained to understand, rather than judge. But death was hardly his favorite topic right now!

Thanks a lot, Rob, he thought bitterly.

"Mark?" Eerin was staring at him. "Don't humans wish to be ready when death comes? What do they do to prepare?"

Mark sank back down onto the couch. All the energy and lightness he'd felt watching Eerin dance had fled; he was tired and depressed.

"Humans do wish to be ready," he said after a moment's thought, trying to answer Eerin's question honestly. "But very few ever are. Some religions have rituals, but usually they occur after the person dies. Most humans' preparations are financial or legal, to provide for their families. To dwell on the idea of death every day would seem morbid to a human."

"It does not seem morbid to Elspind."

He looked thoughtfully at Eerin. "I know. That music you played . . . it was happy!"

"Do humans dance?"

"Sure. Most do, anyway. I love to dance, myself."

"When Mark dances fast and free, does Mark feel afraid?"

"Well, no."

"Sad?"

Mark shook his head.

"Because dancing drives out the negatives, brings up energy. It leaves one strong and clean. Full of life, Mark."

"That's my point!" the human protested. "Full of life. *Not* ready for death."

"Death is a part of life. Mortenwol celebrates the whole of

the pattern." Eerin blinked. "Can we have breakfast now?"

Mark heaved himself off the couch. "Sure. I'm trying to understand, Eerin, but to me, death just isn't something to celebrate."

"No," agreed Eerin, making an obvious effort to slow hin's usual exuberant rush toward food. "It is each day of life that is the happy occasion. The joy of Mortenwol each morning is that hin is alive to dance it again. It is also a commitment to give hinself gladly to life that day. That includes the part of life that is death, if it should choose that day to come. No one can separate them."

I can. Out of deference to the Elpind, Mark didn't say the words, but he felt oddly betrayed, not knowing why.

"It is all tied together: the dance, the music, the feathers," Eerin continued, oblivious to Mark's mood. "The feathers are more than decoration. They come from the tails of the Elseewas. That translates to 'Shadowbird.' " For the last word, Eerin abandoned Mizari to combine two of hin's limited supply of English words. Without teeth, the "sh" sound definitely lost something in the translation.

Eerin switched back to Mizari. "This beautiful, multicolored bird lives in the mountains of my world. Their feathers are rare, so they become family treasures, handed down from generation to generation. They are priceless; no amount of money can buy one. It is a sign of hin's family's rich heritage and high esteem that hin was given six to have for hin's very own," Eerin finished with pride.

Mark was glad to pursue the seeming change of subject. "Why are the feathers so scarce?" he asked. "Has the bird been hunted too much?"

"No. Hin's people do not eat flesh, and rarely hunt unless in the case of a rogue predator. It is forbidden to kill an Elseewas, Mark. Their feathers can only be found, not taken."

Eerin stopped talking for a moment as they entered one of the dining areas. The Elpind waited impatiently, hopping a little from foot to foot, as the human got his food.

When they were seated at the table, the Elpind continued, "The Elseewas is an important symbol to Elspind. The adult bird lives only six days. We feel a certain kinship to it, since the Elpind adult lives only six years, at most, after the Change."

Mark wondered how Eerin could sit there, calmly eating and speaking so matter-of-factly about what seemed to him to be a tragically early death. *It's normal for them,* he reminded himself again. *I can't judge the Elpind culture by my feelings. Remember, understanding, not judgment.*

"Six days?" he said, carefully neutral. "That's not long."

"The Elseewas grows very rapidly, mates, hatches one brood, then dies," said Eerin. "But it sings so marvelously and dies with such grace and passion that it symbolizes the way we, too, wish to live and die."

The Elpind's golden eyes grew faraway and hin stopped eating for a second. "Elspind say that to see the death of an Elseewas changes one's life forever. Hin has never been so fortunate."

Mark didn't want to ask, but he had to. "How do they die?"

"They drown."

"Drown? A bird?"

"They fly out over a body of water and perform a . . . well, we call it a dance. It is an incredibly acrobatic effort. Parts of the Mortenwol symbolize that last flight. Then, when the bird is spent, it plunges into the water. Some speculate that it dies in the air and merely falls, but those who have seen it say that isn't true. They say the Elseewas seems eager for its last adventure and dives to find it."

All of a sudden this talk of last flights and death plunges was too much for Mark. "Uh, excuse me, I'm through," he said, getting up to ram his tray down the recycling chute with more force than necessary.

He turned around to find the Elpind studying him carefully. Mark cleared his throat.

"Uh, we've got advanced first-aid training this morning. If we go now, we can practice a bit . . . you know, name the items in the kit for each other . . . before the instructor gets there."

Eerin waited until they were in the hall before hin spoke.

"The CLS team that prepared hin to leave Elseemar warned of this. They told hin not to speak much of our culture's way of facing death because it would seem callous to many. They said the young of most species often have not even seen death yet."

Mark stopped. "You talk like there are dead bodies lying around everywhere on your world." He could not keep the bitterness out of his voice. "Have *you* experienced death personally? Lost someone you love? Believe me, I have."

"Hin has seen death," replied the Elpind calmly. "One of hin's siblings died in infancy, when the gland that produces the juvenile hormone began to function. It is a risky time. Another died during the Change, which is not uncommon. And hin's parents died, of course."

Mark stared at the alien. "What do you mean, of course?"

Eerin regarded him incredulously. "Hin *told* Mark the adult Elspind die within six years of the Change. Thus, after the parents bear the young, it falls to the oldest siblings to raise the younger, until all are through the Change. Every family goes through two stages, a parent-family, or 'pinlaa,' and a sibling-family, which is called a 'pinsa.' A pinlaa prepares for as much as two years for the coming deaths of the han and the heen so that all is done with dignity."

"I'm sorry," Mark muttered. "I should have realized."

The Elpind regarded him sympathetically, evidently realizing his distress. "Mark has watched a family member embrace death?"

Mark nodded numbly. "First my father. I was very young; I hardly remember. But"—tears welled up despite his efforts to control them—"just a few months ago, my mother . . . " He trailed off, unable to finish.

Eerin's voice was kind. "Did Mark make a fine farewell ceremony? Mark said humans have death rituals."

The young man shook his head. "I wasn't there," he said in an agonized whisper. "I wasn't with her . . . "

Eerin reached out and awkwardly patted the human's arm. The golden eyes were troubled. "Hin will speak no more of death. It is time to go for lessons."

Mark blinked rapidly and took several deep, steadying breaths. *Dammit, Kenner, get hold of yourself! This is no way to relate to a nonhuman culture, by creating taboo subjects!*

"No, it's all right," he said as soon as he could trust his voice, "I should have realized about your parents when you told me about your lifecycle the other night. And anytime you want to talk about the Mortenwol, or the Elseewas, or anything else in your culture, you go right ahead. We've got to learn about each other, that's what you're here for, right?"

"Yes."

"Well, your ways are what work for you, and if every Elpind knows hin's going to see hin's parents die . . . well, if dancing helps you prepare for that, then dancing is the thing to do. If I could have prepared for my mother's death"—Mark's voice trembled—"it would have helped me, I know."

Animation came back into Eerin's eyes. "Mark Kenner will be a great interrelator," hin announced firmly.

The Elpind turned away and headed down the corridor with hin's customary skips and hops without seeing Mark shake his head soberly. The human followed, wondering whether he should tell Eerin of his plan to leave StarBridge once this project was over.

It would be too hard to explain, Mark decided. And it really didn't matter anyway. Negatives, Mark was discovering, had little claim on Eerin.

Three days later, once again in the observation dome and once again after the Mortenwol, the subject of life and death on Elseemar resurfaced . . . but this time it was Cara Hendricks asking the questions, during her formal interview with the Elpind.

She's really good, Mark thought, watching her work. Overhead the stars provided a stunning backdrop, and since the transparent plas-steel dome went all the way to ground level, he could look out across the asteroid's rock-strewn, desolate surface, lit only by the starlight. He turned away from the disturbingly close horizon, bounded by the mountain peaks of the Lamont Cliffs, to look down at his friends as they sat together on the floor, cross-legged.

Cara's camera hovered over her shoulder, but she seemed oblivious to it; her whole attention was focused on Eerin. As a result, the Elpind had also forgotten the camera. *Cara is the most fascinated listener hin has encountered here,* the young man realized, amused. *And Eerin is loving it!*

Mark was relieved to find himself more relaxed than he'd thought he might be. He'd dreaded the idea of losing his composure again, especially in front of Cara, when the inevitable discussion of Elspind and their death rituals surfaced. At first he'd planned to absent himself.

But his interest in alien cultures that had given him the dream of being an interrelator in the first place had won out over his unease, and now Mark was glad. It helped to be nothing more than an observer—it wasn't the same as discussing the painful topic firsthand. He was learning a lot about the Elspind that he hadn't known.

"What is your home like, Eerin?" had been the young journalist's first question.

Eagerly the Elpind had described Lalcipind, "Beautiful Gathering Place of the People" in the foothills of a great mountain range: the simple homes nestled beneath the tall trees on the hillsides, the clear, swift-flowing rivers that ran down into the lush valley below where the crops were grown. Eight walks-under-the-sun-and-under-the-moons away lay the sea. Eerin had made the journey once to gaze upon its endless expanse from the top of a steep cliff that dropped straight down to the rocks and the heaving water.

There were deserts on Elseemar, too, the Elpind told them. These vast stretches formed a wide girdle of hot, arid land that bordered the mountain ranges on the central continents.

"Tell us about your people's First Contact with the CLS" was Cara's next request.

Mark knew the story from the CLS's viewpoint, but was fascinated now to hear it from the Elpind's. "Eight years ago a Heeyoon scout ship suffered life-support failure and made an emergency landing on Elseemar," Eerin said. "The WirElspind, our governing body, decided to welcome the Heeyoon . . . and in the ensuing years, they and the other CLS representatives have since opened the portals to the universe for hin's people."

Hin is so poised! Mark thought. The realization brought back to him something he'd almost overlooked in getting to know the Elpind; that Eerin was a visiting head of state, accustomed to sitting on the Council and helping to make decisions affecting an entire planet.

"I know that you weren't born at the time of the first encounter, but can you describe the mood of your people at that time?" Cara asked.

"Hin has heard the Tellings from that time," Eerin said, then went on to explain that at first the strange beings with their magical-seeming tools had seemed godlike, but that the Heeyoon and subsequent CLS visitors had been careful to dispel any such notions. "It was a shock for us to realize that we were not the only ones," Eerin said. "Hin's people experienced both fear and wonder."

"Some CLS members have criticized the Heeyoon crew for not leaving your world as soon as they realized it was inhabited by intelligent beings, since by their continued presence they ran the risk of bringing unwelcome change—some have gone so far as to call it contamination—to your world. What is your opinion on that, Eerin?"

"Hin's opinion is one with the WirElspind—the Great Council—in thinking that the CLS contact is a good thing for our people. Someday it may be possible to trade with other worlds. At the moment, Elspind value the cultural interchange between our world and the CLS representatives. We are learning a great deal." Eerin regarded the journalist unblinkingly. "Hin values the opportunity to learn, Cara."

The journalist nodded. "What about the other Elspind? How do they currently feel about the CLS contact?"

"The Elspind—our name means 'People of Life'—support the government in its decision," Eerin said, obviously choosing hin's words with great care.

"But there was trouble on Elseemar recently," Cara pointed out. "Trouble from a group of Elspind, correct?"

"*Not* correct," Eerin said firmly. "Those who caused the trouble were not the Elspind, but the Wospind—the People of Death. Outwardly they appear like us, but inwardly their minds and hearts are in conflict with the People of Life."

"How do the two groups differ?" Cara asked. She was leaning forward intently, obviously relieved that Eerin was willing to discuss such a potentially touchy subject.

"The Wospind fear that our old ways will be totally destroyed by the contacts with the off-worlders. They do not believe that contact with the CLS can prove beneficial."

"They claimed responsibility for the destruction of one of the main laboratory buildings near your village, didn't they?"

"Yes." Eerin shifted restlessly.

"Can you explain where they come from, and what their position is to my viewers?"

For the first time, the Elpind seemed reluctant. "The Wospind rose as a separate group only after the CLS representatives came to our world. From the first they argued against off-world contact. The dissenting families began to move away from our villages and towns in large groups, going higher into the mountains or even near the edges of The Long Desert, isolated places. There they promised they would cling to our traditional life-style. Their protests grew ever louder."

"And what is their goal?"

Eerin hesitated. "Before hin can explain their demands, hin must first give a brief"—the Elpind's mouth turned down as hin considered—"a brief Telling. The word does not translate well. History . . . legend . . . myth . . . all those words combined, and more, that is a Telling."

Cara nodded. "I think I understand. Go on, please."

"Long, long ago, our Tellings say, the people lived much longer than they do now. Long enough so most Elpind parents survived to see their last child weaned and thriving before death ceased their dancing forever." Eerin's speech had fallen into that rhythmic cadence Mark had noted before. "In those days, long ago, the years of an Elpind's life as a hin, a neuter, were twice what they are today . . . or so our Tellings record."

"But something changed?"

Eerin nodded. "The Elspind do not know what caused the lifespan to shorten. But over generations, it grew less and less. At the request of the WirElspind, the CLS scientists at the mountain laboratory have been researching the problem, to see if the lifecycle can be restored to its original length."

Mark straightened, listening intently. *I didn't know about this! Eerin never mentioned any of this!*

"If the CLS researchers succeed," Eerin was continuing, "Elspind would be able to look forward to time for many more Tellings, time to learn, time to accomplish more. Time enough so Elpind parents can leave strong, healthy children instead of infants behind."

"And the CLS scientists are close to finding a solution?"

Eerin nodded. "Hin believes so. The scientists have been working with Elpind herbalists and healers. Together they created a substance named 'Elhanin,' meaning 'life-more-long.' It would cause the Change to be delayed, thus extending the time we remain hin. Early small-group testing was promising. Hin's own sibling Lieor volunteered to be among the first large test groups."

Mark felt as if a weight he hadn't even known he'd carried was suddenly lifted. Perhaps Eerin didn't have to die so tragically young. Medical science had failed his mother, but if it could give years more life to an entire planet of people . . . well that would be wonderful!

"Is the substance available yet?" he blurted eagerly. "Can *you* get it?"

Cara gave him a reproving glance.

"Sorry," he said, realizing he'd interrupted.

"Hin does not know the answer to Mark's question," the Elpind said. "Hin does not know what will happen to the schedule now, or if, in fact, any of the research projects will continue. There was other research concerned with the lifecycle," Eerin explained. "Postponement of the Change was the first to bring results—because it was the easiest, they said. Elhanin would also lengthen life after the Change. It would slow down the rapid Elpind metabolism," Eerin said, and shot Mark a triumphant glance, obviously pleased at remembering the technical word. "The researchers are also investigating ways to make the Change, Enelwo, safer, so that not so many will die then."

"According to my sources, many of the researchers survived," Cara told the Elpind. "Perhaps they can continue the work."

"That is a choice currently facing the WirElspind . . . whether to ask that the research be continued."

"What influence will the Wospind play in that decision?"

"Possibly a great deal," Eerin replied. "The Wospind feel that tampering with the lifecycle nature has given us is wrong." The Elpind sighed, an almost human-sounding sigh. "We of the WirElspind attempted to reassure the dissenters that Elhanin would only be available to those who wished to take it. But they did not believe us. They also feel that no Elpind should have to make that choice."

"How did the Wospind get the name 'People of Death'?"

"One of the members of the WirElspind, First Speaker Alanor, began referring to them as Wospind, saying angrily that if they were not in favor of longer life, they must obviously be in favor of death. Use of the name became common . . . even the Wospind themselves now sometimes use it, as a challenge and insult to the Elspind."

"And it was the Wospind who destroyed the lab," Cara said. "To stop the research, right?"

Eerin nodded. "But the destruction of one lab cannot stop the growth of knowledge on Elseemar. Hin hopes the Wospind will come to realize that soon, and cease this recent violence."

"They weren't violent to start with?"

Eerin shook hin's downy head. "At first their protests were peaceful. The Wospind petitioned the WirElspind for a seat on the Great Council, so they could have a voice. But the WirElspind ruled that they were not entitled to representation, since they were a group of believers scattered over many places. Our representatives are appointed by province. The Wospind protested this ruling bitterly, and with growing anger."

"How did you, personally, vote on that issue, Eerin?" Cara leaned forward intently.

Eerin was reluctant, but finally responded, "In this instance, hin was not in agreement with the majority."

"Was that ruling what began the Wospind's violence?"

"No. Three cycles ago, six of your months, a new Wopind leader arose. Orim is said to come from Lalcipind, hin's own village. This new leader is extremely radical, urging violence as a way to gain the Wospind's ends. It was Orim who led the attack on the CLS laboratory."

The Elpind was now plainly restless and uncomfortable, and Cara, seeing this, hastily brought the interview to a conclusion. Mark watched as she thanked the Elpind and promised to provide hin a preview of the film later. Then, with Mark's promise to join hin in a minute, Eerin bounded off for breakfast.

"Do you want to eat with us?" Mark asked.

"No, thanks. I'll program something in my room. I want to take a look at this morning's film, do the edit on the interview, and get it transmitted today if I can. This material's too important to carry home like the rest of my documentary. I'm looking forward to watching the playback of the Mortenwol," she added. "That was simply amazing."

"I know," Mark agreed. "I actually look forward to getting up in the morning now, just to see it." They both laughed.

"Well, join us later if you want," he added. "We'll be getting a rundown later this morning from Rob on the student leaders we're to meet with on Berytin."

Mark and Eerin's pair project assignment was to work with the student leaders of one of StarBridge's satellite testing schools on one of the Drnian worlds, analyzing and lowering, if possible, the school's unusually high dropout rate.

"I've been meaning to ask you about that particular assignment," Cara said. "I mean, in light of the fact that you've decided to, uh . . ."

"Drop out myself?" Mark grinned. "I think it's an extremely ironic assignment and no accident, but I like it. And I won't have any trouble talking about the StarBridge ideals to those kids; I believe in them as much as I ever did. I'm just not cut out to be an interrelator myself, that's all."

Cara was shaking her head,

You don't know, Mark thought. *I'm really not. And I can't tell you the real reason I like this assignment—that I'm relieved as hell because it's one where nobody's life or death is going to hang on any decision of mine.*

Smiling, he escorted Cara out of the observation dome, then went to find his pair partner.

CHAPTER 6

◆

Departures

A crowd gathered to see Cara, Mark, and Eerin off when their time came to leave StarBridge. Cara filmed the occasion, smiling a little mistily as she focused on Eerin, who was gamely modeling the StarBridge jacket hin had received. The human-sized garment hung in limp folds over the Elpind's thin body, but hin's eyes were brighter than ever as Eerin nodded and thanked hin's well-wishers, all the while clutching the jacket around hin proudly.

It's a good thing I don't have to say good-bye to Mark and Eerin until tomorrow, Cara thought. *I don't think I could stand two more good-byes today.*

Someone touched her shoulder. Cara turned to see Rob Gable behind her, another StarBridge jacket in his hands. "Here," the psychologist said, holding it out, "a memento of your visit."

"Thank you, Rob!" Cara exclaimed. "I'll treasure it." Quickly she draped the midnight-blue folds over her shoulders, then struck a pose. "How does it look?"

He nodded, making a circle with thumb and forefinger. "But how are you going to manage to film yourself wearing it? Your documentary won't be complete without this shot."

"This footage is just for me," she told him. "To commemorate the greatest experience of my life—and the shortest month. I only wish I were arriving instead of leaving—then I could start all over again!"

Rob gave her a hug. "Don't let this be good-bye," he said. "Come back and see us again, okay?"

"I wish I could," she said earnestly. "I'll try."

He smiled understandingly. "Take care, Cara."

"I will, Rob." The journalist turned away from the doctor and looked at the crowd surrounding them in the shuttle dome. It seemed to Cara as though every student she'd so much as spoken to in the hallways was there to say farewell.

"The shuttle's ready," Rob announced, pointing up the ramp at the school's engineer and pilot, Janet Rodriguez. The striking woman with the vivid auburn hair was beckoning to her. "Here, I'll get—" Rob groaned theatrically as he picked up her carry-on bag. "What I'd better get is an a-grav unit! What have you got in here? Rocks?" He gave her a mock-suspicious look. "You sure you're not swiping the school's radonium? We need it to power this place, or we'll all be breathing vacuum!"

She laughed. "Come on, I didn't shoot *that* much film!"

"You couldn't prove it by me," he grumbled, his dark eyes twinkling. They began walking toward the shuttle. Mark and Eerin were already halfway up the ramp.

Cara paused in the hatchway, looking back at the crowd and Rob, feeling tears threaten again. "Rob, I . . . "

The psychologist read her expression. "I've learned that there are times when it's not a good idea to look back, and this is one of them," he said. "Mahree learned that the first day she spent alone after the *Désirée* left her on the Simiu homeworld. 'I had to learn to look forward, Rob, not back,' she told me. And she was right, as Mahree usually is."

Cara smiled at this unusual personal revelation from the media-shy psychologist. The doctor's trust that she would not reveal his confidence was a gift more tangible than the jacket she wore. "Thanks," she said. "I'll remember that."

The hatch slid shut.

Minutes later, as the glowing domes of the asteroid receded behind them, Cara unobtrusively wiped her eyes, then glanced at Mark across the aisle from her. She never had gotten the whole story on him, and she regretted that—not that she wanted to know it for professional reasons anymore, but her curiosity was still aroused.

Why is he leaving? she wondered, not for the first time. *Is it because he's so depressed over his mother's death? He told me he'd made up his assignments, so it's not academic failure . . .*

She also knew that he'd split with Sulinda Carmel, his girlfriend. According to Cara's sources, Sulinda was telling her friends (at least the eight or ten closest ones) that the breakup was just as well, since Mark Kenner had some serious maturing to do before he became an interrelator or anything else.

That was just typical breakup talk, of course, but Cara still found it hard not to be disappointed in Mark. *From what I've seen of him with Eerin, he's good at what he does,* she thought. *But maybe he's just not cut out to take the pressure of a diplomatic job. If so, I ought to try to admire his honesty, but it's hard not to think of him as a quitter . . .*

She remembered Rob Gable again, and reminded herself that the psychologist obviously saw something worth fighting for in Mark, or he'd never have arranged this pair project for him. *Give the guy a break, Cara,* she thought. *Don't judge what you don't understand . . .*

Cara looked out again. Only seconds had passed since takeoff, but already she could see the stark, jagged mountains on the asteroid's horizon, dark against the star-spattered void of space. Looking down, the four domes were just brightly lit circles.

"It's nice that we'll be traveling together for a little while," Cara said, breaking the silence in the shuttle. "Even if it's only until tomorrow morning, when we go into hibernation."

Mark nodded and smiled warmly. "It will certainly make Captain's Night a lot more pleasant." Traditionally, every embarkation from a space station generated a ship's party called Captain's Night, at least on the big passenger liners. Interstellar travel took weeks and months, even now with the ultra-fast, Mizari-designed Stellar Velocity drive; crews and passengers alike looked forward to the dressy affairs.

"Is Eerin going into hibernation, too?" asked Cara.

"Hin will not," said the Elpind decisively—in English.

"Oh!" She was a little startled. "Eerin, I didn't realize your English was so good now. I didn't mean to ignore you."

The Elpind nodded graciously.

"You'd think I'd be used to it by now, but I'm still always surprised by how quickly Eerin learns," Mark said. "Hearing a word seems to be about the same for an Elpind as having it engraved right into hin's brain . . . it's there for good."

Cara gave him a mischievous smile. "And can you say the same about your progress with Elspindlor?"

Mark laughed. "After hypno-sessions every night for weeks, and a couple of hours of practice each day, I'm getting there," he said. "If I were on Elseemar right now, I could definitely ask for food, water, or the nearest rest room."

"Well, you've certainly mastered the essentials, then," Cara said, straight-faced. "I'm proud to report that I could do the same on Shassiszss!"

Both humans laughed, then Cara turned back to the Elpind. "Eerin, if you're not going to hibernate, what will you do with yourself for the six weeks it will take you to get to Berytin?"

"Hin will learn from the computer," the alien answered carefully in stilted English. "Many lifecycles would not be . . . " hin paused, searching for a word.

"Enough?" Mark suggested.

"Enough," repeated Eerin, "to learn all its Tellings."

"I can assure you that Eerin will make a pretty good dent in it, though," Mark said, smiling fondly at his pair partner.

The trip up to the space station took only a few minutes. Their tiny shuttle mated with an air lock at StarBridge Station, then they boarded the passenger liner S.V. *Asimov*.

A steward led them to the small cabin that Eerin would occupy while hin's companions slept. Mark would share it with the Elpind until time to go into hibernation, while Cara had a temporary berth across the narrow corridor.

"Almost as soon as we depart we'll make the transition to metaspace," the steward explained. The S.V. *Asimov* was an Earth-owned passenger transport; he was human. "Three hours from now Captain's Night begins. Main festivities in the common lounge forward. You two will be hibernating tomorrow morning, so you know not to eat anything after midnight, right?"

After showing them where to stow their hand luggage, he gave them each a layout of the ship, and left.

Cara studied the flimsy. *Asimov* was shaped like the diamond on a pack of cards. The forward "point" was taken up by the control room, officers' cabins, and storage lockers. A round room in the wide center of the diamond contained the hiber units, eighty of them. Directly aft of it, and extending in an oblong to the point of the diamond opposite the bridge was the hydroponics section, crew quarters, and a series of different-sized cargo holds that could provide various types of storage environments. The largest cargo hold and the engineering deck curved beneath and ran nearly the length of the diamond shape to form the liner's underbelly.

Small cabins, forty in number, backed against the reinforced plas-steel sides of the four "walls" created by the side points on the diamond. The open spaces in the side points and the space around the hibernation room offered a large mess area, a gym, a small infirmary, and two viewing lounges with high-density storage for thousands of music disks, books, and holo-vids, plus numerous computer links for public use.

The largest open area in the ship was the big lounge that lay between the hibernation chamber and the forward passage that led toward the bridge.

Mark looked up from his copy of the layout. "I've heard they have a great buffet for Captain's Night. Eat, drink—at least until midnight—and be merry, dancing the night away. How about it, Ms. Hendricks? Will you be our date?" He bowed gallantly.

"Our?"

"Eerin and I are partners, you know." He turned to the Elpind. "This will be a unique part of your exploration of other cultures, Eerin. You'll love it." He laughed. "And we sure won't have to teach *you* to dance!"

Cara thought of the exuberant moves of the Mortenwol and grinned, too. "I would be honored to accompany the two of you to the dance . . . as long as you promise me, Eerin, that I don't have to leap into the air as high as you do."

"It is a promise," agreed the Elpind solemnly.

In the privacy of her minuscule cabin, Cara changed into a red dress that showed off her slim waist and had a swirly skirt perfect for dancing. A gold belt, gold sandals, and a touch of gold sparkle in the sable hair that she fluffed naturally around her face completed the look. On impulse she left the tiny gold sensor patch on her cheekbone. Though she didn't plan to do any filming tonight, she suspected her face would feel naked now without it . . . and it certainly coordinated with her outfit.

"You look wonderful," Mark said sincerely, the minute she opened her cabin door to him.

"So do you." Cara eyed him admiringly. He was wearing a well-cut, black, one-piece outfit. The ivory silk jacket over it made his shoulders look even broader. Something was missing, however. "Where's Eerin?"

"In one of the viewer lounges checking out the computer links. Hin didn't want to sit around and waste time while I got ready. We'll go pick hin up."

"I don't see how Eerin crams so much information in one brain," Cara said as they headed toward the lounge. "Hin must have another one secreted somewhere. Have you figured it out?"

Mark shook his head. "I'm just glad to let the computer take over the job of answering hin's questions for a while."

"Constant, huh?"

"Well, during our two weeks together, I was interrogated on everything from Earth history to my bodily functions. One morning, I had to name every plant and tree in the Earth section of the botanical dome, a predicament my Simiu botany teacher of two years ago thoroughly enjoyed witnessing, I can tell you!"

Cara was laughing, her reaction encouraging Mark to go on.

"And food!" he said with a comical groan. "Not a bite went in my mouth that I didn't have to describe, from growth cycle to preparation!"

"That's not true," protested Cara, giggling. "I ate with you two lots of times. Eerin only did that at lunch and dinner. Breakfast, hin was too hungry to talk . . . "

Mark rolled his eyes at her attempt to set the facts straight. "I think I had to take half of StarBridge apart to show Eerin how this thing worked or what that thing looked like inside. Whew!"

"I know, I saw," Cara agreed with a chuckle. "In spite of

it all, you seem to really like Eerin."

"I do. Very much. Hin is honest and open-minded and enthusiastic about everybody and everything. A positive attitude, you know. Just being around Eerin has helped me a lot these past couple of weeks," he added thoughtfully, then looked embarrassed.

"Mark." Cara stopped him in the corridor with a hand on his arm. "I, uh, heard that you lost your mother a few months ago. There was never a good time to tell you how sorry I am, but after tomorrow, we won't see each other, so it's now or never. I just wish I could express . . . "

Mark put his hand over hers and gave it a squeeze. "I know. And thanks," he said quietly. Instead of continuing down the corridor, he leaned back against the bulkhead. Cara could see he had something on his mind. Once they reached the party there'd be no chance to talk privately.

"What is it?" she asked.

He shrugged, obviously ill at ease, suddenly seeming much younger than usual. "I meant to talk to Rob about this before we left, but I chickened out. Eerin's been good for me in a lot of ways, but I don't think I've been good for hin. I think Rob made a mistake pairing us."

"Why?"

"Hin's culture, with so much emphasis on death . . . the Mortenwol every day, you know . . . "

She nodded.

"Well"—he bit his lip—"I haven't really been able to relate to Eerin the way I should have, just because the whole subject of death makes me . . . uncomfortable. To put it mildly. And Eerin sensed how I felt. Hin would have been stupid not to . . . I wasn't very subtle with my reaction."

"I think that's understandable, given your situation," Cara said comfortingly. "I'm sure hin knows why you feel as you do . . . "

He shook his head. "I worry that by not accepting a part of Elpind culture, I might make Eerin feel . . . rejected. As if I disapproved of hin."

"Why don't you ask Eerin if that's how hin feels?" Cara suggested. "You said hin was honest. You'll get an answer you can deal with."

Mark grimaced. "That's the obvious solution," he admitted. "But since Mom . . . died . . . I haven't been dealing with things very well. I've been evidencing what Rob calls 'displacement' and 'avoidance' behaviors." He smiled wryly as he quoted.

"That doesn't mean that pattern of behavior has to continue," she pointed out. "You can start changing things by talking to Eerin, little by little, about painful subjects. Hin will understand, I know hin will."

Mark nodded, his hazel eyes thoughtful. "You're right," he said slowly, then added, "I was so relieved to learn the other day that Eerin has a good chance at a longer lifespan. I just hope they get that Elhanin research under way again quickly."

"You'd better hope the WirElspind doesn't decide to bow to the Wospind's pressure," Cara said.

"They won't!" Mark exclaimed. "Surely they'll ask that the research be continued! It's not as though anyone's going to *force* the Wospind to take the Elhanin."

"Where does Eerin stand personally on this?" asked Cara. "Did you get the impression hin would choose to take it?"

Mark looked startled. "Of *course* hin would," he said quickly, then frowned. "At least . . . I hope so. Eerin's too smart not to take advantage of something so wonderful. Maybe I'll ask hin about that, too."

He stood considering for a moment, then smiled and straightened up. Ceremoniously he offered her his arm. "Enough gloom and doom. Are you ready to party, Ms. Hendricks?"

Cara grasped the crook of his elbow and gave it a little squeeze. She smiled brilliantly. "Ready, willing, and able!"

I should get some rest, Cara thought, hours later, then chuckled inwardly. In just another three or four hours she'd be deep in hibernation, resting for the next three months.

The buffet was delicious, making it torture to stop nibbling from it when midnight came. The music and the sound system that delivered it were both excellent, and Mark, she discovered, was a terrific dancer. Fast or slow, it didn't matter—he had an instinctive feel for the rhythm and knew just how to take her along with him.

The two humans had spent the entire evening together, because Eerin, after a few minutes of watching the dancers crowded in the center of the noisy lounge, had adamantly declined to try the activity. Hin had returned to the viewing lounge to continue with some computer research that the Elpind declared (obviously loving the new English word) "mesmerizing."

The crowd was congenial, and Cara spent nearly as much time chatting as she did dancing. The journalist found herself wishing she didn't have to go into hibernation so quickly. Having time to get to know some of these people better would have been a wonderful opportunity.

She tried out her fledgling Mizari on a youngster away from his homeworld of Shassiszss for the first time and was pleased that he was so impressed. She met an elderly Heeyoon male whose name translated as "Nightsinger"; he wanted to hear all about her trip to StarBridge. They conversed by voder. A Terran fiction author, whose name she recognized, talked writing with her, and a tall, dark-haired, fortyish man from the colony world of NewAm cut in on Mark to dance with her several times.

"His name is Ryan and he's going to Earth to bring his fiancée back out with him," she told Mark as they kept time to an intricate beat. "They've corresponded for twelve years by holo-message and now they're going to actually meet and get married. Isn't that romantic?"

"Then what's he doing dancing *your* feet off?" Mark grumbled, with an air of assumed (*or could it be genuine?* she wondered) jealousy.

Cara laughed. "You are a *flirt*, Mr. Kenner," she accused.

"Never!" he maintained, twirling her until she was breathless. "I'm always sincere when I'm with a beautiful girl."

They both liked the *Asimov*'s Captain. The party had officially begun with the First Mate's introduction of Captain Lee Loachin to the crowd, and Cara had been mildly surprised when a petite woman with exotic Asian features stepped forward to accept the polite applause. She was small-boned and delicate in her sparkling blue evening gown, but the way she held herself and the level look in her dark eyes spoke of steel fiber. Cara guessed she was somewhere in her fifties.

The Captain circulated through the crowd. *Friendly, but reserved,* Cara decided, watching her. *Don't forget, this is just part of her job.* But when it came their turn to meet her, Loachin's face grew suddenly animated.

"You are the two we picked up from StarBridge Academy! Are you students there?"

Mark shook her offered hand. "Mark Kenner, Captain. Yes, I'm a student there. This is Cara Hendricks, journalist. She came out from Earth to do a documentary on us."

"And now you are going back?" the Captain said, shaking Cara's hand, too. "What did you think of the place?"

"Of StarBridge? I was impressed," said Cara. "It's everything you hear about it and more."

"Good," Loachin said emphatically. "I have a granddaughter who's being profiled this year. Her dream since she was practically a baby has been to go to the Academy. That's why I always notice who we pick up from StarBridge on this run, so I can ask them about the school."

"We'd be happy to answer any questions you might have," Mark offered, and the three of them spent a pleasant half hour chatting before the Captain was called away.

But it was Mark who made the most interesting contact of the evening. His hazel eyes shining with excitement, he called Cara over as she stood chatting again with Ryan. Coiled beside him was a stately, beautifully patterned black and silver Mizari. And hovering near them both was one of the insectoids from the planet humans had dubbed "Apis."

Dr. Zenez, the StarBridge dietician that Cara had seen on her first day there, was one of the wasplike Apis. This being was of the other Apis group, resembling a meter-long bee with a large, furry body. Black strips circled her honey-colored "fur." Her fore and aft limbs looked incongruously delicate in contrast to the sturdy, fuzzy little bundle that was her torso. Stubby wings that beat so fast they seemed to be merely vibrating kept her aloft in the air.

"Cara, I'd like you to meet Esteemed Sarozz and his traveling companion and colleague, R'Fzarth. Cara Hendricks, from Earth, a journalist," Mark said.

Cara respectfully made the Mizari greeting gesture she'd learned, while the young man went on, "They're bioscientists,

Cara, and guess where they're headed? Elseemar! The CLS is sending them out to organize the survivors of the medical research team and see what can be salvaged of their data."

"The loss of the researchers there was tragic," said Cara, allowing her voder to do the work this time rather than struggling herself for the Mizari words. "Did either of you have friends among the victims?"

No, the Apis said, via her voder, but the Mizari nodded an affirmative, the light glimmering in soft colors off his iridescent headscales with the movement. "A dear friend, with whom I had worked for many years," Sarozz said. His tentacles waved in agitation.

"I'm so sorry," Cara said.

"Your friend would probably be glad to know that you are going to carry on the research," Mark suggested softly.

"Indeed he would," agreed the Mizari. "He learned to care deeply for the gentle Elspind. I know he wished to find a way to allow them to live longer."

"Are you apprehensive about going there?" Cara asked. "Do you think there'll be any more trouble?"

"We have been fully apprised of the Wospind and their protests," answered the Apis, R'Fzarth, "and, of course, the team will be on guard now as it was not before." The voder projected a thin, reedy voice. "But we do not anticipate trouble again of that magnitude. They have made their statement and now will surely realize they cannot actually stop progress through violence. It never works."

"Cara, I want to take them back to meet Eerin," Mark said. "Hin can answer a lot of their questions about Elseemar."

Cara went with the three of them, curious about Eerin's reaction to meeting replacements for the medical research team. But if Eerin had any reservations about more scientists going to Elseemar, hin did not display them in front of Sarozz and R'Fzarth. They entered into a lively discussion on the flora and fauna of the mountains around Lalcipind where the lab was located.

Mark enjoyed testing his knowledge of Elspindlor, and he, the two scientists, and Eerin all chattered away in that language. Cara was stifling a yawn and trying to decide whether to go back to her cabin, or the lounge, when Captain Loachin appeared to invite Eerin forward for an introduction to the crew and passengers as a visiting dignitary.

"It was a great party," Cara said, sighing, several hours later as she walked with Mark and Eerin back toward their cabins. The *Asimov*'s arbitrary "morning" had arrived. "And I'm so tired, I'm actually looking forward to hibernation."

Mark nodded. "I haven't enjoyed myself like that in a long while. You're quite a dancer."

"So are you," Cara said. "Thanks for teaching me that new tango-glide."

He bowed and grinned. "Definitely my pleasure." Cara held out her hand, but instead of shaking it, Mark gave it a gentle squeeze, then held it for a second before letting her go.

She colored a little, then managed a smile. *Better watch yourself, girl,* she thought, *he'd be easy to fall for, and that's all you need!* "Good night, Mark," she said.

"Good night."

Alone in her cabin, she rested for a few minutes, then changed quickly into the comfortable coveralls that she would wear while hibernating. Then she repacked her carryon, carefully checking the autocam before tucking it into her folded clothes, and stowed the bag in one of the two lockers provided for that purpose inside the cabin. Others might use this cabin during the three months that she slept, but the sensor plate of the locker she chose would open only at the touch of her palm.

Before long, it was time to report to the hibernation chamber. Cara stepped out in the hall to find Mark and Eerin waiting, with a white-coated medical attendant.

"You'll have to say good-bye to your friends here," the woman told Eerin. "Only those going into cold-sleep and authorized crew personnel are allowed in the hiber room."

Eerin blinked, and the Elpind's beautiful golden eyes looked sad. Cara hesitated, wondering how she should say good-bye to the little alien. A hug was what she felt like giving, but she'd never so much as touched Eerin, and she didn't know how the alien might view such a gesture.

Eerin solved the problem for her. Hin leaped over, with that marvelously graceful energy, and held out hin's hands.

Eerin's bony forearms were turned with the underside of wrists and forearms held up.

"Hold your arms out," instructed Mark, "except turned the opposite way so that your arms fit over Eerin's."

"This is a parting between those who are close," the Elpind said slowly, in hin's stilted English.

"Oh, Eerin, thank you. I'm honored." She placed her arms carefully over Eerin's so that, wrist to elbow, vulnerable skin to vulnerable skin, they fit together. The Elpind was warm to the touch, and the soft down tickled just a bit.

"Cara has enriched hin's time."

Tears stung Cara's eyes. It was a beautiful farewell phrase, belonging, as it did, to a race that placed such a high value on the use of time.

"You have enriched my time, too, Eerin. I'll always remember you." Gently she disengaged and stepped back, suddenly feeling let-down and even wearier than before. It really was over now, her great adventure.

Mark touched the Elpind gently on one shoulder, and Cara realized they must have already said their good-byes in the cabin. *At least theirs are only temporary,* Cara thought. In a month Mark would be awakened, and they would share their pair project assignment. The journalist tried not to feel envious.

The hibernation chamber was cold—not as cold as the unit itself would be, but still, cold. Cara shivered and looked around curiously. It was much like the one on the ship she'd come out on, the S.V. *Marion*.

A double row of units, sixty in all, lined the circular room, with wedge-shaped master control panels filling in the corners created by the rectangular units themselves. Another twenty units were grouped in the center of the room, set in deep grooves in the flooring and strongly form-welded to center stanchions.

Small windows were set into the side and top of each unit. Face after sleeping face could be dimly seen, each one composed, oblivious, and somehow very vulnerable to Cara's stare. She shivered again, feeling like an intruder into their privacy.

"Let's not say good-bye," Mark said. "I'll be back on Earth within the year. Is it all right if I call you then? Maybe we could get together . . . catch each other up on the news."

Cara smiled at him warmly. "I'd like that. I don't think I could handle another good-bye. When I see you, you can tell me all about the pair project on Berytin."

He nodded. "I didn't have time yet to have that talk with Eerin, but I will as soon as I get out of hibernation. Thanks again for the advice last night."

"You're welcome," she said softly.

The technicians were getting restless.

Cara smiled awkwardly. "Well . . . see you on Earth, okay?"

He nodded once more, with a quick smile, and then turned to follow the technician to the other end of the chamber. Cara turned to the one waiting for her.

"Have you done this before?" asked the technician, leading her to an empty unit on the first row. "Do you want me to explain how it works?"

"I've done it before," she reassured the woman. *And I'm going to do it again someday. I'm going to see the Fourteen Known Worlds—every one of them. I'm coming back out here, I swear it.*

Cara remembered Rob's admonition to look forward, not back. "I'll remember, Rob," she muttered.

"What did you say, honey?" the technician's voice broke into her musings.

"Nothing." She smiled at the white-coated woman. "I'm ready."

CHAPTER 7

◆

Rude Awakening

Mark dreamed he was being shaken like a bug in a jar. Shouts and thumps reached him; there must be trouble somewhere in his dream, but . . . who cared? Awareness stumbled woozily through his brain like a drunk looking for a place to lie down.

Something jabbed him, hissed, then a sudden wash of molten fire scalded his insides. Mark tried feebly to push away the rough hands jerking at him. His head smacked something solid, and the double message of pain, from his head and from his gut, jolted him awake.

Peering painfully through slitted eyelids, he saw that he was half in, half out of the open hiber unit.

My head hit the top, he thought groggily.

Hands yanked at him again, dragging him over the side of the unit. He dropped limply to the deck, and the fire rushing through his veins abruptly reversed course, exploding in his stomach. Mark threw up violently, ridding himself of the scanty contents of his stomach in gasping heaves. He gagged on bile as tears streamed down his face.

"Here," said a woman's voice. "Put this under your tongue."

He felt her hand, warm on the chill skin at the back of his neck. Obediently Mark lifted his bowed head, fighting renewed nausea from the slight motion, and, with an unsteady hand, helped guide the pill to his mouth.

The little pill dissolved almost immediately. It left a burning sensation on the underside of his tongue, but somehow it took away the vile taste. Seconds later the awful nausea eased away, too. Mark sighed shakily, wiped his mouth, then rubbed his swollen eyes.

"You okay? They could kill someone, yanking people out of hibernation like this," commented the woman.

"What . . . what's wrong?" Mark asked. He blinked furiously, trying to focus. "What's happening?" Despite his grogginess, he sensed the charged atmosphere around him, a confused miasma of fear, anger, and urgency. "Who are 'they'?"

"We've been hijacked," she answered flatly, and he recognized her white jacket as belonging to a hiber tech. "Terrorists. Listen, there are other people who need help. You okay now?" She was gone before he could answer.

Hijacked? Terrorists! The words shocked clarity into Mark's brain. He opened his eyes wide.

He was kneeling on the hibernation chamber's deck. Most of the units were still closed, but several gaped open and empty. Scattered around him, like so much debris, were their former occupants. Some were sitting, some were lying curled up or sprawled out, others leaned on each other. The tech who'd just helped him knelt by one of the prone figures several meters away.

Only two people were on their feet. One of them was busy dumping a Chhhh-kk-tu out of a lower-tier hibernation unit. The other stood by the door with a gun trained on the room.

Shit! Mark's heart contracted, then began to race as he stared incredulously at the two upright figures. The hijackers were Elpind!

Elspind, dammit! Use the plural. It was a ridiculous time to be concerned with alien grammar, and part of his brain realized that dimly. Mark took slow, deep breaths, trying to calm his thudding heart, steady his trembling.

The hin near the door rapped out a command to the other. Mark recognized only a few words. He'd never heard

Elspindlor spoken so rapidly and colloquially before.

Where's Eerin? he wondered. Surely . . . surely *Eerin* couldn't be part of this! He tried to reject the thought out of hand, but it lurked in the back of his mind like an uninvited guest.

"Get up!" shouted the Elpind with the gun in Elspindlor. "Everyone . . . *up*!" Hin waved the gun for emphasis. Mark got to his feet with a grunt, fighting dizziness. His head pounded, nausea threatened again, and he was stiff and sore all over. Shaking off hibernation was never pleasant, but this was worse than anything he'd ever experienced.

He gestured to the other passengers, some of whom were looking at him, and slowly, they began following his example. They understood the gun and the gesture, if not the language.

They staggered, several holding on to each other for support. Mark counted five who still sat or lay on the floor. The second Elpind prodded one of the sitters at the other end of the hibernation chamber. "Get up!"

Oh, God! Mark sucked in his breath as he recognized one of the still-prone figures. *Cara!* Until now, he'd assumed that she was still in one of the units. He had to get her up. Slowly, careful to make no sudden moves (*the first rule when taken hostage*, his memory supplied automatically, *make no sudden moves*), Mark shuffled across the chamber until he was beside her.

It flashed through his mind to wonder why he and these other people had been singled out to be awakened, but he didn't have time to ponder that question, or any other. Cara came first. He could feel the gun like a physical touch on his body as the Elpind holding it swung it around, training it on him as he clumsily knelt.

The journalist lay on her stomach at the base of one of the control panels, turned away from Mark. Her legs, with bare, dark feet poking out of the blue hibernation coverall, sprawled limply.

Mark swallowed hard as he knelt by her. "Cara?" *Oh, God, be all right! Please!* Even though he could see the slight movement of her back as she breathed, his hand shook as he slid his fingers beneath her shoulder-length bush of hair.

Then he sighed with relief. Her skin was warm, her pulse,

strong and steady. *Fell back asleep, that's all.*

"Cara!" Mark shook her shoulder, glancing back at the chamber door. Their fellow hostages were being herded out the door; only three or four still remained in the room. He shook the girl hard, wishing he could just scoop her up and carry her, but at the moment it was touch and go as to whether he could haul himself up and out of the room. "Come on, Cara! Wake up!"

She muttered drowsily and stirred.

"It's Mark, Cara. Come on." Grunting with effort, afraid that they'd both topple over, Mark somehow dragged her to her feet. Slinging her arm around his neck, he slipped his own tightly around her waist, in a grim parody of their time as dancing partners. Cara sagged against him, mumbling.

"Walk, Cara. That's it. C'mon, walk." Alternately dragging her and guiding her irregular, stumbling steps, Mark got them across the chamber and out the door. The group followed one of their captors, while the other Elpind brought up the rear.

The *Asimov*'s large common lounge wasn't really crowded, but the couches and chairs were all taken. Some of them were occupied by people he recognized, people he'd met at the Captain's Night party, but Mark didn't see anyone wearing a blue-and-white crew uniform.

Steering Cara to a space on the floor against the outside wall of the hibernation chamber, he let her slip to the carpeted deck, then dropped down beside her. His body was immensely grateful to be sitting down again.

We need food and water, he realized, though his stomach spun rebelliously at the thought. The fast before entering hibernation, as well as the sleep drugs themselves, left people weak and dehydrated. *Got to try to think clearly,* he reminded himself, trying to remember all his StarBridge courses on dealing with crisis situations. All prospective diplomats learned hostage protocol. It seldom happened; interstellar distances made terrorist raids rare, but they weren't unknown in the CLS.

"Mark?" Cara was finally coming around. She sat up woozily. "What's going on?"

"Trouble." Mark took his first good look around the room and caught his breath. Eerin stood quietly with four other Elspind at the front of the room, watching him and Cara. Hin's golden eyes were huge and sad.

Mark closed his own eyes, biting his lip. *Eerin is* ***not*** *part of this. I refuse to believe it!*

Cara was looking, too. Even groggy, the journalist in her recognized the significance of people with guns on a passenger ship.

"We've been hijacked!" she gasped . . . then had enough sense to shut up. Heads were turning their way. Seconds later her dark eyes widened again as she realized who their captors were.

"Elspind?" she whispered. "Why? What about Eerin?"

Mark shrugged, but a cold lump of suspicion was congealing in his stomach as he remembered the two scientists they'd met at the party—and why they'd been traveling to Elseemar.

What if these guys are Wospind? He hoped he was wrong, hoped these terrorists had no idea and couldn't care less that Sarozz and R'Fzarth were on this ship. Still dizzy, he forced himself to scan the room again. The Mizari and his Apis colleague weren't present. Narrowing his eyes, Mark turned his attention back to the terrorists.

The one to Eerin's right seemed heavier built, but that was largely due to a much denser coat of soft-looking honey-brown hair . . . as if the down on Eerin had thickened into fur on this Elpind. The skin, like Eerin's, was orange and leathery. This Elpind had green eyes instead of gold, but they were as large and round as Eerin's and had that same luminous quality.

The most noticeable difference between this Elpind and Eerin had nothing to do with physical form. Two of the terrorists wore a scarlet, loose-fitting tunic that fell nearly to their knobby knees. The left side of the garment was decorated with the emblem of a bird, a bird with outspread wings of bright, varicolored feathers. Its head pointed down toward the hem of the tunic.

As if it were diving . . . Mark thought foggily, then memory suddenly surged back. *Oh, my God! That's an Elseewas, that bird that does a suicide dive into water at the end of its life. Eerin wears Shadowbird feathers when hin dances the Mortenwol.* Eerin had said the bird was an important symbol to hin's people, but seeing its death plunge worn as a badge sickened him.

He focused on the other tunic-clad hijacker. Virtually hairless, the natural angularity of these painfully thin people was very evident here. The peach-colored skin had a healthy glow and was tight and smooth, not leathery-looking, over the bony outlines. This one wore a tunic like the other except it fell open down the middle.

Mark recalled what he knew of the three Elpind genders. *The males have fur, but the females are smooth, almost hairless. So that furry one is a heen, or male, and the orange-skinned one is han, or female. That's why they're wearing clothes when the neuters don't. They're sexual beings.*

Cara poked him in the ribs. "Who's the leader?" she whispered. Just as she spoke, another figure entered the lounge from the narrow passageway leading forward to officer quarters and the bridge.

"Never mind," amended Cara grimly. "I know."

Watching this newest addition to the group stride over to the side of the room where Eerin and the others stood, Mark agreed with Cara. "Stride" seemed a strange verb to apply to a light-boned, fragile-looking Elpind, but it fit this one. It had nothing to do with size or solidity or weight; the word applied because every move the newcomer made claimed confident space.

Mark stared at the downy, uncovered body the color of old ivory. Another neuter. He noted the quick glance the Elpind gave to hin's compatriots. It was a look that said, "I'll handle the decision making from now on." The Elpind's eyes were the color of old brass.

The leader turned toward the passageway and gestured. A petite Asian woman entered the lounge. Captain Loachin.

Beside him, Cara gasped, and Mark clenched his hands into fists. One of the woman's beautifully tilted eyes was swollen shut and a large, livid bruise marked her left cheekbone. Her uniform was disheveled and bloodstained. Studying her, Mark decided with relief that the blood wasn't her own.

The Captain stepped forward without urging, her posture straight and unbending as she began speaking in perfect Mizari.

"Some of you know what I'm about to say, but those of you who have just have been awakened do not. Five days ago, just two days after docking at Station Four that orbits Arrooouhl, the Heeyoon mother world, *Asimov* picked up a distress call on the continuously monitored emergency frequency. As regulations decree, we dropped out of metaspace to respond, and found a small shuttle with CLS markings apparently drifting powerless. We grappled it alongside."

Mark noticed that Eerin was translating the Captain's speech for the brassy-eyed leader.

"When these people came aboard, we discovered that the distress message was a ruse. They ordered us to take them to Elseemar. When my navigator tried to resist, their leader, who calls hinself Orim"—her voice faltered for the first time—"shot and killed him."

Mark and Cara gasped, both recognizing the name. *Shit, they're Wospind all right!* Mark thought. *The People of Death! But if that's the case, what the hell is Eerin doing with them?*

Loachin had paused, obviously fighting to regain control. When she continued, her voice was once again even. "Several weeks ago a medical research lab was destroyed on Elseemar. Many scientists working there were killed. Two of our passengers . . ."

Dammit, I knew it! Mark thought.

" . . . Esteemed Sarozz, a Mizari, and an Apis named R'Fzarth, are scientists who have been sent out by the CLS to organize the survivors and see what can be salvaged of the research data. These two passengers, Orim has told me, are the reason this ship was chosen by these hijackers."

Loachin paused again, this time for breath that escaped involuntarily in a small sigh. *She's exhausted,* Mark realized. *These last five days must have been hell for her*. His admiration for her cool control increased.

"These people call themselves the Wospind and claim responsibility for the recent violence there. They have taken R'Fzarth and Sarozz into special custody, and announced that the CLS must meet their demands, or there will be further violence. We are approximately one hour away from Elseemar. That is all I know at the moment."

She gazed out across the lounge, and a different, almost pleading note entered her calm voice. "Obviously, we arc in grave danger. I ask the passengers to please remember that not only your lives, but the lives of others, depend on your actions in these next hours. I caution you to move slowly, speak quietly, and try to restrain your fear. Remember that our captors do not speak Mizari. Do not attempt to antagonize them or make demands. They have warned me that any such actions will bring speedy reprisal, and they have already killed once."

She swallowed. "I have been attempting to persuade the Wospind to allow my crew to bring you food and water as soon as possible. Again, the best thing you can do for yourself and others is to remain as quiet and cooperative as possible."

A low murmur of fear and consternation went through the small crowd. Captain Loachin waved to quiet them. "Berytin, our next scheduled destination, was notified when we changed course to investigate the faked distress call, but Orim has allowed no communication since. Currently, no one knows our location. All we have to depend on is each other," she finished quietly. "I am counting on each one of you to remember that."

Then the woman stepped back and, obeying the female Wopind's gesture, moved over to stand by the han.

The next person on the agenda, the Wopind leader hinself, stepped forward and Eerin moved with hin. The gun trained on hin's back, held by another of the neuters, was suddenly visible.

"Mark!" Cara whispered.

"I see it." Mark was ashamed of the relief he felt. Eerin was a hostage too, in as much danger as the rest of them. He tried to catch his pair partner's eye so he could smile encouragingly, but Eerin, appearing suddenly agitated, even desperate, deliberately looked away.

"Call forward the spokesman," the Wopind leader ordered Eerin loudly in Elspindlor. The mellifluous language, with its many "L" and vowel sounds, seemed at odds with the hard glint of Orim's eyes and the harsh tone of hin's voice. Mark found he could understand the words—though the speed at which the sounds flowed over each other confirmed that Eerin had spoken slowly during their Elspindlor practice sessions.

"The one you have named is not appropriate," Eerin argued, using the same language. "The CLS will expect the Captain to deliver the Wopind demands."

"The Captain is only the Captain," the hijacker snapped, the fanatic light in hin's eyes altering to a frightening glare. "The passenger roster lists one person who is a trained negotiator. If heen speaks, the CLS will listen. Heen must speak for our people. Call the negotiator forward! Now!"

Mark's heart took a sudden plunge as he realized why Eerin was arguing. *Oh, God, no! Trained negotiator? Please, anything but this!* But he knew instinctively that there was no denying the madness in Orim's eyes. His worst nightmare was coming true. *Don't argue with hin, Eerin,* he thought numbly. *It's too dangerous. Do what hin tells you.*

As if in response to his thoughts, the Elpind looked out over the passengers, hesitated a moment longer, then hin's golden eyes met Mark's. "Mark Kenner," called the Elpind in English. Hin's voice was heavy. "Mark Kenner, please come forward."

"*Laris mian!*" Orim demanded in Elspindlor. "*Laris mian,* come here, Mark Kenner!"

"No!" Cara grabbed his arm frantically. "Mark!"

"It's all right, Cara," Mark said. She hadn't understood the Elspindlor, of course, couldn't know why he was being singled out. "They just want a spokesperson, that's all." His heart was still slamming, but reassuring her had steadied him a little, he found, as he slowly climbed to his feet, careful to keep his hands away from his body. The adrenaline now pouring into his system also helped, clearing a little more of the drugged haze from his mind.

As he picked his way through the crowd, Mark could feel the gun trained on his chest. He could barely keep from staring fixedly at the weapon's snout, and it was with difficulty that he transferred his attention back to the Wopind leader.

He forced himself to regard the Wopind without flinching, but also without seeming to challenge hin. Eye contact was a touchy thing in hostage situations. Some species regarded a direct stare as an open insult or challenge, others took the lack of it as a sign of duplicity. Mark had to walk a very thin line, knowing as little as he did about Elpind body language and cultural mores.

Dealing with fanatics is the most dangerous of all possible hostage situations, he remembered. *God, help me do and say the right thing . . . don't let anyone get hurt because of my mistake.*

Orim's eyes held his for long seconds, then finally hin said fervently: "Mark Kenner is a StarBridge interrelator." The terrorist had to use the Mizari rendering for the last word. "Hin has been told that the CLS places great value on beings who possess the ability to help one culture relate successfully to another. Hin has heard that StarBridge trains its students to communicate with skill and insight, in the hope that they will weave peace between the worlds."

Mark had to admit that he'd never heard it put more succinctly—or more poetically. "That is correct," he replied in Elspindlor.

Orim glanced sharply and accusingly at Eerin. "Mark Kenner speaks our tongue far more fluently than hin was told."

"I don't speak it well," Mark said, deliberately slurring and slowing his delivery—he certainly didn't want to get Eerin in trouble if hin had tried to keep him safe by understating his language skills to the Wopind leader. "But I am learning. I will do my best."

"Mark Kenner will listen to the words of Orim, then render them to the CLS representatives on Elseemar," Orim directed.

Mark nodded. "I will do my best," he repeated.

"The off-worlders will listen to Mark Kenner when heen repeats the words of Orim. They will listen for two reasons: first, because they are strong words upon which many lives will hang, and, second, because they are relayed by a StarBridge interrelator."

I'm a dropout, not an interrelator, Mark thought, but, knowing that it would gain him nothing positive to disagree with Orim, he stifled his instinctive protest. "Orim will first address these beings," the Wopind said, indicating the captives.

"I will translate," Mark said obediently. *Good,* he thought. *Orim's making a speech will give hin a chance to ventilate.*

Encouraging terrorists to relate their grievances at length was a good delaying tactic . . . and would also help the hijackers to release some of their anger and pent-up frustration—hopefully without inciting them to further violence.

Mark knew from his course in handling crisis situations that the longer a hostage situation continued, the less likelihood that more hostages would be injured or killed. If Elpind terrorists reacted like humans or other intelligent species who had attempted to gain their ends by hijackings, a phenomenon called "the Stockholm Syndrome" would set in.

Simply stated, the longer hijackers were exposed to their captives, the greater the tendency for them to develop a rapport with the hostages, empathize with them. Hijackers actually grew fond of their captives, and no longer wanted to harm them. Bizarrely enough, the converse was also true; there were documented cases where former hostages had defended and testified on the behalf of their former captors.

Of course it was impossible to predict whether the Wopind hijackers would react in the same way . . . especially when they could not communicate with their captives.

Orim drew hinself up to hin's full height. "Hin is Ri-El Orim," hin announced, then paused as Mark faithfully translated. Not knowing how much Mizari the Wopind might understand, Mark resolved to be meticulous in his translations. "Hin is the leader here. We have been forced to take this way of gaining the CLS's attention, so the universe will at last comprehend the injustice that is even now transpiring on Elseemar."

The leader paused. Mark was relieved that the Wopind leader was speaking slowly, punctuating hin's speech with forceful gestures.

"On Elseemar we have always lived in peace as one people. This is no longer true. Our way of life is threatened, and we have become the Wospind in order to defend it. In time, all the people of Elseemar will thank us."

Mark glanced quickly at Eerin when Orim paused, noting the glare of pure hatred the Elpind gave the oblivious Wopind. *Not all of them, Orim,* he thought grimly.

"Ever since they arrived uninvited on our world, the CLS representatives have been trying to change us. And lately, they have not been content to change our society and our ways; their scientists have been working to change our lifecycle as well. We know, even if the Great Council has forgotten, that death must come whenever it wills and to whomever it chooses. The splendor of Elpind life is found in the courage to meet death, the willingness to seek adventure in every moment up to and including death. The CLS would have us shy away from that splendor, would have us conspire in a pitiful attempt to prolong life—as if Elspind feared to grapple with the ultimate truth of death."

Orim's eyes glowed with passion as hin spoke. Mark had to struggle to translate the entire speech, sentence by sentence. Several times he was forced to pose a word in Mizari to Eerin and receive a suggested translation before he could render Orim's meaning. But, as promised, he did his best.

"Once in orbit," Orim/Mark continued, "this ship will contact the CLS sociological team on Elseemar, who, in turn, will communicate with our Great Council, the WirElspind. We will demand that the WirElspind immediately revoke its support of CLS involvement on Elseemar and specifically forbid further research on the Elpind lifecycle. Furthermore, all off-worlders must leave Elseemar in their shuttle immediately. Until these conditions have been accomplished, this ship, the *Asimov*, will circle Elseemar." Hearing the next words, Mark broke off, mute with horror, but when Orim glared and one of the heen gestured with the gun threateningly, he reluctantly finished, "and one passenger will be killed every six hours."

Cries of fear and protest broke out in the lounge, but quickly stilled to tense silence when the armed Wospind raised their weapons and trained them on the crowd purposefully.

Orim appeared to be enjoying the reaction hin's words caused, reveling in hin's sense of power, Mark realized sickly. *I don't think hin is really sane . . . or rather, hin is the Elpind version of a sociopath, he thought. A being without a conscience.*

His StarBridge training told him that he was dealing with the most dangerous type of hostage situation of all—fanaticism. *Oh, God, why me?* he wondered bitterly, feeling so tired and beaten that his knees buckled. But the jab of a gun muzzle in the small of his back straightened him up in a hurry.

"Once the CLS and the WirElspind have agreed that all research will stop and the CLS representatives and scientists have left Elseemar," Orim concluded, raising hin's hands for emphasis, "the executions will cease, and this ship will be released to continue its journey. We hope, of course, that there will be many, many passengers left to do exactly that."

There was a hint of truly sick mockery under this last that made Mark's mouth twist as he relayed the information.

"Right now," the translation continued, "the Wospind hold the nonhibernating passengers and some of the crew in the two smaller lounges to the rear. Other passengers, as you know, we left in hibernation. But this group"—here the Wopind beamed upon the people in the common lounge fondly—"is special. This group has been selected, some from hibernation, some from the passengers already awake, for a special purpose."

The passengers did not dare cry out again, but several huddled together, clutching each other. Tears were streaming down many of the humans' faces, Mark noted. He had to fight back the urge to leap at Orim, kill hin with his bare hands.

"Once the shuttle containing the CLS scientists has achieved orbit, this group will be ferried to Elseemar and held until we have verified that every alien has indeed left our world. Then, and only then, we will allow one more contact with the CLS. We will take this group to a prearranged location and leave. Then a rescue ship will be permitted to land so this group can also leave. On its way, it can pick up the orbiting CLS representatives and scientists."

The Wopind's gaze moved around the lounge slowly. "When the alien taint is finally removed from our world, even the Wospind will be no more, for we will no longer be needed; all of Elseemar will be Elspind once again, united at last!"

It's obvious that hin has very little conception of interstellar distances and travel time, Mark thought, biting his lip. *It will take* **weeks** *to get a big CLS ship out here from Shassiszss to pick us all up. And that's too long for one of the small shuttles to orbit without running out of fuel. Orim's condemning the CLS scientists to death with hin's demand.* He wondered whether the Wopind leader knew that.

He began sifting and analyzing the speech, remembering that he would have to relate it to the CLS representatives. He imagined himself translating it into either of the two alien languages he spoke fluently: Mizari or Heeyoon. Could he do it? Would he be able to convince the CLS reps and the WirElspind that Orim was deadly, as well as serious? Should he try to negotiate with the Wopind himself on behalf of the hostages?

A flurry of movement from the entrance to the lounge made him look up again. He saw a hijacker, another heen, gesturing the black and silver Mizari into the lounge.

Sarozz! Oh, God, no! Tell me this isn't what I think it is! Frantically Mark glanced around him, caught Eerin's eye. Hin looked as sick as he felt. The human closed his eyes and forced himself to breathe evenly. *Please,* some portion of his mind was praying, imploring to anyone or anything that would listen, *please, no! Please!*

"So that the CLS will be convinced when they hear hin's words from the mouth of Mark Kenner, hin has arranged a demonstration of sincerity," Orim announced. "The images made now will be transmitted to the CLS when the communications link is established."

"You bastards!" Captain Loachin growled, unable to restrain herself. She tensed, as if about to throw herself forward.

"Captain!" Mark warned, his voice quiet but carrying. She subsided, her mouth tight with agony. The passengers muttered, distressed, but didn't dare move.

"One other participant is required," Mark heard the Wopind announce over the noise. Automatically he translated. Then, "Call the journalist forward," Orim ordered.

Mark stiffened. *No! Not Cara!* He tried to get the protest out of his mouth, but he was too late, as if it would have mattered anyway what he said. Even as he struggled to speak, Orim impatiently took matters into hin's own hands. "Cara Hendricks!" hin shouted. "*Laris mian,* Cara Hendricks!"

CHAPTER 8

♦

People of Death

The silent han marched Cara back to the locker where her camera was stored, and all the way, she struggled to overcome a sense of surreal horror. Film an execution? The idea was barbaric . . . sick. By the time she returned to the lounge, sensor patch once more on her cheekbone and the autocam floating by her side, Cara was filled with such burning anger and outrage that she faced the Wopind leader unflinchingly.

"I will help as much as possible by filming your speeches and transmitting your demands to the CLS," she said as Eerin translated. "But I *won't* film Esteemed Sarozz's death! Don't you understand that you'll only be hurting your cause if you go through with this?"

Orim's eyes flashed at her refusal, and Mark frantically shook his head. Cara's mouth tightened and she folded her arms across her chest, staring stubbornly at the bulkhead. She didn't care what they did to her, she wouldn't be a party to this. Her anger gave her strength, stiffened her resolve. Maybe, if she stood her ground, the Wopind would back down.

"Cara Hendricks," a voice called. The journalist turned to

see the doomed Mizari, Sarozz, regarding her anxiously. "Ms. Hendricks, your stand, while honorable, is also extremely foolish." The scientist spoke slowly and distinctly, mindful of Cara's limited Mizari. Also, whenever she had obvious difficulty, Mark translated. "I beg you, please reconsider. You must not anger our captors. In doing so, you put your own life in peril—as well as the lives of our fellow passengers. The thought of my own death I can bear, but the thought of other deaths on my behalf . . . " The Mizari's tentacles atop his wedge-shaped head made an eloquent gesture of despair. The movement sent silver ribbons of light dancing around his head.

"Esteemed Sarozz." Her Mizari was adequate to her thoughts, but not her voice; it broke. "I just . . . can't."

Orim watched coldly as the Mizari and the human argued.

"If they kill you for refusing, that will not save me," Sarozz pointed out. "Nothing can save me. I have known for days that my death is inevitable, and I am prepared. Please, Ms. Hendricks . . . do not endanger yourself."

Tears welled up in Cara's eyes. "But if I refuse," she managed to say, "perhaps they'll change their minds."

The Mizari shook his head, obviously familiar with the human negative. "My death is in Orim's eyes. It will be quick, and painless. I am ready. Please, Ms. Hendricks . . . "

"All right," somehow Cara managed, then slowly, formally, she bowed to the Mizari in the fashion of his people, bowed as deeply as she could, trying to convey her respect and admiration for his courage. Then she straightened back up, activated her camera, and braced herself.

Sarozz's lidless black eyes held Cara's; he did not look at his executioner. But Cara did—she made sure this shot included both the scientist and the Wopind leader who, with hideous and sadistic deliberation, slowly aimed his weapon.

Esteemed Sarozz lifted his head proudly. Light glimmered in soft colors off his iridescent headscales and floated like a reflected halo about his head as the small tentacles moved.

The Wopind fired. A beam of sizzling energy seared the Mizari's head, instantaneously charring his brain.

Screams rang through the lounge. Sarozz, however, made not a sound. There was only a horrendously delayed *thud* when his black and silver body seemed to give up waiting for the destroyed brain to send it a message to fall . . . then fell anyway.

Silent tears rolled down Cara's face, but she wasn't aware of them. Numbly, she filmed the length of the Mizari's still body, his blackened head, then Orim's satisfied expression. Numbly, she prepared the camera to transmit the images she had just filmed.

"Cara."

She looked down, noting absently that Mark knelt by the body with one of the *Asimov*'s blankets. Shaking out its blue and white folds, he let them settle gently over Sarozz's ruined head. Then he looked up and called her name again.

The journalist simply stared at him. Dimly, she wondered why she felt nothing.

Mark rose and gently put an arm around her, leading her back to where his hijacker guard gestured him to stand. Cara leaned against him as her knees began to shake. "Take it easy," he whispered. "You had to do it. He understood, Cara . . . "

Now it's your turn, Mark, she thought. *Now they're going to make you speak for them, as they made me film for them.*

Feeling returned in a rush as she realized that she was now experiencing the same compassion for Mark that Sarozz had felt for her. The terrible aching knot in her throat abruptly loosened, and she began to sob. Mark held her tightly, and the feel of his arms was all that kept her from collapsing. "Shhhhhh," he whispered, muffling the sounds she was making against his shoulder. "Shhhhhh . . . "

Orim took three of them to the bridge: Captain Loachin because she insisted so loudly, Cara to transmit the film of the Mizari's death, and Mark.

The bridge was guarded by two more Wospind with guns, a female and a neuter. That made eight hijackers Mark had seen so far, and he knew there were more in the two rear lounges, guarding the other passengers and crew. The *Asimov*'s navigator was dead, and the First Mate and the Engineer had been forcibly removed from the bridge during the takeover. Only the Communications Officer and a second-class engineering tech supervised the bridge as the ship orbited Elseemar on automatic.

The Communications Officer established contact with the CLS main transmitter on the planet below, and Captain Loachin stepped forward to verify the ship's identity.

"We're glad to hear from you, Captain." The speaker in the holo-tank was a Heeyoon. "Berytin reported that your schedule had changed. Is everything all right?"

"No, it is not. We've been hijacked and are being held hostage," Loachin said tersely. "The hijackers have conditions the CLS and the WirElspind must meet before we will be released. Communicating with these Wospind has been difficult, since they do not speak Mizari, but fortunately, one of our passengers, a StarBridge student named Mark Kenner, speaks Elspindlor. He will relay their demands."

"Hold just a moment. I'm transferring you," the wolflike being directed. "This linkup will be audio only." The screen went dark, and a moment later, a new voice came on. "Go ahead, *Asimov*."

Mark stepped forward under the watchful eyes of the Wopind leader. The moment was here. His hands shook, and all his desperately rehearsed words jumbled together in his mind.

"Go ahead, *Asimov*. We're receiving you."

The language was Mizari and the pure inflection of the vowels meant that the speaker was a Mizari. Thinking of Sarozz, Mark's throat tightened, but he resolutely drew courage from the scientist's bravery. He couldn't let Sarozz's death be in vain. "This is Mark Kenner," he said steadily. "I'm a StarBridge student who has been pressed into service as a temporary spokesperson for our Wopind captors."

He checked the chrono. "Fifteen minutes ago, one of your own people, a Mizari named Sarozz, was deliberately murdered aboard this ship. He died very bravely. Please prepare to receive visual transmission."

Cara handed the autocam to the Communications Officer, who made the transmission. In close orbit as the *Asimov* was, the message would be received immediately, but playback would take a minute or two. Mark waited.

"*Asimov*, we have received and viewed your transmission." The voice was now heavy with restrained grief. "This development unfortunately comes as no surprise. Last week one of our shuttles, along with a Heeyoon pilot, took off unauthorized.

We figured the Wospind must have forced Swifthunter to pilot them off-world. Is he aboard? Is he unharmed?"

"I'll ask."

Mark looked back at Orim, switched to Elspindlor, and asked the question. "Yes, he's here," he replied a moment later. "He's being held in the starboard lounge, which is why I haven't seen him. They say that as long as he pilots them home safely, he'll be released unharmed."

"Thank the Spirits of the Sands for that, at least. I have sent messages to the WirElspind, and Shassiszss, explaining what has happened. Are you ready to relay the terrorists' demands?"

"I am," Mark said. "This is what they want . . . "

Minutes later he had faithfully related all of Orim's words as precisely as he could translate them. "Do you understand?" he asked. "Did you get all that on record, uh . . . what's your name?"

"Zahssez," the other said. "Affirmative, to both questions."

"Remember," Mark warned, "that unless you and the WirElspind act *immediately*, Orim intends to kill another passenger six hours from now"—he glanced at his watch—"uh, actually, five hours and twenty-three minutes from now. There are over a hundred and fifty passengers aboard, many of them children. Please, tell them to hurry!"

Zahssez's voice sounded heavy. "Mark, you have to make them realize that our field researchers are scattered all over the main continent. We fully intend to comply with Orim's demands, believe me, no matter what the WirElspind decides, but retrieving all those people will take time! More than six hours." He hesitated. "Can you talk them into extending that deadline? Or releasing the *Asimov* and taking only a few hostages aboard the shuttle, in return for our promise to begin evacuation immediately?"

"I don't know," Mark said dully. "I'll try."

"May the Spirits be with you," Zahssez said. "Our invocations certainly will be. We'll be standing by for your next transmission."

"Understood," Mark said. "*Asimov* out."

As StarBridge Academy's Counselor, Rob Gable had received calls in the night before. Since any transmissions that could wait until business hours were automatically delayed until then, anything that came through at night always meant bad news.

Sometimes it was a student in trouble (Rob still had nightmares about the call he'd gotten from Mark Kenner in the wee hours of the morning, when he'd discovered Jon's body), sometimes it was notification of death or disaster on somebody's homeworld.

Consequently, middle-of-the-night calls always brought him wide awake in a heartbeat, and this time was no exception. His terminal beeped twice, and then he was up and jamming his feet into ancient sweatpants, almost before his eyes were fully open. "Rob Gable here," he said, yanking the pants up, then activating the unit's visual channel, "who is it?"

"Rob, I've just received a very distressing message." The holo-vid screen on his wall resolved into the school's Chhhh-kk-tu Administrator. "I'm afraid it's bad news."

"What is it?" He braced himself to hear that something terrible had happened to Mahree, or Claire, their daughter. Or was it Mom, or one of his sisters? Fear gripped him so tightly he could hardly breathe. He found himself bargaining with God. *Just don't let it be Mahree or Claire. I can stand anything else . . .*

"It's about Mark and Cara and Eerin," she began. Rob's knees sagged with relief, even as guilt washed over him for feeling it.

"What happened to them?" he demanded hoarsely.

"The *Asimov* was hijacked by some kind of radical Elpind group. They've apparently pressed Mark into service as their spokesperson, because he knows Elspindlor. Rob,"—Kkintha's furry face, with her Siamese-cat mask, was full of apprehension—"the hijackers have already killed two people. They forced Cara to film one of the executions."

"Oh, God, how terrible!" he whispered. "Those poor kids!"

"Here's the transmission from the *Asimov*, plus the subsequent recording of Mark's conversation with the CLS Liaison on Elseemar," Kkintha said. Rob sank slowly back onto his bed as he watched, eyes widening with horror. Then the sound of Mark's strained young voice as he spoke to Zahssez made him bite his lip hard. *Dammit, this is my fault. I made him go out there . . . if it hadn't been for me and my bright ideas—*

He ran a hand through his sleep-rumpled hair, his habitual gesture when thinking hard. "We've got to do something. How much more time is left on that deadline? We've got to have experts working on this. Hostage negotiations are too delicate to be trusted to a bunch of scientists and sociologists, no matter how well intentioned!" Frustrated, he slammed his fist into his palm as he paced.

"Rob . . . " The Administrator held up a small paw while she looked at the chronometer. Obviously she was doing some quick calculations. "Rob, more than five of their hours were up before I got the message relay from StarBridge Station. There's no time for us to do anything before that next deadline."

"Dammit, Kkintha, I can't just sit here." He looked at her gravely. "We've got to try and help. After all, we're the ones who made the decision that put Mark and Eerin on that ship."

"I should have known that a psychologist would be an expert at uncovering inner guilt," the Administrator said sourly.

"Maybe Mahree can help," Rob said hopefully.

"Perhaps she can," Kkintha said, brightening a little. "I shall have a call put through to her. Where is she?"

That was a good question, and Rob had to think about it for a moment, mentally adding up dates and travel times. "She should be back on Shassiszss by now. There was a big trade conference coming up, then she has a review of colonization activities by Earth and the Heeyoon."

Rob paced impatiently while she put her assistant to work on the frequently frustrating job of tracking down the former Secretary-General of the CLS.

Kkintha's people did not pace, but her little clawed fingers groomed her chest ruff until it stood up in tufted disorder. "Do you think she will handle this personally?"

"I doubt it," Rob said. "Mahree isn't experienced in hostage situations. But she'll be able to make sure the best people are put to work on this crisis." But he spoke distractedly, his mind far away. The psychologist was remembering Mark's face when he'd agreed to be the Elpind's pair partner.

Kkintha doesn't know the half of it when she talks about guilt, he thought. *When I think about Mark's expression the day he told me that he never again wanted to run the risk of making a mistake that could hurt someone . . .* The doctor shuddered. What if his recommendation to Kkintha ch'aait that Mark Kenner be paired with Eerin turned out to be the young man's death sentence?

Or what if he breaks under the strain? he thought, resisting the urge to lash out and smash one of the knickknacks resting on his bookshelf. *Other people . . . a whole shipload of people . . . are depending on Mark. But what if he can't prevent more tragedy from happening? Another failure could destroy him . . .*

"Rob?"

He whirled around to face the screen. Kkintha was back. "I just spoke to the Council Secretary for the Cooperative League of Systems. The Council's in session," (it was midmorning on Shassiszss) "but he's paging Mahree. She should be available in a few minutes."

As Rob waited tensely, suddenly the screen rippled, then Kkintha's anxious features were replaced by a woman wearing an embroidered blue shirt and dark blue trousers. Long brown hair hung in a thick braid over one shoulder. Her face was strong-boned, with features that just missed being handsome, rather than pretty, and brown eyes that were too old for her apparent age.

Motherhood had softened her angular frame, rounding her slightly from the coltish girl Rob had first met fifteen years ago, though she was still small-breasted and slender. "Hello, Rob," she said, and smiled.

"Mahree . . . " He smiled back, feeling his throat tighten. "It's so good to see you. How is Claire?"

"She's fine. She's staying with Shirazz during this trade conference." Her eyes narrowed as she took in his bare chest and disheveled hair. "Something's wrong. What?"

Briefly, Rob explained the problem. "From the way Mark translated Orim's requirements, there's no way those researchers can get off-planet in time to prevent this deadline—and even if they take off in time to prevent a fourth casualty, there's no way they can survive in a tiny shuttle with limited fuel long enough for rescue ships to reach Elseemar. Their orbit will deteriorate and they'll burn up in the atmosphere. Can you find out if there are ships in the area that could be diverted to Eerin's world and arrive soon enough? Passenger ships, League ships . . . whatever?"

"I'll get my staff on it immediately," she promised. "And I'll personally speak to this WirElspind Council, if the researchers can put me in touch with them. Perhaps something can be worked out with them . . . some kind of hidden landing place for the CLS people to hide out until the rescue ships arrive . . . "

"I'm sure they can use any help you can offer," Rob said. "Those hostages and the researchers planetside are going to need every scrap of CLS support you can dig up, sweetheart."

"If you've got a fourth-year student there, he's had a lot of crisis negotiation training," she pointed out, trying to comfort him. "He ought to be able to handle it."

"He *can* handle it," Rob said grimly, "but he doesn't know he can. He might not be able to take the pressure, Mahree. Mark wasn't in good shape when he left here."

"I see . . . " Her expression was grave. "I'll do everything I can, Rob."

"I know you will." He smiled faintly. "I wish you were here."

"If I were there, I'd be as powerless as you are," she pointed out, practically, but then her mouth softened. "I'd better get started," she said, and her hand moved toward the controls of the computer link. "I'll call you when I know something concrete, darling. I love you . . . "

Rob had to clear his throat. "And I love you," he returned, but she'd already cut the connection.

CHAPTER 9

◆

Tightropes and Thumbscrews

Four hours later, Mark was so exhausted that he could barely sit upright in his chair, and so frustrated that he could barely keep from screaming. He looked across the table in the Captain's staff room at Captain Loachin, studying the woman's sallow face, seeing the dark shadows of exhaustion ringing her good eye and the livid coloration of the bruised one.

I'm worn out after three hours of trying to deal with the Wospind, he thought, *and they've never touched me. How has she made it through five days of this?*

Negotiations with Orim were not going well. The Wopind obviously didn't trust Eerin, though hin had allowed the Elpind to sit beside Mark and assist the human with Elspindlor vocabulary, as the human struggled to negotiate in a language that was still (despite the total immersion he'd had since he'd been awakened) awkward for him.

Lee Loachin, recognizing that Mark had more training in negotiations than she did, had let him take the lead in their discussion with Orim. Together they had managed to secure a few concessions—such as food, water, and supervised lavatory visits for the hostages. But the Wopind leader still hadn't budged on the important issues.

"Let's go over this one more time," Mark said. He was getting hoarse, despite the water he'd been sipping. "Please, Ri-El Orim"—he was careful to use the Elpind honorific—"remember that the CLS officials will be asking me whether you are willing to make concessions in return for what you want to accomplish, and I want to be able to tell them yes, because then you'll stand a *much* better chance of getting everything you want."

The Wopind leader glared at Mark, then hin blinked and sat back in the padded armchair that was usually the Captain's seat. After a moment's silent consideration, Orim said, "Hin will listen, but hin promises nothing."

Well, that's more than hin has agreed to so far, Mark thought, slightly encouraged. "Ri-El Orim, you need to keep in mind that the CLS will be far more likely to listen and obey your demands if you present them with a show of good faith on your part." (He had to ask Eerin for a translation of "good faith.") "If you do that, I can practically . . . " Glancing at Eerin, he asked for a translation of "guarantee," and the Elpind provided one. "I can practically guarantee that they'll be willing to do as you wish and leave Elseemar forever."

Especially since they already told me they would, Mark thought dryly. He took a sip of water from the glass before him. "So, if you would agree to let most of the passengers go, then you, I, your people, and several of the other hostages could take your shuttle down to Elseemar. That would really impress the CLS as a gesture of good faith on your part."

"How many other hostages?" Orim asked after a long minute.

Mark tried to stifle the surge of excitement he felt. *Hin really is listening this time!* "The fewer you keep, the better it will appear to the CLS," he said carefully.

"Hin must have her"—Orim indicated Loachin—"and the member of the WirElspind, and the journalist, to record that hin is keeping hin's agreements." The Wopind fell silent, obviously considering. "Hin will require at least ten more."

That's better than I'd hoped for! Mark thought, keeping his expression carefully neutral as he nodded slowly. "May I translate for the Captain?" he asked.

Orim nodded.

Quickly Mark related the Wopind's terms in English. The woman's tired eyes brightened slightly. "You're finally getting someplace!"

"Gently, Captain," Mark cautioned her with a quick, noncommittal glance at Orim. "We don't want Orim to know that we're pleased with the number."

She nodded. "Of course I'll volunteer to remain a hostage," she said. "The First Mate can take the *Asimov* on to Berytin. Ask Orim if the Wospind will accept members of my crew, rather than passengers, for the ten hostages. I know my people will volunteer. Under the circumstances, it's their duty."

Mark quickly translated the Captain's request. The Wopind considered for a moment, then snapped, "Three crew only. Seven passengers."

"How about half crew, half passengers?" the human counteroffered. "Five each."

Orim's brassy eyes held his for so long that Mark thought that he might have wrecked it all, but finally, hin nodded. "Five and five," hin agreed.

Mark wanted to shout with relief, but forced himself to nod impassively. "So if the CLS team agrees to leave Elseemar immediately, you will allow me, Eerin, the Captain, and Cara, plus ten other hostages, consisting of five crew and five passengers, to accompany you to the surface of Elseemar, where we will remain as your guests until you are satisfied that your demands have been met," he summarized.

The Wopind leader shook hin's head. "In addition to the CLS representatives leaving, hin must have the WirElspind's promise to end the research forever," hin said.

Shit, Mark thought. *For a second I thought I might get away with it.*

"We have been informed that the WirElspind is currently in session," he said. (He had to ask for a translation of "in session.") "Perhaps they will have such an agreement for you. But I would like to give the CLS your guarantee that if the off-worlders leave Elseemar by the time of your six-hour deadline," he repressed the urge to look at his watch—"then you will extend that deadline to allow us time to hear from the WirElspind. It is not fair to make my people suffer if your people cannot reach agreement," he concluded, pushing a little, greatly daring.

"Hin will consider extending the deadline," the Wopind said after a long pause.

All right! Now we're getting somewhere! Mark thought.

"Ri-El Orim," he began, "if you—"

The soft chime of the intercom interrupted Mark. Captain Loachin, after a glance at Orim for permission, said, "Yes?"

"Captain, this is Rogers." It was the voice of the Communications Chief. "We have a call coming in from the WirElspind."

Without being told, Mark translated the man's message.

Orim climbed to hin's feet, the gun once more prominently displayed, then gestured them brusquely out the door. "Go back to the lounge," hin ordered Eerin. "The heen and han only will come to the bridge."

The Elpind hesitated, then went, accompanied by the guard who had been posted outside the door. Mark and the Captain preceded Orim through the corridor and onto the bridge.

As they passed by on their way to the communications console, the young communications tech on duty glared at Orim, hatred in his blue eyes. The other two Wospind on the bridge raised their guns meaningfully; the man slowly subsided.

Quickly the Wopind leader motioned for Mark to take one seat before the communications console, while hin took the other. The Heeyoon communications operator nodded to them. "Stand by, *Asimov*."

As they waited, the holo-tank rippled, then an Elpind neuter's image appeared. "Hin is Ri-El Alanor," the Elpind said. "First Speaker of the WirElspind."

"Greetings, First Speaker Alanor," Mark said. "This is Mark Kenner. You have a message for us from the WirElspind?" he asked hopefully. *Maybe they've agreed to meet Orim's demands,* he thought. *Maybe this nightmare will be over soon. Even if I have to spend time on Elseemar as a hostage, knowing that the* **Asimov** *is safe and that rescue ships are on the way, I could stand that.*

"Hin has no message for Mark Kenner," the Elpind official said sternly. "Hin has instead a warning for Orim!" Hin leaned forward, fury evident in every line of hin's body. "Orim, the

Wospind are a disgrace to our people, a weed that must be wrenched up, allowed to wither without mercy! The WirElspind knows the names of those who have followed you aboard that ship. Their families, as well as Orim's family in Lalcipind, are at the moment being taken captive! We intend to give back to the Wospind what they have done to our CLS friends—tenfold, Orim! Does hin listen and hear the words of Alanor?"

As the First Speaker's tirade had begun, Mark had sat frozen, stunned to hear an Elpind speaking so threateningly. Before the WirElspind representative was half through, the young man was shaking his head and looking at the board before him for the "end transmission" control. *No!* he wanted to scream. *Don't! I was finally getting someplace with hin, and you're ruining it! Dammit, the thumbscrew approach doesn't work with fanatics, anyone will tell you that!*

Beside him, Orim was trembling with rage.

"First Speaker," Mark said hastily, "Orim has—"

"Orim has *nothing*!" the Wopind said shrilly, leaping up, stabbing the air savagely with the muzzle of hin's weapon. "The WirElspind will suffer for this, and Alanor will watch the consequences of hin's words! Obviously, the WirElspind doubts hin's resolve, hin's sincerity—well, they will be convinced! Hin will not wait for the deadline!"

Even though Orim was shouting in Elspindlor, hin's anger and intention to commit further violence was evident to everyone on the bridge. "Orim!" Mark said. "Please—"

The Wopind turned on him, and Mark shrank back in his seat before those mad, burning brass eyes. Quickly the Wopind spoke to the armed female. "We need more pictures. Bring the journalist, Cara Hendricks, and this time bring *two* prisoners. Hin will see that they meet Wo before the eyes of this one!" Hin gestured furiously at Alanor, who was silent with shock. "Bring the Apis here, and one other"—hin glared at Mark—"and make sure that other is human!"

No! Mark's mind screamed. *No! God, don't let this happen!*

Alanor was silent, perhaps realizing what hin's anger had done. *You fool!* Mark thought savagely, then the holo-tank rippled, and the face of the Heeyoon was back. "*Asimov*," he began, "what's happening? What—"

"They're going to kill two more hostages!" Mark yelled in Mizari. "Get Alanor back to say hin didn't mean it!"

"But—" the Heeyoon stammered.

And the communications tech cracked.

"You idiots!" he yelled, lunging for the comm board. "*Do* it, or we'll all— Ahhhhhh!" His scream was mortal agony as the high-energy beam from Orim's gun drilled a neat hole in his back. He fell against the comm station. Mark leaped to get out of the way of the deadly beam, and crashed against Rogers, the Communications Chief. The man lurched forward.

Perhaps the han who'd stood so many long hours guarding the bridge thought the Comm Officer was attacking her. She fired wildly, as if she'd never handled a gun before, missing him and destroying the comm station and several panels of instrumentation in the process. And then Rogers was on top of her, and they were rolling on the deck, wrestling for the gun.

"Stop!" Loachin was screaming. "You'll wreck the ship!" Orim was turning to fire on Rogers. The woman launched a desperate high kick at the Wopind's head, stiffening her whole body into a projectile. The impact ruined his aim, sending the deadly beams sweeping over the bridge. Part of the navigation board and most of the engineering board melted into a charred mess. Warning alarms sounded, and lights flashed red on the still-intact controls.

The third Wopind on the bridge, the other neuter, wavered less than a second between targeting Loachin or Rogers. By the time he chose Loachin, it was too late; Mark was on hin.

The Wopind was wiry-strong and fast, but Mark had been well trained in the martial arts. A calculated pressure grip and a follow-up, strong twist and jerk sent the gun sliding across the bridge. Mark forced the Wopind facedown on the deck and straddled hin.

Only then was he able to look up and realize that Orim lay dead across Loachin's legs, blasted by the gun Rogers had wrested from the han guard.

Loachin pushed the Wopind off and staggered to her feet. One look at the bridge controls was sufficient. "*Shit!*" she yelled. "We've got no power! We can't maintain orbit without power! We're going down!"

Rogers was already at the ruined comm board. "No communications, Captain, internal or external!"

Loachin turned to the StarBridge student. "Mark, get back to the passengers, spread the word, tell them to secure for a crash landing. If you see the First Mate, tell him to get up here!" She slid into the pilot's seat and began testing what remained of the controls, rattling off orders to the Communications Chief, who had taken the navigation console.

Mark whirled on the remaining Wospind. "This ship is going to crash on your world in just a few minutes." He mimed an explosion. "You go and tell the rest of your friends that if they want to live, forget guarding the hostages and find a place that will protect them!"

The han and the hin looked at each other, at Orim's body, at the nearly destroyed bridge, then bounded off down the passageway.

Mark raced after them, skidding to a stop just inside the common lounge.

"Listen!" he shouted. Pandemonium, created by the panicked arrival of the two Wospind a second before, was already breaking out. "Listen to me! Secure for crash landing! Secure for crash landing!"

"Where's the Captain?" a woman yelled. "What's—"

Rogers, the Communications Officer, appeared suddenly at his shoulder. "I'll take over here. You see if you can find the First Mate. All right," he shouted at the screaming crowed, "secure yourselves for emergency landing. Use the hiber units!"

A few people obeyed, but most just milled, all babbling at once. As Mark whirled back toward the door, Cara grabbed him. "Mark, what happened?"

"Orim's dead, and we're going to crash!" He shoved her in the direction of the hibernation chamber. "Get us a unit! Where's Eerin?"

The Elpind materialized next to Cara. "Here!"

"Both of you! Find a unit."

Mark pushed through the crowd. He wasn't the only one who remembered that the central part of the diamond-shaped passenger liners had the greatest number of reinforcing layers. People were jostling and elbowing their way into the hiber room as the cry went up all over the lounge: "We're going down!"

The *Asimov* bucked, leveled, bucked again. Fresh screams erupted.

Oh, my God! We're hitting atmosphere already!

Mark was forced to move aside for a big Simiu bent on clearing a path into the hiber room for a wizened little Apis and realized the two had just entered the common lounge with a clot of people from the rear, smaller lounges. He battled his way through them and suddenly spotted the uniform of the First Mate headed straight for him.

He grabbed the man's arm. "Sir! The Captain needs you on the bridge. Crash landing!"

"I'm on my way." The man hardly paused. "Find a safe place!"

Mark turned, expecting to find the way easier now that he went with the flow of the crowd . . . but the tide of people was changing direction. Again he had to push and elbow his way through. As soon as he made it into the hibernation chamber he knew why. Every unit was full!

The ship heaved again, and Mark joined several others in a tangle of arms and legs that rolled across the slanting floor.

"Mark! Over here! Over here!"

Automatically he tracked the voice and saw Cara waving frantically to him from one of the second-level units.

"Over here, Mark! Get in!"

His body was moving before his mind caught up. It propelled him there, climbed up, hesitated when he saw both Cara and Eerin already there, but slid in anyway.

Lying on their sides with the skinny Elpind in the middle, the three of them were tightly jammed into a hiber unit designed for one person. Mark fumbled over his head to let the top down, checking, at the same time, the location of the manual catch that would open it from the inside. They would need that if they survived.

If.

"Oh, God, Mark . . . " Cara whispered. "We'll burn up."

"No," he corrected her. "The special insulation material that protects against the effects of metaspace works against friction, too. We've already entered atmosphere."

The ship pitched violently, and instinctively Mark reached

out. Two human hands, one dark-skinned, one light, met across the down-covered body of the Elpind. Mark held on tight, closed his eyes, and pressed his face against the back of Eerin's fuzzy, warm neck.

A hard, uneven, side-to-side wobble was suddenly the ship's predominant motion. *She's going to pull it off! The Captain's landing us!* Mark thought triumphantly. He recognized the motion as a sign that they were very low now . . . and in the same moment he gauged the sense of forward motion that penetrated even into the hiber unit. *Oh, shit! Too fast. We're going too fast!*

His heart rattled off a hundred heartbeats in the last, long, too-long second. The suspense alone was killing him.

Dammit! Crash, if you're going to! Just get it over with! he silently screamed.

The S.V. *Asimov* obeyed.

CHAPTER 10

◆

Death Rites

The first slamming impact would have bounced Cara and the others like a child's ball, spattering them against the lid of the hiber unit, except for the unit's emergency air-cushion that was triggered by impact. Even so, she lurched against the padded side of the unit as more bruising bounces were accompanied by grinding, tearing noises. The unit tilted, then there came a final, massive jolt that abruptly ended all sensation of motion.

A long, breathless minute passed.

"It's over," Mark said in a strangled voice. He stirred, and his face appeared over the Elpind's shoulder, worried hazel eyes studying both of them. "Cara? You okay? Eerin?"

The Elpind squirmed. "Hin is well."

"I . . . I'm fine. Are you?" Her throat was raw, and she could barely whisper.

Mark nodded and took a deep breath. "We've got to get out of here. Hit the manual release on your side, Cara."

We're alive! We made it, all three of us. As her fingers groped at the lever, Cara tried to feel joy, or even relief, but she only felt numb.

Mark pushed back the top of the unit, then climbed out. Seconds later Eerin followed the human over the side. Cara shifted in the sudden roominess and sat up. The unit was steeply tilted, leaving her feet far lower than her head.

"Cara? Here, let me help." Mark's head reappeared over the side. Cara looked at the hand he held out, the hand she'd gripped like a lifeline during the crash, and realized she didn't remember letting go of it.

"Cara!" He regarded her anxiously. "You okay?"

She nodded, then slowly, conscious of dozens of bruises, she clambered out. As she did so, she spotted the autocam wedged in a corner of the unit, and grabbed it.

Her bare feet encountered a wildly tilted deck as Mark steadied her down. Cara turned and regarded the hibernation chamber with mingled horror and awe that any of them had survived.

The whole compartment tilted steeply to port. The deck was littered with broken light panels and smashed instrumentation. The few remaining light panels glowed a dim, eerie orange, the result of the emergency power cells.

Behind her, Cara heard grunts and groans as several other survivors sat up in hibernation units that practically hung from the ceiling due to the *Asimov*'s pronounced slant. There were dripping sounds and a soft hissing, and somewhere to her left, someone whimpered mindlessly, like an injured animal. But despite these faint sounds, the most notable thing was the thick stillness, an unnatural quiet, that made her shiver.

The chamber seemed to have shrunk. Cara peered through the red gloom toward the "down" end and realized that part of the compartment had buckled inward; bulkheads and overhead supports met in a crazy tangle. What had been an orderly curving wall of sleep units was now a crunched and twisted disaster. Here and there through shattered viewpanels Cara could make out a splayed hand, a still, huddled shape, a blood-streaked face.

"Oh, God. I hope none of them are still alive. If they are, we'll never be able to get them out. We'd need equipment . . . " Mark trailed off, shuddering all over as he turned away to look back at the units on the wall where they had been. Some of them were damaged, too, but nothing like the ones on the starboard side.

Cara reached out to him in the same instant as the Elpind. *Screaming won't help,* she told herself sternly as the three of them briefly clung together. *Screaming won't help at all. Think of something practical to do.*

It occurred to her then that the authorities would need a complete record. Activating the camera steadied her.

"I guess we should search the ship . . . try to locate any other survivors . . . " Cara attempted to swallow. Sometime during the crash she must've screamed—only that would explain how raw her throat felt. She stared at her human companion. Even in this light, he was pale. "Mark, are *you* okay?"

He nodded, taking a deep breath, and she could sense him doing the same thing she was: trying to push away the emotional reaction to this carnage until there was time to deal with it.

"Hin will examine these units for survivors," Eerin said.

"I'll check the lounge." Mark's voice was a little steadier. "Everyone watch for first-aid kits. Or any of the crew."

"I'll come with you," Cara told him, reluctant, for the moment, to let Mark out of her sight.

"Wish I could remember that layout . . . up near the crew quarters, I think, but maybe near the storage lockers . . . " He was mumbling almost to himself, and Cara realized he was still talking about the medical kits. She waited for him to move, but he didn't. Finally she took his arm.

"Mark," she said, "let's go."

"Yeah . . . " But still he didn't move. Cara realized that he was afraid to leave the chamber. She thought she could guess why. "Do you think it'll be worse out there than in here?"

He nodded somberly. "This compartment is supposed to be the safest, strongest part of the ship. If the hiber chamber looks like this . . . "

"We'd better find out the worst," she said after a moment.

Mark nodded and led the way, stooping low to get through the doorway's distorted frame. Cara followed, and found his fears well-founded. The destruction in the hibernation chamber had been only a preview. What she saw as she emerged into the remains of the *Asimov*'s forward lounge was the real thing.

A blast of hot, dry wind blew into the lounge from a huge rip in the bulkhead. Outside they could see a patch of naked rock and sand, sizzling beneath a pale, greenish blue sky. Cara stepped to the lip of the tear and gazed out. *This is Elseemar,* she thought dazedly. *I'm on an alien planet.*

Loosely packed soil, dark brown and sandy-looking, streaked with red, stretched away as far as she could see. Boulders, some of them nearly as large as she was, studded the uneven ground.

It's a desert, she realized. *Eerin said Elseemar had them.*

Deep gouges scored the desert floor. The *Asimov* had slid a long way, a careening, crooked slide as first one side of the diamond, then the other, had grated along the ground. Shading her eyes against the harsh daylight glare, Cara let her eyes follow the tortuous path the ship had taken. Scattered everywhere, like confetti along a parade route, were bright colors: cushions from the lounge furniture, bed coverings, luggage and clothes from the wrecked cabins, tapes in their glossy containers, shoes, toys.

Cara squinted, staring harder, then abruptly closed her eyes, swallowing against nausea. Some of those bright bundles were *people,* flung out on the desert as carelessly as their belongings. Faces of the people she'd met at the Captain's Night party flashed through her memory, and she shuddered. Which ones would she find out there on the sand?

Mark had taken a quick look over her shoulder out the torn side, then moved away. Cara knew what he was doing behind her—searching for survivors in the destroyed lounge. Steeling herself, she turned to help him.

A ragged line of people, those lucky enough to ride out the crash in the padded, undamaged units, were by now trickling out of the hiber room into the lounge. A brawny male Simiu headed the line.

Cara stepped out of the way as he moved toward the giant fissure in the side of the ship, then gracefully leaped over the ragged plas-steel rip, landing effortlessly on the desert floor. He stood on all fours, looked around, then he turned and waved, beckoning the next being in line, an Apis. Spreading her wings, she flew through the hole to land beside him.

Ignoring the humans and other beings from the hiber chamber who now crowded to see out, the big alien and his small companion moved away, out of sight.

"Cara! Over here!" Mark was across from her on the port side of the lounge, with Eerin beside him. The two were struggling to move aside a metal storage locker that had been full of holo-vid cassettes. The bolts holding it against the bulkhead had ripped loose, and it had fallen over.

From the urgency of their movements, Cara guessed that someone was trapped beneath it, and she dashed across the uneven deck to help.

Grunting with effort, they managed to shift the huge thing to the side slightly. Their shoving uncovered two beings wedged into the corner made by the fallen cabinet—two male Wospind in red tunics. One heen lay facedown and obviously dead, the back of his head crushed to a bloody ruin. Biting her lip, Cara looked away, watching Eerin as hin crouched down in the newly cleared space by the other one.

The other male Wopind lay on his side, half across the dead one's legs, his own legs and the whole lower half of his body still trapped beneath the heavy metal cabinet. Cara saw his back move as heen breathed.

"It looks like most everyone got out of the lounge before we crashed, or else they were thrown out during it," reported Mark quickly. "I only found four people. Well, five, counting heen." He pointed at the dead Wopind. "This one"—nodding at the second Wopind—"makes six, but he's different—still alive."

"Should we try again to get this cabinet off him?"

"I don't think we can. And even if we could . . . " He shrugged and shook his head.

Cara nodded. The Wopind surely had serious internal injuries and bleeding, not to mention the obviously broken bones.

Eerin said something in Elspindlor, and incredibly, the Wopind opened huge sea-green eyes. They were unfocused and cloudy with pain, but after a moment, heen spoke in a weak, raspy croak. "Heen-see . . . " he gasped—or that's what the word sounded like to Cara.

Eerin repeated the word, sounding upset. Moving quickly but carefully, hin unhooked the fastenings on the Wopind's loose tunic, then laid back the flap. Cara stared incredulously.

"A baby! Damn!" Mark exclaimed. "I never saw any of them with a baby!"

Cara's heart lurched with pity. "It's so little," she breathed. The alien infant, softly fuzzy and the same light honey-brown color as its parent, was about the same size as a kitten, though longer and thinner. The baby clung to the wiry mat of its father's chest hair with its hands and feet just the way Cara's kitten back home had hung from her clothes by its sharp little claws.

And it was just as hard to get loose. At Eerin's touch it uttered a series of piercing wails and dug in deeper. Eerin hastily let go. The baby whimpered pitifully.

"Hin's afraid," said Mark.

Eerin looked up at them, speaking English for Cara's benefit. "This one is a hinsi, because it is so small it is still nourished by the father's feeding glands. The child appears to be six or seven of your weeks in age."

Feeding glands? The males suckle the infants? Cara's eyes flicked to the hijacker's hairy chest. She didn't see anything that looked like nipples, but the tunic and the baby itself obscured part of her view.

The Wopind stroked his child, making soft, crooning sounds. Clearly the effort was costing him. He paused a moment to look up at Eerin with those huge, pain-filled eyes and uttered a few more gasping words.

Eerin reached across the injured hijacker and beneath the dead one's tunic, groping under the body between chest and floor. Cara realized immediately what hin was searching for.

There was no trouble plucking this baby off its parent. Eerin's hand emerged with a tiny, fuzzy white creature dangling from it, totally limp.

"Is hinsi . . . dead?" She could hardly say the word.

"No. Hinsi breathes." But Eerin looked grave as hin examined the little creature, gently moving its limbs with a forefinger. "Hin believes hinsi is hurt."

"I'll hold hinsi," Cara offered, reaching down. Eerin hesitated a moment, then handed the baby to her.

Warm and silky soft, the infant felt incredibly fragile in Cara's hands. She could feel its rib cage and even its sharp little hipbones. Sudden tears stung her eyes. Carefully she eased it up to cuddle in the crook of her elbow.

The other child had quieted. Weakly, the father disentangled the fierce grip of its tiny orange hands and feet. Eerin reached to help, then lifted the baby away from the Wopind's chest. The child began wailing immediately.

The Wopind spoke in that low, weak voice again.

Eerin, trying vainly to soothe the sobbing baby, looked up. "The father says this one's name is Terris and the other is Misir. This one knows death is close, and heen begs us to take and care for the hinsi."

Mark sighed, edging around until he was able to kneel in the small space next to his pair partner. Absently, he reached out to run a gentle finger down the spine of Terris' narrow back. "Of *course* we'll look after them. We won't just leave them lying on the deck! We'll take care of them until help comes."

Cara was surprised by Terris' reaction to Mark's touch. Shivering all over, the baby swiveled hinsi's little head to regard him with big green eyes like its father's. Hinsi's crying ceased, until it was just a soft whimper. Mark didn't notice the infant's sudden fascination with him.

Eerin shook hin's head, looking dubious. "Heen wishes us to take them to a settlement," hin explained, "where we can find a nursing male to care for them."

"We happen to be in the middle of a desert, thanks to heen and heen's bunch." Sudden bitterness colored Mark's voice. "The babies are stuck here with us. All we can do is—"

He broke off, surprised, because the hijacker reached out a long-fingered, trembling hand to tug at his pants leg. The dying alien whispered a word, gasping with the small exertion.

"Pocket," translated Mark, leaning over to check the Wopind's tunic.

The baby began to cry again. Cara saw the father give it a worried look, but he made no move to take the child back.

"He's got a plotting map!" Mark drew forth a small, wafer-thin instrument and quickly activated it. "With the whole planet in memory! Let me see if the location sensor's working. Where'd he get this thing, anyway?"

"The CLS has placed satellites in orbit around Elseemar, and maps were made from the images they produced," Eerin explained over the baby's crying. "The researchers all have them."

"Then I'll bet he took it off the kidnapped Heeyoon, the one the Wospind forced into piloting for them."

Terris' steady cries were bothering Cara. She reached around Mark with her free arm, intending to pet the child, as he had done, to quiet it, but at the approach of her hand, it went into a yelping fit.

"Eerin, are you sure that baby's not hurt, too?" Mark asked, giving Terris a concerned look. Then the tiny light he'd been waiting for blinked on, and his attention returned to the map.

"Hey, all right! The sensor's working. Here's where we are." He pointed. "Thank God we're not in the middle of the desert; we're about fifty kilometers from its edge. There are mountains not too far away, and settlements all through them."

The young man glanced down at the injured hijacker. "Maybe there's one close enough to make your request possible—and get us some help for the survivors. Eerin, look at this map and see if you recognize the names of any of the closest settlements." He held the instrument, since Eerin's hands were full with the squirming baby, where both hin and the hijacker could see the small square display.

Eerin began to question the Wopind.

Hin's questions, Cara decided, watching the exchange without understanding a word, were designed to spare the fading alien as much as possible; the questions were long while the whispered answers from the hijacker were extremely short. *Yes or no answers,* thought Cara. *Maybe a coordinate here and there.*

Whatever they were, Eerin, and Mark, too, seemed satisfied each time. Bright flickers leaped from point to point on the map's tiny grids as Mark's fingers carefully touched one programmed key after another.

After several questions they paused to let the injured Wopind rest a moment. He was noticeably weaker. Mark looked up at Cara.

"There are three settlements within reasonable walking distance," he told her. "Two of them were founded by Wospind leaving the cities and moving deeper into the mountains. In fact, he says the group that took this ship was using the larger of the two for a base camp for a while. Then they moved closer to Lalcipind where they could take action against the WirElspind, keep an eye on activities at the medical research lab—"

"You mean destroy it," Cara interrupted.

"Eventually, yes." Mark frowned. "We don't know what kind of communication Orim might have maintained with hin's former base camp. Even if none, it would hardly be a good idea to walk into a Wopind settlement and ask for help."

"I agree. What about the third place you mentioned?"

"He called it a 'nahah.' That's the Elpind word for a very small, walled settlement. They cultivate sestel, wilbre vines, and mreto nuts. Sometimes the population is no more than one big extended family."

Eerin indicated hin had another question to ask, and Mark broke off to listen. The hijacker started to answer, then his face twisted in a spasm of intense pain. He tried to speak, but choked instead. Then he began to cough in hard, painful spasms. By the time the attack ended, the Wopind was limp. His eyes were closed, and his breath came in wheezing gasps.

Oh, my God, he's going to die—right here, right now, Cara thought. The Mizari's death had been planned, and quick. She found that in some ways it was infinitely harder to watch this being struggle for life—and lose. "Isn't there anything we can do?" she pleaded softly.

Mark glanced from the father to the crying child in Eerin's arms, then looked up at her and shook his head sorrowfully.

"There is something hin can do," Eerin said. "Hin has a duty to perform for anyone who is dying."

"What is that?" Cara asked, wondering if Eerin meant promising the hijacker a proper burial or something.

"Hin must dance the Mortenwol," Eerin told them, then rose decisively.

Mark looked down at the Wopind, who lay listening with a look of anxious hope on his face. "Dance the Mortenwol?" He gaped at Eerin. "You mean . . . right now?"

"Yes."

"Uh . . . Eerin, that's not a good idea. The human survivors of the crash won't understand why you're trying to comfort one of our captors. They might think you're a Wopind, too. I don't think you'd better."

"Heen wishes to witness the Mortenwol that will attend

heen's death," Eerin explained, obviously surprised by Mark's protest. "It is necessary that heen's last wish be fulfilled."

"Eerin, the Mortenwol right now could stir up trouble. Remember, humans reserve dancing for times of joy. If any of them see you dancing, they might also think you were mocking their sorrow. Do you understand 'mocking'?"

"Yes. And hin is sorry if any humans are upset. But if our positions were reversed, hin would expect this heen to dance the Mortenwol, and hin can do no less."

Mark glanced over his shoulder. The lounge was empty at the moment. "Well, maybe you can do it quickly . . . and quietly. Do you have to use the kareen?"

"It must be done properly," Eerin insisted.

"The music will draw people, Eerin. This could create bad feeling."

"Hin will dance the Mortenwol," Eerin said firmly.

Mark sighed. "Dammit, Eerin! We've got a lot to do, finding medical kits, searching for other survivors, and, now, caring for these babies." He glanced down at the Wopind, who appeared to have lapsed back into unconsciousness. "This hijacker won't know whether you dance for heen, or not. He's too far gone to care."

"Heen will know. Heen will care." Eerin looked mulish. It was the first time Cara had seen the Elpind show strong emotion.

"Hin promises to hurry. It will not take long," Eerin declared, and, without further argument, handed Terris to Cara and bounded off.

"Can you manage?" Mark asked Cara, after a single resentful glare sent after the departing Elpind. "Can you handle both babies?"

"Sure," Cara said, settling the again-wailing Terris in her lap. "You go look for the medical kits. And something we can adapt for diapers. I'll stay here."

Mark frowned. "I hope to hell Eerin can get this over with quickly. I guess it's like last rites to hin. But I'm worried that there will be trouble over it."

"I'll explain," Cara said. "Anyone who protests fulfilling a dying person's last wish would have to have a heart of stone. Don't worry, Mark."

He sighed reluctantly. "Okay. I'll check the forward cabins, find the kits, then be back as soon as I can."

After he was gone, Cara shifted the babies again, trying to get a better grip on the struggling Terris (whose thin, monotonous cries were beginning to get on her nerves), without disturbing the unconscious baby. She gazed around the lounge, her eyes avoiding the four other bodies, one Drnian, one Chhhh-kk-tu, one a human woman, and, almost buried beneath debris, a blue-and-white-wrapped form. The tip of Sarozz's black and silver tail was sticking out.

Cara closed her eyes, crying softly. After a few minutes, she resolutely wiped away the tears. She looked back down at Terris' father. The Wopind's eyes were closed, his breathing shallow and uneven.

"Hurry, Eerin," Cara muttered. *"Hurry."*

Sorrow tugged at Eerin's mind, demanding attention even as hin rushed down the warped and broken corridor, but hin forced it down, concentrating only on fulfilling hin's duty. Mark did not understand, and Eerin regretted that, but Elpind tradition must be followed, even at a time like this. The Mortenwol took precedence over personal feelings.

Eerin was angry with the Wospind, angry over the disaster Orim had so maliciously caused, but personal antipathy did not matter when death approached. If Orim hinself had been lying out there dying, Eerin would have done the same for hin.

The Elpind used the manual control to get into hin's quarters. The small living area was relatively intact, and since the Elpind had had the foresight to secure the kareen in the storage webbing whenever it had to be left unattended, the sturdy little music board was unharmed. Gathering it up, hin grabbed the case of feathers and a cushion, then headed back for the lounge.

As Eerin went, hin tried to sort out hin's feelings, in preparation for the dance to come. Anger, guilt, and a great sense of shock were uppermost in hin's mind. These feelings had been present in Eerin since the moment the Wospind boarded the *Asimov* and pointed their guns. That hin's own people should threaten to hurt others, innocent others, and then should actually carry out that threat—!

Hin was not on Elseemar to see the ruins of the lab, the bodies being carried out, Eerin thought. *Perhaps seeing that would have prepared hin . . .*

And now hin also knew sorrow. Eerin knew instinctively that the crash had been very bad; from the moment the *Asimov* had halted, hin had felt the dark presence of Wo hanging over the ship. Death on Elseemar was an all-too-familiar presence, and not usually frightening. But so many deaths, and all unprepared for! Eerin knew that hin would be dancing the Mortenwol for *all* the *Asimov*'s, dead, not just the hijacker. It was the only comfort, the only tribute, hin could render . . . even if Mark Kenner could neither understand nor appreciate the gesture.

Eerin also felt sorrow for the impending deaths of the two infants. Why had the Wopind asked hin and the humans to take suckling children? Heen must know there was no chance the babies could survive without food long enough to reach a settlement. Hope, Eerin realized, must live very strongly in a parent's heart. But hin could not share the hijacker's hope; Eerin knew the babies were doomed.

Hin headed back toward the common lounge at a near run, hoping the hijacker still lived—yet part of the Elpind almost wished heen would be dead.

Mark is right, Eerin admitted to hinself. *Dancing for a hijacker will be seen as an inappropriate thing to do by those passengers who suffer under a new and heavy burden of grief.* Hin was learning firsthand how overwhelming sorrow could be when Wo came without warning.

Cara, with both infants in her arms, looked up as Eerin entered the lounge. "Hurry," she urged. "He's still alive, but barely."

Eerin nodded and went straight to the dying male. "Hin has returned," said Eerin loudly in Elspindlor, kneeling to slip the cushion under the Wopind's head. "The last Mortenwol begins." But neither the words nor lifting his head for the cushion roused the failing Wopind.

"Journey-taker," Eerin said sharply, using the ritual words for the dying and shaking the red-clad shoulder, "behold your last Mortenwol!"

With a moan the Wopind slowly opened his sea-green eyes.

Eerin sensed heen's gratitude, for the hijacker was beyond speech by now.

Eerin jumped up and, with a quick motion, wove hin's Elseewas feathers into a headband. Moving to the center of the wrecked lounge and checking to be sure of the Wopind's clear view around the fallen cabinet, Eerin nodded with satisfaction to see the hijacker's gaze still fixed on hin. The Elpind laid the kareen at hin's feet, wound it, then touched it into life.

The first note sounded. *Elseemar . . .* it seemed to sing to Eerin. Despite the circumstances of this Mortenwol, hin rejoiced to be dancing it while breathing the air of home.

Hin sprang into the air, savoring the lighter gravity. Before leaving Elseemar, gravity had been a thing never noticed. Now, after the constant drag of the slightly heavier environment at the Academy at StarBridge and aboard ship, this normal gravity felt like flying itself.

Eerin began the first pattern. *This is for the journey-takers,* hin thought, letting hin's meaning encompass all the others around the broken ship who were, like the Wopind, even now meeting death, letting it reach to those whose breath had already stopped, letting it touch even the babies, soon-to-be journey-takers.

El is life and Wo is death, and each completes the other. Hin slipped into the second pattern. *In the quick flight of a Shadowbird, El becomes Wo. Let it be, let that knowledge grace the fullness of each moment . . . let it ever be so.* The words of the ancient Telling for journey-takers, their rhythm in harmony with the swooping movements of the second pattern, ran through Eerin's mind.

And it will ever be so! Eerin leaped up, relieved to feel hin's old gladness at the surety, freed by the total acceptance of that surety.

Eerin rejoiced.

This was only the second time Cara had seen the Mortenwol, and she marveled again at the lightness, the elegant delicacy of the movements. Gone was the bouncy abruptness she associated with normal Elpind movements. Gone was her awareness of Eerin's bony frame, each limb marked by knobby, protruding joints. Instead, as she watched, the girl felt she saw a long, creamy feather taken by the breeze.

"What's it doing?" demanded a voice. Cara started and looked behind her.

A big, heavyset man was peering through the rent in the *Asimov*'s side. He had great smears of red blood on his shirt, but seemed unharmed himself. As Cara watched, he clambered back in, glaring from the dancing Elpind to the babies in Cara's arms. A doll dangled from one hand, as if he'd forgotten he held it. It, too, was covered with blood. His dark eyes beneath thick brows glittered feverishly.

Cara swallowed, and quickly laid the two babies down on a nearby chair cushion. "Eerin's not one of the terrorists," she said, moving so that she was between the newcomer and the oblivious Elpind. "Hin is fulfilling the last request of that hijacker over there, who is dying. It's kind of like the Elspind version of last rites," she explained, but he ignored her.

"The goddamn bastard is *dancing!* Dancing, because that sonofabitch over there is still alive!" he snarled.

Involuntarily following the man's gaze, Cara glanced down at the Wopind. His huge eyes, riveted on Eerin, seemed lit with green fire, life in all its raw energy blazing up in them.

But even as she watched, his body suddenly trembled violently, shaking for several seconds, then went limp and still. The Wopind's fiercely exultant stare, still directed at the spot where Eerin had just lifted into a spiraling turn, grew fixed and glassy. Heen's eyes still shone, but now only with the reflection from the emergency lights overhead.

Cara swallowed painfully. "There, he's dead now, you can see that," she said. "Eerin will stop dancing now."

The fury on the man's face made him look barely human. He flexed powerful hands. "My wife is dead," he snarled. "And my little girl." His gaze moved to Eerin, who had just landed after the dance's final leap, and was gazing at them in surprise and consternation. "So every one of those bloody murderers needs to be dead, too. Not *dancing!*"

He spat out the last word, hunching his shoulders, tensing like a big cat. Cara saw the flicker of madness in his eyes.

"Run, Eerin! Run!" she screamed, flinging out her arms in a futile effort to stop him.

With an inarticulate roar, the grief-crazed man slapped her out of his way as he would have a bothersome insect. The blow to the side of her head made Cara grunt with pain. Lights danced crazily behind her eyes; her ears rang. The lounge blurred around her as she fell, spinning in an orange-and-white whirl.

Struggling to remain conscious, she screamed again as she saw Eerin go down beneath the man's huge bulk. The Elpind cried out in fear, then was silent.

"Rob," Mahree Burroughs said quietly, "I have news, and I'm afraid it's not good."

It was morning at StarBridge Academy. Rob had showered and changed into a business suit; this morning he faced a trip up to StarBridge Station to meet with an eminent Drnian government official whose son Rob had encouraged to withdraw from the Academy . . . he just plainly wasn't interrelator material. The father was the one who was taking it hard; the youngster had confided that he'd really rather be a physicist.

Now he stared at Mahree, trying to brace himself. *Dear God, what's happened?* Aloud he said steadily, "Okay, tell me."

"All contact has been lost with the *Asimov*, and the ship seems to have vanished."

"How?" Rob said, baffled. "Weren't they orbiting Elseemar?"

"They were, but they're not anymore. Reports are confused and incomplete. I spoke with the CLS Liaison on Elseemar, and he told me that the ship was in communication with one of the WirElspind leaders, who was stupid enough to threaten the Wospind." She shook her head and sighed. "And then the terrorist leader began yelling threats and orders. Some kind of altercation broke out on the bridge. Mark was shouting that more hostages were going to be killed when communications were cut abruptly—first visual, then audio. For a moment they could hear the sounds of a struggle, and . . . " she hesitated, "weapons firing."

"Oh, God . . . "

Mahree sighed, her dark eyes shadowed and weary. "Zahssez told me they tried for over an hour, but couldn't reestablish communications. Their mapping and weather satellites indicate that the *Asimov* is no longer orbiting Elseemar."

"Where could they have gone?"

She frowned. "I don't know. Could the Wopind leader have ordered the ship to another destination?"

"Where?" Rob said. "They'd be taken into custody."

"Could they be heading for Sorrow Sector?" she asked, referring to the sector of space where the criminal elements of many planets took refuge and based their illegal activities.

"The Wospind? They're fanatics, not crooks," Rob pointed out. "I can't imagine that they'd go there."

"I suppose that it's also possible that the crew was finally able to regain control of the *Asimov* from the hijackers, and take it on to Berytin," Mahree said. "But if that happened, why didn't they notify the CLS base on Elseemar?"

Rob shook his head, baffled. Then a sudden thought made his stomach knot. "Mahree . . . could they have blown the ship up?" he asked, his mouth dry with fear.

She shook her head again. "I asked, and the satellites recorded no evidence of any explosions in space."

"At least that's something," Rob muttered.

"I've requested communications operators on all nearby planets and stations to notify my office immediately if there is any word from, or about, the *Asimov*. I'm afraid we'll just have to wait until they initiate contact."

Rob knew as well as she did that interstellar space was just too *big* to make any kind of a search operation possible. He nodded numbly. "Thanks for trying, Mahree . . . "

"Let me know if there's anything else I can do, Rob."

"I will." He looked up at her, meeting her eyes across the parsecs, and tried to smile. "I love you."

Minutes later, when he related the bad news to Kkintha ch'aait, the little Chhhh-kk-tu sighed aloud, rubbing her paws in distress. "Oh, Rob . . . this is terrible."

"Mark has no one left back on Earth, I know that. But Cara does. Do you want to call Cara's family or do you want me to?"

"It is my job," she said, "but they are human, so I would appreciate it if you were with me when I speak to them."

"Sure," he said. "My appointment can wait a little while. This is an emergency, after all." For a moment he wondered what time it was on OldAm's East Coast. Cara had told him she lived in . . . Atlanta, that was it. Would it be the middle of the night there? *Probably*, he thought grimly. *It figures. Bad news always comes in the middle of the night, remember?*

The *Asimov*'s forward passageway was badly warped, heavily damaged. Some of the supply lockers that lined the spaces between crew cabin doors were bent and jammed shut; others had sprung permanently open in the crash. The locker marked "Medical Supplies" was one of the latter. Mark found several med-kits and stuffed them into the front of his coverall. He also found a pair of socks and shoes that were only half a size too big, so he pulled them on. Walking through the debris with bare feet was becoming increasingly hazardous.

His next goal was to look for possible survivors in the forward crew cabins, but, anxious to know Captain Loachin's fate, Mark decided to check the bridge first. He was gripped by a cold foreboding that the task wouldn't take him long.

Mark quickly discovered that reaching the control room from inside the *Asimov* was impossible. The primary hatch was warped and would not respond to the controls, not even to the little-used manual release. The secondary hatch opened partway on his third try, but there was something blocking it.

He tried to peer around the obstruction. No good. Only silence answered his repeated calls.

Mark hurried back down the corridor to the second cabin on the starboard side. On the way to the bridge, he'd passed its open doorway and noted another huge rip that had penetrated the ship's outer skin.

Carefully avoiding jagged edges, Mark crawled through the gash in the ship's side and dropped down on the desert floor. After the murky red dimness of the emergency lighting, the glare of daylight was painful. He jogged far enough away to avoid most of the wreckage, then headed for the forward point of the diamond, the nose of the *Asimov* where the bridge was located.

Seeing the ship from this perspective, Mark's heart contracted. *How the hell did we survive?* he wondered. He'd realized from the interior that it had to be bad, but it was still a shock to see the reality.

Captain Loachin had done a valiant job, trying to land a

craft that had never been constructed to land. Handling her ship like a glider, belly flopping it down on the desert floor . . . no pilot could have done more. But their speed had been too great, their angle too steep, and the bulge of the cargo storage in the underbelly too curved to allow a successful belly flop. The *Asimov* had tilted from side to side, then slammed over to starboard, almost completely ripping off the starboard point of its diamond shape. The port side was in better shape, mostly intact, though very battered.

And the bow of the ship had been virtually plowed under when it had impacted with a massive boulder that had stopped the vessel's slewing, out-of-control slide across the desert. The *Asimov*'s momentum, when it met the obstacle in its path, had crumpled the bridge back in on itself, folding the ship's nose like an accordion between the solid rock in front and the thousands of metric tons hurtling behind it.

Mark stared at the building-sized boulder. Though rough rocks from pebble size to man height littered the hard-packed desert floor, there was nothing else this size anywhere in view. *Where the hell did you come from?* Mark demanded of it silently, angrily. *Why did you have to be right here?*

He remembered feeling that last, awful jolt while lying in the hiber unit. Captain Loachin and all the others on the bridge would have already been dead then, smashed in a millisecond and dead even before the impact of their fatal collision could travel through the length of the ship.

Loachin's face, not bruised and drawn from exhaustion as he'd seen it that last time, but beautiful and wearing the warm smile of Captain's Night, rose in Mark's memory. He hoped she'd never realized just how badly her vessel was tearing apart, how many people were dying as it careened across the desert.

Struggling to maintain control, Mark hurried back. There still remained the necessity of checking the forward cabins.

Every cabin he entered threatened to make real his old nightmare of opening a door to find bloody death behind it. Grief and fear coiled tighter and tighter inside him, and even the relief of finding all the starboard cabins empty didn't release the tension.

Behind him from the lounge he could hear the first sweet,

shrill notes of Eerin's kareen. The joyful music sliced through the graveyard quiet like an intruder's attacking knife. Mark quickened his pace, anxious to get back to his friends.

The first and second port-side cabins were also empty, but in the third one was the body of the beelike Apis, R'Fzarth, the other one of the two scientists headed for Elseemar. *The Wospind must have left her here when when they took her companion, Sarozz, out to the lounge to be executed,* Mark thought sickly.

They'd tethered her to one bolted leg of the bed by a thin wire around her compact, fuzzy torso, but she'd been in flight, probably trying to dodge flying debris, when she died. A long, large spear of broken light panel had impaled her against the wall behind the bed. Wings outspread, she looked hideously like an oversize lab specimen—except for one thing. The force of the blow from the spear had driven her backward farther than the tether could reach, and the thin wire had sliced her neatly in two. The lower part of her body lay on the bed.

Mark studied the pitiful scene for a moment, felt absolutely nothing, turned away to leave . . . then dropped to his knees, hand pressed to his mouth, gagging.

Tears filled his eyes, and this time he couldn't fight them back. Mark wept for Captain Loachin, for the mutilated Mizari lying back in the lounge, and his Apis companion who'd met her death all alone, for the orphaned babies—for all those who had died, whose bodies would never be found. His sobs came from deep in his chest, so deep that they were painful, and some of them were for himself. *What could I have done differently?* he wondered. *Could I have prevented this?*

As soon as he could find enough control to do so, Mark wiped his eyes and nose, then rose shakily to his feet. He moved toward the bed, intending to take R'Fzarth down from the wall and cover her body.

A shrill scream suddenly echoed through the dead ship. "Run, Eerin! Run!"

Whirling, Mark raced out the door and down the corridor. *What's happening? I shouldn't have left them. I knew better. You don't dance in the face of this much death. Not where humans are involved, anyway. God, let me be in time!*

He burst into the lounge, only to see a large, heavy-shouldered man throttling Eerin. The wiry Elpind was struggling, flailing wildly, but the huge man ignored hin's blows.

"Stop!" Mark shouted, but the man ignored him. Dragging the weakening Elpind up off the floor, he shifted his grip to hin's shoulder and drew back his right hand, the edge of his huge palm aiming knifelike at Eerin's throat. From his self-defense training, Mark recognized the blow, knew that it would crush the Elpind's windpipe, killing Eerin.

Mark saw it as if it were happening in slow motion. Only meters away and already at a full run, he knew with a cold certainty that there was no way he could reach them in time.

CHAPTER 11

◆

The Apis and the Simiu

From out of nowhere, rescue came.

She must have been watching from outside and flew in, Mark decided later, when there was time to think. "She" was an Apis, one of the wasp-resembling type like StarBridge's dietician. Her meter-long body seemed small and fragile next to the man's bulk.

The insectoid alien darted at the man's head, beating her wings furiously in his face. She never actually touched him, but the human drew back instinctively, throwing up his hands to protect his eyes.

"Stop it!" Mark yelled, startling the man further as he seized his shoulders, dragging him off Eerin. His opponent broke Mark's hold and turned, amazingly fast for his bulk. A second later the younger man found himself down on his back while the huge man screamed curses in his face and tried to throttle him. Managing to pull a knee up to use for leverage, the StarBridge student gave a mighty heave and shoved his attacker off.

Mark rolled, coming up to his feet, but he stumbled over Eerin's kareen, and before he could regain his balance, a powerful hand yanked his ankle. He fell heavily.

The Apis moved in again, and the fingers around Mark's ankle released as the man again shielded his face from her beating wings. Still on the ground, Mark levered himself up on his hands and one knee. His foot lashed out, catching the man squarely on the point of his chin.

The man fell back on the bloodstained carpet and was still.

Breathing heavily and trembling from leftover adrenaline, Mark crawled over to the Elpind, who lay unmoving.

The golden eyes were open . . . and alive. "Eerin? You okay?"

"Not hurt." But the Elpind made no immediate move to get up. One hand rubbed gingerly at hin's thin neck, and there was a shocked look in the golden eyes that hadn't been there even during the height of the crisis with the Wospind.

Mark immediately turned to Cara, who was sitting up, looking every bit as shaken as the Elpind. "He hit me!" she cried, tentatively touching the side of her face. It appeared swollen, though her coloring hid any bruising.

"Are you hurt?"

"No, I'm all right. But he nearly scared me to death." She took a deep breath. "My God, he was going to *kill* Eerin!"

"Where are the babies?" Mark looked around the lounge. In the silence, he could hear Terris crying.

"Over there." She pointed to one squirming, squalling bundle of fur and one limp, silent one who lay on a cushion. Wavering to her feet, she stumbled over to them, then looked up, relieved. "They're okay. Terris is just mad."

"Sit down for a minute and get your breath," advised Mark, suspecting that she was more shaken than she let on. He managed to right the couch, and she sank down on it gratefully. Eerin joined her, for once content to sit still.

Mark turned his attention back to their rescuer. The Apis had settled down onto the deck, and was watching him curiously, patiently, from her faceted eyes. Mark hastily made the Mizari greeting gesture and addressed her in that language, knowing that she could "hear" him through the hairs on her antennae that could pick up sound waves. "Thank you for helping us." Past her, through the rip in the *Asimov*'s side, he could see a large crowd of onlookers peering in and muttering. But no one made any move to help.

Mark bent over the man who lay on the floor.

Their attacker was breathing normally, and the student sighed with relief. The man's obviously expensive clothes were heavily bloodstained, but none of it was his own. Mark carefully checked the burly neck for displacement and found no signs of damage. Only then did he allow himself to sink down on the floor and rest for a moment. "He's okay," he told Cara. "Just knocked out."

He regarded the Apis, who was still watching him. *She's old,* he found himself thinking. At StarBridge, the Apis students had all been young, and none of the instructors had been past middle age, as the insectoid race measured it . . . but this one had a dry, shriveled appearance that made him suspect that she was quite elderly. His already considerable respect for her courage increased. *The only person with enough guts to jump in and help, against a guy dozens of times her weight, and she's old, too!*

Mark bowed again to the Apis, bowed deeply to indicate his great respect, then said in Mizari, "I am very grateful to you. I think you saved Eerin's life."

She moved closer on slender legs, her wings waving slightly, then touched her forehead, above her eyes. Mark saw that her voder, which she customarily operated with her antennae, was cracked. Detaching it, she put it on the deck between them. "Oh . . . " Mark said, picking it up and examining it. "That's too bad. It doesn't look like it's repairable."

"What are you doing?" a harsh voice demanded loudly. "Do not touch her!" A reddish blur came sailing through the gap in the *Asimov*'s hull, then leaped so it landed between them.

Even before the Simiu halted, Mark realized who it had to be. No other species could take the sibilant Mizari and make it guttural.

"She helped my friend and me with some trouble," Mark said, backing away slightly. The big alien looked angry enough to deliver a challenge, and Simiu challenges were nothing he wanted to incur. He held up his hands, demonstrating that they were empty. "I was just thanking her."

The Simiu snorted. "She does not require your approbation, *human*. She gained the highest honor before you were born!"

Oh, shit! If this Simiu isn't honor-bound or related to the

Harkk'ett clan, I'll eat my socks, Mark thought bitterly. He wanted to groan aloud. *A Harkk'ett . . . that's all we need!*

The great majority of Simiu, including, of course, the Simiu students and teachers at StarBridge Academy, liked and respected humans . . . but Mark knew that some of the aliens felt very differently. Descended from or honor-bound to the Harkk'ett clan that still harbored a fifteen-year-old honor-debt against the crew of the *Désirée*, these Simiu bore a grudge against the human race . . . and never missed a chance to express it.

As Mark struggled for something conciliatory to say that wouldn't sound too abject, the Simiu gestured imperiously, and the little Apis took wing and joined him. Moments later both of them were gone. Mark noted with grim humor how quickly the crowd scattered to let the big alien through.

"Eerin, there's *got* to be some way to get this baby to stop crying!" Behind Mark, Cara sounded frustrated to the point of exasperation.

Mark went back to his friends. Eerin, looking ruffled and dejected, stood by the couch where Cara sat. Hin made a helpless gesture. "Hin is sad to tell Cara," the Elpind said in careful English. "The hinsi will die."

"Why?" Mark demanded, shaken. "What do you mean?"

Eerin regarded him steadily. "Nursing Elpind infants must eat every few hours or they will soon weaken and die."

Cara shook her head impatiently. "Eerin, surely there's something we can fix for them as a substitute formula! Just to keep them alive until help comes. I mean, what do Elspind do if the father sickens and can't nurse, for instance?"

"Parents often prepare supplement feedings," the Elpind admitted. "They are kept for the father to use if his feeding gland becomes infected, or if a nonnursing heen must feed the child in his absence."

"Okay, so look and see if these two fathers brought any with them." She nodded at the hijackers. Mark saw that Terris' father was now dead, which came as no surprise, but still saddened him.

Eerin dropped down and began going through the pockets of the dead hijackers. A moment later the Elpind straightened again. "Supplements!" hin announced triumphantly, holding up a large handful of thin, tubular objects, bright green in color.

"Okay!" Mark said, immensely relieved. "Go ahead and give Terris one of them. You know how, don't you?"

"Yes," Eerin said slowly. "But there is something else. A nursing infant will not accept food from other than a heen. If a father dies before a child has completed nursing, the child must be given quickly to a family, a pinlaa, that has a nursing male."

"But . . . both heen are dead," Cara said. "You mean that unless we can find another heen to give Terris the food, hinsi won't take it?" She glanced quickly at Mark, her skepticism plain. He couldn't blame her for doubting Eerin . . . it sounded crazy to him, too.

Eerin nodded bleakly. "Hin is afraid that is true. Hinsi will not accept nourishment from females or neuters. They become upset and stop eating, sometimes refusing to begin eating again, if they are separated for any appreciable length of time from a heen. In our lifecycle the chemistry of a hinsi is linked to that of a male."

"But only for a few days . . . " Mark began.

Eerin shook hin's head sorrowfully. "Elpind infants' metabolisms are"— hin searched for the English word, gave up and used the Mizari—"are *genetically programmed* to interact with the metabolism of a heen." Hin sighed. "Babies whose fathers die must be given to a heen if they are to survive, and from that time on, the child is a member of the new family. Hin lost hin's youngest sibling in just that way."

"Oh, shit . . . " Mark muttered, and leaned over to stroke the sobbing baby in Cara's arms. The moment he touched the child, Terris quivered all over, half turned on Cara's shoulder, then stiffened and positively *leaped* across the small space between the two humans.

"Umph!" Mark sat back on the couch, reflexively reaching up to catch and hold the baby, but Terris was already attached to the student's coverall like a burr, hinsi's sharp little nails piercing the material. Mark could feel them pricking his skin lightly. With one last, loud sniffle, Terris burrowed hinsi's head against Mark's chest. Blessed silence ensued.

"Well . . . damn!" the young man whispered, in awe, not

anger. He stared down at the baby, his mouth half-open with surprise, then reached up to stroke hinsi. Terris' big eyes closed contentedly. Mark found himself grinning foolishly. "I think I've just been adopted," he said.

"Mark is correct," Eerin said, hin's golden eyes beginning to shine again. "Apparently Mark being male is enough to satisfy Terris . . . it does not matter to hinsi that Mark is not Elpind. It is hard to believe . . . but, under the circumstances, extremely fortunate. Now Terris may live, if hinsi will take food from Mark."

"Lucky for Terris," Cara said softly, a shadow crossing her face as she looked down at the unconscious Misir. "Mark, try feeding hinsi."

The Elpind snapped the end off one of the supplement tubes, and thick grayish liquid oozed out of the tip and down the straw. Mark took it and touched the oozing tip to Terris' mouth. The baby looked at him, seeming puzzled, with those huge eyes. "Come on, Terris," he coaxed softly. "You'll like this stuff."

Terris twisted hinsi's head away.

"It's all right," Mark soothed. "C'mon . . . " He stroked the baby's silky back with one hand, offering the straw with the other. "Eat something, Terris." *You have to, Terris,* he added silently. *I can't stand any more death! Please!*

A long sandpaper tongue, a miniature of Eerin's, emerged cautiously from the baby's mouth and touched the gray slime that oozed from the straw.

"That's right!" Mark urged. "Come on, Terris."

Suddenly Mark felt the straw tug in his fingers as the baby pulled the first inch of the straw into hinsi's mouth. Hinsi began sucking eagerly, little orange cheeks going in and out as the baby rapidly emptied the feeding straw.

"Attakid, Terris!" Mark cried, beaming, and Cara grabbed his arm and squeezed it, echoing his smile.

"Retribution," someone said flatly.

Startled, Mark looked up. The man who'd attacked Eerin was conscious again. The student watched him warily as he climbed to his feet, all the while glaring at the feeding Elpind baby.

"That's what murderers ought to get. Retribution. Not dinner!" Hatred filled his eyes. Mark tensed, ready to shove Terris into Cara's arms and defend Eerin and the children if the man caused further trouble.

But Cara beat him to it. Quickly handing Misir to Eerin, she leaped up to confront the man, her back stiff with outrage. "I think you'd better leave," she said coldly. "Eerin is not one of the hijackers, and these babies are not murderers."

The man pointed at the babies. "Murderers' spawn," he mumbled. "Same difference."

Cara shook her head. "You know better than that." Her voice was firm. "Listen, we're very sorry about your family, but that's no excuse for attacking innocent people! Now I think you'd just better go away and get hold of yourself."

"There will be retribution," the man insisted, but somewhat to Mark's surprise, he began shuffling away. He watched them, and they watched him, all the way out of the lounge, until he climbed down over the broken edge onto the desert floor outside and disappeared.

"Oh, Mark . . . " Cara sank back onto the couch.

Mark let out his breath. "Remind me to call you the next time I'm in trouble." Then he added sincerely, "No, I mean it, Cara. That was damn good."

She shook her head. "Lucky, that's all. What do you think he means by that retribution stuff? Do you think he'll try something?"

"He's crazy with grief right now. Let's just keep the babies . . . and you, too, Eerin," he added, nodding at the Elpind, "as far away as possible from him, for the moment. He'll snap out of it." He looked down at Terris. Still clinging tightly to Mark's coverall, the baby had fallen asleep with the empty straw dangling from hinsi's mouth. Mark drew it out gently.

"Here are some more," called a voice from outside the lounge. A tall, blond woman peered at them through the rent in the ship's side. "Some guy named Reyvinik is calling a meeting. Outside, up front, in a few minutes. There's a giant rock . . . "

"I know which one," Mark said grimly. "We'll be there."

Sixty-three people, including the two Wopind infants, survived the crash of the *Asimov*. Only two of the ship's crew were among those sixty-three, and they were among the twenty-four who were injured, several critically. Seventeen of the survivors were children, many of whom had lost the parent or parents they were traveling with.

These were the grim statistics reported by the person who'd assumed the leadership role. He identified himself as Jorge Reyvinik, chairman of the largest plastic compounds conglomerate on Earth. With iron-gray hair and a severely trimmed beard, piercing black eyes and a commanding manner, he looked every bit the powerful executive.

Mark remembered seeing him at the party on Captain's Night, but after the hijacking, Reyvinik hadn't been in the common lounge where the terrorists kept their "select" group. *He must not have been taken out of hibernation, or else they kept him in one of the smaller lounges with the other nonhibernating passengers,* Mark decided.

The meeting was emotional. Some of the survivors wept; some babbled; almost all asked questions of Reyvinik as if he were an official flown in to offer direction, not just another passenger who'd crashed with them.

"Will rescuers be looking for us?" was the question most urgently asked.

"I doubt it," Mark called, speaking up for the first time. Everyone turned to him, and he rose to his feet from where he'd been sitting on the ground. Exhaustion was taking its toll; he felt as though he'd been awake for a year, and it was a challenge for him simply to stand up. "Mark Kenner, from StarBridge Academy," he introduced himself. "I was the one the Wospind picked to negotiate for them, and as a result, I was on the bridge when the ship started to go down."

"Can you come up and tell us what happened?" Reyvinik called, beckoning. Wearily Mark walked to the front of the group. Resolutely, he kept his eyes from the smashed, folded-under nose of the *Asimov* as he began relating what had happened those last few minutes. As he spoke, he realized that Cara had moved closer and was filming him.

When he'd finished, Mark sat back down, hearing the crowd murmur until Reyvinik raised his hand for quiet. "So now we know," the older man said. "Communications were destroyed first, so it's probable that no one knows where we are—or even that we've crashed. Simply waiting could be suicide; it appears to me that we've got to actively seek help."

Mark nodded. Reyvinik had cut through to the heart of it. "The question is," the executive said, "where we ought to look for that help. Has anyone ever—"

He paused as Mark waved for his attention. "I was there when one of the hijackers died," he began, "and he gave me and Eerin"—he pointed to his pair partner—"this—" Mark broke off as he heard the sudden chorus of fearful exclamations. "Look!" "It's one of *them*!" "A terrorist—I thought they were all dead!"

"They *are* all dead," Mark said firmly. "Eerin is my pair partner, and we were sent out from StarBridge together, en route to Berytin. It was pure coincidence that Eerin was on board when the hijackers took over the *Asimov*."

Cara spoke up. "I can verify that. I left StarBridge with both Mark and Eerin." The gold sensor patch and her autocam gave her an air of authority. The suspicious, angry murmurs quieted.

"I met Eerin on Captain's Night," Reyvinik said firmly. "And I also can attest that Mr. Kenner is telling the truth. Go on, please." This last was addressed to Mark.

"Anyway, this dying hijacker asked me and Eerin to take his child"—Mark pointed to Terris, clinging to his coverall and fast asleep—"to a nearby settlement. To help us get there, he gave us a plotter map."

Reyvinik leaned over, and Mark handed the little instrument up to him. The executive studied it, frowning, checking their location, then listening intently while Mark summarized the information the dying Wopind had given them.

"I think the injured, any elderly or handicapped, and the children need to stay here for now, with enough people to care for them," said Reyvinik firmly, "but we must send out at least two teams to try and reach these settlements on the map."

"But the main water tank was ruptured," one elderly man spoke up. "All we have is the auxiliary tank to depend on. What if the ones who stay behind run out?"

"If our supplies run low, we can consider moving into the mountains and leaving a trail so rescuers can locate us," Reyvinik said. "But let's hope we don't have to try and cross the desert with the injured and children."

"I'll volunteer to lead a team," a Heeyoon survivor said. "My home is near a desert; they are not unknown to me."

"Good," Reyvinik said. "Anyone else? We should send out a couple of teams toward these settlements. On foot it'll take several days to get to any one of them."

Mark looked over at Eerin and spoke quietly. "When the teams reach these settlements, will the Elspind be able to contact the CLS to tell them what's happened?"

Hin nodded. "Yes. Some villages have CLS researchers stationed there, as part of the sociological program, and they have communications devices, of course. But even the villages that have no CLS researchers can pass messages quickly, either by our system of messenger runners, or, over very long distances, by releasing trained messenger birds. Hin's people will do everything possible to help."

Reyvinik called for agreement to his proposal and got it.

"We'll send a team to each of the two largest settlements that are within reasonable walking distance," he decided. "Once we have both team leaders, I want each of them to choose their own group from volunteers."

"I'll lead a team," said a middle-aged woman. "I'm an archaeologist, and I've spent a lot of time in desert climates." She looked over at Eerin. "Maybe Eerin can give me some background on Elseemar's flora and fauna."

"That is a good idea," said the other, Heeyoon, team leader.

Mark wasn't listening, however. Reyvinik's phrase, "the two largest settlements," had given him pause. "Wait a minute," he said, waving his hand. "Mr. Reyvinik . . . wait a minute!"

"Yes, Mr. Kenner?"

"Those two largest settlements . . . they're Wospind enclaves," Mark said. "The hijacker told us so. They're the *last* places off-worlders should be heading on Elseemar."

Eerin was nodding agreement. "To walk to the nahah would be much safer. The people there are Elspind, and they will help."

Reyvinik looked at them, then slowly shook his head. "You can't be sure that hijacker told you the truth, Mr. Kenner. The nahah is probably the Wospind enclave, and he told you to go there so that his child would be raised by his own people."

Jorge's mouth tightened as he deliberately glanced at the wreckage of the *Asimov*. "Remember, these people were willing to die for their beliefs; it seems reasonable to me that they wouldn't have any compunction about lying for them."

A chorus of "That's right!" and "Of course he was lying!" and "You can't believe a terrorist!" followed the older man's declaration.

"I'm sure the hijacker was telling the truth!" Mark protested. "He swore he was! Dammit, the Wopind was *dying* and all he wanted was for his child to live. He wasn't plotting against us on his deathbed!"

One black man glared at Mark, shaking his head. "Don't be naive, Kenner," he said sarcastically. "That guy would've said anything to get you to take his kid where he wanted it to go. Besides"—he gave Eerin a hard look—"I still think it's a pretty farfetched coincidence that old Eerin here just happened to be on the ship that the Wospind decided to hijack."

"According to the map, we can reach the nahah two to three days before we'd get to any of these settlements," Mark pointed out. "It's crazy not to go there." He gave the group a hard look of his own. "Don't forget, time is survival."

"*You're* crazy to listen to a terrorist" was the response from several sources.

"They are people without civilized ethics, by definition," said a Chhhh-kk-tu. "You cannot expect truth from them."

"He lied so you would take his child back to its own people," said a woman with a baby of her own in her arms.

"Hell, that's what I'd do," said the black man. Heads nodded all around the ragged circle.

Reyvinik looked at Mark. "Frankly, I'd consider it a higher duty, if I were leaving a helpless child behind, to provide for the child. Whatever I had to do!"

"I want to be found, but not by *them*," said another survivor. "Alien fanatics! They'd probably kill us on sight."

Reyvinik listened carefully until the group ran down. "Does anyone else have anything else to offer?"

"Hin's people are not liars," Eerin spoke up for the first time, loud and firm. "Hin is ashamed of what the Wospind did, and hin apologizes for their actions . . . but hin still believes that the Wopind hijacker spoke the truth today. The nahah is the best destination."

"The Elpind is correct," said a loud, harsh voice. It was the big, ruddy Simiu. "Elspind are a truthful people, much the same as my own." The big alien glared at the black man. "Humans, of course, can comprehend little of such honor, but I assure you that it exists in this culture. The hijacker was undoubtedly telling the truth."

The black man's lips tightened, but he remained silent.

Reyvinik chose not to acknowledge the Simiu's insult. He gazed off at the hazy rim of mountains for several minutes, then finally spoke again. "There are good arguments on both sides, and it's a risk either way. I suggest a compromise. Mr. Kenner, will you volunteer to lead a third party to the nahah? That way we'll have covered all the bases."

"All right," Mark said steadily.

Quickly the three leaders chose teams. Mark, of course, selected Eerin and Cara. Then the Elpind gave the Heeyoon and the archaeologist an accelerated course in Elpind plants and animals.

"Mr. Kenner," said Reyvinik, when Eerin was through, "I'd like there to be at least five in each party." Each of the other two teams had seven members.

Mark hesitated, glancing over the crowd. From their expressions, it was obvious that no one else was eager, or even willing, to accompany him. He was about to tell Reyvinik he was happy with his team, small as it was, when the elderly Apis suddenly swooped over the gathered crowd and landed at his side!

Mark regarded her steadily. "Uh . . . I appreciate your gesture, but this is going to be a very difficult journey, uh . . . "

"Her name is R'Thessra, and she is too kind for her own good!" came the Simiu's harsh voice. "She has already had to protect this human who could not defend himself . . . " He glared at the insectoid alien, who regarded him without budging. "Now, apparently, she thinks to make a career of it!"

There were chuckles around the circle.

"I wouldn't want to endanger her," Mark said. "I know she is not young . . . " He trailed off delicately, wondering how the hell he was going to extricate himself from this one.

"She is strong and fit," snarled the Simiu. "And I will accompany her." He glared at the circle of survivors. "I shall see that this group reaches its destination. The rest of you will find only Wospind where you are heading."

Reyvinik smiled wryly. "Your name, Honored Simiu?"

"Hrrakk', if it is any business of yours, human." The name had the distinctive Simiu click on the end.

"Mark, will you take R'Thessra and Hrrakk'?"

Mark sighed and nodded. *I can't insult R'Thessra, and I have to admit, Hrrakk's strength and agility are bound to be a plus . . . but his antihuman attitude is already a royal pain.*

"Fine. That's settled. Let's get some rules laid down for basic organization," Reyvinik said.

It was agreed the walking teams would leave as soon as dusk fell and that, until then, everyone would work together to make sure that the *Asimov* was left in the best possible shape.

Mark was assigned to the group that moved all the injured into the central location of the common lounge and made them as comfortable as possible.

Another, larger team worked at extricating the dead from the wreckage. The bodies would deteriorate rapidly in the heat and, to prevent disease, must be preserved. This was accomplished by placing them in the hibernation containers, which they then activated, powering the units with the ship's solar-powered emergency batteries.

Cara worked with the team that foraged the ship for usable supplies. Food and water shortages were critical. The food servos were now useless, though a few blocks of their basic protein or carbohydrate presynthesized material proved salvageable. Chunks of them would be unpalatable, but edible. They found some fresh vegetables, raised in the hydroponics section as a supplement to the processed food. Most of their rations would come from the *Asimov*'s survival kits.

In the end, the food was rationed out equally, but most of the water was left with the injured, the children, and those who would care for both until help arrived. The walking parties, it was assumed, would find water in the mountains. They were given only enough to ration their way through the short desert portion of the hike.

Clothing, blankets, items that would be useful for camping, medical supplies—all these were collected and divided by Cara's hardworking team.

The journalist assigned herself an additional task. She made a complete circuit of the broken ship, filming wreckage and bodies for the record the authorities would need.

Knowing she would find people out there on the sand that she'd met and liked, Cara steeled herself as she set out. But her professional composure eroded as she recognized face after face, now emptied by death.

Worst of all was when she found Ryan. Cara remembered the times they'd danced together, and could hold back the tears no longer. She filmed his body, thinking of his fiancée, even now waiting eagerly back on Earth, and hoped fervently that the woman never saw this footage.

Cara filmed survivors, too. Their faces, blank with shock, or twisted with raw grief, or tight with pain, were just as hard to bear. Finishing, she wished she could turn her memory off as easily as she'd just ordered off the autocam.

By the time she was finished, she was wrung out, but she forced herself to walk with her head up, her shoulders straight. When she reached the shadow cast by the wrecked ship, she found her friends kneeling on the sand in the middle of a small circle of sorted supplies, methodically cramming two knapsacks.

Mark looked up as she drew near. "We're almost ready. Did you finish filming?"

She nodded, looking around the immediate area. The fear that she'd find, upon returning to her group, one more small body had been haunting her.

"Where is Misir?" she asked, dreading the answer.

Mark caught the tone in her voice and glanced up at her quickly. "The baby's still alive, Cara. But still unconscious." He waved at the pile of supplies. "We were lucky. Our luggage was intact. Time to get changed for the journey. Wear a couple of layers with white on the outside if you can, to protect yourself from the sun. And find something to put over your head." He held up a pair of socks. "Bring extra shoes, and all the socks you can. Changing shoes and socks on a long hike helps prevent blisters."

Cara looked at the outfit Mark had chosen for their trek, loose, white exercise pants, a fuzzy-looking beige sweater, and, over it, a long, loose white shirt.

"Won't that sweater be too hot?"

Mark shrugged. "Don't forget, it gets cold at night in the desert. But I picked this material mostly for Terris. It's almost the same color and texture as hinsi's father was. Easy for hinsi to cling to, also." The baby was still fast asleep.

"I'm surprised they don't fall off when they sleep like that," Cara said. Opening her suitcase, she pawed through it, pulling out her sturdiest clothes. Her hand brushed the silky material of the red party dress and she jerked it away, remembering Ryan again.

After she had changed and packed her chosen clothing, including "borrowing" several pairs of socks from two women who were staying with the ship, Cara rejoined the group, finding Hrrakk' and R'Thessra there ahead of her. The Apis seemed impossibly frail next to his solid bulk. *They're certainly the oddest couple there ever was,* she thought.

Hrrakk' was the largest Simiu Cara had ever seen. His broad, heavy shoulders and the hard planes of muscle in his more lightly furred haunches spoke of a dangerous strength. The top-knotted tail that Simiu carry straight up usually gave them an unintentionally perky or playful look . . . or so Cara had thought when describing the Simiu students at StarBridge. But there was nothing playful about this one; his tail was just another part of his wary alertness.

A rich, bronze mane flowed over the Simiu's shoulders and ran up the back of his head to become a flame-colored crest. Around one massive ankle was a coppery circlet of the sort favored by some Simiu clans. Embedded in it was a huge, deep red gem. The anklet gave Hrrakk' a rakish, rather barbaric air.

When he saw the alien sit down nearby, Mark stood up and made the gesture that was the Simiu greeting sign. It wasn't returned. Hrrakk' squatted on the sand, regarding the humans with unblinking—and unfriendly—violet eyes.

*He's **got** to be from the Harkk'ett clan,* Cara thought sourly, remembering all the pleasant, friendly Simiu she'd met at StarBridge. *Why did we have to be so unlucky as to be stuck* *with him? Dammit, this trip is going to be hard enough!*

Mark squared his shoulders. "It's time to go," he said, in Mizari. "Let's stay within sight of each other, in case anyone needs help. We'll set the best pace we can and with luck, we'll reach the nahah before the other teams reach those Wopind settlements. Maybe the Elspind can help us keep the other two teams from falling into Wopind hands."

His eyes met Cara's with a question, and she nodded to show she was understanding his Mizari, sending him an encouraging smile at the same time. The stiffness in his back told her how uncomfortable he was, taking on the role of leader.

Mark brought out the little plotter map, extending it toward the Simiu. Cara thought for a moment Hrrakk' wouldn't take it, but finally he did. The little instrument was almost lost in the Simiu's huge palm.

"According to the map," Mark was saying, "we'll only have one hard night's hike in the desert to contend with. We'll have to take shelter during the day, but tomorrow night another few hours should see us into the heights. We've got sufficient supplies to take us that far, and there ought to be water in the mountains."

The journalist nodded, thinking of the supplies her work group had divided among the walking teams. Knives, firestarters, a folding multitool, lightweight plastic rope, dual-purpose sheeting, water purification tabs—even makeshift diapers for the babies. The *Asimov*'s large and well-stocked survival kit had provided enough that each of the three teams had a fair share.

"Does anyone have any questions?"

The Simiu did not deign to answer. Contemptuously, he tossed the map back at Mark, who fumbled and nearly dropped the little instrument. The young man flushed, but said nothing.

"I have a question, Mark," Cara said. "Can I carry Misir until hinsi wakes up?" *If hinsi wakes up,* she amended the question silently. She knew that if Misir awoke, she'd have to give the baby to Mark, so he could try to feed hinsi.

Mark nodded, and Cara went to pick up the child, wrapped in one of Mark's blue pullover shirts. Reyvinik came by to wish them luck, then they were ready to leave.

"Let's go," Mark said quietly, then turned and walked slowly away, checking the little plotter. He glanced back once to see whether they were following. They were. Hrrakk' was last of all, but finally he rose off powerful haunches and strode forward on all fours, moving, as Simiu did, like a big dog . . . or a lion. Mark turned back to the ragged line of mountains and began walking in earnest.

Cara followed, and did not look back.

CHAPTER 12

◆

The Desert

Hrrakk' might have been the last to get moving, but Cara soon found herself bringing up the rear. Mark and Eerin set the pace, though the Elpind's tendency to bound rather than walk meant that hin often paused impatiently while Mark caught up.

The Simiu overtook the group easily, loping four-footed, but then he ranged far out to the side. He was neither leading nor following, and his aloofness proclaimed that while he might be going in the same direction, he did not necessarily view himself as a member of the group.

The Apis stayed with Cara, alternately skimming close to the ground, then lifting higher into the air and circling, as if scouting their path. Cara suspected R'Thessra was deliberately holding back to keep her company.

It was a relief to be away from the dead, a relief that Cara guiltily admitted to herself. She felt less tired, more hopeful, and she looked down at the unconscious baby in her arms and sent it a strong thought. *Live, Misir! Try! Life's worth it!*

Cara watched the scenery around her . . . not that there was much to see. Scattered rocks, with occasionally one large enough to qualify as a small boulder, studded the flat, sandy ground. Pale greenish gray tubular plants that fanned out at the top like the Simiu's tail were the only vegetation, and appeared drab and ugly in the failing light.

She liked the mountains, however. As the sun slipped out of sight behind them, the wavering illusion of distance that glare and heat haze had cast vanished. Appearing much closer now, the mountains stood in sharp relief against the darkening sky.

Cara's eyes searched the sky as evening progressed, and she was finally rewarded. There it was, the first of Elseemar's four moons, already up and well into its nightly journey across the sky. It had been too pale to notice before, but now it cast a weak light. She knew from Eerin that when all four moons were up, the night would be brighter than the brightest moonlight back on Earth. Cara was eager to see the multishadow patterns that gave Elseemar its name—"Shadow World."

After the first three hours, Mark called a water break. "Everybody thirsty?" he asked rhetorically, unfastening his canteen. It was one of five allotted to them from the ship's emergency supply.

"We're not counting swallows," Mark told them. "In survival class they teach that you actually need less water if when you do take some, you drink until your thirst is satisfied."

He called out an invitation to the Simiu while Cara drank, but there was no answer from Hrrakk'. The alien had paused when they did, but sat some distance away, his back to them.

"I don't think he'll stay with us long," Cara muttered. "We're going too slow for him."

"As long as the Apis is with us, I think the Simiu will be nearby," Mark said. "I think he must feel some sort of obligation toward her, the way he acts."

"Maybe. Any ideas as to what that obligation could be? I mean"—she smiled—"they're not exactly related."

He shrugged. "I'm betting that there's some story between them, but she *can't* tell us"—he glanced at R'Thessra, delicately sipping from a cup with her long, tubular tongue—"and Hrrakk' *won't*, so we'll probably never know."

"I know that honor is important to Simiu," she said. "But . . . "

"Honor isn't just *important* to them, it's *everything*—their whole culture is based on it," Mark said. "The ancient Japanese honor-code couldn't even begin to approach the way Simiu regard it, although it's the closest parallel we have on Earth."

"We should have given him one of the canteens to carry, if he's too damned stubborn to accept water from us," Cara said, with mingled irritation and concern.

"I guess he'll take it when he gets thirsty enough," Mark said, then glanced sideways at the big alien. "I've got to quit letting his attitude get to me. I'm just not used to aliens disliking me merely because I'm human. That's something I never encountered at StarBridge . . . guess I'm getting my eyes opened."

He pulled a pair of socks out of his knapsack and the hijacker's map out of his pocket. "Let's change socks, Cara. The more frequently you change, the less chance you'll get blisters, and we can't afford any. How are your feet?"

She burrowed through her own pack. "Tired, but not sore."

"How about your feet, Eerin?" he asked.

"Hin has walked farther than this at one time before."

"Not on sand, I'll bet."

"Mark is correct. But hin's feet are fine."

He glanced at R'Thessra. "How about you? Doing okay?"

The winged alien wriggled her antennae vigorously and buzzed.

He smiled at her. "Does that mean yes?" She repeated the motion and sounds, and he grinned and nodded. "I guess it does. Let's check the map."

Cara peered over his arm at the small instrument. Mark had set it for hourly input and update, so now their own position glowed on the map as a tiny red dot. It looked impossibly far from the white flicker that was the mountain nahah. But at least they were on course.

"Everybody okay? Ready to go?" Mark asked.

The journalist wished grumpily that he'd quit prefacing his questions with "everybody." The Apis couldn't answer, the babies couldn't answer, Eerin was uncharacteristically silent, and the Simiu wasn't present to answer.

"Ready," she said with a sigh.

The little group walked steadily for hours in the vast quiet of the desert. As the night and the silence grew deeper, Mark began to feel that even his breathing was too loud.

The four moons in their separate orbits were all up, each at a different point in the sky. Their light was far easier to bear than the eye-hurting glare of day, but it seemed unnaturally bright, and thus disturbing to a human. It brought home as nothing else could have done that he was here, on an alien world, one of only a handful of his own people. He felt very isolated.

The moons' light was so bright it washed out all but the brightest of the stars, and Mark found himself missing those points of light. At StarBridge, he'd gotten used to having the stars as constant, close-appearing friends. Their lack made him feel even lonelier.

It's the shadows, he thought. *They're the most alien thing of all . . .*

The intensity of the moons' light gave them a sharp-edged clarity, and as the moons moved, objects cast multiple shadows . . . double, triple, and even quadruple shadows, each cast in a slightly different direction. They shifted and flowed eerily in the colorless clarity of the night, sometimes overlapping to form pools of lightlessness deeper than dark.

As he walked, pushing himself to maintain a steady pace, feeling the brief surge of energy that eating and resting before embarking on their journey had given him trickle away, Mark found himself wondering whether Elspind believed in the supernatural.

Are there ghosts on Elseemar? he mused groggily, half drunk with weariness. *I never saw a more appropriate place for them. And even if the Elspind don't become specters after death, there are certainly enough off-worlders who died here today to provide plenty of haunts . . .*

Biting his lip, he brought himself up short. *Talk about morbid, Kenner!*

To distract himself, he pulled back his shirt flap and checked Terris. The baby slept soundly. No distraction there.

Mark looked ahead thoughtfully at Eerin's back, silvered by the moonlight. As the hours had passed and Mark tired, the Elpind's light, quick step kept hin ever farther ahead of the human.

"Eerin," Mark called softly. His voice sounded strange, echoing in the silence. Eerin dropped back to his side.

"We haven't had a chance to really talk since the hijackers pulled me and Cara out of hibernation," Mark said. "Let's use Elspindlor, okay? I need to keep practicing; it will probably be useful at the nahah."

Eerin nodded, but waited for the human to speak first.

"Uh . . . tonight, you've seemed kind of . . . quiet," Mark began. "Is everything okay? Are you sure that guy didn't hurt you?"

"Hin is not hurt," Eerin hesitated. "But . . . Mark was correct to advise hin not to dance. Hin thought hin was only risking hin's own life. But Cara could have been hurt . . . or the hinsi."

"But they weren't," Mark reassured the alien. "And I have a feeling you needed to dance the Mortenwol very badly. For yourself, not for the hijacker," he clarified.

Amazement colored the Elpind's tone. "Mark knew that?"

"Not at the time. I didn't stop to think about the hell you'd been through and the fact that you probably hadn't had the chance to dance it in several days, not since the Wospind boarded. But even before I went into hibernation, the Mortenwol was something I wanted to talk to you about."

"Hin thought that Mark did not enjoy discussing the death dance, or the reasons for it."

"Well . . . I didn't," Mark confessed. "But I was wrong not to be more accepting. The Mortenwol is an important part of your culture . . . and I'm trying to understand it, I really am. Death just isn't something I'm handling very well these days." He took a deep breath. "The only way I got through the hijacking and the events of today was concentrating on saving those who still lived—and not thinking about the ones who died."

"Today was difficult for all, including hin," the Elpind said gently. "Mark must believe that hin's people do not rejoice in death. But Elspind try to be ready, more so than Mark's people . . . that is the largest difference between us."

"It's certainly a big one," Mark admitted.

"But it is not death that Mark is having a difficult time accepting," Eerin added quietly. "It is life. Mark cannot celebrate life when heen is running from it. Running from everything, even StarBridge."

Mark gaped at the Elpind, speechless. *Damn! Rob Gable*

couldn't have put it any more plainly! "I didn't think you knew that I was leaving the Academy," he said finally.

"Hin knew. But that decision is only the most visible sign of Mark's running, is it not?"

The human studied the Elpind thoughtfully. The huge eyes shone back at him in the bright moonlight, steady, full of faith. "I hadn't really thought about it like that," he said at last.

They walked together in silence for a while.

"Eerin?"

"Yes?"

"Is it my trouble accepting your beliefs that's bothering you, making you so quiet?"

"No. That is not it."

"Then what's wrong? Can you tell me?"

The Elpind hesitated, obviously distressed, then finally blurted, "Hin is sorrowful and angry that hin's own people would intentionally harm others, *kill* others. It is shameful!"

"There are twisted criminal people on every world," Mark told the Elpind. "I've even heard legends that the person who controls Sorrow Sector, the big boss, is a Mizari, so even *they* aren't perfect—though most of them I've met seem to come damn close. But Orim's and the other Wospind's actions don't mean that off-worlders are going to judge the Elspind by them."

The Elpind gave a very human-sounding sigh of relief. "That is comforting to hear. Tell hin, Mark . . . "

"Yes?"

"During the meeting after the crash, Mark told of how Orim's decision to kill two passengers ahead of the deadline brought about hin's downfall, and the crash of the ship. But what caused the Wopind's sudden anger, hin's decision? Mark did not say."

"I guess I can tell you in private," the human said, lapsing into English. "I'm afraid your WirElspind really made a mess of things, Eerin."

"Explain, please."

Mark did. Eerin shook hin's downy head sorrowfully. "Hin has no difficulty seeing how it must have been. Hin has known Alanor for years. Now hin must also feel shame for the stupidity of hin's people. The First Speaker has never been what hin would call . . . insightful." Eerin's voice was dry.

"Well, stupidity was certainly not Orim's problem. It's a shame that hin was so radical," Mark said. "Hin was obviously extremely intelligent, organizing the Wospind the way hin did, plotting to steal the shuttle and figuring out how to lure in the *Asimov* . . . I suppose Orim made the Heeyoon pilot tell hin everything about how the weapons worked."

"Orim had obviously practiced," Eerin agreed bitterly.

"Yes . . . " Mark was still thinking. "I wonder where the guns they used to hijack the ship initially came from? A couple of those weapons were Heeyoon, but most of them were of human manufacture. Stolen from the *Asimov*'s arms locker, I guess."

"Perhaps the Heeyoon shuttle also had an arms locker."

"I guess it's possible, though CLS-sponsored missions to a world aren't supposed to," Mark said. "I guess we'll never know. Orim is dead. It's too bad . . . I talked hin into letting the *Asimov* go, you know." *I really did,* he thought, suddenly remembering all those hours of negotiation that had finally begun to pay off—until Alanor's words had destroyed his efforts.

"Hin has no difficulty believing that," Eerin said. "Mark Kenner is a StarBridge interrelator."

"Soon to be a StarBridge dropout," Mark reminded the Elpind lightly. "But thanks for the vote of confidence."

"Hin has always believed, contrary to the opinions of most of the WirElspind, that giving the Wospind a voice in the Great Council is the right path to take," Eerin said regretfully. "Perhaps *now* the WirElspind will listen."

"Not if Alanor is any example, they won't." Mark's voice was grim. "But you're right in saying that if the Wospind and the Elspind don't start talking, compromising, then this Elhanin issue is only going to get worse before it gets better."

Eerin nodded. "Hin will do what hin can to bring about such talking," the Elpind promised. "Hin believes that the question of whether to take Elhanin should be every Elpind's own choice."

"I agree. You said your sibling Lieor wanted to take it. Would *you* take it, Eerin?" Mark asked, gazing intently at the Elpind in the moons' light.

The Elpind's gaze was equally level as Eerin shook hin's head. "No. Hin will not. Hin wishes to experience hin's life-cycle as nature intends hin to live it."

Mark swallowed a dozen protests. He didn't have the right to try to change the Elpind's mind. But oh, how he wanted to!

He was still groping for words when he felt a vigorous wiggling and squirming against his chest. Mark looked under his shirt flap. A pair of round, alert eyes looked back.

Terris made an expectant sound, plucking at Mark's sweater with surprising force for such a small creature. The high-pitched sound was repeated, this time louder.

"Hinsi feels hunger," Eerin observed.

"No kidding! I'm glad it's this sweater and not the hair on my chest that hinsi's yanking," Mark said, and stopped. "Feeding break," he announced to Cara when she caught up. He changed the baby's diaper, then dug one of the straws out of the knapsack.

There was no hesitation this time. Mark was barely able to get his fingers out of the way after breaking off the tip before the infant's jaws clamped the straw and began to suck mightily.

Mark stroked the baby's head affectionately, but he couldn't help glancing at the bundle in Cara's arms. No sound or movement yet from Misir. Something was seriously wrong with hinsi, and he hoped Cara was steeling herself to face the little Elpind's death. The thought made his own throat tighten painfully.

"Let's go," he said abruptly. "I'll feed hinsi as I walk."

Hrrakk' had not paused with the others, and now he was substantially ahead. Mark contemplated the Simiu's four-footed amble that was surprisingly rapid, though Hrrakk' didn't seem to be pushing. *If he gets much farther ahead, he'll be out of sight,* he thought.

Maybe he'd been wrong in thinking Hrrakk' would stay with them as long as the Apis did. R'Thessra had stayed beside Cara, and the Simiu had paid her no attention at all. *If he gets out of sight, it may be that that's the last we'll see of him.*

Mark wasn't sure how he felt about that. If Hrrakk' chose to stay with and become part of the group, however, there was one thing he did know. The question of "who's in charge" would, inevitably, come up, in spite of the fact that Reyvinik had given Mark the designation of team leader. He dreaded the thought of such a confrontation.

Against his chest, Terris squirmed again and exhaled gustily. The straw was limp.

"Hey, good work, Terris," said Mark softly. The baby regarded him with a bright, penetrating gaze, then reached up to brush hinsi's fingers against his chin, almost as if hinsi were patting him. Touched, Mark stroked the infant's back, took a deep, cleansing breath, and quickened his step just a little.

Three of the four moons were already gone. The last one floated low in the sky, about to sink out of sight behind the mountains.

Mark had kept his eyes on it for a while now, watching it dim, using it as a beacon, and trying not to notice the growing ache in his legs. Finally, though, he looked behind him to check on Cara and the Apis. That was how he caught the first ray of the rising sun in his eyes.

There was nothing to soften the impact as the glaring curve of Elseemar's star leaned up over the flat desert horizon. Mark narrowed his eyes with an involuntary wince, and when he looked again, carefully shading his eyes, the whole burning disk had popped up into view.

"Don't slow up," called Mark, more to himself than to the group. His throat felt dry and sore, but he didn't suggest another water break yet. Their five canteens weren't large, and their one water break in the night had emptied one, and most of another. "It won't get hot for a while. Let's keep going just a little longer."

Three of the longest hours of Mark's life crawled by. The ache spread from his legs to his whole body. Sweat slicked his skin and made his clothes clammy. He was exhausted and thirsty to the point of pain.

Halting, he pulled out the almost-empty canteen and the third, still-full one and waited for Cara to catch up. She was plodding doggedly, not looking up, concentrating on not breaking stride. Her Apis shadow looked bedraggled. Even Eerin drooped.

When the canteen came back to him, Mark held it up in the Simiu's direction. Hrrakk' had not, after all, pulled completely out of sight. In fact, he seemed to be drifting closer, though they were still too far apart for Mark to see the Simiu's face. He hoped Hrrakk' could make out the canteen; his throat hurt too much to yell this time.

But once again there was no response.

Mark sighed and repacked the now half-full third canteen.

"Can we stop now?" Cara's voice had a pleading note.

He nodded. "We've done better than I'd hoped." Wiping his burning eyes, he added frankly, "And I'm beat."

Cara looked relieved. She studied the immediate area. "Over there," she said, pointing. "Those rocks are high enough to give us a decent lean-to if we angle our sheeting off them."

Mark nodded and pawed through his knapsack for the dual-purpose sheeting that was standard survival gear.

"Mark can make shade," said Eerin, "but even so, the temperature will be too hot in the middle of the day."

Mark looked sharply at the Elpind, wondering if he'd just imagined a strange note, like dread, in his pair partner's voice. He saw nothing in the golden eyes, however, but the Elpind's normal curiosity and eagerness to solve a problem.

"The silver side of the sheeting reflects sun. It will make shade that's cooler than natural shade," Mark explained. "But you've got a point. Survival courses say not to rest on the surface of desert ground if you can help it. If we could dig a meter-deep east-west trench, the sand at the bottom would be as much as thirty or forty degrees cooler. Trouble is"—he frowned—"digging a trench big enough for all of us would take a lot of time. Especially with only one digging tool."

"It would take more than time and tools," Cara said. "It would take a hell of a lot of energy. Which I don't have at the moment."

"We'll compromise," Mark said with smile at Eerin. "We'll dig a *shallow* trench, and hope that will be at least ten degrees cooler, okay?"

Mark, Cara, and Eerin rigged two lean-to shelters, then took turns scooping up the soil in their shade to a depth of about thirty centimeters. It was worth the extra effort—under the reflective sheeting, in the trench, it seemed almost comfortable. While they worked, the Simiu squatted on his haunches some distance away, watching.

"Here's an invitation he can't refuse," Mark muttered as they finished. Then he called out in Mizari for Hrrakk' to join the group in the newly made shelters.

The huge alien slowly rose and moved toward them, but he stopped again about thirty meters away from where Mark stood. Cara and the others had already crawled under the sheeting; they watched from the shade.

"What's he doing?" asked Cara.

Hrrakk' had taken a two-handed hold near the bottom of the smooth trunk of a large plant. He heaved upward, trying to yank it out of the ground. The plant quivered and lurched under his assault, but remained firmly embedded in the ground.

"Rarely are Elspind caught in the desert; we avoid it if at all possible. But there are some old Tellings that mention these plants can make a shelter," Eerin offered. "Elspind cannot pull them out of the ground, however. We must dig."

"Shelter?"

"Actually, it is the hole that is left that provides the shelter. The roots of the tasrel plant go very deep."

"This one may have to be dug up, too," Mark said, watching the Simiu struggle. "Dammit! Why can't he get under the sheeting with the rest of us?"

Then he sighed and added, "Oh, well, maybe this is a chance to build some goodwill." Grabbing the multitool, he trudged over to the Simiu, who ignored his approach. Hrrakk' was still heaving mightily with no sign of progress.

"I'll help you," Mark said, loosening the soil around the plant with the tool. "Maybe if both of us pull . . . "

The Simiu didn't reply, but he paused while Mark knelt and grabbed the trunk just below the spot where Hrrakk' had it in a death grip. The plant's stem was as big around as the human's forearm, and it bushed out roundly with pale, tubular shoots from its top all the way down to the ground.

Hrrakk' gathered breath and timed his next powerful heave to coordinate with the human's effort. Together they pulled and strained and tugged and panted . . . then heaved again.

The bushy growth began to rock loose and then came up so suddenly that Mark sat unexpectedly on his backside. Terris yelped indignantly at the jolt. Chuckling weakly, Mark released the trowel attachment on the multitool and, still sitting, began to dig at the hole.

The alien plant's root system had grown both deep and wide, deep to tap into the cool moisture that lingered far below the hot sand, widespread to trap the maximum amount of scant evening dew. The depression that the pulled-up roots left was a good one, but not large enough to hold an adult Simiu. The sandy ground was well loosened, however. Mark, with the digging tool, and Hrrakk', with his powerful muscles, were able to enlarge the hole to the required size in a few minutes of concentrated labor.

Still, the Simiu had not spoken.

The sand infiltrated Mark's clothes and stuck to his sweaty flesh. He hurt all over, and he was trembling now with exhaustion. With a painful grunt he pushed to his feet as soon as the Simiu stopped scooping sand.

Hrrakk' didn't even look at him. He was already clambering into the hole and pulling the bushy stalk over it as a cover.

Mark shrugged and turned away. *So much for goodwill.*

"Mark!" Cara's yell carried surprise and unmistakable joy. "Look! Misir's awake!"

It was true. The infant's eyes, golden like Eerin's, were open. Cara was ecstatic. "I knew it! I knew this baby would wake up!"

Cara loosened the blue jersey wrapped around the baby. Four little limbs waved feebly in the air, and four people—two humans, an Elpind, and an Apis—shared delighted looks with one another. After so much death, there was incredible triumph in the stirring of this tiny spark into flame; it lent them energy.

"Terris, buddy, are you ready for some company?" Mark asked. "I'll bet little Misir is hungry."

Eerin had the straw out already. Cara dropped a gentle kiss on the baby's fuzzy head. "I'm going to miss carrying you," she said softly, "but it's time for Mark to take you."

The young man scooped up the fragile creature carefully.

A terrible screech and a wild scrabbling at his chest nearly caused him to drop Misir. Then a spitting fury of honey-brown fur landed right on the sick baby.

"Terris! Stop! Stop it, Terris!"

Mark tried to pull the frantic child off Misir with one hand. Cara reached under the struggle and slid the infant to safety as soon as Terris' grip loosened. She clutched it to her chest as it began to whimper weakly.

"What the hell was that all about?" Mark demanded, trying to soothe Terris, who was still screaming indignantly.

Eerin shook hin's head worriedly. "Hin has seen this happen only once before. Usually a nursing heen adopts the hinsi of a dead father with no difficulty; both infants thrive. That particular time, however, the child born to the nursing heen rejected the new infant so violently that the adoption had to be canceled. A different heen had to be found for the orphan."

"You said you've only seen this once. But have you heard of it happening to other people?"

Eerin nodded reluctantly. "It is rare, but hin has heard others speak of it."

"What causes it?"

"No one knows; it is a thing that cannot be predicted. Perhaps, in this case, by accepting Mark's different body chemistry, Terris has already made all the adjustment hinsi can handle."

"Let's try again," Cara suggested. "Maybe we just caught Terris by surprise."

Mark nodded. "Look, Terris," he crooned softly, leaning over to gradually close the distance between the two children. "A sibling for you. See the baby. We're going to . . . "

Terris squalled in renewed frenzy, twisting and clawing at Mark. Cara pulled Misir back hurriedly. Mark stared at the babies, frustrated and exhausted. "Shit! What now?"

"Mark will not be able to care for both hinsi," Eerin stated the obvious.

"But . . . we have to feed Misir!" Cara's eyes filled.

"There's only one other heen available, and that's Hrrakk'," Mark said slowly.

"Oh, God," Cara said. "Do you think he would do it?"

Three pairs of eyes, brown, golden, and faceted, watched Mark anxiously.

"He'll have to," Mark said grimly. "I'll tell him so."

Crawling out of the shelter after the relative coolness was

like plunging into a furnace. Mark could hardly bear to breathe as he wavered to his feet.

Cara peered up at him from under the sheeting. "He can't refuse. You helped him with the plant," she pointed out. "Honor would say he owes you one."

"Maybe," Mark said, and stumbled toward the Simiu's "shelter." This was the confrontation he dreaded . . . or close enough. Falling, more than kneeling, at the edge of the Simiu's hole, he spoke in Mizari to the uprooted plant that covered it.

"Honored Hrrakk'! I must speak with you."

A fierce-looking head rose up out of the sand. The fleshy leaves draped over it would have looked laughable, if it had been anyone else's face. But the Simiu's violet eyes held only disdain and impatience.

"The Elpind baby who's been unconscious since the crash . . . hinsi is finally awake."

"Of what concern is that to me, human?"

Mark quickly explained the problem. "There are only two males in this group. The baby's got to be fed, and will only take food from a male," he concluded, finally. "Since I can't take Misir—that's hinsi's name—that leaves you."

"No," said Hrrakk' flatly.

Mark was stunned. "But . . . unless you do, Misir will die!"

"I have seen that child," Hrrakk' said. "It will die no matter what. There is no honor in attempting to prolong a life that has no hope."

"But . . . we have to *try*, Honored Hrrakk'!"

"I do not have to try. I am going to sleep." Hrrakk' started to slide back down in his hole.

Desperately Mark gathered nerve he wasn't sure he had for the leadership showdown. "Everybody pulls their own weight on this trip, Hrrakk'. You knew that before we started out. You're part of the group, like it or not. You *can't* refuse to help!"

The glitter in the alien's eyes was now clearly one of anger, and the bronze crest on top of his head flattened. Mark could see the flash of his enormous canines as the alien's muzzle lifted in what was almost a snarl of challenge. "You are impugning my honor, human, and that is not wise. Be warned."

Mark glared back, his initial nervousness lost now in his own anger. "Maybe Misir *is* fated to die, but you'll never know whether hinsi could have lived, unless you help! Refusing this request is like going over there and killing that baby with your own hands! Where's the honor in that?"

Hrrakk's eyes narrowed, but he controlled himself with a palpable effort. "You know nothing of Simiu honor! Leave now!"

Mark's eyes wavered, then fell. "You are right, I am not well versed in the nuances of the Simiu honor-code," he admitted. "But"—his eyes returned to lock with Hrrakk's—"I will learn more of the Simiu," he promised fiercely, "and someday I *will* know whether your honor-code truly demanded that you refuse to help."

He knew that judging alien actions in terms of human morality and ethics was wrong, but nothing could make him regard the prospect of Misir's death as anything but a tragedy. Mark glared at the Simiu. "Someday I will know," he repeated, then scrambled to his feet, and, despite his weakness, stood firm. "Until the day when I will know," he switched into the highest Mizari dialect, the tongue of formality, "I grieve. I sorrow for your honor, as well as my own, that, between us, we must let the child die."

Mark felt Hrrakk's stare boring into his back as he walked away. He shook his head as he crawled back into the shelter. Cara's eyes widened with horror. "Oh, Mark! He couldn't refuse!"

"Well, he did." Mark looked at the Elpind. "Eerin, you've got to try to feed hinsi. At least you're an Elpind. Maybe that's all that will matter this time. The baby may be too weak to care whether you're han or heen or hin or anything else."

"Hin cannot. The chemistry is wrong. Hin has told Mark."

"We have to *try*!"

Eerin gave him a tolerant look underlaid with sadness, but made the attempt. Hin's careful and repeated efforts to coax the straw into the baby's mouth, however, proved futile. Misir's jaws remained locked shut.

"Okay." Mark sighed. "You were right." He stared at Misir, trying to think of a solution.

"It is Elpind biology," Eerin said miserably. "Hin cannot—"

"Give me the child," a deep voice broke in. Hrrakk' reached down into the shelter and practically snatched Misir, holding the baby against his massive chest with one hand.

The Elpind missed only a beat before reaching up and handing over the feeding straw as well. Mark admired hin's poise. His own mouth was hanging open, and he hastily shut it.

"Sleep!" barked Hrrakk'. "We must travel again soon." He turned and marched back to his hole.

"Do you think he'll be gentle with Misir?" Cara asked worriedly. "Hinsi is so tiny . . . "

Mark was tempted to go see for himself but, given the Simiu's temper and unpredictability, feared that any interference might cause Hrrakk' to change his mind again. "Since he took the child, honor demands that he treat it well," he said slowly. "Simiu clans are very nurturing, I know that." He yawned despite himself. "Cara . . . Hrrakk' was right. We've got to sleep."

Mark and Eerin took one shelter, Cara and the Apis, the other. It occurred to the student that the Elpind would be very impatient with this time wasted; there was nothing to occupy hin's attention while the rest of the party slept. The layover couldn't be helped, though; even the Elpind seemed eager to stay out of the sun.

Mark pulled off his socks and boots, groaning as the sweaty socks peeled from the sore bottoms of his feet. He massaged them, wiggling his toes vigorously.

"I hope Terris didn't sleep so much during the night that hinsi can't sleep now." Mark lay down, squirming into a comfortable position in the trench. Terris levered up from his chest on pipe-stem arms, inspecting the shelter alertly.

Mark watched that unbridled curiosity, so like Eerin's, with a smile, but part of his mind was with the Simiu. "Wonder what made Hrrakk' change his mind?" he asked his pair partner.

"Mark does not believe it is something he said?"

"Maybe. I was really angry, and I let him know it. But there's a lot we don't know about Hrrakk' . . . " He tried to concentrate on an odd, nebulous feeling he had about Hrrakk', but couldn't hold it long enough to define the thought. Sleep was falling over him like a muffling blanket.

Mark closed his sun-sore eyes and knew nothing more.

CHAPTER 13

◆

The Intruder

Mark dreamed, and it was his old nightmare. Slowly, slowly, he came to a door. Blood seeped out from under it onto his bare feet. *Jon is dead. My fault!*

Only this time, when he opened the door, there was a broken ship behind it and, around the ship, dozens and dozens of bodies. Each body was his mother's.

The roar of a wild animal suddenly shattered both the silence and the dream, and Mark woke, heart pounding. Outside he could hear a voice cursing and screaming incoherently in English. There came another wordless roar, then a guttural stream of Simiu words that Mark, of course, couldn't understand. *Hrrakk'! What's going on? Who's out there?*

Terris squawked in fear as Mark bolted up and scuttled out of the shelter, his heart slamming.

He was halfway out of the lean-to when he heard the solid smack of flesh meeting flesh. He looked up, frozen with shock.

The burly man who'd attacked Eerin back at the ship sprawled unconscious on the ground. Over him stood Hrrakk', clutching the Elpind baby in one huge hand, the other hand still half raised and ready to strike again, and strewn on the ground—

Oh, dear God, No!

—were shards that glimmered bright green in the late afternoon sunlight. The babies' feeding straws. Broken.

A piece of green tube still lay in the palm of one of the man's outflung hands, thick, gray fluid coating the lax fingers.

Cara emerged, rubbing her eyes, then gave a choked, horrified cry. "Oh, no! Look what that bastard did! Are there any left?"

Eerin was already searching. "No," hin said grimly.

Feeling sick to his stomach, Mark knelt and helped the Elpind look a second time. *What are we going to do? We're still days from the nahah!*

Not a single straw had survived.

He scrabbled through the pieces, trying to find any of the liquid that wasn't befouled with sand, but the man had done a thorough job, crushing the pieces and squeezing out the liquid onto the thirsty sand.

Guilt and anger churned inside Mark. He rose, crossed over to Hrrakk', and looked down at the unconscious man. A red mark showed clearly on his face where one powerful blow from the Simiu had knocked him out. *Too bad,* Mark thought coldly, *that Hrrakk' didn't kill him.* He was too angry to be horrified at his wish.

"What happened?" he asked in Mizari.

"Do you not have eyes, human? I awoke when I heard this honorless *thing* babbling as he ripped the straws to shreds. Where were you?"

Mark wished he had a better answer than the obvious one. The supplement straws had been in his knapsack, beside him in the shelter. If only he'd awakened when the man had reached in . . .

But Eerin had been there. Mark swung around to the Elpind. "Eerin . . . where were you?"

Hin hesitated. "Hin was asleep also," the Elpind finally admitted.

Cara's eyes widened. "But—Eerin—I thought Elspind never sleep!"

"There are certain times in the lifecycle that an Elpind's body must gather energy in the same way as a human's does . . .and certain conditions that cause that need also. Great heat is one of them. Hin fell asleep, just as Mark did." The Elpind seemed apologetic.

"Well . . . are you okay?" Mark asked worriedly. He had the feeling there was more that Eerin wasn't telling him.

"Hin is fine," Eerin said hastily.

"What are we going to do about the babies?" Cara asked.

"The first thing we can do is give them some water," Mark declared. "Living beings die of dehydration long before they do of starvation. If the hinsi aren't getting their liquids from their feedings, they'll have to have water."

They managed to rig a feeding straw from a bit of plastic wrapper, then gave Terris water. Hinsi sucked it up eagerly, but Misir would only take a few drops from Hrrakk'. "I awoke earlier, when this hinsi stirred," the Simiu said, "to change hinsi. At that time, I gave the child the remainder of the earlier feeding in the middle of the afternoon." The Simiu shook his head. "It is unfortunate that I then slept again," he said with a black glare at the intruder.

"Well, at least hinsi has had something today," Mark said, but the big alien shook his head, and his violet eyes were bleak.

"The feeding did not stay down," Hrrakk' reported.

"Oh," Mark said. Cara looked ready to cry.

Terris squawked and burrowed in Mark's sweater, making hinsi's distinctive "I'm hungry" noise. "Uh-oh," Mark said, stroking the baby. "Hinsi's hungry. We've got to figure out something to feed these babies!"

"There is nothing," Eerin said sadly. "Their systems cannot tolerate any of the substances we have. They will die."

"Not if I can help it!" Mark said grimly.

"It is Elpind biology."

"I'm sick of hearing about Elpind biology!" the human snapped. "Dammit, Eerin, these babies didn't live through that crash just to die here in the desert. We're going to keep them alive until we reach the nahah!"

Mark saw the Elpind's golden gaze soften and give way in affectionate understanding of a friend's stubbornness. He smiled in rueful acknowledgment at his pair partner.

"Let's try mashing up one of our concentrate bars with a little water," Cara suggested.

He nodded. "They might eat that. We'd better have some food and water ourselves." Mark felt as if every bit of moisture had been baked out of him while he slept.

"I'll get the concentrate," Cara volunteered.

Mark nodded, then sighed, studying the man at his feet. "He shouldn't be out this long. He must have walked all day in the heat to catch up with us. Probably dehydrated. Bad sunburn, too. I guess we'll have to give him some of our water." He heard the reluctance in his own voice.

It galled him to share their small supply with this man, but he had no other choice . . . did he? Mark resolutely pushed away temptation and fetched the canteen. Carefully he dribbled a little water between the man's cracked and blistered lips, seeing him swallow eagerly. Tight-lipped with anger, Mark gave him more, begrudging every swallow. He took the canteen away after a few sips, then sat back on his heels.

The man struggled up and stared dully around him, until his wandering gaze stopped on Terris, clinging to Mark's chest. "Murderer's spawn . . . " he whispered, eyes brightening with hate. "Kill the murderer's spawn. Retribution . . . eye for an eye, life for a life . . . " His words trailed off into inarticulate mumbling.

"What is he saying?" Hrrakk' asked.

"You don't want to know," Mark said. "He's crazy . . . not responsible for his own actions."

"Like Simon Viorst who, sixteen years ago, caused the death of one of my people after they had welcomed in friendship your vessel *Désirée*?" growled Hrrakk'. "Not responsible like that?"

Mark shrugged. "Yeah, I suppose so," he muttered.

"You humans excuse the most heinous crimes with that phrase 'not responsible'!" Hrrakk' glared at him, the violet eyes filled with contempt. "Of *course* this honorless *dragkk'* is responsible! Who else walked through the desert with death filling his thoughts and the wish to kill the innocent driving him?" The Simiu gave a disgusted grunt. "I only regret that I did not strike harder, and thus remove this one from his miserable, honorless existence when I had the opportunity."

I was just thinking the same thing, Mark thought sourly. "Well, unless you want to kill him now in cold blood, that opportunity is past," he said bitterly. "I guess we're stuck with him. We'll have to tie him up and take him along."

"We could leave him here in the desert," Hrrakk' suggested.

"We could, but how do we know he won't sneak up on us again?" Mark asked. "Besides, Honored Hrrakk' "—he held the alien's gaze with his own—"that would be the same thing as murder, and you know it as well as I do."

The alien nodded. "I do," he conceded. "My honor would not permit that, even had you been willing."

He was testing me! Mark's lips tightened angrily. "Sorry to disappoint you," he said aloud. "Maybe I have my own kind of honor, ever think of that?"

The man did not resist as they hauled him to his feet and bound his hands behind him, nor did he speak again. His eyes seemed slightly more lucid, however. "Do you know what you've done?" Mark demanded angrily. "You destroyed all the babies' food! Now they may die!"

The man's expression remained blank. Mark could not tell if he even heard the accusation.

"Why did heen do it?" Eerin asked, speaking for the first time as Cara returned with the food.

"I think he's cracked from the grief," Mark said, taking a bite from the concentrate bar the journalist held out.

Elpind curiosity surged forth. "Hin does not see cracks," said Eerin, looking hard for some.

"Mark means that he's gone insane," Cara translated automatically. She waved a hand before the man's face, trying to get his attention. "Hey, what is your name? I'm Cara. Can you hear me?"

No response.

The next half hour was a flurry of activity. They took down and stowed the sheeting. Cara and Mark ate several of the dry, tasteless food bars that were standard survival ration while the Apis sucked juice from a hydroponics-grown orange, and Eerin stuck the sucked-dry pulp under hin's tongue after the Apis was through. Everyone except Hrrakk' drank several healthy swallows of water, including Terris and the new addition to their group. Misir took only two tiny sips, despite all their efforts.

Both babies adamantly refused the liquefied concentrate. Terris made a face and spat it back out, then turned hinsi's head away. Misir simply would not suck, and drops they squeezed into hinsi's mouth drooled or gagged back out, even when Hrrakk' stroked the downy throat to engage the swallowing reflex. In Misir's case, Mark suspected the results would have been the same, whatever the food.

Hrrakk' gently rubbed the baby's fragile arms and legs. The massage started Misir's limbs moving feebly. Next the Simiu held the infant up to his massive shoulder, rubbing the tiny body against his fur. He was trying to encourage the child to take hold with hands and feet for transport.

Misir nuzzled hinsi's head against the Simiu's thick, coarse hair. Instinct stirred, and all four limbs reached out and grasped as they were supposed to.

But only for a second.

Misir's body sagged and fell. Fortunately, Hrrakk' had cupped one huge hand beneath the child, and caught hinsi.

No one spoke as Hrrakk' rigged a small sling from the blue jersey, knotted it around the strap of his travel pack, hung it over his shoulder against his chest, then slid the baby inside.

Eerin pulled out hin's kareen. "Hin wishes to dance the Mortenwol," the Elpind said hesitantly.

Mark could think of several reasons to object: time, further depletion of Eerin's water reserves, the possibility that hin's dancing would set their captive off again. But he remembered how important this was to Eerin and merely nodded silently. *We all need a boost,* he thought. *Maybe it will help.*

Out came the feathers of red and green and blue and that breathtaking white one. Eerin flicked them this way and that, and they were a headpiece. Hin wound, then activated, the music board. The first sweet, high-pitched note swelled out.

Eerin dipped hin's downy head in an oddly moving gesture that Mark realized was directed at the two hinsi, then bent, turning slightly. Halfway through the turn, hin rose cleanly, gently into the pellucid air of sunset. Joyfully the music gathered strength, tumbling and trilling and leaping over itself with melodic runs. The Elpind somehow both followed and soared over the patterns. Every movement seemed both crisp and subtle, controlled and yet so free, so known and dearly familiar to the dancer and yet so just-born new.

Mark watched, feeling sadness instead of the energy boost he'd hoped for. *Today it's particularly important to perform the Mortenwol,* he thought, remembering Eerin's half salute at the beginning, then glancing at the feebly moving bundle slung against Hrrakk's broad chest. *Misir may need it . . .*

As he watched, he also remembered last night's conversation with Eerin. Given the choice, his friend would choose an early over a postponed death. He knew the Elpind didn't quite look at it that way, but that's how it seemed to him. *Don't judge,* he reminded himself fiercely. *It's not your place to judge.*

"I wonder," Cara said quietly, watching as Eerin began the final leaps, "whether all Elspind revere life so much."

"Seems to me they revere death," Mark said bitterly.

She shook her head. "I know that's how it seems, but, Mark, that dance is about *life*. That it's good and filled with hope . . . and that today will be a joy to live."

Mark sighed. Cara obviously understood far better than he did—and *he* was the one with the training in relating to alien cultures. *Just more proof that I was right in deciding to leave StarBridge,* he thought. *I really* **have** *lost the empathy that it takes to be a good interrelator.*

The group walked fast and hard, as evening darkened around them, driven by memories of the *Asimov*'s survivors, and by the needs of the hinsi. The mountains loomed over them.

Cara had worried that the bound man *(I'm really tired of thinking of him as "the man," she thought once, exasperated. If he doesn't tell us his name pretty soon, I'm going to give him one!)* would slow them down, but he kept up.

Mark and Hrrakk' flanked him, one on each side . . . and Hrrakk's presence, even more than the stranger's, was the difference in this portion of their journey. Though he'd had absolutely nothing to say since they'd captured the intruder, and regarded all of them, except for the Apis, with an aloof disdain, the Simiu was *there*.

Another difference, this one hard to bear, was Terris. Soon after they set out, hinsi began to cry and whimper in earnest.

Butting a fluffy head against Mark's chest, the baby scrabbled up and down the sweater with demanding fingers and toes. Mark talked to the child and petted it and shifted it to different parts of his body, but nothing worked. Both he and Terris were worn out by the time the group paused for a water break.

But only Terris received sips from their dwindling supply this time. Misir could not be roused. The others had to make do with a less-satisfying source of moisture.

Having noted the sap in the tasrel plant when they were pulling the big one up yesterday for Hrrakk's shelter, Mark tested the vegetation with the analyzer in the survival kit, then, finding that tasrel leaves were not harmful, he used their knife to lop off leaves for them to chew and suck.

"Ugh!" Cara chewed, swallowed, then spat the pulp out on the ground. "It's so bitter." That sounded like whining; something her pride wouldn't allow. "Hey, but it's *wet*!" Resolutely she popped another piece of the stuff into her mouth.

Mark grimaced. "I'll see your 'ugh' and raise you a 'yech.' " He spat out his chewed-up wad with a theatrical shudder.

By the time they had finished with their "plant break," Terris, exhausted from wailing, finally fell asleep. Cara walked more briskly in the silence, and thought they all did.

With the rising of the moons, true night arrived, and, suddenly, so did the edge of the desert.

The desert floor literally ran smack into a wall of reddish rock. The wall stretched as far as the travelers could see on either side, rising straight up for fifteen or twenty meters. Over centuries the desert winds had blasted it with sand, polishing it into smoothness, broken by only a few outcroppings. The moons had risen and shadows danced crazily over the cliff.

"Looks like we climb," Cara said, staring up at it.

"Yeah, and even with the rope and in Elseemar's lighter gravity, it may not be easy." Mark moved along the wall of rock, feeling it with his fingers. "Not much in the way of footholds."

Their team had been given a short length of thin, plastic cord that now bound the man's hands, as well as a much longer piece of the same material that Mark took out. Very lightweight, it was nevertheless as strong as plas-steel cable.

Line in hand, Mark turned, looking thoughtfully at the Apis.

She fluttered excitedly, then darted forward and grasped the end that the human extended.

Hastily, Cara signaled her camera on. She had let the autocam trail along at her shoulder tonight, unused, but now, sensing drama, she began filming again.

With a furious blur of wings, the small and delicate-looking being rose straight into the air. In only a second or two she was higher than the lip of the cliff. Her wings slowed, and lightly she touched down.

Cara beamed. "There are distinct advantages to traveling with an Apis."

Mark was watching R'Thessra move back and forth along the treeless top. "That's step one solved," he agreed, "but if she can't find anything to tie that end around, we're no better off. She's not strong enough to hold it for us."

But apparently the Apis was able to find a projection of some kind to anchor the rope, for she appeared on the edge of the cliff, wings and antennae waving. Hrrakk' picked up the rope and gave it a couple of sharp yanks, then hung his weight on it for a second. It held.

"That's a relief," Mark said. "Who wants to go first?"

"I will go," Hrrakk' said.

"You'll need to rig a climbing harness," Mark said. "I think I remember how. You just—"

The Simiu gave him a contemptuous glance, then, without a word, took off the sling that held Misir, handed the baby to Cara, and swarmed hand over hand up the cliff face. In what seemed like only seconds, he was pulling himself over the top. Mark looked over at Cara and shrugged, grinning. "As I was saying, climbing harnesses are for sissies, right?"

"Or for humans," she amended dryly. "Who's next?"

Eerin stepped forward. "Hin will go."

Hrrakk' leaned over and shouted something down.

"He wants the packs." Mark began quickly tying them to the rope. "He'll empty one up there, send it back down, and we can hoist Misir up in it." In minutes the baby had been hauled to a reunion with hinsi's adoptive heen.

"I think Terris can hang on to me while I climb the rope," Mark decided, buttoning his outer shirt into a sort of pocket to cradle the Elpind baby.

Eerin, in the meantime, had grasped the rope. "Eerin's so light," Cara said, looking up, "that maybe Hrrakk' can just pull hin up."

"That's not a good idea," Mark said. "What you need to do, Eerin, is to pass the rope behind you like this, so you're almost sitting on it, then you just sort of *walk* your way up, leaning back against the rope. Use your feet to fend you off the cliff, as well as find footholds." Eerin tested hin's balance for a moment, then, quickly, effortlessly, the Elpind was climbing.

Cara watched and sighed. "I don't know whether to be envious or disgusted," she complained. "Hin tries something *once* and hin's a master at it!"

Mark nodded. "I guess that's what comes of being a professional athlete," he said.

"Professional?" Cara repeated, surprised at his choice of words.

"Anyone who can dance the Mortenwol every day of their adult lives is the equivalent of a champion gymnast crossed with a prima ballerina," Mark pointed out. "Right?"

"I see what you mean . . . " Cara said, staring up at the clifftop where Eerin was being helped over by the Simiu's firm grasp. She turned back to Mark, a look of near panic on her dark features. "Oh, God, Mark, I'm not sure I can do that."

"You can," Mark said firmly. "You *have* to."

"I guess I do." She fingered the cord lying before her. "Mark . . . what about *him*?" she asked, nodding at the man with no name. He stood passive, empty-eyed, off to one side. There was no sign he'd noticed the struggles of his companions to get up the cliff face—he showed no reaction to anything.

"He goes up, too. If we have to tie the rope around him and haul him up," said Mark. "But quit stalling. You're next."

"Okay. I'll film the rest of this team effort from the top; it'll make a nice change of perspective." They walked over to the dangling rope together, and Mark began rigging it as he had for Eerin. "I'll steady you until you're over my head," he promised, "and Hrrakk' will be there to help you when you get within arm's length of the top. The important thing to remember is to keep your feet between you and the rock when you lean back and let the rope harness support you, so you don't start spinning and bang into a projection."

"Okay," she said nervously, then stepped into Mark's cupped hands, reaching upward for the first handhold.

"Good!" Mark encouraged her. "Test each foothold and handhold . . . the shadows can fool you! Good, that's right . . . "

Cara's world narrowed to the feel of the rope cutting into her shoulders, and running across her rump, reassuring in its strength. Slowly, feeling the rock score her palms and fingers, she climbed, moving from handhold to handhold, foothold to foothold. She was careful not to look down.

It seemed to take forever, but finally, she heard the scuffle of feet just above her head, and looked up to see that she was almost there. As she reached up for the next handhold, an incredibly strong, leathery-palmed hand closed over her wrist and yanked just as she boosted upward off her foothold.

Before she realized it, she was halfway over the edge, then the Simiu grabbed her by the seat of her pants and efficiently (if inelegantly) heaved her over the rest of the way. Cara sat up, breathing hard, and began untangling the rope harness.

"Hey, Cara!" Mark yelled, backing away from the rock face and looking up. "You okay?"

A moment later her face appeared, just as the rope came snaking back down. She waved, grinning broadly.

Mark turned away with relief. The problem of how to get the last remaining member of the group, except for himself, to the top of the cliff looked a bit easier in the light of one human success. He crossed to where the man stood silently.

He was reluctant to remove the man's bonds but saw no other option. *Besides, the guy's been nothing but a zombie for hours now; Hrrakk' knocked all the fight out of him.*

"You're next," he said as he untied the man's hands. "You can go up like Cara. I'll help you."

The hands dropped limply to the man's sides; he stared blankly at nothing.

"Do you hear me?" Mark spoke a little louder and tried to make eye contact. "You've got to get up that cliff."

Still no response.

"Okay. We'll rig a harness, see." He looped and knotted

the end of the rope, hoping Hrrakk', Cara, and Eerin were strong enough to pull the hefty male straight up, if that's what it took. "I'll put this around you. Raise your arms." When the man didn't obey, Mark took his wrist and lifted it.

Sudden animation flashed over the man's heavy features and through his body, and a second later his fist slammed hard into Mark's midsection, driving the air from the younger man's lungs in a startled gasp.

Mark doubled over reflexively, clutching at his middle, desperately trying to suck in air.

Oh, God! Terris! He tried to turn away, shield the baby with his body, but a second jarring blow impacted with his jaw, sending him reeling. Dimly, Mark felt powerful hands grab the front of his sweater and shove him brutally against the rock wall. His head snapped back hard, stunning him again.

Sharp agony flashed through his being, and then a final blow hit him like a thunderclap of darkness, and he blacked out.

CHAPTER 14

◆

The Shadow of Death

"Mark!" Cara screamed, seeing him crumple to the ground. The shadows dancing around him hid the upper half of his body as he lay slumped against the base of the cliff.

The man glanced up at them, his face a white blur. Then he advanced again, hands going out, reaching for Terris as hinsi screamed in fear. "*No!*" Cara shrieked. "Hrrakk', *do* something!"

The Simiu was already halfway down the cliff.

A heartbeat later, there was a *thud* as Hrrakk' dropped the last few meters to the ground. Hearing it, the man looked up, dropped the wailing Terris back onto Mark's body, then began backing away. Without warning, the Simiu leaped, his hand lashing out with blurring speed, striking the side of the man's head; the human fell over backward. Hrrakk' advanced again.

The whiteness of the man's face was now half obscured by darkness—*blood*, Cara thought sickly—and he scooted back on his elbows, then grabbed up a double handful of sand and flung it into Hrrakk's face.

Hrrakk' snarled, hit him again, and this time he lay still.

Cara watched anxiously as the Simiu turned back to Mark

and began examining him. "Is he badly hurt?" she yelled in Mizari. "Should I come down?"

"It is not necessary," Hrrakk' replied gruffly. "The human is stunned, but save for a cut on the back of his head, I do not believe he has suffered serious injury. Lower the first-aid kit."

Hastily Cara stuffed the fourth full canteen and the medical kit into one of the knapsacks, then lowered it down.

She saw Mark stir, then, with Hrrakk's help, he sat up, his head bowed over his knees. The watchers above heard Terris, whom they couldn't see, finally stop crying. The Simiu wet a strip of bandage and began cleaning the back of the human's head.

"Oh, my God . . . " Reaction set in, and Cara began trembling violently as she looked up at the others. "Mark could have been killed—and Terris, that bastard was going to kill Terris, I'm sure of it! I hope to hell Mark doesn't have a concussion!"

Eerin must have had difficulty following her rapid, idiomatic speech, but somehow the Elpind understood. Hin patted the journalist's arm comfortingly. "Mark is strong," hin said. "Hrrakk' would have said if heen was truly hurt."

Cara wondered dully if Elspind did the same thing humans so often did: offer empty words of reassurance, just to make themselves feel better.

"How are you doing down there?" she called to Hrrakk'.

"I'm okay," Mark himself answered, though his voice was weak and hard to hear. "I blacked out for a moment, but otherwise, I'm fine. Thank God Terris wasn't hurt."

"What about your head?"

"I've got a lump and a cut. It's sore, but that's all."

Cara caught a movement amid the shadows. The man was crawling on his stomach, then, as she watched, he climbed to his feet and began staggering away. "Hrrakk'!" she yelled. "The man is getting away!"

"Let that honorless *dragkk'* go," the Simiu snarled, watching as Mark's attacker broke into a staggering, stumbling run and vanished around the curve of the cliff.

Cara's attention shifted from the two at the bottom of the cliff to Eerin as hin rose and fetched the blue bundle that was lying near the other knapsack. Misir lay curled into a quiet little ball in the makeshift sling. Cara felt the baby's diaper, finding it dry. At her touch, the child opened golden eyes, so like Eerin's, and looked at her unblinkingly . . . waiting. *Is hinsi waiting for food?* she wondered, feeling a chill trace down her spine, *or for something else?*

The baby sighed; its eyes closed again.

"Misir is worse." Tears filled Cara's eyes. R'Thessra, hovering next to her, touched the girl's arm with a delicate feeler, and Cara glanced up, grateful for the silent comfort.

"Yes," the Elpind agreed gently. "Hin does not believe food will help this hinsi. There is injury inside the child's body. But Terris must have nourishment."

Eerin rose to hin's feet. "Now that we have gained the mountains—even these beginning mountains—there is sure to be vegetation farther on. Hin is going to go on ahead and attempt to locate some wild sestel, if it grows in this region. It is possible that Terris may be able to drink a broth made from sestel leaves. That is what young Elpind babies are weaned on. Terris is young to be weaned, but it is hinsi's only chance."

"But . . . Eerin, shouldn't you wait for Mark and Hrrakk'?"

"Hin can travel faster alone, and time is short, now."

Cara knew the Elpind was right, but she hated to see hin go. "How will we find you again, if we separate?"

"Hin will find the group. Hin has committed the map route to memory, so hin will come back along that route."

Cara wanted to protest further, but subsided. "Okay," she said. "I'll tell Mark and Hrrakk'." She looked up at the mountains ahead of them. They rose up gently in graduated levels like giant's steps. The narrow plateaus were barren, showing faint red and brown in the moons' light.

"I sure hope there's water ahead," she said, feeling thirst nearly overwhelm her.

"There will be," Eerin was confident, "if these mountains are at all similar to the ones around Lalcipind."

"They'd better be," Cara said grimly. "There couldn't be settlements without water, I suppose."

"Cara is right, of course."

Eerin made no move to go, but stood beside Cara, looking up at the mountains. The huge eyes seemed troubled. *Is it only my imagination,* Cara thought, *or is something wrong with Eerin?*

"Frankly, I'm surprised Mark didn't ask you to go on before this, since you can obviously go much faster than the group can."

"Mark did ask hin before we left the ship," Eerin admitted. "But an Elpind cannot keep going in conditions of heat." A shudder made the down on Eerin's bony frame stir. "Hin must rest then also. This is why Elspind live in the mountains or build their cities beneath the cover of great forests."

Cara gazed at the Elpind anxiously. "Eerin, are you *sure* you're all right?"

"Hin is fine," Eerin said, shortly. "Cara must not worry. Hin will be back."

"Okay. You take care, then," she said awkwardly.

Hin nodded, then bounded away, a silvery blur in the moons' light. Seeing hin leave reassured Cara. Eerin's departure was energetic enough for three humans.

"Ouch!" Mark fought back the urge to jerk away as Hrrakk' finished putting medicine on his wound, then began to bandage the back of his head. In his lap, Terris finished the water in hinsi's feeding straw, then began sobbing pitifully from hunger. Mark stroked the baby gently. "Sorry, little buddy . . ."

Hrrakk's none-too-gentle hands paused in their ministrations. "The child will begin to weaken, soon."

"I know," Mark agreed bleakly.

"Can you stand?"

"I think so . . . " Mark tried, wavered, then made it to his feet. He was touched to notice that Hrrakk' had both hands raised as the Simiu squatted on his haunches beside him. The alien had obviously been ready to catch him if he toppled.

Mark cuddled Terris, snuggling the little body against his face, and relief that hinsi wasn't hurt washed through him again. He looked over at the curve in the cliff face. "Do you think he's gone for good?" he asked, referring to his attacker.

"I hit him hard, this time," Hrrakk' said. There was no regret in his tone. "I do not believe he will return." The big alien indicated the line dangling down the cliff face. "And we will pull the line up after us. We may need it again."

"You know what will happen to him," Mark said, staring into the night.

"I know," the Simiu growled. "Do you by any chance wish to go and look for him?" His gruff voice dripped sarcasm.

Mark shook his head. "No," he said. "He tried to kill Terris, and I can't risk that. Besides, he left; it's not like we abandoned him. And if we searched for him, we'd waste time that might save lives aboard the *Asimov*."

Silently the alien handed him the canteen. Mark limited himself to only a few swallows. "Here," he said, handing it back. "Your turn."

The Simiu hesitated, then took the water. His throat rippled as he swallowed, great gulps of water in one long swig. When he took the canteen away from his mouth, there was only a small sloshing; he'd practically drained it.

Well, he's definitely entitled, thought Mark. *That's the first water he's had since we left.* "Uh, Honored Hrrakk' . . . listen, uh . . . thanks. For saving me and Terris."

"I am going back up now." The alien ignored the human's words. "If you cannot climb, human, I will pull you up."

Mark smiled wryly. *He's never going to change.* "I'll climb," he promised, watching the alien walk away without glancing back, then, just as before, swarm up the rope.

"Hang on tight," Mark said to Terris as he secured hinsi in his shirt. His head was pounding, but the water and the rest had helped. Slowly he secured the line around himself, then, with a hiss of pain as he jerked upward, searching for the first foothold, he began to climb.

Midway up, Mark had to pause. The multiple shadows swirling around him had combined with the pain in his head to make him dizzy. His stomach lurched, and he bit his lip grimly. *You're not going to lose the water you just drank,* he told himself sternly. He swallowed, then began climbing again.

He was grateful that he'd always been active, and that his upper-body strength was good. Otherwise, he would never have made it. He paused again, feeling the pain in his head like a wave of blackness, waiting to overwhelm him.

"Mark? Mark?" Cara was calling him. He tried to answer, but settled for waving feebly. The blackness receded slowly.

He reached up, found another handhold, wedged his toe into another crevice. *Come on, Kenner . . . keep going . . .* Terris whimpered. That gave him the strength to find another handhold, another foothold . . . then another . . .

Two hands abruptly seized his wrists, then Hrrakk' yanked him straight up, pulling him halfway over the cliff edge. Mark managed to turn to the side at the last moment, just in time to keep from squashing Terris.

He lay limp and panting as Cara and the Simiu dragged him the rest of the way over the edge, then flopped onto his back, careful not to hit the back of his head. Mark could feel his feet still sticking out over nothingness, but hadn't the strength yet to move them. Blackness threatened again.

But he didn't pass out. Finally, after what must have been several minutes, he was able to sit up with a groan. "You okay?" Cara asked.

"I'll live." He looked around. "Where's Eerin?"

"Hin went on ahead." Briefly, she explained about the Elpind's search for wild sestel for Terris.

"Thank God there's something we can give Terris," said Mark fervently. "I'm afraid hinsi's weakening. Let's get moving. The quicker we go, the quicker we'll meet Eerin."

"Can you?" she peered at him anxiously.

"Yeah." Mark hoped standing up wouldn't make a liar out of him. He struggled to his feet, then reached for the knapsack, but Cara got it first.

"Just carry yourself," she admonished. "And Terris, of course." She looked up at the folds of mountains. "Think we can climb past those by dawn?"

"Not if we waste any more time," Hrrakk' growled, tying himself back into the blue sling that held Misir. Turning, he loped away.

"We're coming already," Mark said irritably. "I wasn't exactly having fun 'wasting time' down there." He looked around. "Everybody ready?"

The Apis lifted into the air and flew after Hrrakk'.

"I think since half of us have gone already," said Cara dryly, "the answer is 'yes.' "

For most of the night, as the moons swung overhead and shadows scuttled like live things across the rocky surfaces, the group climbed the giant's steps of barren plateaus. Though sometimes they needed both hands and feet on the steeper slopes, none were as high or difficult as the cliff marking the boundary between desert and mountains.

The night air was cool and reviving, but, for Mark, the hike was a nightmare. His head throbbed viciously, and his entire body ached, both from the fight and as sore muscles complained at the unaccustomed climbing.

Every minute of the climb he worried about Terris who, tortured by hunger, alternated between fits of panicky wailing, mournful whimpering, and brief, restless naps.

From the blue jersey that held Misir there was no sound or movement at all. Mark was aware that the Simiu frequently slipped a hand into the sling, and he knew Hrrakk' must be checking for warmth and breath.

Two hours before dawn they topped the final plateau. A narrow valley stretched before them. Small hills rose on either side, and at its far end they could see the hump of a bigger mountain. Behind it, sharply etched in the bright moonlight, rose another range, even larger, and, far away, white-capped peaks shone. Each range was higher than the one before it, as if they'd been neatly set in stepped rows by an arranging hand.

"We won't have to climb them all," reminded Mark, reassuring himself as much as Cara as he checked the map.

"Do you see any water marked out on that thing?" Cara tried to look over his shoulder at the tiny display. Thirst was a torment for all of them by now.

"Not close by and not on a direct route. Maybe they only registered major lakes and rivers," he speculated. "Streams could have been left out. I hope!"

"Mark, I know we're trying to save what's left, but after all that climbing . . . "

"I know," he interrupted, bringing out their last, half-full canteen. "I've got to have some, too."

They all drank—except for the now-comatose Misir—then set off again. Dawn found them halfway through the short valley.

Exhausted, every step jarring his already splitting head, the temptation to stop for sleep became an obsession for Mark. But he found himself pushing on, despite his pain and exhaustion. The thought of Terris and the other survivors was too imperative.

He did allow them a short rest and food break, and they chewed more leaves for moisture. "I know we need to sleep," he admitted, looking at Cara's haggard face, "but I'd like to push on a little farther before stopping, since it will be cooler up here than it was in the desert. Any time we can save could make a big difference," he said, knowing they'd follow his meaning. "Everybody up to a couple hours more walking?" He wondered vaguely if he, himself, was. *I have to be, that's all!*

The Apis hovered expectantly, and Hrrakk' looked capable of marching steadily on forever, if need be. Mark's gaze fell on Cara. To his surprise, she laughed.

"I'm beginning to think my name really *is* 'everybody.' Do you realize I'm the only one who ever answers these rhetorical questions of yours?"

Mark grinned weakly. "Everybody Hendricks, journalist to the galaxy." He pretended to consider it. "It would look good on a byline."

She snorted rudely.

They started up the wooded mountain at the other end of the valley, the bushy, scattered trees seeming a novelty after the desert and the bare plateaus. As they climbed higher, the plant life began to thicken. Mark noticed the Simiu studying their surroundings. Occasionally Hrrakk' broke his loping stride to touch the leaf of a plant or break off a stalk. *Why in hell is he interested in Elseemar's vegetation?* Mark wondered.

It was midmorning when they paused again for a water break. One or two swallows, including some for Terris, and their water was gone, except for a small amount he saved for Eerin. Mark considered trying to analyze these new plants to see if there were some they could chew, but he hated to take the time. "There's *got* to be water soon," he said. "Watch for signs of animal trails; listen for stream sounds, check outcroppings for seepage, and be sure to—"

He broke off as Hrrakk' grunted with surprise and untied the blue sling. There was movement within. Hrrakk' slid the baby Elpind out on one huge palm.

"Oh, no," whispered Cara.

Misir's tiny body was trembling all over, hinsi's four limbs outstretched rigidly. The Simiu cupped his other hand over the baby, cradling it between his palms. In a few seconds the mild convulsion ended, and the child went limp between his fingers.

Gone, thought Mark. But Hrrakk' held out his open palm with the baby draped across it. "Cara," he said clearly. It was the first time he'd addressed one of them by name.

Tears slid down Cara's face as she sank to the ground, cradling the infant. The Simiu watched impassively, but the flame-colored crest on his head lay flat, which Mark knew was a sign of distress. The Apis moved up to Cara's left shoulder, touching her with a quivering feeler. Mark knelt at Cara's right shoulder and looked down.

Misir's round, golden eyes opened. They stared up at Cara, but it was plain their unfocused gaze didn't really see. The child's breathing was irregular and labored.

"Do you think hinsi is in pain?" With one finger Cara stroked the top of the soft head. Tears splashed her hand.

Mark regarded those unseeing eyes. "No . . . hinsi's pretty much out of it," he answered, hoping it was true. Gently he touched the baby's small shoulder, trailing his finger down the twig-thin arm, over an upturned palm no bigger than a coin. Suddenly six tiny fingers curled loosely around his larger one. Though the action was probably nothing more than a reflex, his heart contracted painfully, and he fought back tears of his own.

Cara stroked the infant's head. "It's okay," she murmured brokenly, "it's all right. Don't be afraid."

A quick, visible shudder rippled over the flesh beneath the white down. The baby inhaled sharply, once, and then its jaw dropped. The air *whooshed* back out in a bright, swelling bubble of orange blood that burst wetly and dribbled down the lax chin. The golden eyes began to dim.

Mark held his own breath, realizing the little chest had not rounded again. A deep stillness settled over Misir's fragile-looking form, and the last bit of amber light drained from the open eyes.

Mark slid his finger out of the still gently curved shape of the child's hand, stood up, and walked away.

• • •

Cara felt strange . . . hot and cold at the same time, stiff on the outside while her insides were dissolving away. A large, leathery hand appeared in the field of her blurred vision to lift the body from her lap. "Close the eyes," she said dully.

She sat there for a while, not thinking, just letting the sun soak warmth into her bones. The Apis poked around the base of a tree looking for small insects while Hrrakk' . . .

Cara registered finally what Hrrakk' was doing: digging a small grave with their multitool. He seemed as stolid as ever, betraying no emotion at the nature of his task, but she remembered how he'd spoken her name, how he'd given her Misir to hold one last time. *He has to be hurting, too . . .*

She got up on wobbly legs and went over to him. "Honored Hrrakk' . . . are you all right?" she asked in Mizari.

He grunted and nodded without speaking.

Cara wanted to put a hand on his massive shoulder, remembering how the Apis' touch had brought her such comfort, but she resisted, knowing the Simiu would not appreciate such a gesture from a human. "We all appreciate . . . especially I appreciate . . . that you tried to save . . . Misir." She had to close her eyes and bite her lip to choke back sobs. "Thank you for that," she said. "And . . . thank you . . . for saying my name."

He did not turn around or reply, merely resumed his stolid digging. *But at least he didn't tell me to get lost,* Cara thought. "I'm going to find Mark," she said. "I'm sure he didn't go far. I'll be back . . . soon."

The Simiu nodded silently.

Cara found Mark sitting on a rock, perfectly still, in a little clearing farther along their map route. She studied him for a moment from behind a clump of small trees.

Dried sweat and possibly tears had mixed with dirt to turn his tanned face into a dirty mask, looking doubly filthy in contrast to the whiteness of the bandage around his head. His hair, lighter now from the sun, hung matted and limp. The white shirt, beige sweater, and white pants had resisted dirt and stains better than flesh, but even they looked grimy. Cara looked down at herself, realizing she must look nearly as bad. *My kingdom for a bath and clean clothes . . .*

She stepped out of the trees and moved toward him, and hearing her approach, Mark looked up, his hazel eyes, seeming lighter now in the sun-darkened face, empty and bleak.

Cara regarded him uncertainly. "I was worried about you."

"Sorry. I didn't mean for you to worry. I just had to get away for a minute."

"Where's Terris?"

He patted the lump under his shirt. "Right here, asleep."

She sat down beside him on the sun-warmed rock. "So . . . do you want to talk about it?"

Mark shrugged and looked away. "I was thinking about my mother when she died. Wondering how it was, you know." He took a deep, shaky breath. "Wondering if anybody held *her* hand."

"Mark, you've got to let her go," Cara said earnestly. "I think you know that as well as I do."

Her bluntness evidently surprised him; frankly, it had rather surprised Cara herself. Slowly he turned and looked at her. "And if she knew that you're leaving StarBridge because she died," she continued, after a moment, "she'd feel terrible."

Mark examined his hands, trying to dig the dirt out from under his fingernails without notable success. "That's not why I'm dropping out," he said finally.

"Then why?"

"I'm not sure myself anymore—dammit, Cara, I'm not sure of anything these days! Part of it is that the thought of any decision of mine causing anyone's death—*ever*—makes my blood run cold. Interrelators can face situations where their decisions could mean life or death."

"Situations like this hijacking," she pointed out.

"I suppose so."

"Seems to me you've acquitted yourself rather well, for someone who can't handle pressure. Negotiating with Orim—something that would leave even the most seasoned professional sweating—plus the way you've led us on this little jaunt through the wilderness. Look at the way you were able to talk Hrrakk' into taking the baby."

"For all the good it did," he said bitterly.

"That doesn't negate the fact that you were able to persuade a Simiu who obviously has absolutely no use for humans to do something he didn't want to do."

Mark shook his head. "Whatever made him take that child, it wasn't anything I said. I certainly haven't figured out what makes Hrrakk' tick. There's something about him . . . something he's hiding . . . "

"I've sensed that, too. But, Mark, don't try to change the subject. You've got to admit you've done an interrelator's job aboard the *Asimov* and here on Elseemar."

"I did the best I could," he corrected shortly.

"But that's the point! The *best* we can do is *all* we can do! Sometimes things go wrong despite our best efforts. You're right, sometimes people die, but that's no reason to give up."

"It's reason enough for me," he said tightly. "I *hate* death." His voice warmed with passion. "I really do."

"Since all of us have to die sooner or later, it seems to me you're wasting a lot of energy on something that can't be changed," she said mildly.

"I know. I'm trying to come to terms with it, and I'll think that I have, then something like Misir's death—or finding out that Eerin doesn't plan to take Elhanin, even if it becomes available—will happen, and I feel like someone kicked me in the stomach," he said bitterly. "Eerin says I'm running from life."

Cara thought that over, then nodded slowly. "Maybe Eerin is right. And maybe when you're ready to stop running from life, you won't need to run so hard from death either."

He sighed, but remained silent.

She stirred reluctantly. "I guess we'd better get back . . ."

"You're right."

As they slid off the rock together, she caught his arm. "Mark . . . " she said suddenly, fiercely.

He put his hand over hers, obviously surprised at the urgency in her expression. "What is it?"

"Do you think we'll ever get *home*?" Cara felt her throat tighten painfully. "I've tried not to think about it, but . . . it's getting to me . . . " She gulped. "They've probably called *my* mother and told her . . . "

As she trailed off, unable to say the rest of it, he put his arms around her, the warm, comforting grasp of a friend. His embrace felt good, and she leaned against him for a minute or so. Then, without speaking, she pulled herself free and they left the clearing together.

When they reached the others, the first thing they saw was Eerin. "Eerin," Cara said, "Misir . . . Misir is dead."

"Hin grieves for the small journey-taker," said Eerin softly. The gold eyes were mournful.

Mark looked at the Elpind's empty hands. "Did you find some food for Terris? The sestel?"

Hin shook hin's head. "No," the Elpind said. "At least . . . hin was not sure. There is a growth farther on that resembles the wild sestel hin has seen, but it differs in some ways. Hin thought it would be best to check with Hrrakk' and possibly use Mark's cell analyzer to discover whether it is indeed sestel before giving it to Terris."

"Did you find *water*?" Cara asked urgently.

"Not yet," Eerin said. "But the vegetation is much thicker the higher one goes. There must be water, and we will find it."

Cara started to say something else, but Hrrakk's gruff voice interrupted. "The grave is ready."

The journalist's heart contracted painfully when she saw the grave the Simiu had made. It was completely lined with small rocks, painstakingly placed to make a protective shell. And in the bottom was a deep, soft nest of green leaves. Hrrakk's care with the baby's final bed spoke of his feelings in a way that nothing else could.

The silence was profound as the Simiu placed Misir, wrapped snugly in Mark's blue jersey, into the waiting hole. Cara saw Mark reach beneath his shirt to touch Terris, reaching for comfort in the baby's warm, solid reality.

Hrrakk' scooped a large handful of dirt from the mound at the foot of the grave.

"Wait," Eerin said, and stepped forward. In the Elpind's hand was a long white feather. Cara recognized it and saw that Mark did, too. It was one of Eerin's six treasured feathers from the Elseewas, the only white one hin owned.

"El is life and Wo is death and each completes the other," said Eerin softly in Mizari. The ancient words were oddly comforting. "In the quick flight of a Shadowbird, El becomes Wo. Let it be now, and let it ever be so."

The Elpind knelt and leaned down. Gently hin laid the silky feather on the baby's shirt-wrapped form, a form hardly longer than the feather itself. The white color was clean and pure against the bright blue cloth.

The colors blurred and ran together. When Cara could see again, the grave was a mosaic: dark brown earth and gray rock with only bits of green leaf, blue cloth, and white feather peeping through. Hrrakk' and Mark and Eerin transferred handful after handful of dirt, and soon thc only colors were earth ones.

They tamped the ground down firmly, smoothed it, then Hrrakk' brought a large rock and laid it over the grave, almost obscuring the raw place. Cara was comforted, knowing that no animal would disturb Misir's rest.

The others moved away, but the journalist stood silently for a few moments more. Finally, she wiped her eyes and turned. Mark was putting on his backpack. Beside him was only the Apis.

"Where are Hrrakk' and Eerin?"

Mark sighed and glanced down at Terris. "They've left to look for the sestel. They'll meet us up ahead."

"Why Hrrakk'?" she wondered.

"Why indeed? He said that the leaf patterns in this region vary from the wild sestel around Lalcipind."

"How would Hrrakk' know that?"

"I'm asking myself that very question." His hazel eyes were troubled. "And . . . Cara . . . did Eerin look different to you?"

Cara thought about it. "Just tired. But that's natural. After all, hin covered twice the ground we have today."

Mark wasn't reassured. "Hin asked me for some ration bars. Eerin wouldn't even consider eating one of those before."

"How many of them do we have left?"

"Seven. We're not too bad in the food department, if we can just find some water. Eerin drank what we had saved for hin."

"Good." She looked at Mark, worrying over how tired he looked. "How's your headache?"

"So-so. You ready?" When Cara nodded, picking up her pack, he looked at the Apis. "You ready to go, R'Thessra?"

The elderly alien rose quickly into the air, obviously ready.

Cara checked the position of the sun. It was almost noon. She felt years older than when she'd stopped here for a sip of water, but only an hour or so had actually passed.

She noticed Mark didn't look back at the grave as they left the quiet, sunny clearing.

Neither did she.

CHAPTER 15

♦

New Worries for Old

The travelers climbed steadily for two hours, while the trees grew wider-girthed and the underbrush thicker. Plant colors became more varied, and they began to notice signs of birds and animals.

Mark paid little attention, however, to his surroundings. The sight of Misir's eyes as they'd faded in death haunted him, but he kept seeing them green instead of gold. Terris' eyes.

The baby woke several times as they walked, crying loudly, angrily. But each time hinsi subsided more quickly into weak whimpers, and each time the whimpers subsided more quickly back into sleep.

The sights and even the sounds began to blur together for Mark. He'd done more than a day's worth of climbing since his injury, and only his fears for Terris kept him moving. His head throbbed again, and sometimes he would jerk back into awareness and realize that he had no memory of the past minutes' walking.

Dehydration is setting in, he realized in a moment of lucidity. In survival class they'd learned that a little water will go a long way . . . for a while. Then the negative effects begin to accumulate quickly. Headache and dizziness begin when only six percent of the body's tissues become dehydrated.

Finally he realized that if he didn't stop, he was going to stumble and fall . . . and that might injure Terris. Reaching out, he put a hand on Cara's arm. "Stop . . . " he managed, hardly able to make sounds emerge from his dry mouth. "Got to . . . rest."

Cara folded to the ground right where she stood. "I was . . . going to tell you . . . same thing," she said shakily.

Mark slumped down and pulled off his pack. The Apis hovered over them, alert, watching. Then she flew closer and reached out a slender forelimb to touch Mark. It was the first time she'd ever made such a direct bid for his attention.

"What is it?" he asked in Mizari, concerned.

She bent slightly and trailed one wingtip along the ground as she flew in a circle around them, repeating the action several times until the long grass was brushed in one direction in a clear perimeter. Then she fluttered outside the grass-marked ring and let those large, faceted eyes rove deliberately over the circle, around the surrounding forest, over the circle again, and back to Mark.

"Mark, she's saying she's going to stand watch."

Cara's interpretation was right, he recognized it instantly. "Somebody's got to. Eerin said there are predators." He addressed the Apis in Mizari, barely able to summon enough saliva to produce the sibilants. "R'Thessra, don't you need to rest?"

Slowly, deliberately, she moved her head from side to side. "She's shaking her head no," Mark said. "I guess she learned from us."

"Face it, Mark," Cara said weakly, lying down in a patch of shade. "Everybody else on this trek can outdo us humans: Hrrakk', Eerin, even R'Thessra, as old as she is. Now lie down and sleep."

Mark was too tired to argue. "Thank you," he said in Mizari to the Apis. He lay back, resting his head on his knapsack.

"Wake me if you need me . . . " he mumbled, relaxing, feeling as if his body were going to sink down through the grass, below the soil, clear to Elseemar's . . . Mark was asleep before he finished the thought.

• • •

Terris squalled.

Coming up out of sodden sleep, Mark felt a heavy hand shake his leg. And his shoulder. Then it prodded him in the ribs. He rolled onto his side, then felt something cold and damp trickle down the back of his neck.

"Okay! All right, already! I'm awake." The trip back from such intense sleep was not easy, and Mark felt miserable and still exhausted. Thirst was an added torment. Opening his dry, gritty eyes, he saw the Simiu standing over him, a canteen in his hand. Mark groaned. The slant of the sunlight told him that they'd only slept a couple of hours. No wonder he felt so awful.

The significance of the Simiu's presence suddenly mingled with the sight of the canteen and the cold dampness of the drops on his neck, making Mark's foggy brain function. "Hrrakk'—did you find *water*?"

"Yes. And Eerin awaits us with the sestel," said Hrrakk' impatiently in Mizari. He reached over Mark to hand the canteen to Cara. *Simiu chivalry?* Mark wondered. *Or is it just that Hrrakk' dislikes her less than he dislikes me?*

Watching Cara drink eagerly, Mark heaved a great relieved sigh. "Don't drink too much at one time, Cara, or you'll get sick." He smiled at Hrrakk'. "Water . . . and sestel for Terris! That's wonderful, Honored Hrrakk'! Where?"

The Simiu pointed. "An hour in that direction. Eerin is waiting."

Cara quickly finished and passed the canteen to Mark. Quickly Mark filled Terris' feeding straw and gave the baby some of the cool liquid. A part of him hoped Hrrakk' had used the purification tablets, but as soon as Terris finished the straw (hinsi had emptied it in only seconds), Mark raised the container to his own lips without bothering to ask.

The blessed coolness splashed over his tongue and coursed down his throat, tasting so wonderful that Mark gulped too quickly, even as he realized he had to slow down, or risk sickness. Hrrakk' shook his head at him warningly, and Mark stopped. He changed Terris, then filled the baby's feeding straw again.

As Terris drank, Mark looked over at Cara, grinning, and

she smiled ecstatically back. **FOOD AND WATER!** In his mind's eye, the words were ten meters high in laser-lit capitals to symbolize the giant worry that had just been lifted off his shoulders.

Both of them drank again, then, wonder of wonders, there was still enough left to splash over their faces and rinse their filthy hands.

Refreshed, they started out. Mark quickly realized that an hour's journey to a Simiu constituted more than an hour's fast hike for a human. The spurt of energy the water had given him soon wore off as they climbed farther up the mountain, then hiked along its spine.

The water had also given Terris a brief spurt of energy, which hinsi expressed by crying, then whimpering, but soon the baby lapsed back into sleep. Cara was silent with exhaustion; it was a very quiet group.

The forest, however, grew louder. Small rustlings sounded here and there in the underbrush. A zing or a whir announced the presence of tiny insects in the air, and birdcalls whistled from tree to tree. The foliage was thicker and higher and small beaten trails wound through it, always converging now in the same direction: toward the life-sustaining water.

At some point Mark began hearing a dull, muted droning sound. For a moment he thought it was his ears, that his exhaustion was catching up with him. But as he strained to hear, he realized it was definitely coming from outside his own body. As Hrrakk' made another turn and led them onto a well-defined animal trail, he realized it was growing louder.

Suddenly a piercing, sweet, strangely *familiar* sound cut through every other noise. It was a high, fluting call, and Mark recognized the first note from the Mortenwol. *Is Eerin doing the Mortenwol up ahead?* he wondered.

But the sound was repeated again, exactly the same, and he knew then that it was not the kareen. "Mark, look!" Cara pointed straight up, her voice hushed and excited.

A huge, winged shape sailed into view, silhouetted against Elseemar's chalcedonic sky. Multicolored, with the wings and long tail outlined in black, it seemed like a living piece of stained glass. Mark remembered the black tips on all of Eerin's treasured feathers and their glowing colors.

"Cara! That's an Elseewas! A Shadowbird. That's the kind of bird Eerin's feathers come from."

The bird dipped lower, and Mark could clearly see the deep red wings and body. In the long sweeping tail the feathers alternated: soft blue, deep green, and pure white.

"It's gorgeous," breathed Cara. "I don't know if I mean how it looks or how it sounds," she added, for the bird was singing with long trills and intricate repeating runs.

"Eerin said much of the Mortenwol and its accompanying music is inspired by the Elseewas," Mark said, craning his neck to follow the bird out of sight. The song drifted into silence.

Even Hrrakk' had paused to watch the Elseewas. As they resumed trudging along the path, Mark told Cara what he remembered of Eerin's story about the Shadowbird.

The throbbing beat he'd heard earlier gradually increased to a roar. "That's a waterfall!" exclaimed Mark finally. "Sounds like a big one."

Cara stumbled into a tired trot. "I think I want to stand in it as badly as I want to drink it."

Mark followed eagerly. The worn track sloped down a bit, then suddenly opened out and they were there. *Like a fairyland,* he thought, stunned by the unexpected beauty of the place.

Here, the mountain crest they'd been walking suddenly folded sideways against another higher hump, and down from the taller mountain, over a hanging shelf of rock, plunged a long, narrowly focused fall of water. Nothing broke its fall until it struck the deeply carved basin far below. The pool before them churned white with the force of its unceasing assault. A continuous thunder echoed from the huge rocks that edged the stream, and clouds of mist hovered in the air.

On both sides of the stream, leaning over and pushing between the great rocks, were trees of a variety Mark had not seen before, even in these mountains. *They must need to grow right by water,* he decided.

The trunks were formed by several tightly braided, woody stems, and the branches were wide-flung and flexible, moving slightly with every current of air. Attached by short stems up and down the branches were the most amazing leaves. Each was a bright, translucent yellow, making the tree seem as though it were hung with living jewels.

The trees caught the rays of the late afternoon sun, rays that had to struggle down through more ordinary green layers of taller treetops, and fanned them into flame. The effect gilded the rocks, and even the mist-laden air picked up the golden glow.

Cara had not allowed the alien beauty of the place to distract her from priorities. She was already bending over the water, splashing it vigorously onto her face. Then she pulled off her shoes and waded right in to begin sluicing her arms.

"Remember, don't drink it," cautioned Mark. He began filling the canteens and dropping one of the purification tablets inside each. "Hrrakk', where's Eerin? Where's the sestel?"

Hrrakk' loped off downstream without replying. Looking that way, Mark saw why. He dropped the filled canteens and ran.

Hrrakk' was crouched beside the limp Elpind as Mark raced up. "Eerin is not hurt," the Simiu said. "Merely asleep."

"Asleep?" Mark stared incredulously. "But . . . "

Eerin stirred, then blinked awake.

"Eerin, what's wrong? I thought you must be . . . "

"Hin was merely sleeping," Eerin said serenely.

"But we're not in the desert anymore," Mark protested, remembering Eerin's explanation for sleeping then. "It's not that hot now. What's wrong? Are you sure you're all right?"

"Hin was tired, but hin is now fine," the Elpind said, getting up. "And hin has the sestel. Is Mark ready to try feeding Terris?"

A terrible suspicion grew in Mark's mind. It had occurred to him before, and he'd thrust it aside in the press of all that had happened, but now it sprang up again full-blown. *What if it's not weariness or heat making Eerin need to sleep? Hin said that they sleep sometimes, during certain times of their lives when they need to store energy. Was hin talking about the next major event in hin's lifecycle, which will be Enelwo?*

The thought that Eerin might be facing the Change early was something that he couldn't bear to contemplate. *I should just accept what hin has told me,* Mark admonished himself. *If anything were wrong, Eerin would say so! Don't borrow trouble, dummy.* Terris stirred against his chest, whimpering, and he turned with relief to the matter of primary importance.

"Hinsi's ready," he said. "I just pray this sestel works."

The survival supplies yielded a collapsible pot and fire-starting material. Water from the stream was soon boiling vigorously. Eerin retrieved several leaf-wrapped bundles that had been moistened and laid on a rock near the stream to keep cool and fresh.

"Hrrakk' knew that the wild strain of sestel in this area had an extra leaf in each whorl," explained Eerin. "Heen confirmed that this was the correct variety for this region."

Eerin rapidly picked over the greenish purple leaves, then tossed several of them into the pot. They tumbled in the boiling water, and in seconds the water turned dark as it leached a deep purple sap from the heavily veined leaves.

Cara examined the bubbling pot. "Smells awful!"

Mark took yet another long, cool drink from his canteen and munched a ration bar. "When will it be done?"

The Elpind used a twig to fish out one of the dangling leaves. It hung limp and now nearly colorless. "Soon," hin said. Eerin removed the pot from the fire, setting it aside to cool. "Now to thicken it."

Hin proceeded to strip clumps of clustered white seeds from some spiky green stems that hin took from a second of the leaf-wrapped bundles.

"These seeds will not only thicken the liquid, but add to the nutritional value. Because it will be more filling, Terris will feel more satisfied." The Elpind quickly ground the seed clumps between two rocks and threw the coarse powder into the purple water.

Soon the Elpind pronounced the broth cool enough to drink.

Cautiously Mark scooped up some of the warm liquid in the feeding straw they had been using. Then he gently eased Terris loose from hinsi's sleeping grip on his sweater and settled the child in his lap.

He looked down at the baby and then around the group, wondering if each of them had the same knot in his or her (or hin's) stomach that he did. *This has to work. You're going to eat this stuff, Terris!*

Mark jiggled the baby. Terris woke sluggishly, then jerked and pushed against his hands with a sharp cry. Hinsi's honey-colored body shivered with urgency. "Hey, hey," he soothed.

"We've got food this time." He placed the feeding straw against the baby's mouth.

Terris' snubbed nose wrinkled. The dull, fitful look that had come into the green eyes in the past day changed to one of eagerness. "C'mon, taste it . . . "

Suddenly hinsi's tiny jaws clamped on the straw, and the baby sucked mightily.

Tears rose in Cara's eyes. "That's the most wonderful thing I've ever seen."

You are so right! Mark thought. It didn't take Terris long to finish the first strawful. Quickly he prepared another. As he offered it to Terris and the baby began to slurp, Mark's eye was suddenly caught by the date that showed on one side of his wristwatch. "Well, I'll be damned," he said, and looked up at his companions with a grin. "Guess what, Cara? Today's my birthday! I'm twenty!"

"Well, congratulations!" she said, and gave him a kiss on the cheek. "I'm sorry I don't have more of a present for you."

Mark looked down at the eagerly gulping Terris. "This is the best birthday present anyone ever had," he said quietly.

"I wish . . . " Cara began softly, then she stopped. The sudden sadness on her face made it obvious that she had thought of Misir, left miles behind, but she tried to cover up. "I wish we could bathe," she finished instead, plastering on a smile. "Could we?"

"If we don't waste too much time. There's a cake of soap in the supplies."

Taking turns to allow for the few shreds of privacy left after days together in the wilderness, they sluiced themselves off quickly in the cold, refreshing stream. Cara checked Mark's wound, found it to be healing, then rebandaged it.

Feeling pleasantly wealthy, they repacked their knapsacks, glorying in the several leaf-wrapped bundles of sestel and five full canteens of water.

Mark programmed the waterfall and the stream into the map's grid. Activating the plotting function, he watched as it figured the stream's projected course and displayed it. As he'd thought it might, the hairlike bright line crawled to and merged with the only body of water the grid had previously shown, a small lake that had been off their previous course.

Having detoured to reach the stream, they were now on a direct line with it.

He showed the map to Hrrakk' and Eerin. "This lake is about two hours away, and we can follow this stream all the way. We should get there just before dark, then sleep there. Frankly, Cara and I are still tired . . . we really need a long rest."

Hrrakk' grunted agreement, and Mark thought to himself that even the Simiu was beginning to look weary.

"I've plotted a new course to the nahah, using the lake as a reference point," he added, "and it actually turns out to be a couple of kilometers less than the original one we were following. There's no need for us to backtrack."

Cara had been inspecting one of the yellow-leafed trees, and she came running back with cupped hands. "Look what's growing at the base of those leaves!"

In her hands were fat, round marbles of fruit, and they were as odd as everything else about the trees. At their heart was a gold gumdrop-looking center, but encasing it was an outer shell of firm, spongy texture. It was a much lighter shade of gold and just translucent enough to allow a view of the brighter center.

"Do you think they're safe to eat?" asked Cara. "I'm so sick of those dry nutrient bars."

Quickly Mark checked it with the cell analyzer. Hrrakk' nodded when he pronounced it safe. "None of the poisonous berries on Elseemar grow on trees," he said. "There are several varieties, but they all grow on ground-crawling vines."

Mark was surprised again by Hrrakk's knowledge of this planet, and was tempted to ask how the Simiu knew, but he was distracted by the enticing scent of the globes in his hand. He bit eagerly into the fruit, finding the outer section pleasantly tangy and chewy, while the inner heart had a milder bite, and deliciously washed down the whole mouthful with its juiciness. Mark and Cara gorged on the berries, and the Apis, a fruit-eater by nature, enjoyed a hearty helping as well.

Eerin crammed hinself, too, with handful after handful of the raw sestel stems and roots. Mark had always had to stifle a chuckle at the eagerness with which Eerin ate, but something about this time chilled him. Eerin stuffed the untidy bundles under hin's orange tongue too quickly, too methodically, too . . . too urgently.

Not like a person who's hungry, thought Mark. *Even really hungry. It's like something else is driving this eating fit.*

Eerin seemed to sense his speculative gaze. The compulsive eating stopped immediately, and the Elpind rose. "Hin must dance the Mortenwol before we leave."

There was no white feather in Eerin's headdress this time, but, otherwise, the dance struck a welcome chord of familiarity in the middle of this alien wilderness. From his two weeks of every-morning attendance at Eerin's ritual and the several times since then, Mark knew the movements and their order so well that he sometimes thought he could have danced the Mortenwol himself.

Even now, exhausted, aching, and anxious to get under way again, Mark felt the music call to his blood. It gave him a much-needed surge of vicarious energy, and he found himself enjoying the dance more than he had since first learning what its name meant.

Until Eerin stumbled and fell.

CHAPTER 16

◆

The Shadowbird

"Eerin!" Cara cried, leaping up—but Mark was already there, kneeling by the Elpind's side.

"Hin is fine," the alien was saying. Eerin sat up, then tried to stand, but Mark gently restrained the Elpind.

"Do you feel dizzy?" he asked. "Does anything hurt?"

"Hin is fine," Eerin repeated. "Clumsy only. If hin dances every day, hin must fall sometimes. It is the average law."

"Law of averages," corrected Cara automatically. "Eerin, are you sure you're all right?"

The down-covered Elpind nodded, and Mark reluctantly let his pair partner up. "Hin does not need to finish," Eerin said. "Hin has wasted enough walking time. Let us go."

"Not a waste," protested Cara. "The Mortenwol is never a waste."

Eerin's golden eyes sparkled gratefully.

Mark said nothing, only helped the Elpind pack the kareen and the five feathers back into their respective cases. Cara saw that he was troubled far beyond what the little episode warranted, and she remembered his quizzing her about Eerin right after Misir's burial. *What's going on?*

The group turned their backs on the little gorge and headed down the streambed. *Except for that brief nap—or collapse might be more accurate—we've been walking for nearly twenty-four hours straight,* Cara thought, falling into her usual rear position. *I can hardly believe I'm still on my feet!*

The water and her sluicing in the cold water had refreshed her, but she knew her energy would fade fast. She needed sleep, hours of it. She thought longingly of Mark's promise.

As they walked, Cara found herself watching Eerin. There was definitely something wrong. The Elpind's usual springy gait was a steady plod, and each time the humans took a sit-down break, hin took one, too. The Elpind also ate steadily as they walked. Cara watched as the alien wadded and thrust bundle after bundle of sestel stems under hin's tongue. *It's a wonder hin doesn't get sick,* she thought, concerned.

Cara's unease was heightened by the fact that both Mark and the Simiu were watching Eerin every bit as intently as she was.

After nearly two hours of following the water, a small hill rose up before them.

"Going around would be the long way," Mark said, checking the plotter. "The lake should be right on the other side of this hill. We can pick up the stream again on the other side."

They were halfway up when Hrrakk' yipped sharply. Cara, following his gaze, looked up into the sky and gasped. The Shadowbird soared by overhead, a splash of brilliant colors against the pale blue of Elseemar's sky. The bird voiced that high-pitched musical cry that was so similar to Eerin's kareen.

"Elseewas!" cried Eerin. Hin leaped into a bounding run. "The lake!"

Mark sprinted after the Elpind. "Hurry, Cara! Come on!"

Waving her camera on, Cara forced her tired legs into a run as she followed the others over the crest of the hill and halfway down the other slope, skidding to a stop where the group paused. The lake spread out before their view.

It was small but apparently very deep, for the water shaded to a vivid blue in the middle. Reflections from the surrounding yellow flame trees (as Cara had come to think of them) slanted across its smooth surface, giving the illusion of a sapphire set in a golden brooch.

What are we watching for? Cara wondered, then she remembered Mark's story about the Elseewas. She shaded her eyes from the setting sun to scan the sky. *Is this one going to do its final dance and then its suicide dive?* "Do you think it's making its last flight?" Cara asked the Elpind.

"Perhaps. If so, we will be privileged. It is said that to see the death of an Elseewas is to have one's life changed forever," Eerin said quietly.

"There it is!" Mark cried, pointing. The sun had nearly set by now, and the first moon was clearly visible. But even in the fading light, the bird seemed to glow as it soared against the sky. The last, slanting rays from the setting sun struck sparks of scarlet fire off its wings.

The Elseewas looped in a slow glide around the lake's perimeter. It flew low, just clearing the tops of the trees. Its song was soft and low, a bittersweet dirge.

It's saying good-bye, thought Cara. *Good-bye to all the earthly pleasures of life, like food and warm breezes and a tree to shelter in.* She thought suddenly, painfully, of Misir.

The bird wheeled majestically over the lake, turning on its side and swooping so low that the tip of one red-feathered wing ruffled the calm surface of the water. Cara held her breath, thinking this must be the moment when the Elseewas would sink down farther and drown.

But the bird leveled out, then, flapping its wings powerfully, it rose into the air again. The full-bodied, mournful notes of its song ceased. Again the bird shrilled a single note, but this one was the leaping-up, joyful note they had heard so many times during the start of the Mortenwol.

Cara gasped as the Elseewas suddenly angled sharply up. Driving like pistons, its powerful wings cut the air, propelling the creature higher and higher. Now its song split into tumbling trills, and its body spun and twirled in aerial somersaults through the sky. A bright reflection of its colorful, carefree beauty flashed back and forth across the surface of the lake.

The song trembled in the air, and the bird soared upward in a tight spiral. Cara strained her eyes, waiting for it to climb out of sight.

But just before it disappeared, the Shadowbird spread its wings to their furthest, slowed, then arced over in a seemingly impossible turn that was nearly a backward flip. For a long, long moment the Elseewas hovered, its song altering from melody to more of a penetrating call.

Cara imagined she heard urgency in the sound and an eager anticipation. *It sounds the way you do when you shout to someone on the other side of a door, "Open up! I'll be right there!"* she thought.

The Elseewas tilted gently so that the variegated tail pointed up and its sleek, red head pointed downward. Once more the mighty wings beat air. The first stroke propelled the bird into a dive, the second and third gave that dive hurtling speed. The red wings folded tightly to its body as it plunged down . . . down . . .

It was a long way down, and all the way that wild, glad cry rang from the Shadowbird's throat.

A ruby reflection trembled to the surface of the water like a welcoming spirit, and the bird burst through. A small plume of water was flung up, then fell back with a quick splash and a watery exhalation almost like a sigh. Darting ripples danced out from the center and then rings of slower, larger ones floated farther out and gently disappeared.

Silence spread over the lake like benediction.

Cara felt Mark's hand slide around hers and grip tightly.

Eerin woke when the third moon, Elrans, rode a high apex in the sky. With the angles of Aanbas, the first-to-rise, and Orood, the last-to-set, they made an elongated triangle overhead, and nested in the center of the triangle was the tiny fourth moonlet, Inid. The night was a chiaroscuro of black and white as the shadows skittered.

The Elpind shifted restlessly as yet another of the eleven sacred points on hin's body erupted into fiery pain. Eerin reached cautious fingers to take inventory. Yes, the sixth slirin was open. One more day—perhaps less—before Enelwo.

Eerin watched the shadows flit across the sleeping shapes of hin's companions and touch the back of the tall, light-haired figure standing watch. They were comforting, these shadows, and hin was glad to be, if not home, at least on Elseemar.

The thought of home brought a different pain. In the wide valley dotted with softly shaped hills and nourished by the deep waters of the rivers Rainel and Rainwo, the Change was a known thing. At the opening of the first slirin the call went out to all the family, and feasting began. At the last moment, just before all strength fled, the one-who-was-to-Change danced the last Mortenwol that would ever be danced as a neuter, and all the young hin of the family joined in. And when the slisrin began to weep in earnest, the elder siblings, those who had already become han and heen, began the vigil.

All these things were done and always had been done, and many times Eerin had seen in hin's mind how it would be when the word went out, "Eerin nears Enelwo."

Now it would not be so.

Eerin looked at the sleepers, at Mark's guarding figure again. These companions had become dear, but they were not Elspind. They could not know how it felt to dance to the threshold of one's second birth. They could not comprehend the chasm that separated hin from han and heen, nor the many-sided whirl of joy and terror at crossing it.

Was there any way to explain the comfort of even Wo's dark presence through the journey, a comfort formed of long and close association, a comfort resting on the total absence of something Eerin saw clearly in the humans? Hin doubted it. This fear of death in them, it was so much darker than Wo itself.

The Elpind sat up and reached for the nearby stash of sestel stems, hastily rolled a round wad, and slipped it under hin's tongue. With shaking fingers hin prepared a dozen more while the words of an ancient Telling echoed in hin's memory:

"The hunger before Enelwo is first one of preparation, then of strong need, and, finally, a craving that beats like a pulse through the body. The hunger that rises after Enelwo is many times more a craving: deeper than the bone, swifter-rushing than the fevered blood, and sweet, very sweet. To eat will quench the fire of hunger; to mate will also soothe, but will also kindle greater fire. By the mystery of rizel do shadows cast shadows."

Eerin thrust another wad of sestel beneath hin's tongue, rose, then slipped like a silent white shadow to Mark's side.

The human started when hin appeared. "You're not supposed to sneak up on the person standing watch," he complained.

Eerin looked up into the face that had become so familiar. "Mark Kenner was still very tired when hin awoke heen for Mark's turn at watch . . . but that time is past, is it not? Why does Mark not sleep again?"

"I was supposed to wake Hrrakk' for watch an hour ago," the human admitted, "but by then I was wide awake. I keep thinking about the Shadowbird, seeing it again in that final plunge." Mark studied hin. "Eerin . . . what's wrong with you? Tell me, please."

The Elpind hesitated. The time had come to tell hin's pair partner, and Eerin dreaded to see pain enter Mark's eyes. Heen would regard the Change only as a prelude to Wo, not as life's greatest adventure.

Seeing the Elpind's reluctance, Mark spoke again. "You're about to go through Enelwo, aren't you?"

Eerin sighed. "Mark is correct."

The young man nodded, then looked away. "I knew it. Are you scared?"

"No."

"But why is it happening early? Three whole years early!" On the last words a hint of the anguished resistance Eerin had been expecting touched Mark's voice.

"It is not unknown for Enelwo to come early."

"Three *years*?"

"There are some factors that are often associated with an early Change," hin admitted. "Elspind live in the cool river valleys in the midst of mountains. Only for one brief period during Elseemar's cycle about the sun does the temperature in those valleys rise unpleasantly high. It is then that the hin who will mature during that cycle experience Enelwo. The desert . . . is always hot. No hin would go there lightly."

"You're saying that it was the desert heat that triggered this early Change? That it altered your hormonal balance?"

"Hin believes so. The stress may have been a factor, also."

"Shit!" Mark stalked away a few meters and stood with his back to the Elpind.

Eerin saw the tension in his body and did not follow.

After a long moment of silence Mark said, still with his back turned, "Being held captive by the hijackers all those days, that was stress no one could have predicted or, once it began, stopped. But, when we . . . when I was choosing volunteers for this team . . . *Why?*" He whirled back around. "Why didn't you tell me what could happen? Why didn't you stay with the ship?"

"The ship was in the desert," Eerin pointed out gently. "The heat would still have been there. And the stress."

"Yeah, but staying with the ship wouldn't have been as physically taxing as hiking across the desert," Mark pointed out.

"Hin wished to go with Mark. Hin wished to be a part of the effort to help bring rescue to the *Asimov*. It was people from hin's own world that caused the crash; there was a debt to pay."

Eerin looked at the human pleadingly. "Mark must believe that it does not matter what caused Enelwo to come early. Hin is now ready to experience the next step in hin's lifecycle; that is what matters. Hin is . . . " Eerin searched for a word to describe the emotions hin felt, the restlessness, the eagerness for the new beginning. "Mark, hin is excited!"

Mark looked intently at the Elpind. "But the Change can be dangerous for your people, right?"

"True. El and Wo step close together at that time."

"Will it be more dangerous, this Change, because it's coming so early?"

"Hin does not know." Mark's mouth twisted with what hin had come to know meant unhappiness. "But all is progressing well," Eerin added, to reassure the human. "The hunger and the craving for sleep come from the body's drive to store energy for the exertion to follow. And the slisrin are opening as they should."

"The what?"

"Does Mark wish to see?" Eerin moved so that moonlight shone full on hin's left side and gently pulled apart the swollen, painful edges of an finger-long slit just above hin's left hipbone.

"This is a slirin. There are eleven and each one must open in preparation for Enelwo. From the slisrin will flow the lacmore, which is secreted from glands deep beneath the skin. Six of hin's eleven slisrin have now opened."

Mark looked closely, then nodded. "How long?" he asked.

"Perhaps another day. Maybe less."

"Your family is supposed to be with you during this time, aren't they?"

"Yes," hin admitted with regret.

"Is there a ritual connected with Enelwo?" Mark asked.

"Just the final Mortenwol as a neuter before hin goes into the Change, then, during Enelwo itself, hin's older siblings would keep vigil while hin is helpless in the throes of Enelwo."

"Eerin," Mark said, sounding very solemn, "I will stand vigil. Cara too, probably. I know it won't be the same, but at least you'll know you're not alone."

"Hin is grateful," Eerin said slowly. "Especially in light of the way Mark feels about this Change coming early."

The human shrugged. "I'm doing my best." He hesitated. "Uh . . . listen, you'd better tell me what to expect."

Eerin explained the sequence of events that would take place as the physical preparation of hin's body accelerated, then what would actually happen during the Change.

"I understand," Mark said when the Elpind was finished. "And I'll remember what you have told me. I'm trying to be happy for you, Eerin." He sighed. "I just wish you'd had the opportunity to take Elhanin . . . I know you wouldn't have taken it to extend your normal lifetime, but maybe you'd have taken it to give yourself all the time you rightfully should have had."

"No, hin would not have," Eerin said. "Hin knew this might happen, and yet hin refused the Elhanin when it was offered."

Mark stiffened. "When it was—" He stared hard at the Elpind. "You had the chance to take Elhanin?"

Eerin nodded silently.

"When?" Mark asked.

"It was offered soon after the crash."

"By whom?" the human demanded. "R'Fzarth and Sarozz were dead, and they were the scientists aboard . . . " He trailed off, and Eerin saw the realization dawn in the hazel eyes. "Hrrakk'," he said. "It was Hrrakk', wasn't it? He's some kind of botanist."

The Elpind nodded. "A very highly regarded one, apparently. Though working out of heen's own laboratory on Hurrreeah, Hrrakk' was collaborating with the CLS medical research team.

At their request, heen was on the way to a medical conference on Shassiszss to speak on the potential of Elhanin. But heen's ship developed a problem, and heen was transferred to the *Asimov*."

"So the Wospind didn't know he was aboard," Mark said. "If they had, they'd have killed him, too."

"Hin believes that is quite likely," Eerin said sadly.

"And he has Elhanin with him?"

"Yes. A sample he was going to use as an exhibit for the other scientists' analysis. Hrrakk' offered the sample to hin soon after the crash, knowing the effect of heat on Elpind neuters. But hin refused it, and hin does not regret that."

"Okay," Mark said. "I understand . . . and I respect your choices, Eerin." He smiled wryly. "I may not *agree* with it, but I respect it. I'll do everything I can to help you get through Enelwo."

Eerin regarded the human curiously. "Mark has changed from that night we spoke in the desert," hin said thoughtfully. "Mark is no longer cherishing heen's anger at life."

"You mean that I'm not running away anymore?" Mark said.

The Elpind considered silently. "Perhaps Mark is still walking away, but heen is definitely no longer running."

The human chuckled dryly. "Well put, Eerin. I had a long talk with Cara after Misir died, and that's part of my change, I think. She helped me put things in perspective. But the main thing . . . " He took a deep breath. "Eerin, you said that to see the death of a Shadowbird is to have one's life changed forever. Well, I don't know about that, but I do know I've been doing some hard thinking since we left that lake."

"Hin can see that."

"I want to stop running . . . and being afraid."

"Hin understands. Mark wishes to live life the way one dances the Mortenwol."

Mark thought that over. "Something like that. I'm trying to change. Do you think I can?"

"Mark Kenner has great strength and courage. And great understanding that comes from the heart. Hin has seen this."

"Thank you," said Mark softly. "I have not. But I'm going to start trying to feel it. I'm going to try to let go a little more, trust my instincts more, and, most of all, try to celebrate life the way your people do."

"Hin is very glad to hear this."

Mark smiled and broke the mood. "You know, this has answered a lot of questions that were bothering me, especially about Hrrakk'. I'd been wondering why he knew so much about Elseemar's plants, how to recognize wild sestel and so forth."

"It is the wild sestel that is the basis of Elhanin," Eerin said. "Hrrakk' told hin so."

"Really? But how—"

The Elpind shook hin's head. "For the answers to Mark's questions, heen must ask Hrrakk'."

Mark grimaced. "As if he'd tell me. He thinks humans—and particularly *this* human"—he tapped his chest—"are the lowest of the low. But you're right, it's his secret, so I should discuss it with him, not you."

Eerin sighed heavily. "Hin must sleep again now." The Elpind looked up at the moons and shivered, feeling the strange and heavy fatigue again. "Mark should sleep again, also."

The next morning Mark awakened to sprinkles of rain that soon became a downpour. Even with wet socks rubbing new blisters on his feet, he set a fast pace for the group. If they could maintain it, they would reach the nahah on the following day.

As he had yesterday, Mark watched his pair partner intently. His hope that the cooling rain might revive Eerin somewhat went unrealized. Eerin's voracious eating persisted, and the Elpind appeared very worn. Hin's golden eyes were dull, and hin seemed totally self-absorbed.

"Okay, Mark," Cara had said to him when she'd awakened and seen the Elpind this morning, "something is obviously wrong with Eerin. What's going on?"

"I was going to tell you," Mark assured her. They were alone save for Terris; the other members of their party had gone off for what they euphemistically referred to as their morning "constitutionals." Mark went on to explain as he sat cross-legged on the grassy ground, the warm rain dripping off his nose and hair, and feeding Terris.

Cara had listened in silence, then nodded thoughtfully. "That's too bad," she said. "But as long as Eerin isn't sorry about it,

I guess it would be silly for me to get upset."

Envying Cara her quiet tolerance, Mark had sighed. *If only I could feel that kind of acceptance* . . . "There's more," he'd added. "We were right about Hrrakk' keeping secrets . . . " He went on to tell her all that Eerin had revealed about the Simiu. "Do you think I should ask him about it?" he concluded. "Let him know that I know?"

"I don't know," Cara said. "He's perfectly capable of just ignoring you, he's good at that. But if you sense that the moment is right . . . maybe you should try it."

Just then Hrrakk' and R'Thessra returned, and, by mutual unspoken agreement, they dropped the subject.

Late afternoon found them wending their sodden way through a thick stand of tall, interlacing, heavily needled trees. Suddenly Eerin began making sounds that, in a human, would have been deep gasps.

Mark halted immediately. "Eerin, what is it?"

"Hin miscalculated the time until Enelwo." Eerin panted, swaying slightly. "Nine of hin's slisrin are now open."

Mark's heart was pounding. "Should we stop?"

The Elpind nodded. "But not here. Hin must still dance the Mortenwol for the last time as a neuter, and hin wishes that to be under the sky." While it was a bit drier under the canopy of intertwining branches, it was also quite gloomy.

"Eerin, maybe it's not a good idea for you to dance the Mortenwol," Mark protested. The Elpind appeared ready to collapse at his feet.

"It is tradition. The one-who-is-to-Change dances only once after the slisrin begin to open, and that is at the last moment before all strength is gone. Hin must be prepared for a new life or for death. Whichever Enelwo is to bring, hin *must* be prepared!" Exhausted, Eerin plopped down on the wet ground, but the golden eyes were full of determination.

Seeing his premonition fulfilled when Eerin could no longer stand, Mark crouched down next to the Elpind. "I understand the importance," he said. "But are you physically capable of it? If you fell and injured yourself . . . "

"Hin will be able," insisted Eerin, bracing hinself with hin's hands to stay upright.

"But you can't even walk!"

Hrrakk' spoke up in Mizari. "I will carry the Elpind. Place hin on my back."

Eerin gave the Simiu a grateful look. Mark gently took hold of the Elpind's bony arm, feeling the slickness of the water-soaked down, then helped Eerin up. He lifted the alien onto Hrrakk's broad back, the way he would have placed a human child on a pony, watching as hin twisted hin's fingers in the rippling bronze mane.

Even Terris, from hinsi's clinging point just below Mark's left collarbone, squawked with interest at the proceedings.

They walked on, continuing past sunset. At some point the rain stopped, though it was hard to tell when, because water continued to drip steadily from the leaves.

Another hour brought them out from under the trees and to the base of a huge vertical cliff. The wind had risen, sending the cloud cover scudding away in ragged clumps, and they could see that the first two moons were already up. Shifting striations moved across the face of the cliff as the moonlight picked out crevice after crevice. The only sound was the soughing of the trees in the wind that had sprung up.

"So beautiful," breathed Cara.

Mark shivered, hating the feel of his wet clothing in the cool breeze, but he was as awed by the sight as Cara. He understood why Eerin wanted to get out under open sky to dance the Mortenwol.

He looked over at Hrrakk' and his rider. Eerin had sagged a little more with each passing hour until, now, hin did not so much sit as sprawl across the Simiu's powerful back, eyes closed. Hin's creamy fluff was slicked down in bedraggled whorls.

"Let's hurry and find a place to stop where Eerin can dance," said Mark. Privately he felt sure that even with Hrrakk's help these last three hours Eerin had miscalculated; hin's strength was already gone.

Going over the top of the rocky cliff was unthinkable, but the map showed a way around in either direction. The group walked for fifteen minutes parallel to the rock face and past tumbled heaps of boulders along its base. One boulder stood out larger than the others in front of them. Mark rounded it first.

"This is it," he said immediately. "If Eerin's going to dance the Mortenwol, this is the place."

The small meadow hung on the very side of the mountain. Here and there, scattered in the thick, springy grass, were clumps of time-smoothed rocks, but there was plenty of open space. The third moon had joined the first two now, and in the increased light Mark could see wildflowers on skinny stalks. They swayed gracefully in the breeze and cast dancing, multiple shadows across the grass.

From its high perch the meadow commanded a spectacular view of valleys and mountains rolling away as far as could be seen. Their color was lost in the black and white contrast of Elseemar's night, but the hard, radiant clarity of the scene, then a sensation of blurriness as shadows shifted, and then another freeze into clarity gave a surrealistic beauty to the whole that day could never have matched.

Hrrakk' stopped, then, with Cara's help, slid the limp Elpind off his back.

Mark took the kareen out of his knapsack. "We're here, Eerin," he said, reaching for the Elpind's shoulder, "time to dance the—"

"Mark, listen!" Cara broke in. "Do you hear something?"

"Like what?"

Without replying, she crossed the little meadow to the edge where it seemed to drop off into the air. "Hey, there's a path over here. It comes right up the side of the mountain."

Mark joined her. It was true. What looked like a sheer drop from the other side was actually a steep, but passable, series of slopes down to a valley floor. A narrow, switchback trail snaked up them.

"We're fairly close to the nahah now. I'll bet the Elspind roam all over these mountains looking for those mreto nuts Eerin told me grow at this altitude," he said. "It's possible that we won't have to walk all the way to the nahah to find help; it might find us."

Mark peered down the trail. "What did you think—Cara!" He jumped back from the edge, pulling her with him. "Somebody's coming up the path!"

"I knew I heard something!" Cara said excitedly. "Here's the help you were talking about!"

"Let's make sure that's what it is, first," Mark cautioned.

He hustled the group back to the boulder at the far edge of the meadow, and they hid behind it. Eerin had no trouble keeping up. Oddly, hin had come out of sleep almost like hin's old, energetic self.

It's the determination to dance the Mortenwol, decided Mark, noting a feverish light in the huge eyes.

"There may be some hin to dance with," Eerin said hopefully.

A round, creamy head rose up into view over the edge of the meadow, and then the body, and then another head behind it, and then a whole file of aliens climbed steadily up and into the meadow.

Mark counted twelve. The downy, unclothed bodies of nine marked them as hin. The other three, clad in loose, long tunics, were heen.

One of the heen turned so that he faced their hidden watching group, and in the bright moonlight Mark saw clearly the emblem on his tunic.

"Oh, shit . . . " he breathed.

They were Wospind.

CHAPTER 17
◆
The Change

Voices speaking Elspindlor carried distinctly through the still night as Mark and his companions crouched, hidden, and listened. "The time has come," said one of the Wospind. "Hin must dance now."

"The search can wait a few hours," said another. "There is only the one group left to find."

Mark shivered, and sudden fear made him faintly sick. *Oh, God, they've captured the two other teams! And now they're looking for us! The other parties must have told them we were headed for the nahah. Are they going after the* ***Asimov****, too?*

He watched, his mouth dry with fear, as the Wospind piled their weapons at the base of one of the large boulders. They were armed as Eerin had described to him once, with weapons the Wospind had revived. They were ancient weapons from days long ago when Elspind had fought over territory and even mates: short, jagged-toothed steel spears, slings, and long steel knives that reminded Mark of an ancient Roman *gladius*.

One modern weapon lay gleaming anachronistically amid the old-fashioned arsenal: a repulsor gun. Standard issue to CLS sociological teams, repulsor guns were designed to deliver a stunning shock, but not injure a target seriously. They were used on primal worlds to protect researchers against wildlife.

Suddenly the distinctive sound of a kareen shrilled forth, and Mark looked back at the meadow. The male Wospind were now seated, but all nine of the neuters, with feathers on their heads, stood in a loose circle.

"Don't tell me they're all going to dance the Mortenwol!" whispered Cara. He glanced at her out of the corner of his eye and saw her activate her camera.

"Only the hin are going to dance," Eerin told them in a hushed voice. "That means that one of them nears Enelwo. Hin sees! There is the one who begins the Change." Eerin pointed, just as each dancer erupted into that first, soaring leap.

The Wospind danced with the same grace and ease that Eerin always did, and the energy of the Mortenwol poured off them with an intensity that was nine times multiplied. The sweet, high music of the kareen echoed and reechoed off the rocky mountainside, floating away on the breeze like a chorus of ghostly voices.

Which one did Eerin say is beginning the Change? It was hard to watch any individual as they dancers wove in and out of their patterns, but Mark tried. Finally he saw one that was different from the rest. Hin still glistened from the afternoon rain, while the others appeared to be dry.

No, not rain, Mark realized. *That's the fluid that comes out of the slisrin. It's all over hin!*

Reflexively, he glanced at Eerin, and saw that his pair partner also glistened in the moonlight. Clear drops of liquid slicked Eerin's down.

Mark's throat tightened as he watched Eerin, who was observing the dance with a sad, hungry yearning in hin's eyes. He knew why. By the time they were safely away from the Wospind, it would probably be too late for his friend. Eerin would enter Enelwo without having danced the last Mortenwol as a hin.

And if hin dies during the Change, he realized, *hin will have met death without being prepared.*

"Eerin, I'm sorry," Mark whispered. "We can try going back into the woods. Can you dance without the music?"

"Do not worry. Hin is watching the Mortenwol and dancing in hin's heart," Eerin said. The Elpind's courage touched Mark. Clumsily he patted the alien's shoulder.

Hearing the change of melody that signified the end of the Mortenwol, Mark looked back at the dancers. In unison, the circle made that final leap and wafted back to the ground. One, the glistening one, sagged to hin's knees.

That's right, Mark thought, *Eerin said they wait until the last minutes to dance their last Mortenwol as neuters*. In response to an imperious gesture from a large, darkish-colored neuter, several Wospind dashed over to the fallen Wopind and lifted hin. In seconds, carrying the one-who-was-to-Change, the group was heading away, out the other end of the meadow.

"Hin is the leader of the group," Eerin said, indicating the one who'd made the commanding gesture and who now walked alone at the head of the disappearing column. Then the Elpind gasped and sagged against the rock. "It is time," hin whispered.

"Thank God the Wospind are going to be stopping for the same reason we are," said Mark. "At least it gives us time to plan. Let's go back a little way. I want to be damn sure this mountain is between us and them tonight."

Cara looked at him sharply. "You think they're looking for us?" She hadn't understood the overheard Elspindlor, of course.

"I know they are," Mark said grimly, and explained.

"Damn! Mark, we can't hole up and hide from them, we have to keep going! If everyone else has been captured, that means it's *really* up to us to notify the CLS about the *Asimov*! They're depending on us!"

Mark indicated Eerin, who was gasping shallowly, hin's golden eyes glassy with shock or pain. "We've got to stop for a while, Cara," he said.

Looking somewhat abashed, she nodded. "You're right. Maybe by tomorrow they'll be gone."

Mark nodded and helped Eerin stand. "Eerin, do you want to ride on Hrrakk's—"

But the Simiu didn't wait for a response. He simply marched over and stood waiting. Mark picked up the limp Elpind, placed hin on the Simiu's back, then prepared to walk alongside to hold the alien on. By that time, Eerin was unconscious.

• • •

Cara and R'Thessra led the group to shelter in the shadow of the huge cliff, behind two huge rocks that formed a natural windbreak. Cara gazed apprehensively up at the rocky expanse towering over them. *I hope nothing drops down on us during the night,* she thought, then realized suddenly that the same hope held true for the Wospind.

We're really in a mess, she thought with a sigh. *After Eerin goes through the Change, what are we going to do?*

"Here we are, Eerin," Mark's voice reached her, still hushed even though they were some distance away from the meadow now, and the Wospind had been traveling in the opposite direction. "Let me help you off."

She watched as Mark and Hrrakk' eased the Elpind down on the grass within the shelter of the boulders. Eerin trembled violently. In the moonlight hin gleamed with moisture.

The journalist moved over to the Elpind. "Eerin, is it all right to film you during the Change?" she asked.

Eerin tried to speak, but no sounds emerged. Instead hin's long, broad tongue shot out like a snake's. It was furled so deeply that the two edges met at the top of the curl and the whole formed a small, hollow tube. Then the tongue snapped back into the Elpind's mouth.

Cara gasped and recoiled.

"It's okay, that's normal," said Mark quickly, though he looked a little shaken himself. "It's the beginning of the breathing reflex, that's all."

"The what?"

"You'll see. Eerin told me last night what to expect, more or less. This means hin's pretty far along. It really is time!" He gave a quick glance at her camera. "Go ahead and film this, if you want. If Eerin doesn't want it recorded, you can always erase the footage later."

Eerin thrashed, turning on hin's side. Hin's legs drew up, the sharp knees pressed against the downy chest. The Elpind's arms wrapped around hin's legs. Eerin's eyes were wide and abstracted, almost glassy. The two humans watched in mingled fascination and anxiety. The Simiu and the Apis stayed on the other side of the clearing, but they, too, watched.

"Going inward," Cara whispered.

"What?"

"Eerin's eyes. Like hin's looking inside instead of out."

"Oh. Yeah."

But at that moment, the Elpind squeezed hin's eyes shut. Strain wrinkled the round face, and then Cara couldn't see Eerin's expression anymore because the head pulled down, tucking in tighter and completing the curved shape of the Elpind's body.

A sharp, quick tremor, different from the other trembling, raced over the alien's form. Suddenly thick, milky fluid sprayed up from the hollow between Eerin's neck and shoulder.

"Oh, God, Mark!" Cara jumped as the liquid spattered over Eerin's body and the ground, almost hitting her shoes. She backed away, wide-eyed, as the miniature geysers continued to erupt, spraying out in rhythmic pulses.

"That's the eleventh slirin," said Mark. "The big one."

Smaller jets of fluid began to spurt from points all over Eerin's body. The breeze shifted a bit, and the odor reached Cara. She clapped a hand over her mouth, gagging, fighting not to be sick. The exudate smelled like a cross between badly soured milk and cheap perfume.

Beside her, Mark was also trying to control his nausea as he grabbed her arm and pulled her back, upwind.

Tears flooded Cara's eyes, and she suddenly found herself crying. She sank down on a low-lying rock, sobbing bitterly. Mark put an arm around her shoulder, and she leaned against him, gasping out words between sobs. "Oh, Mark, I'm sorry . . . but I just realized . . . this whole thing is so . . . so . . . *strange*, and Eerin might *die*—and the poor thing didn't even . . . get to dance . . . the last Mortenwol!"

He hugged her. "I know. I feel bad for hin, too."

She burrowed her face against him. "It's not . . . just Eerin. Mark, what if the Wospind find us? How did they find out about us . . . from torturing the others? Maybe they *killed* them!"

"I don't know," he said softly. "Eerin told me that Orim was the one who inspired them to violence, and Orim's dead. Who knows what that new leader we saw today is like?"

Cara blotted her tears on his shirt, snuffling as she fought to stop weeping. "I keep thinking I'm never going to see home again, Mark."

"I know." He pulled her close to him, so her head rested against his chest. His heartbeat was strong and somehow comforting. "I've been worrying that I'll never see StarBridge or Rob again. That's the closest thing I have to a home or a family now."

Suddenly something poked Cara's cheek, and she drew back, startled, choking on a last, strangled sob. It was Terris, who'd awakened from a sound sleep to find something strange invading hinsi's territory. Hinsi squawked indignantly.

"Terris, Terris, Terris," Mark complained, "the first time I get this woman in my arms this whole trek, and you wake up and spoil it."

Cara managed a feeble smile, then she remembered something. "Oh, damn!" she muttered furiously, turning back to the Elpind.

"What is it?"

"I just realized that for the last five minutes I've been wasting footage on your shoulder and my sniffling."

"Everybody Hendricks is back on the job," Mark said dryly. "I knew my grimy charms couldn't distract you from your journalistic duties for long."

Cara barely heard him, fascinated as she was by what was happening to Eerin. The geysers were sputtering out. The fluid that came from the slisrin now was even thicker, and it poured steadily instead of spurting.

The Elpind's body moved slightly, and Cara held her breath. *What now?* But the movement was only a relaxation of the tight muscles, a boneless abandonment so complete that Cara knew she'd just seen Eerin lose consciousness.

Oh, God, she thought. *What must it be like to undergo something like this? Like giving birth . . . only you're even more helpless . . .* "Is Eerin breathing?" she whispered.

"The tongue makes a breathing tube," said Mark. "That's how they keep from smothering in the fluid, which Eerin said is called lacmore. It's a survival reflex."

Yes, she could see now. With the loosening of the taut curl, Eerin's face was no longer totally buried in hin's chest. Thick, milky fluid had already seeped over the facial features, obscuring them, but the long orange tongue stuck out, furled into a tube.

As far as Cara was concerned, that frozen tongue just added to Eerin's overall deathlike appearance, but she didn't say so. At least the regular whistling sound of the Elpind's breath was comforting.

The liquid flowed steadily over Eerin's body. Hin lay in a white, viscous puddle, but the puddle was no longer spreading. The minute Eerin had become totally soaked with it, the fluid had begun to adhere to itself, it seemed. It no longer seeped onto the ground.

Layer by layer the exudate built up, until all the scoops and hollows of Eerin's outline were filled in. Hin became a featureless, slightly oblong shape on the ground, nothing more.

"I'm going to take a closer look," Cara said.

Hrrakk' and the Apis were also moving in for a closer inspection. She'd nearly forgotten about them in her absorption with what was happening to the Elpind.

The Simiu circled the cocoon, looking it over thoroughly, then nodded in seeming satisfaction. Cara realized he'd probably seen this before, if not firsthand, then at least in holos his colleagues would have made on Elseemar and sent to him on Hurrreeah. Hrrakk' would know if anything wasn't happening the way it should.

Cara moved closer, trying to breathe through her mouth. The smell was still appalling, and her stomach churned, but she was determined to get a close-range look.

The lacmore no longer flowed; it had hardened. *No,* Cara decided, *not hardened, exactly. It's jelled!*

Now Eerin was nothing more than a dark, indistinct shape in the center of the gelatinous mass. The only break in the surface of the cocoon was where the orange tongue poked through.

Cara listened for a minute to the rhythm of the whistling breath that came through the tongue-tube. "Eerin's breathing seems slower now than at first. A lot slower!" she said in careful, worried Mizari to Hrrakk'.

"That is normal," the Simiu grunted. He went to sit against a rock on the other side of their windbreak and R'Thessra followed him. Cara went back to Mark. She glanced back at Eerin one more time. No change. She waved her camera off, her stomach rumbling suddenly with hunger. The journalist fetched the canteen and some of what she'd dubbed the flame-grapes that she'd gathered as they walked along the lake boundary after the Shadowbird's death plunge. She and Mark shared them silently.

Time went by, and Cara slipped off the rock to sit on a piece of the sheeting to protect her from the damp ground. Eerin's cocoon remained the same, only that whistling intake of breath indicating that their friend still lived inside there. Thinking of such profound changes made Cara shudder, even as a huge yawn caught her unawares.

"So what are we going to do about the Wospind?" she asked, swallowing another yawn.

"I think the best thing *you* can do is get some sleep," Mark said. "The time Enelwo takes varies, but it should be over by late tomorrow, if not before. We can talk about what to do in the morning."

She gave him a surprised glance. "Aren't *you* going to sleep?"

"No, I promised Eerin I'd take the place of hin's older siblings and keep a vigil. I couldn't sleep anyway," he said.

"But we walked all day," she protested.

"If I find myself getting sleepy, I'll wake Hrrakk'," Mark promised.

"Okay," Cara murmured. "Wake me . . . if anything happens."

Lying down, she pillowed her head on her arms, then lay watching Eerin's cocoon until she fell asleep.

Mark's concentration on the problem of the Wospind was compromised by his fear for Eerin. Every time the shadows played over the cocoon Mark thought he saw movement of the dark shape within, but it was always just a trick of the moonlight. His body ached with tension, and he could think of little besides the question uppermost in his mind: *Will Eerin survive?*

He let his gaze shift thoughtfully to the Simiu. Hardly more than an hour had passed since Cara went to sleep and already Hrrakk' had gotten up twice to check the cocoon. Eerin had told him there was nothing anyone could do if something went wrong during this stage, but it was comforting to Mark to know that if it did, he and the Simiu would discover the fact together. *We're both keeping vigil,* he realized. *I wonder whether Hrrakk' gave Eerin a formal promise, too?*

Rising, he strolled around the small, sheltered nook that Cara and R'Thessra had found, grateful for the huge rocks that kept the night breeze off. His clothes were finally dry, but it was cooler tonight. His shadows leaped and rippled around him.

The Simiu looked up as Mark squatted in front of him. "What is it, human?" He kept his voice low in deference to the Apis, who slept, wings stilled, on the ground next to him, but it was still gruff, still cold and noncommittal.

Mark sighed. "Good evening, Honored Hrrakk'," he said, determined to be polite, even if the Simiu wasn't. "You might notice that *I* don't address *you* as 'Hey, Simiu!' "

"That word is one that *your* kind saddled my people with," the alien said coldly. "Unfortunately, since my language is difficult for most species to pronounce, that distasteful human appellation has fallen into common usage throughout the CLS."

Mark was taken aback. "None of my Simiu friends at StarBridge ever said they found it distasteful."

"It likens my people to *animals* that live on your world," Hrrakk' said scornfully. "Animals that *your* kind ate in some cultures, and used to perform vivisection on in others. Would you be flattered, in my place?"

"I guess I wouldn't," Mark said, shaken. He knew that Simiu were strictly vegetarian and were repelled by the human habit of eating meat (though synthetic protein had almost replaced that practice, at least for those living off-planet; shipping animal products was prohibitively expensive). "I'm sorry, I never thought of it that way. If you'll teach me how to say your species' name properly, I promise I won't use that word again."

Hrrakk' shrugged. "You might as well. Everyone else does."

"Uh . . . listen, Honored Hrrakk' . . . " Mark hesitated, then brought up the subject on his mind. "We need to figure out how we're going to elude the Wospind and still get help from the nahah. Have you given it any thought?"

The Simiu nodded. "I have a plan."

Damn, but he's so self-righteous! "Okay, let's hear it."

"The Elpind will be very weak, unable to walk for at least a full day, after heen or han emerges from the cocoon."

"Go on."

"If Enelwo continues to go well, Eerin will emerge shortly after dawn. I will carry the Elpind, and we will walk most of the day. That should bring us nearly to the nahah. At that point we will split up; R'Thessra and I will leave the group."

Mark was already shaking his head no. He was faintly surprised at himself, because a few short days ago he'd wished the Simiu would stay with the ship, join another group, do anything but come with him. But despite the alien's continuing distaste for humans, he'd proved an invaluable help, and Mark knew it.

Hrrakk' ignored his protest. "I am sure Eerin has told you by now that I am one of the researchers connected with the development of Elhanin. My name is known to many of the Wospind. If they discover me, my life is forfeit, just as Sarozz's was."

"Couldn't you give them a false name?" Mark suggested.

The Simiu's glance was scathing. "My name is an honored one! I will not dishonor myself or my clan by doing such a cowardly, honorless thing!"

"Okay," Mark backed down in a hurry. "I'm sorry. I didn't mean to impugn your honor."

"After you have left R'Thessra and me behind, the Apis and I will head for a prearranged meeting place, known only to you," Hrrakk' said. "You and the others will continue to the nahah. Then you humans will hide outside, sending the Elpind in alone. Eerin will determine whether the nahah is safe. If it is, heen or han will return for you. You will send a signal to me—a fire made with green branches, for example—so I can see the smoke from a distance. Then R'Thessra and I will wait for CLS pickup by shuttle at the spot we have agreed upon."

"And if the nahah is in Wospind hands?"

"Then you must lead Cara to join R'Thessra and me in the mountains. At that time, we can determine what to do next."

"Where does that leave Eerin?"

"Wospind are also Elspind; I do not believe they would harm one of their own. Eerin can deny all knowledge of the group, claim that after the crash hin walked alone to the nahah. Later, after the Wospind are no longer suspicious, Eerin can leave, try for another, non-Wospind refuge, then contact the CLS."

"What about Terris? I can't take hinsi into hiding."

"Eerin can take the child into the nahah. There will be a family who will take hinsi."

It was a decent plan, Mark had to admit. It smacked a little too much of sacrificing Eerin for his taste, but nothing was perfect.

"Okay," he said, and stood up. "It's a good plan."

Mark turned to go, then stopped. "One more thing. About R'Thessra . . . "

"Yes?" Hrrakk' was impatient.

"Is she a researcher, too?"

"No. But her younger hive-sister was. I held an honor-bond with R'Fissis, who was killed in the Wopind attack on the lab. R'Thessra was on her way to Elseemar so that she could mourn her sister and end her days on the same world where R'Fissis died. When I learned R'Thessra's identity, honor demanded that I protect her, as I was not able to protect R'Fissis." Hrrakk's crest flattened. "I fail to see that this concerns you, human."

"It doesn't really. I just wanted to know whether she'd be in danger from the Wospind, too."

"We are all off-worlders. We are all in danger from them."

"Yeah. Well, I know you don't think much of human honor, but we do have our own kind. So I'd like to propose an honor-bond between *us*—you and me."

The Simiu drew himself up. "What do you mean?"

"If anything happens to me, I'd like you to look out for Cara. If anything happens to *you*, I swear to you that I'll do my best to care for and protect R'Thessra."

The Simiu looked at him oddly, and did not reply.

"Is it a deal?" Mark asked.

Slowly, the alien nodded. "We have an honor-bond, human, though before this journey, I would have said such a thing was impossible."

"Thanks, Honored Hrrakk'." Mark walked away.

Cara awoke before dawn when Mark nudged her. Groaning, she straightened up stiffly. "How's Eerin?"

"You said to wake you if there was any change. Go take a look."

"Incredible!" Cara said a moment later as she squatted next

to the tongue-made breathing tube. Breath was coming and going rapidly now. The lacmore was beginning to ooze, dripping off the surface of the cocoon.

"Hrrakk' said Eerin should emerge just after morning light," said Mark.

"Did you sleep at all?"

"No, I promised Eerin I'd keep vigil. But I feel okay. I rested, lying down, a lot."

"You should have awakened me," she chided. "I'd have sat up and watched."

"You looked beat. Besides, I had Hrrakk' to talk to," he said dryly.

Cara looked at him. "You're kidding, right?"

"No, actually I'm not. We had a long talk. He's worked out a pretty good plan—better than anything I came up with." Briefly, he related the details.

"That seems workable," she admitted after he finished. Cara glanced over at the Apis. "That's awful about her sister." Rising, she crossed the small clearing to join the insectoid alien. R'Thessra's dark, faceted eyes fixed on her, and she allowed her antennae to droop.

I think she knows Hrrakk' told us, Cara thought. It seemed to her that the Apis' gesture with her antennae was an acknowledgment of a grief that had been private until now.

The journalist bent slightly and, very gently, touched one of the alien's forelimbs. "I'm sorry about your hive-sister," she said in Mizari. "I grieve for your loss."

In return, R'Thessra touched the human's cheek. Cara smiled at her. "Come over to the cocoon. Something is happening."

For the next hour the four waited impatiently. The breathing tube wheezed with ever-quickening rhythm, and the lacmore began to slide off in great, messy globules. It stank, but not as badly as it had when fresh. *Or my nose is getting deadened,* Cara thought wryly.

"You know," Mark said in English as he sat, arms wrapped around his knees, gazing intently at Eerin's cocoon. The Apis and the Simiu waited nearby. "I feel as though I'm losing a friend . . . someone I've known for a long time."

"Well, you are, in a way. Eerin explained how strong the mating drive is after the Change," Cara agreed with him. "It won't be the same between you two. But you can still be friends . . . you'll just have to be friends in a different way."

Mark's hazel eyes warmed. "You're right. It will just take a little while to make the adjustment. I have to give it time."

He turned to regard the journalist just as earnestly as he had Eerin's shrouded form. "You know, Cara, you have a gift for understanding all kinds of people. You ought to think about becoming an interrelator. The CLS needs people like you."

His words sparked something that had been growing inside her ever since she'd first journeyed to StarBridge and seen her first alien. "You know, nothing would please me more," Cara told him. "I've discovered that alien cultures interest me more than anything on Earth. But . . . " She frowned. "I'm too old to start at StarBridge. And what about my journalism?"

"You're not too old. Look how much Mizari you've learned in just a short time. You could use your journalism talents, too; interrelators often integrate the skills of several fields. The minute you get home I want you to send a message back to Rob. And when I get back to the Academy, I'll talk to him."

Cara took a deep breath. "My mother would have a fit. After this, she's going to want me to stay firmly planted on Earth." *We **have** to believe that we're going to get home,* she thought. *We have to believe it, so we can keep going.*

"Is your camera on?" Mark asked suddenly.

Instantly Cara transferred her whole attention back to the cocoon. The tip of Eerin's bony shoulder was suddenly protruding through the lacmore.

"It's been on," she answered. "I wanted to get the breathing and the dripping. I can compress the data later. Look, I can see the whole outline clearly now."

"I just thought of something," Mark said. "Eerin will need clothes for the first time. All the han or heen wear them."

Cara fetched the long-tailed shirt that had been her headgear in the desert, and they laid it out, ready.

Now the lacmore was running off in little streams. Eerin's shoulder, then the round head, then the angular hipbone appeared.

"I feel strange knowing this before Eerin does, but hin's a han." Mark's voice was hushed. "A female."

"How can you tell?"

"Look at the skin."

Cara studied the emerging figure. The patches of skin that showed were smooth and tender-looking as a baby's. "That's right, the females are hairless."

In a few more minutes almost all of the Elpind was visible. Cara threw her shirt over the curled body, studying Eerin's face. It looked unchanged to her, except for the texture of the skin and the fact that the top of the head was bald now instead of downy. *The skin's a paler orange,* she decided.

The Elpind's tongue suddenly snapped back into Eerin's mouth, and a few moments later, the huge, golden eyes opened.

"Welcome back, Eerin," Mark said gently. "El won."

"Mark . . . " Eerin's voice was unchanged, though weak. Han's eyes were cloudy with fatigue, but an affectionate light warmed them.

Eerin looked back at Mark and Cara. "Eerin is han," the Elpind announced. Sudden excitement strengthened the thin voice.

Cara felt tears in her eyes and knew she had a silly grin. "You sure are."

"This is so . . . interesting . . . " Eerin said. The golden eyes brightened. "Han feels so different. As if han has always been female. Han feels . . . complete."

"You're very fortunate, Eerin," Cara gave Mark a sideways glance. "You definitely got the luck of the draw."

He sighed exaggeratedly and rolled his eyes.

After another hour Eerin was able to sit up and eat, then, strengthened, han announced that she was ready to go. Soon Eerin was astride the Simiu.

"No talking on the trail today," Mark warned as they started out. "Listen for anyone approaching."

He kept a rag that he'd soaked in sestel broth ready to give Terris to suck on if they had to hide suddenly. Despite his lack of sleep, Mark was alert as they walked, tight as a drawn bowstring.

As he walked, he tried to think of contingency plans to complement Hrrakk's, in case the Wospind reappeared. But each time he visualized falling into Wopind hands, his mind went blank. All he could remember was the mad gleam in Orim's eyes. *It's terrifying, trying to deal with fanatics,* he thought grimly. *If all Wospind are like Orim, they'll kill us on sight anyway, so what's the use of contingency plans?*

In the late afternoon the group skirted another of the mountain cluster's seemingly endless humps and began a downhill slope through the woods. Through the wide-spaced trees, Mark could see a stream and a small emerald jewel of a tiny valley. He consulted the map.

"One more climb," he whispered. "The straightest way is across this little valley, and up that ridge over there." He pointed it out. "Midway down the other side is the nahah. We can make it by dark." He was too weary and tense to be excited.

"We made it," breathed Cara. She sat down and removed her socks, changed them. Mark took the opportunity to feed Terris.

"Not yet, we haven't," he cautioned, still speaking softly. "Since we haven't seen any Wospind, I'm concerned that maybe they're at the nahah, waiting for us." He glanced around uneasily. "In that valley, we'll be in plain sight. I hate to lose the tree cover."

"Maybe we should skirt the valley, staying in the trees," Cara suggested. "But if we're going to do that, I'll volunteer to get some water at that stream. We're almost out."

"I don't know"—Mark frowned—"skirting the valley will take a lot of extra time. It looks so peaceful . . . " He glanced over at the Simiu uncertainly.

"If anyone comes, we will see them from a distance," Hrrakk' pointed out.

"Okay," Mark said finally with a sigh. "The valley it is. Everybody ready? Let's go."

Cara groaned. "Those famous words again. I'll be so glad when I don't have to hear them anymore."

Cautiously they ventured out through the shorter, bushier underbrush that bordered the little valley. The silence was reassuring. Cara glanced longingly at the little stream. "You sure I can't go get some fresh water?"

"We can make it on what we have," Mark said firmly.

That's where the Wospind took them.

CHAPTER 18

♦

Death Dance

With scarely a sound, their attackers emerged from their hiding places amid the thick underbrush on the verge of the forest. Between one moment and the next, the travelers found themselves surrounded by more than a score of Wospind. Red tunics of the heen and han made bright splashes of color against the varied greens of the vegetation as they stepped into view. All of them carried weapons—the saw-toothed spears, the long, swordlike knives, or slings filled with heavy rocks.

The moment he saw them, Mark stopped dead—they all did—instinctively crouching into fighting stance, hands and feet ready. But when he saw how they were outnumbered, he straightened slowly back up, bracing himself for the quick spear or sword thrust that would end his life. *Terris!* he thought, hastily pulling aside his outer shirt, so their attackers could clearly see the child clinging to his sweater. He knew that even Wospind wouldn't intentionally harm a baby of their own species.

The small army of Wospind rippled, and the one they had seen before, the dun-colored neuter, stepped forward. In hin's hand, hin carried the repulsor gun. Its muzzle was pointed straight at Mark.

The human struggled to speak, but no words emerged. All his hard-won knowledge of Elspindlor seemed to have deserted him as the leader approached, hin's pale green eyes fastened coldly on Terris. "It is not enough that off-worlders corrupt our people with forbidden ideas," the Wopind burst out angrily. "It is not enough that, because of them, hin's sibling, Orim, is dead. Now they also steal our children!"

"Wait a minute, I didn't—" Mark began, but the hin, though giving a start of surprise at hearing the human speak hin's own language, ignored him, beckoning to one of the others. A red-clad male stepped out of the group, pointing his spear at Mark's throat in an unmistakable warning to be silent.

The Wopind leader grabbed Terris, who squalled, terrified, and clung to Mark with all hinsi's strength as the hin tugged one-handed. The sweater stretched, pulling the student forward, but the baby would not let go.

Mark reached up with the intention of soothing hinsi, intending to detach Terris himself, but the menacing guard evidently misinterpreted his movement. Bounding forward, the guard jabbed at Mark's throat with the spear, and the human, feeling the sharp point graze the skin, leaped back reflexively.

Pandemonium ensued.

The heen rushed again at Mark, this time intent on spearing him, but recoiled suddenly as R'Thessra flew between them, wings beating furiously in the Wopind's face. Screaming with mingled fear and rage, the guard thrust at her, but missed.

Several other Wospind charged in to help Mark's attacker and the next moment the air seemed filled with flashing spears and swords!

A hard-flung stone whizzed by Mark's head, barely missing him, just as he heard the *thwup* of the repulsor weapon. Another stone hurtled at him, straight for his face.

Mark ducked, stumbled, then found himself falling. He rolled to protect Terris, hearing, as he did so, Hrrakk's snarl of rage. Suddenly the Simiu roared in pain and fury. Mark came up on his hands and knees, then immediately froze as a hand grasped his hair; something cold and sharp touched the back of his neck.

The human could move only his eyes, and he struggled to focus on the melee before him. Abruptly the blur of movement halted, then resolved into concrete images that burned into his brain.

The Wopind leader, repulsor gun in hand, stood looking down at two bodies lying on the ground before hin. One was a female in her red tunic, the side of her head sunken in and bleeding sluggishly, and the other was . . . the other was R'Thessra.

Oh, God, no!

The Apis lay on her back, wings crushed beneath her carapace, forelimbs jerking uncontrollably. Mark could see no wounds. The Wopind leader must have shot her, and the charge in the repulsor weapon had flung her down so hard that her wings had broken—and something inside her, too, evidently, for even as the horrified student realized what had happened, the little alien jerked once more, then was still.

Cara was crouched beside her, vainly trying to offer help or comfort. "Oh, no!" she gasped, and began to sob.

Between the journalist and the Wospind stood Hrrakk', his enormous canines bared in a full Simiu challenge, his left hand up and ready for battle. His right arm hung limp and helpless, the result of the jagged spear protruding from his muscled shoulder.

Hrrakk' glanced sideways, and the human saw pain flood his violet eyes as the Simiu realized R'Thessra was dead. The big alien did not budge, however, but snarled his challenge again. "Touch her and die!" he growled in Mizari.

He's defending Cara. Is it just because of his honor-bond with me? Mark's intuition told him that it was more than that.

In the sudden silence of the tableau, Terris' crying was the only sound.

Mark cautiously turned his head to see who was holding the weapon against the back of his neck. It was one of the hin. Mark said in Elspindlor, "I am going to stand up now. I will not fight or resist," then slowly, deliberately, rose to his feet. The point of the Wopind's sword now rested against the small of his back.

It's a standoff, Mark realized. *They don't really want to kill us, or they'd already have done it. What the hell am I going to do now?*

Quite suddenly, he knew. "Wopind leader!" he called out.

The other regarded him coldly.

"You said that I stole your hinsi, but you are mistaken," Mark cried. "This child was given to me by one of your people who was dying, with the plea that I would care for and nurture hinsi, and carry hinsi to safety, where hinsi could be cared for by other Elspind. I see that I have succeeded in doing that."

Gently, regretfully, Mark soothed Terris for the last time, then carefully detached the baby from his sweater. Hinsi lay cuddled in his palms, blinking up at him trustingly with those enormous eyes. Mark's throat tightened as he took a step toward the Wopind leader.

The sword did not bite into his back, so he took another, then another. Slowly, one step at a time, he crossed the ground that separated him from the hin. When he reached the Wopind, he halted, feeling tears break free and run down his face.

"Good-bye, Terris," he whispered, and held out the baby.

The Wopind leader stared at him, then inspected Terris closely. "You came from the off-world ship that hin's sibling Orim brought down out of the sky?" hin asked, as if doubting it suddenly.

"I did," Mark said.

The Wopind leader glanced back down at the baby, lying quietly, contentedly, across Mark's palms. "You have cared for hinsi since the ship came down?"

"I have," Mark said. "Hinsi's name is Terris."

"Hinsi appears . . . healthy."

"I did my best to care for hinsi as well as any adoptive father could," Mark said.

Slowly the Wopind reached out and scooped the baby out of Mark's hands. Terris immediately began to wail, stretching hinsi's twiglike little arms out toward the human.

Mark's attention was arrested by a labored moan and gurgle from the direction of his feet. He looked down at the injured Wopind. "Hrrakk'," he said in Mizari, "did you hit her?"

"No," answered the Simiu, pain evident in his voice—whether pain from his wound, or for his dead friend, Mark did not know. "One of the stones from her own people's slings struck her."

I have to establish common ground, Mark thought. *It was*

only when I was able to convince Orim that I totally understood and respected hin's goals that I got anywhere negotiating with hin. Can I do the same thing now? An idea was forming in his mind. "Your friend here is dying," he said to the leader. "Someone must dance the Mortenwol for han."

The Wopind leader looked down at the gasping female. "What do you know of our ways, off-worlder? What do you know of the Mortenwol?"

"I know that this one has the right to have someone dance the Mortenwol for han—and that none of your people have moved to do so," Mark said, holding the leader's eyes with his own, putting into his gaze all the conviction and intensity he could muster. "Therefore *I* will do it!" he cried, raising his voice so all could hear. "I will dance the Mortenwol for han, and then you will see what I know of your ways!"

The entire group of Wospind—Mark saw that now there were at least fifty or sixty—stood watching him, silent with astonishment.

The student hesitated. *I'll bet there are some kind of ritual words I should say!* he thought frantically. *But I wasn't there when Eerin danced for the hijacker.*

Before his pause became awkward, though, Eerin was suddenly there, staggering a little with weakness, Mark's knapsack in her hands. When she reached his side, she swayed and had to grasp his arm for support, but then she drew herself up, and together, they faced the Wopind leader.

"Mark Kenner knows much of our ways," she said. "Heen's Mortenwol will honor the journey-taker." Eerin looked up at Mark, her golden eyes full of trust and hope. Then she knelt, with his help, beside the dying Wopind. "Journey-taker!" she said in a loud, formal voice. "Behold your last Mortenwol!"

The stricken female's amber-colored eyes opened, then widened incredulously as they regarded Mark. Hastily the human picked up his knapsack and removed Eerin's two cases, then he fumbled out the kareen and wound it.

He opened the other case and fished out the two deep red feathers, the dark green one, the two soft blue ones. Adrenaline made Mark's hands tremble, and he dropped the green feather. He retrieved it hastily. *How the hell am I going to manage this?* he wondered. He'd been going on instinct, trusting his gut feeling, but now the craziness of what he was attempting, the near impossibility, was catching up to him.

How was he, an ordinary human, going to manage a dance that would challenge a ballet dancer or a null-grav gymnast? Still his hands moved, sweating and awkward, weaving the feathers together as he had seen Eerin do so many times.

Mark reached up and set the chaplet of Elseewas feathers on his head. A stir went through the Wospind surrounding him. Terris was still crying, and the pitiful sobs tugged at Mark's heart. He forced himself to ignore hinsi and concentrate as he stepped into the middle of the little circle, within sight of the dying Wopind, the kareen in his hands. The Wopind leader must have gestured behind the human's back, for suddenly all of the onlookers stepped back, leaving a good-sized space.

Mark turned back to Eerin and the others. First he gazed at the dying han, and said, "I am dancing for you, journey-taker," then he bowed his head in the direction of R'Thessra's corpse. "And I am dancing for you, my departed friend."

Quickly, before he could lose his nerve, Mark laid the kareen off to one side and his fingers went out, pressing its four sides at once. The little music board's low, powerful throb emerged. Mark took a deep breath. *Mortenwol,* he thought. *Death dance. And if you screw this up, that's just what it will be—for you and for everyone else!*

Carefully he tapped the spidery symbol in the middle of the little music board, activating it. Then he straightened and stood waiting. A kaleidoscope of sensations washed over him; the springiness of the meadow grass, the smell of alien blood, the sun's heat, the wispy brush of the feathers. The headpiece weighed nothing, but at that moment, it seemed to Mark that the weight of an entire world was pressing him down.

The kareen's first high, clear note rang out. Mark remembered the Elseewas, seeing its last flight in his mind. The note swelled out sweet and pure into the air, slowly at first, and then with the sudden throb that had always been Eerin's cue to leap for the stratosphere.

But I'm too heavy to do that, he thought desperately. *Even in Elseemar's lighter gravity, I'm too heavy . . . I can't do it . . .*

Shit, Mark thought. *I have to try!* He closed his eyes and spun, then threw his arms up over his head and followed them into the air.

The jar of the landing traveled through his entire abused body. Mark stumbled, almost losing his balance. He clenched his jaw, forcing himself to see Eerin's body moving in his mind, as hin had floated lightly through the patterns of the dance. He strained to remember the sequence of steps.

The second, upward-swelling note sounded, the one that meant melody was coming. *Back one, two forward, side-hop and spin, reverse and alternate.* Frantically reviewing the pattern that went with the first melodic theme, Mark heard the music tumble out. He floundered after it, already two beats behind. His feet had lost the rhythm; that meant that *he* was lost . . . had lost this desperate gamble . . .

How does Eerin do it? How?

The image of Eerin in Mark's mind suddenly flowed into and merged with the image of the Shadowbird. They became one, flying and dancing together, the music lifting them, pulling them, whirling them. Mark gave up trying to remember the patterns, and simply let his body follow that soaring image, half bird, half Elpind, that filled his mind.

The first melodic run was ready to repeat. Mark opened himself to the music, spreading his arms to echo the image in his mind that the rippling notes conjured up. The first downbeat reached him, and miraculously his body knew, or remembered, he wasn't sure how, and he stepped back smartly, keeping the rhythm.

A breath, and then it was forward—*and forward again—and, yes, knees bent slightly now, and now sideways, and yes, that fits, that's right, then spin and . . .*

The pulse of the music, a hot wildness just beneath the sweet overlay, captured him, ensnared him. It had always called to his blood, even when watching, and now, somehow, it *was* his blood, flowing over him, through him. The music/blood swirled and flowed and ran free. Mark's feet followed surely, unerringly.

The trills and runs wove their familiar patterns, and Mark followed the Eerin/Shadowbird that danced in his memory. *Feel it, the life they both love, the life that includes death, but does not end there . . .*

Joy sprang up in Mark. Miracles surrounded him: pumping heart, heaving lungs, light feet, swift-rushing blood, but they were nothing . . . nothing compared to the wonder of his sudden freedom. Now *he* was the Shadowbird, unfettered, and he flew wild and beautiful and free above the fear, above the sorrow, above the anger.

Faces filled his mind, his memory: Hrrakk's when the Simiu had stood by to steady him in the desert, Cara's bent over the dying Misir, Terris' trusting green eyes. R'Thessra, touching Cara gently, tenderly, and Eerin, leaning over a small grave, hin's treasured white feather in hand. There were other faces, too: Captain Loachin's, Rob Gable's, Esteemed Sarozz's—

—and his mother's.

This time, her memory did not bring pain, for Mark knew that she had understood, and loved him, and forgiven him—as he had finally forgiven himself.

The faces whirled in his memory, as his body whirled in the dance, and a great love for all of them welled up in him. Why hadn't he heard it before in the music? Love, strong and steady, was the beat that held the patterns in place.

The music began to rise toward its final crescendo. A new note, one saved for the final moments of Mortenwol, slipped out from beneath a trill. It swelled, closer and closer to breaking free, closer and closer to owning the song.

Yes, take it, urged Mark. *Take me!*

And when it did, when the music said it was natural to become part of the air, Mark let go completely, leaping higher than he had ever thought he could, letting the sweet, pure vibration of the final note lift him beyond all reason. For a moment he hung suspended, half convinced that he would never come down.

Then his feet were back on the ground, and the echo of the final note floated away into the sky like the smoke of an offering. Mark was breathing harder than he ever had in his life, great, tearing gasps that hurt his chest, but felt wonderful, too.

The circle of Wospind stood in silence. Every eye was on him. Terris' cries were the only sound to be heard. Panting, Mark turned to regard the Wopind leader and stared deep into hin's green eyes.

Then the hin walked toward him, still carrying the baby. The leader stopped in the center of the circle, hin's eyes still fixed on Mark's face. "What is heen's name?" the Wopind asked.

"Mark . . . " He struggled for breath, forcing himself not to bend over, swallowing back the saliva flooding his mouth. "Mark Kenner."

"Hin is Hilnar," the Wopind leader said. "And the journey-taker, Liron, who now embraces Wo, received and cherished han's last Mortenwol, Mark Kenner." At this point, Terris, still howling as hinsi clung to the down on Hilnar's chest, turned and saw Mark. Hinsi's wails strengthened.

The Wopind looked down at the baby, then carefully plucked the infant off hin's chest, one-handed because the child did not attempt to cling to hin. "Terris cries for hinsi's adoptive father," Hilnar said, and handed hinsi back to Mark.

Astonished, smiling incredulously, Mark took Terris and snuggled hinsi against his chest. He stroked the child, whose wails ceased. Exhausted, Terris immediately went to sleep.

Hilnar nodded, hin's green eyes glowing. "The quiet is welcome, is it not?"

"It is." Mark looked over at his friends. Cara was standing there openmouthed, but Eerin was nodding, as though saying, "I knew you could do it!"

"In the quiet," Mark added, "it is easier to talk. It seems to me that we have much to talk about, Hilnar."

The Wopind leader regarded him unblinkingly. "Mark Kenner has shown that it is possible for off-worlders to understand Elpind customs and rites," Hilnar said at last. "Heen's Mortenwol, while different from an Elpind's, still contained the joy that is the essence of our culture. Hin did not think that was possible, not from an off-worlder. Now hin must consider all that hin has seen today."

Hilnar paused, then added, "And after hin has considered, we will talk."

Cara sat amid the shadows, keeping vigil over R'Thessra's body. Her tears had dried long ago, but her heart still ached. *I hope she knew how I felt about her*, she thought sadly. *My respect, my admiration for her. She always thought of others before herself. And to think we never exchanged a single sentence . . .*

They'd made no grave for the Apis. "If we can, we'll take her to Lalcipind," Mark had said as they wrapped the fragile body first in its own wings and then with a piece of the sheeting. "She would want to rest near her hive-sister."

The "if we can" reflected their current situation. Hours had passed since Mark had performed the Mortenwol, night had fallen, and still they did not know what the Wospind planned to do with them.

Eerin had spoken with their captors and learned that the other parties from the *Asimov* were being held in one of the Wopind settlements, two days' journey from this small valley.

Hilnar was now the head of all the Wospind groups, having taken the leadership after Orim's death. Eerin's informant had also told her that when Hilnar was informed of the crashed *Asimov*, hin had immediately sent out a party of heen and han (mindful of the dangers of the desert heat to hin) to take water and food to the downed *Asimov*. The Wospind party had orders to escort all the survivors back to Hilnar.

Cara couldn't decide whether Reyvinik and the others would be better off with the crashed ship, or with the Wospind. But from what Eerin had learned, the Wospind had not harmed any of the off-worlders except for R'Thessra and Hrrakk'.

She glanced over into the next patch of shadows. The Simiu slept there, the deep wound he had received from the Wopind's spear now poulticed and bandaged, as Hrrakk' himself had directed.

Cara was still amazed that Hrrakk' had obviously been prepared to die defending her. And yet, the Simiu was still his taciturn self. When she and Mark had finished ministering to his wound, he'd turned his back on them and lain down without a word.

If I live to be a hundred, she thought, *I'll never understand Hrrakk'!*

Now she shivered, rubbing her arms against the chill of the night breeze, wishing they'd lit a fire. It would have been comforting. The Wospind had fires. She could see them halfway across the meadow, small, red hearts of heat.

Cara knew there were guards surrounding them, there had to be. But the Wospind had been careful to stay out of their way, allowing their captives to move as they wished about their own small, separate camp, permitting them to come and go freely to the stream for water. The journalist's first thought when evening fell had been that perhaps they should try to escape, but upon further consideration, she hadn't even brought up the suggestion.

For one thing, Eerin was still too weak to walk far, and Hrrakk' could no longer carry her. Cara, having seen the Simiu's wound close-up, was frankly surprised that the alien could move at all. But they'd already known Hrrakk' was tough.

And Mark, of course, was exhausted. No sleep last night, and then the Mortenwol today. He lay close beside her as she sat on their one remaining piece of sheeting, curled on his side, deeply asleep.

Remembering the way he'd danced the Mortenwol, the journalist smiled faintly, ruefully. The spectacle of a lifetime, and she'd totally forgotten to activate her camera!

Shadows shifted again as tiny Inid climbed higher still in Elseemar's sky. Cara looked up at the four moons, watching them silently, remembering R'Thessra, then thinking of Eerin and her face as she'd watched the human's Mortenwol.

Mark stirred in his sleep, and Cara glanced down at him. His hair glimmered ghostly silver in the moonlight. How ridiculous he'd looked, with Eerin's feathers jammed down over his head! And that awful beginning, that first awkward leap, the stumble . . . she'd wanted to close her eyes and not have to watch. But somewhere during that first long measure, he'd suddenly begun to dance, really *dance. Then something came alive in him,* Cara thought.

Not for one minute had Mark's dance been Eerin's. But what Mark's dance had lacked in grace and airiness had been more than balanced with . . . Cara searched for the right word. *Passion*, she decided. It had been the difference between the wafting dance of a feather and the leaping-up of a fierce flame. They'd all felt it.

Waves of joy had radiated from the whirling figure, waves that had eased Cara's grief as she'd crouched by R'Thessra's crumpled body. She felt sure that, in finally understanding the Mortenwol, Mark had made peace with himself.

Cara sat staring up at the moons, thinking of all that had happened since she had first set out for StarBridge Academy so many months ago. The thought of the school, of going there to learn about other species, made her pulse quicken a little.

I've certainly gotten a crash course in the Elspind, she mused. *And tomorrow, all of us are going to get a crash course on the Wospind . . .* Her unintentional choice of words made her smile grimly. *I just hope that "crash" isn't the operational word again.*

Mark stiffened, then jerked in his sleep, mumbled something indistinct in Elspindlor, then moved restlessly against her hip. His legs drew up, then thrust down, as though he were leaping.

He's dreaming, Cara realized. *Dancing the Mortenwol in his sleep . . .* Gently she stroked his hair, his cheek, her touch as light as one of Eerin's Elseewas feathers. Finally he relaxed and slumbered deeply again.

CHAPTER 19
♦
The Interrelator

Mark awoke the next morning when Terris began squawking hungrily in his ear. He sat up, reaching automatically for the canteen containing the sestel broth, and fed the baby. As he changed hinsi, he examined the downy little form, and decided that the child was definitely larger than when he'd first seen hinsi.

"You're growing, Terris," he whispered. "Getting big."

The thought that his days with the child were now definitely numbered made his throat tighten painfully. He was glad of the distraction when he heard his name called.

Looking up, he saw Eerin coming across the meadow toward him. A male Wopind walked close by her side. Yesterday the Elpind had been so weak, so drooping, but today she moved with all Eerin's old energy—and more. The heen at her side could scarcely keep his eyes off her.

Mark scrambled up and stared as she stopped before him. In the warm light of early morning, the Elpind seemed positively luminous—han's peach-colored skin had a definite sheen to it, a glow that almost matched the one in the golden eyes. Eerin seemed radiantly alive in a way he'd never seen before.

"Eerin, you . . . you look so different! You're . . . glowing!" Mark stammered. He couldn't get over the difference from the wan, feeble creature of yesterday.

Eerin bounced happily. "Han will be desirable to a heen now, will han not?" At first the human thought her question was rhetorical, but then he caught her sideways glance at the heen.

Mark studied the male Wopind. He was about Eerin's height, with thick, tan-colored fur and eyes just a shade darker than his friend's.

"This is Reenor," Eerin introduced, giving her escort a dazzling glance. "Heen changed the same night han did. Mark remembers."

He certainly did. "It's nice to meet you, Reenor," Mark said, feeling rather like the older brother of a teenage girl being introduced to the first serious boyfriend. The air between Reenor and Eerin fairly sizzled with mutual attraction.

"We came to ask Mark to dance the Mortenwol with us," Eerin invited.

"Are you sure you're up to it already? Yesterday . . . " Mark trailed off, shaking his head and smiling. From the joyous look on Eerin's face, han was up to anything.

The Elpind nodded. "Once again it will be done every morning, just as before Enelwo. Come, dance with us!"

"I couldn't," Mark protested. "I'd feel silly. Yesterday, when I started, I was so clumsy, and . . . " He trailed off. "And I don't have the same need driving me today."

"Mark is learning. From what han saw yesterday, heen will learn very well indeed. And, remember, it is not the steps, but the feeling as one does them that makes the Mortenwol." A challenge shone in the golden eyes. "Yesterday, Mark *understood* the Mortenwol, han could tell. Has Mark forgotten everything heen has learned?"

The human smiled slowly, remembering. "No, I haven't." He took a deep breath. "Eerin, I would *love* to dance the Mortenwol with you two."

"This time, my camera's going to be on," Cara announced, having just come back from a wash at the stream. "I'm not missing the chance of a lifetime twice!"

Mark grinned. "Okay, 'everybody,' let's go."

Minutes later Mark stood between the two Elspind in the middle of the grassy meadow, beneath the dawn sky. At the first high, sweet note of the kareen, Mark's heart rose within him. Together, he and his pair partner—and, he suspected, Eerin's soon-to-be mate—spun and leaped and wove the patterns.

As they finished Mark realized that several of the Wospind, drawn by the sound of the kareen, had come to watch. He recognized Hilnar. The leader beckoned to him. "Hin is ready to talk," Hilnar said. "Mark Kenner will please bring heen's companions."

As Eerin and Mark walked back together to fetch Hrrakk', the human hesitated, then blurted, "Eerin, I don't mean to tell you what you should or shouldn't do, but Reenor—heen's a Wopind!"

"Han knows that," Eerin replied, her golden eyes bright. "But Mark must understand . . . the fire of the rizel burns, and there is no denying it. The fire within han awoke the moment han saw Reenor, and it burns even now."

Suddenly Eerin was reciting. "The hunger *before* Enelwo is first one of preparation, then of strong need, and, finally, a craving that beats like a pulse through the body. The hunger that rises *after* Enelwo is many times more a craving: deeper than the bone, swifter rushing than the fevered blood, and sweet, very sweet."

The Elpind gazed at Mark. "The Telling continues to describe rizel, the act of mating. Rizel is the next great adventure, and han is eager for it." Eerin's golden gaze deepened, as han searched Mark's eyes. "Mark did not understand the Mortenwol until heen danced it. This feeling is one that Mark can perhaps never completely share, but han asks Mark to accept."

The human remembered how the blood had rushed through his body, remembered that shining moment when he'd felt able to love all the worlds and beings in the universe. He smiled at his friend and nodded.

Eerin skipped happily. "Mark Kenner is a great interrelator," han said, repeating her favorite declaration.

Mark took a deep breath and squared his shoulders as he looked up the hill at the Wospind leaders who awaited them. "Well, I'm going to do my best," he said softly.

The travelers gathered with Hilnar and the other Wopind

leaders (including, Mark was interested to note, Reenor) beneath several large trees in one corner of the meadow. Armed Wospind stood guard outside the perimeter of their small circle, as they all sat on the ground.

"Hin received a messenger bird this morning," the Wopind leader began as soon as they were all settled. "The group hin sent to reach the ship has arrived there. They will depart tonight with the survivors of the crash to begin the journey into the mountains." The Wopind gazed around the circle. "Hin has given orders that the prisoners are to be well treated, and that they must not be harmed."

Mark gazed straight at hin. "And what are your plans for the off-worlders, once you have them all within your grasp, Ri-El Hilnar?"

The Wopind leader hesitated. "At first, hin was planning to follow the example of Orim, and insist that the CLS take them and never return to Elseemar."

"But that plan has changed? How?" Mark prompted.

"Now hin is not sure. Hin has seen that at least one off-worlder truly understands our world, our ways. If there is one, there could be others who respect our culture."

"I assure you that the CLS prides itself on respecting the cultures of worlds it contacts," Mark said. "I come from a school where students spend at least five years learning to respect and preserve the cultures of other peoples."

The Wopind glanced up, startled. *To hin, five years is a third of hin's life,* Mark thought sadly.

Hilnar indicated the others in the circle. "Do these friends of Mark Kenner's also speak Elspindlor?"

"No, they do not," Mark said. "If you wish to address them, I will translate."

"Reenor speaks the language known as Mizari," Hilnar warned. "Hin will be told if Mark Kenner does not translate accurately."

"I understand," Mark said.

"First, tell hin their names."

Mark hesitated. *Oh, shit!* The moment he had been dreading worst of all was here. "This is Eerin, as you may already have discovered," he said quietly, indicating the han who sat at his side. (Reenor, not surprisingly, sat on Eerin's other side, as if basking in her glow.) "Han and I have been friends for many days now. Han was with me at the school I told you of."

Quickly Hilnar turned to the Elpind and asked Eerin to describe han's impression of StarBridge. Mark listened as she told the Wopind leader of all the things she had learned.

"And this one?" Hilnar turned next to Cara.

Mark introduced the journalist, who smiled and greeted the Wopind leader in excellent Mizari, exhibiting admirable coolness.

All the while that Mark translated automatically for Cara, his mind was racing toward panic. *What the hell am I going to do?* he wondered. *Any second Hilnar's going to ask me to—*

"And who is this?" the Wopind leader asked, indicating Hrrakk'. Mark took a deep breath, then said to the Simiu, "Hin wants to know your name."

The violet eyes were grim. "We had this conversation once before, human. Tell Hilnar that I am Hrrakk', of the Harkk'ett clan!"

The student bit his lip, then said: "This is Honored Hrrakk', of the Harkk'ett clan, from the world called Hurrreeah."

For a moment he thought he was going to get away with it, then Reenor said urgently to Hilnar, "This is one of the scientists, Ri-El Hilnar! Heen heard this one's name spoken by the off-worlders in the nahah when they communicated with their leaders. They did not realize that heen understood their tongue. They worried about the fate of the scientist, Hrrakk', who was traveling to Shassiszss, to show some of the accursed Elhanin to other scientists. It is almost certain that heen has brought Elhanin into this camp!"

Hilnar drew hinself up, glaring at the Simiu. "Is this true?" hin demanded, then ordered Mark to translate. Miserably the human did so. Hrrakk' stared straight at the Wopind leader, then deliberately nodded. "It is true," he said.

The human glanced back at Hilnar, who was glaring furiously at the Simiu. "How dare this one bring that substance into our presence?" demanded the Wopind leader. "Heen is one of those who wishes to subvert our entire way of life!"

"Ri-El Hilnar," Mark began, "can you tell me exactly what your position is, regarding the Elhanin, and what you would like to see done about it? I have had some experience"—he repressed a sigh as he remembered Orim—"in negotiation. Perhaps I can help your people resolve their problems. I would like to help, because I like and respect your people. I respect *you* as a strong but rational leader."

For the next half hour, Hilnar and Reenor between them summarized the Wospind's position, already familiar to Mark from his time with Orim. The human paid close attention to everything they said, searching for ways to establish common ground, trying to think of possible compromises between the WirElspind and the Wospind position.

Thank God that Hilnar is a reasonable person, he thought as he listened. *Hin's no Orim. Hin takes hin's traditions very seriously indeed, but hin is not a fanatic . . .*

"Let me restate what I understand of what you have told me," Mark said when the Wospind finished, "so that you may correct me if I err. You believe that the WirElspind was wrong to request help from off-worlders in changing the Elpind lifecycle. You acknowledge that CLS contact may be a good thing for the people of Elseemar in some ways, but that the benefits are outweighed by the threat this research presents. Am I correct so far?"

Hilnar nodded. "The splendor of El is found in the willingness to seek joy and adventure in every moment up to and including Wo. Nothing must be allowed to interfere with that willingness! We do not wish to become as Reenor has told me the off-worlders are: afraid of Wo, fearing it more than anything."

Mark took a deep breath, then glanced up at the sky, remembering the flight of the Elseewas. "Hilnar, you feel concern that the off-worlders will change you," he began. "I don't believe that will come to pass. Your feelings about the Mortenwol are too deep, too profound, too *true*, to be easily overturned. You are underestimating the power of your own culture, your own truths.

"I tell you this, because, when I first came here to Elseemar, I was so afraid of Wo, and of El, too, that I was going to give up the work I had trained for at StarBridge. I was going to quit, run away, because of my fear."

Mark's hazel eyes held the leader's green ones. "But your planet, your people, your beliefs, have changed me. Yesterday, you saw me dance the Mortenwol. I have come to understand how your people feel about El and Wo, and I am attempting to adopt those ways of looking at the universe. Your world changed me, an off-worlder, not the other way around. And if I am permitted to live, and leave Elseemar, I will go back to StarBridge to complete my training. I will live El to the fullest, as your people have taught me."

"But Mark Kenner is only one of many," Hilnar pointed out. "And Mark must leave Elseemar, heen has said so."

"If you permit us to leave, yes, I will someday leave this world," the human said. "But if you wish, I would stay as long as necessary to convey your convictions, your wishes, to the CLS and the WirElspind. I could negotiate on your behalf."

"Does Mark believe that heen could convince the WirElspind and the CLS to stop the research on Elhanin?"

Mark hesitated. "I would not be honest if I told you that I believed that that was within my ability. But one thing I am *certain* of"—he fixed the leader with a steady gaze—"I am certain that I will be able to gain both the WirElspind's and the CLS's pledge that Wospind, if they do not wish to take Elhanin, will *never* have to do so. No one will give Elhanin to your children, or coerce them into taking it. This is a promise I am certain I can gain for you," he declared, knowing that he spoke truth.

All along, Eerin had told him that the life-extending drug would only be offered to those who chose to take it.

"Mark Kenner does not know the WirElspind," Hilnar said. "They will not make such a pledge, ever."

"Give me the chance to try," Mark pleaded. "I know that I can gain that pledge. If not, the CLS research will be suspended, because the CLS does not support tyrannical actions on the parts of planetary governments." He took a deep breath. "Hilnar . . . give me the chance to try. I can do it!"

The Wopind leader's green eyes remained unconvinced. "Hin can see that Mark is in earnest, but hin recalls that the WirElspind hates our views, our beliefs. They will not even allow the Wospind a seat on the Great Council."

"They will now," Eerin said suddenly.

The Wopind leader looked at her in surprise. "What?"

"Before han changed, han was a member of the WirElspind," Eerin told hin. "Now it is time for han to choose han's successor to take han's seat." Eerin gazed at Hilnar. "Lalcipind will need a new representative. Is that not the home-place of Hilnar, as it was for hin's sibling, Orim?"

"That is true," Hilnar replied.

Eerin fixed the Wopind with a steady gaze. "Ri-El Hilnar," the Elpind's voice rang out dramatically, "Ri-El Eerin of the WirElspind names hin to take han's seat on the WirElspind!" Han pointed directly at the Wopind.

The leader was plainly taken aback.

"And when han relates to the WirElspind the foolishness of Alanor, when hin spoke to Orim, threatening hin, goading hin into further violence," Eerin added solemnly, "there will be yet another seat available. Han will do everything in han's power to make sure that seat, too, goes to one of your group. Surely at least one Wospind was born in Caselmar!"

Mark dived back into the fray. "Hilnar," he said, "even if you do not wish a longer lifespan, think what you are doing in saying that no one should have that choice! You are doing exactly what you are afraid will happen to you. Do you wish to impose your beliefs on all the people of Elseemar? Isn't that something that could be left to each individual, that choice?"

"But if the longer lifespan is offered, our people will lose all dignity, all nobility, in the fear of Wo," Reenor said.

Eerin shook her head. "There will be many who will not choose the Elhanin. Before we left the *Asimov*, Hrrakk' offered han the drug, and han refused. Han does not believe that han is greater or more courageous than other Elspind. Hilnar, there will be a *choice* for our people. Hin can educate hin's children as hin wishes and sees fit."

"Drug!" Reenor echoed. "An unnatural substance, created from off-world chemicals—poisoning the bodies of Elspind, as well as their minds! Such a substance cannot be tolerated!"

Eerin shook her head. "Han spoke badly just now. Elhanin is *not* an off-world chemical. Hrrakk' told han it is made from wild sestel."

"Is this true?" Reenor turned to the Simiu and hastily translated Eerin's speech into Mizari.

"Yes. Elhanin is extracted and concentrated from the wild sestel," the Simiu said. Automatically, Mark translated each of the big alien's sentences. "Long ago, your legends say, the

Elspind lived longer. That was because, in those days, they foraged for their sestel.

"As time went by, the Elspind began to transplant sestel to grow as a crop. As generation upon generation passed, the Elspind depended more and more heavily upon cultivated sestel . . . sestel that gradually lost some of its properties as it evolved into a domesticated plant. As the sestel grew larger, more tender, juicier, more flavorful, the substance within the plant that extends the Elpind lifespan grew less and less. Now it hardly exists at all in the sestel grown by your people."

Mark turned to Hilnar. "Your people wish to return to the old ways, isn't that so?"

The Wopind nodded slowly.

"Well, if the Wospind stay up here in these remote mountains, foraging for most of their food, eating wild sestel, your people will be increasing your lifespan—slowly but surely! Almost as if you were taking Elhanin! Am I right, Honored Hrrakk'?" he demanded, and hastily translated.

The Simiu nodded. "Of course, the Elhanin is such a concentrated form of the chemo-influencer found in wild sestel that the Wospind would not notice a change for perhaps ten or more generations. But such an alteration would occur, I believe."

Turning back to the Wopind leader, and translating rapidly, Mark watched the impact of the Simiu's revelation. Hilnar was definitely shaken.

"Ri-El Hilnar," the human said, pressing this new advantage, "we have spoken together today in peace. We have been able to discuss your beliefs and wishes like reasonable people. I believe that we have both learned a great deal. I know that you have given me much to consider, and I hope that the same is true for you."

Slowly, deliberately, Mark made the Mizari bow of respect to the Wopind. "That gesture is a mark of highest respect within the CLS-member worlds. I give it to you because I have learned today that Hilnar is truly a great leader for hin's people."

He took a deep breath. *Now go for it*. "Ri-El Hilnar, are you now convinced that Eerin and I earnestly wish to help your people? All that we ask is an end to the violence Orim began, and the chance for the *Asimov*'s survivors to be sent safely home.

"In return for your promise that this will be so, Eerin has

promised you a seat on the WirElspind, and han's support in gaining other seats. You have my solemn word of honor that I will negotiate a pledge for your people from both the WirElspind and the CLS—a pledge that the Wospind will never have to be exposed to or take Elhanin unless they choose to. Your beliefs and wishes will be forever respected."

Hilnar stared at him, hin's green eyes thoughtful. "Hin will agree to cease the violence. Hin was never one to love the hurting of others, as Orim was, so that is not a difficult vow to make. Also, hin will agree to release the survivors of the *Asimov* to the CLS . . . with one exception."

Hin pointed to the Simiu. "The scientist who has profaned our camp by bringing Elhanin into it must not be allowed to carry on heen's work. Hin will give Hrrakk' a choice. Remain here with us forever, or die. Either way, heen will no longer be a threat to us."

Mark's breath caught in his throat. "No, Hilnar, that is not acceptable. Hrrakk' must be allowed to go free, too."

"The scientist profanes our camp with what heen carries," Hilnar maintained stubbornly, green eyes shining with a cold glint that suddenly reminded Mark of Orim. The human felt a chill at the back of his neck. "Heen is an enemy to our people. Heen wishes only to study us, not to help us."

"You have observed that I have come to love Terris," Mark said, patting the sleeping child beneath his shirt. "And that observation was what led you to agree to talk with me, is that not correct?"

Hilnar indicated assent.

"You are wrong about the Simiu, and I will tell you why I know that," the human said steadily. "There was another baby, named Misir, who also survived the crash. But unlike Terris, who was unharmed, poor Misir had injuries within hinsi's body. Despite the best of care, hinsi died, which made us all grieve."

Mark paused for effect. "The person who gave Misir the best of care was Honored Hrrakk', Hilnar! He carried and cared for little Misir every bit as conscientiously as I cared for Terris. He grieved when Misir died, we could all see it. Hrrakk' *does* care about the people of Elseemar!"

Hilnar glanced questioningly at Eerin, who quickly verified the human's account, adding to it a few details she had observed. Reenor gazed levelly at the Simiu, then addressed him in Mizari. "Tell us of this Misir," he said.

Hrrakk' looked stubborn, but Cara touched his arm, the unbandaged one. "Please, Honored Hrrakk'—tell them. Or I will."

The big Simiu sighed deeply. "There was a Wopind infant named Misir," he began. "I could see that the child had serious internal injuries, but the human, there"—he jerked his head at Mark—"convinced me to try and save hinsi. I did my best, but the child died." Hrrakk' paused, then said in low voice, "I still miss hinsi."

Reenor and Hilnar hastily conferred softly as heen translated the Simiu's words. Then the Wopind leader turned to Hrrakk' and Reenor translated as hin spoke: "We will let you go free, but only if you relinquish the Elhanin to us, so we may see it destroyed."

Hrrakk's muzzle wrinkled slightly, scornfully, and he growled, "I refuse. What you demand would not be honorable. You have no right to deprive me of my freedom, and therefore it would be dishonorable of me to *buy* my freedom from you!" His crest stood straight up, in challenge mode. "Instead I *demand* that you execute me immediately. Waste no more time trying to coerce me into dishonoring myself!"

Mark wanted to bury his face in his hands. *Oh, shit,* he thought. *What now?* Cara made a soft sound of shocked distress as she realized for the first time the threat the Simiu faced.

The student straightened his shoulders and gazed at Hilnar. "Ri-El Hilnar," he said, "what if *I* destroyed the Elhanin? Would that satisfy you?"

The Wopind leader nodded curtly. "As long as it no longer profanes our camp, hin does not care who destroys the Elhanin."

"Honored Hrrakk'," Mark said in Mizari, holding out his hand, "give me the Elhanin, please."

"Why?"

"So I can destroy it. The Wospind don't care who does it, and giving it to *me* won't be any dishonor to you. It won't be like you're giving in to the Wospind."

"The answer is no. I would rather die than give up the Elhanin. My honor demands it."

Mark glared at the Simiu. "Dammit, Hrrakk'! The Elhanin is a *thing*, it's not alive! Being willing to die for Cara or R'Thessra was honorable, but dying over a sample of Elhanin is just plain *stupid*!" He snorted disgustedly. "And don't tell me I'm wrong. I know I'm right! Giving me the Elhanin won't damage your precious honor!" *Besides,* he thought, *you can always go back to your lab on Hurrreeah and make more, and you know it as well as I do!*

"What do you know of Simiu honor, human?" Hrrakk' demanded, and there was a glint in the violet eyes Mark couldn't read.

"You have taught me a great deal about it," Mark said quietly. He extended his hand again. "Now please, Honored Hrrakk' . . . give me the Elhanin."

Long moments crawled by. Mark did not budge. Violet eyes and hazel regarded each other unblinkingly—

—and then Hrrakk' sighed loudly and reached for the anklet he wore. With a quick twist of his fingers, he removed it. Fumbling left-handed, he pressed a hidden catch, and the massive red gemstone swung up. Within was a tiny vial. The Simiu held the bracelet out to Mark. "Here you are, human."

"One more thing," Mark said, picking up the tiny vial of Elhanin and clutching it tightly, "I have a *name,* Honored Hrrakk', and it's *not* 'human'! It's Mark Kenner."

The glint showed in the violet eyes again, and this time the human recognized it for what it was . . . amusement. Slowly, solemnly, the big Simiu made the formal greeting gesture of his people, touching his eyelids, muzzle, and chest, then extending his hand toward the human, head inclined slightly. "I shall remember that in future, Honored InterrelatorKenner," Hrrakk' said, using the most formal of Mizari dialects.

Hilnar accompanied Mark down to the stream and watched solemnly as the human poured out the tiny vial of powder into the racing water. Hin nodded hin's satisfaction. "Thank you, Mark Kenner, for preventing violence." The Wopind leader pointed past the meadow and over the last hill. "Hin's people have been keeping watch over the nahah, because there is a CLS research team stationed there. Hin and hin's people will escort Mark Kenner and his friends there, and then we will leave."

"Don't go too far away," Mark reminded the Wopind leader. "You've got to claim that seat on the WirElspind that Eerin promised you."

"Hin will not forget," Hilnar promised. "Is Mark's team ready to go now?"

"Yes . . . yes we are," Mark said. He could hardly believe that the long journey would finally be over, and that they were going to make it.

Together, they walked back to the little group. "Honored Hrrakk'," Mark said, "we are free to go. The Wospind are going to escort us to the nahah personally. There's a CLS team there. They have a communications device. Can you walk?"

"I can, Honored InterrelatorKenner," the Simiu said.

Cara was staring at Mark, hands on her hips. "This is too much," she complained. "First I had to learn *Mizari* to keep up with what's going on. Now, dammit, am I going to have to learn *Elspindlor*, too? Or are you going to tell me what the hell's been happening?"

Mark started guiltily. He'd translated for everyone today except the only other human. Cara was right to be irritated. He gave her a conciliatory smile. "I'm sorry," he said.

"I'm smart enough to pick up on the change in atmosphere, at least," she told him, her stern expression softening into an answering smile. "And I know why Hrrakk's no longer in danger. I also know that the Wospind are going to let us go . . . I think. What I don't know is *why*.

"As for what's happening between those two"—she nodded over at Reenor and Eerin, who stood staring deep into each other's golden eyes—"don't bother translating anything they say. It would obviously be incredibly sappy."

"You're probably right," Mark agreed.

"But can I *please* get an explanation of how you got Hilnar to agree to let us go?"

Mark grinned and held out a hand. "Ms. Hendricks, if you'll be my walking companion on the way to the nahah, I'll tell you everything I know."

"Is it going to be that short a walk?" She grinned back and slipped her hand into his.

Mark looked at Hilnar. "Let's go. There are a lot of people depending on us to reach that nahah."

Epilogue

Mark stretched lazily on the end-to-end pallets that made a human-sized bed. The thick walls and low windows of his room gently filtered the early morning sounds: birdcalls, leaves rustling against the house, the distant sound of flowing water.

Odd to find an atmosphere of restful peace in a town that never sleeps, Mark thought, smiling to himself. He himself had done a lot of sleeping lately.

He was in Eerin's family home in Lalcipind. Though a major population center and host to the WirElspind, Lalcipind was, in its own way, as wedded to the natural elements as the little nahah.

A wide valley, caught among foothills even greener and more rolling than those he'd hiked half a continent away, held communal fields and gardens, public areas, and gently landscaped parks in its lush palm. On either boundary ran the mountain-born, swift-rushing rivers, Rainel and Rainwo. Hillsides rose in all directions away from each of the two rivers, and homes melted gracefully into the rocks and trees of the gentle slopes.

I'll miss this place, Mark thought. Was it only a week ago that he'd danced the Mortenwol for the first time? Soon he would join Eerin and Reenor and Lieor in the large courtyard and dance it as part of the morning ritual. By now it felt as though he'd done it all his life.

He had a kareen of his own, now, and two Shadowbird feathers, both gifts from Eerin's family, but Mark knew he would not dance the Mortenwol every day after he left Elseemar. *Maybe on special occasions,* he thought. Mostly I'll dance it the way Eerin had to on the night of han's Change . . . in my heart. That's where it matters most.

Today he and Cara were scheduled to leave Elseemar aboard a CLS shuttle. He'd fulfilled his pledge to Hilnar, seen hin installed in the WirElspind, along with Morana, Alanor's replacement, also a Wopind.

Terris stirred on his chest and chirped at him hopefully. "Food," Mark translated. "Coming right up, Terris!"

He held the baby close while Terris slurped at the supplement-filled straw. Leaving Terris behind would be the hardest thing, and he dreaded it. Even the Mortenwol each day hadn't been able to relieve the grief he'd felt, knowing that he must leave hinsi. But this was hinsi's home, where hinsi belonged, he knew that.

At least you'll have the best of homes, Mark thought, gazing down at the baby.

Eerin and Reenor had agreed to raise Terris as their own, keeping hinsi on supplement straws until hinsi was ready to be weaned, rather than giving the child to a family with a nursing male. Mark and Reenor had worked together to prepare Terris for yet another parental switch. Transferring hinsi back and forth for short periods and holding hinsi while they sat together during feeding times, they'd now persuaded Terris to eat for either of them.

Absently Mark stroked the child, thinking of all that had happened. Most of the survivors of the *Asimov*'s crash had already left Elseemar on a specially detoured ship, the S.V. *Hawking*. Mahree Burroughs, Mark had gathered, was the person responsible for the ship's rapid arrival. After their little party had left the wrecked ship, only five more people had died, which, under the circumstances, had to be considered good news.

Elspind and Wospind both had searched for the man who'd

attacked Mark's group, then run away into the desert, but, so far, had found no trace of him.

One of the brightest memories of the past days had been Eerin and Lieor's reunion. Mark had very much enjoyed getting to know Eerin's sibling. Eerin's entire family had welcomed both humans with great warmth. Even the crusty Hrrakk' had softened slightly when he was around them.

Five days ago, Eerin and Reenor had joined as lifemates. Mark and Cara had attended the ceremony, the first off-worlders ever to be invited to attend an Elpind wedding.

Their joining had taken place on the bank of the river Rainel, just as Aanbas, the first moon, rose into the night sky. Members of both joining families had chanted in unison the ancient Telling that Eerin had quoted to Mark on their first night together at StarBridge. The sound of the rushing water had been a fitting counterpoint to the solemnly rhythmic words:

"El is life, and Wo is death, and each completes the other. We are Elspind, the people of life, for the life of the people endures even as death swallows us one by one. Our lives are cast like the shadows of the four moons from the ever-shining light of the people. We are born for the rizel. In the rizel, life is taken, each from the other, and given, each to the other, and El walks so far ahead of Wo, there is no catching."

Today, there would be another ceremony: today R'Thessra would be buried next to her hive-sister in the mountain graveyard where many of the victims of the laboratory's destruction now rested.

There was a light tap at the door. "Mark?"

"Come in, Eerin," the human called.

The Elpind's golden eyes held excited curiosity. "Zahssez of the CLS waits in han's courtyard. Heen says Mark must come quickly. A call from StarBridge is coming in for Mark!"

Mark bounded down the hillside as eagerly as any Elpind. For once, an Elpind had trouble keeping up with a human.

When he reached the CLS office, the holo-vid tank was already filled with two familiar faces. "Rob!" Mark yelled, grinning. "Administrator ch'aait!"

The psychologist and the little Chhhh-kk-tu were as happy to see Mark as the student was to see them. For several moments there was a confused babble of mutual greetings and, on Rob's and Kkintha's part, profound relief to find him well and in good spirits.

"I'm fine!" Mark assured them. "And so are Cara and Eerin! This is Terris," he said, holding up hinsi. "Isn't hinsi cute? I've been taking care of hinsi," he said, and explained briefly.

Rob Gable grinned broadly. "Does this make me a grandfather?" He winced theatrically. "I'm not ready!"

"How have *you* been?" Mark wanted to know, seeing the traces of sleepless nights still present on the psychologist's face.

Rob shook his head ruefully at the younger man. "Does it show that much?" He pushed back his dark, curly hair and leaned forward so that his image filled the entire holo. "See these gray hairs? Every damn one of them has *your* name on it! I've been a wreck, worrying about you!"

Mark shrugged, suddenly sobering. "You were right to worry, Rob. It was touch and go there for a while. But we made it through."

"So I understand," the doctor said grimly. "And . . . Mark . . . listen, if you want to tell me to take a flying leap out the nearest air lock for getting you into such a mess, go right ahead. I won't utter a word of protest."

"Hell no, Rob, don't be silly," the younger man said firmly. "It was my choice to go. And," he said thoughtfully, "it was the best choice I could have made, all things considered." He grinned wryly. "I wouldn't have missed it for the world. I've really come to love Elseemar."

"So we heard," Kkintha ch'aait said. "They are saying many things about you."

"Nothing too awful, I hope," Mark joked.

"Hardly," Rob said. "What's this I hear about your single-handedly bringing peace to Elseemar?" The doctor shook his head. "First Tesa on Trinity, now you on Elseemar."

"Come on, Rob, it's hardly that," Mark protested. "I managed to get people talking a little, that's all."

"Spoken like a true interrelator." The doctor's dark eyes held Mark's intently.

Mark grinned. "Okay, you win. I knew you'd guess the truth as soon as you saw my face, I could never keep anything from you"—he chuckled suddenly, remembering a few school escapades— "well . . . hardly anything!"

"Don't start confiding past transgressions now, either," Rob pleaded. "I'm too old for any more shocks. But . . . do you mean it? My gamble paid off? You're not going to quit?"

"Not on your life," Mark said. "These last days, I've enjoyed the little taste I've had of being an interrelator. Nothing's going to stop me from coming back to StarBridge and finishing my training!"

Rob gazed at him solemnly. "Nothing? Not even the chance to stay on Elseemar for a year as the CLS interrelator there?"

Mark's mouth fell open. "What?" he managed to say after a moment. "You're kidding, Rob, right?"

"He is not joking, Mark," Kkintha ch'aait said, her tiny fingers grooming her chest-ruff excitedly. "Both the WirElspind and the CLS team have specifically requested that you help them in establishing communications with the Wopind groups. Would you be interested in the job?"

"*Would* I?" Mark's heart leaped within him. "But what about the rest of my training?" he asked, uncertainly.

"You'll of course receive credit for your work on Elseemar," the Administrator said. "And then, when your year is up, you can return to StarBridge to make up any courses that you need for graduation."

"Well, Mark?" Rob Gable asked. "Want the job?"

"I sure as hell do!" the student exclaimed.

Kkintha looked up at the psychologist inquiringly. "More of your human colloquialisms, Robert? Does that by any chance constitute an affirmative response?"

"It sure as hell does," Rob said, grinning broadly. "Congratulations, Mark. We're proud of you."

The new interrelator grinned back. "I'm kind of proud of myself, actually," he admitted. "But I couldn't have done it without Cara. Rob, I think I've just about talked her into applying for StarBridge. I'm betting she'll be the best interrelator the school's ever seen."

"We'd be delighted to have her, of course," Rob said. "You tell her that."

"I will," Mark said. "Talk to you soon, Rob."

That same afternoon, Mark, Cara, Eerin, and Hrrakk' attended R'Thessra's burial service. It was after the brief ceremony that the Simiu scientist told Mark that he, too, had been asked to stay on Elseemar to help the scientific team reconstruct their work on the Elhanin.

"It seems, Honored InterrelatorKenner," Hrrakk' said in his usual taciturn, gruff tones, "that we will be working together in an effort to educate the Elpind people about Elhanin and how it is produced."

"That'll be the biggest challenge of all," Mark admitted later to Cara as they stood together in the courtyard of Eerin's home, her travel case lying on the flagstones between them, "working constantly with Hrrakk'!"

The journalist grinned at him. "By the end of the year," she predicted, "you'll either be the best of friends for life, or Hrrakk' will swear a new honor-oath."

"Oh, yeah? What?"

"To strangle any human he meets on sight!"

They both laughed, then abruptly sobered as the reality of their leave-taking suddenly descended. "Damn, Cara, I'll miss you. You've been . . . more than a friend," Mark said softly. "I only wish . . . " He hesitated, then stepped around the travel case and put his arms around her. Bending his head, he kissed her gently on the mouth.

Cara slid her arms around his neck, and when the kiss finally ended, she rested her head against his shoulder, fighting back tears. "That was nice," she said shakily. "Why didn't we ever do that before?"

Mark shook his head ruefully. "I don't know. I ought to have my head examined!" A sudden thought occurred to him. "This isn't good-bye forever, remember. You're going to be coming to StarBridge, right? So I'll see you there next year . . . "

Cara stepped back, wiping her eyes. "You've enriched my time, Mark," she said quietly, and then, trying for a lighter touch, she pointed to her battered knapsack, filled with keepsakes from Elseemar, and her travel case. "Now, how about helping me carry my stuff down to the shuttle?"

Mark nodded and picked up the travel case. "Got your camera?" he asked, already knowing the answer.

"Of course," she said. "I can't wait until they see my footage back on Earth!"

"You'll probably win a Pulitzer, this time," he said.

"Don't think the thought hasn't crossed my mind," she said,

grinning at him. "My only regret is that I didn't get your first Mortenwol on film. It was . . . indescribable."

"I'm glad you didn't, actually." He smiled wryly back. "Don't you think it was one of those things where you really had to be there?"

Together they started out of the courtyard, but then Cara suddenly halted, grabbing his arm. "Oh, no, you don't," she said. "We've got a tradition to keep up, here, and you know how important tradition is on Elseemar."

"What?" he asked blankly. "What tradition?"

"Your famous words, remember?"

"My famous words?" He began to chuckle. "I'm stumped. Tell me!"

" 'Everybody' is ready," she quoted, smiling. " 'Let's go!' "

Afterword

StarBridge launched successfully, *Silent Dances* (which, as I write this has just reached bookstore shelves) appears to be safely in orbit, and now *Shadow World* is counting down for takeoff. Time is rushing by at stellar velocity . . . it seems only yesterday that I suffered a bout of temporary lunacy and decided to begin a series of books set in my own science-fiction universe. But that was 1985, and now it's—*gasp*—1990!

Serpent's Gift, Book Four of the series, will be out in mid-1991. It's a book centered around StarBridge Academy itself. The school is in trouble—big-time. Will the Academy have to shut down because the school's radonium supply is inexorably altering, turning the entire asteroid into a gigantic time bomb? Or will the entire StarBridge project go bankrupt before it can explode?

Rob Gable, Kkintha ch'aait, Dr. Blanket and Esteemed Ssoriszs all have their hands (or equivalents!) full, trying to save the school, as well as a valuable archaeological site recently discovered beneath the Lamont Cliffs. The relics buried there may provide a clue to the fate of the mysterious Mizari Lost

Colony—but only if the lethal radonium-2 doesn't destroy them first. . . .

Book Five is *Silent Songs,* where Kathy O'Malley and I return you to Trinity. Most of our old friends are back—Tesa, Lightning, Thunder, Meg and Bruce—with some new additions. Jib is Tesa's former StarBridge roommate, trying his wings as an interrelator trainee. Kheera is a Simiu who has been sent by the Harkk'ett clan (under the prodding of Ambassador Dhurrrkk', of course, after the events of *Silent Dances*), to make reparation to the people of Trinity. Only problem is, she doesn't want to be there. (Angry, resentful Simiu make *wonderful* companions, as we've just seen in this volume!)

Tesa has enough headaches just trying to keep the peace between Kheera and the others, but, before long, her life becomes even more complicated. Our deaf interrelator has to contend with *two* more First Contacts—a telepathic race of creatures native to Trinity, plus an aggressive, technologically advanced species determined to conquer the planet!

Here's hoping you'll enjoy those books, as well as the ones you've already read.

Before I close, a couple of quick acknowledgments. First of all, for help on *Shadow World*, I would like to thank Dr. Gary Weaver of the School for International Service at the American University, Washington, D.C., campus. He provided invaluable information and insights into hostage situations and how negotiators are trained to handle them.

And, finally, the biggest thanks of all goes to *you*—the *StarBridge* readers. Getting this series off the ground has meant the hardest, longest stint of work I've ever done (anyone who doesn't believe writing is *hard work* should try it!), as well as the most rewarding experience of my career.

Many of you have written to tell me you're enjoying *StarBridge* and are looking forward to the next book. A number of you have posed thoughtful, insightful questions that have sparked ideas for additional novels, if the series is extended beyond the initial five books. Reading these letters has been incredibly gratifying—it makes all that hard work worthwhile. I answer each letter personally (just a reminder, a stamped, self-addressed envelope is a BIG help!), and the warmth and encouragement expressed has been wonderful. Thank you all so very much!

—Ann C. Crispin
June, 1990